WHITE MIST DOG

SAGA OF THE MOUNTAIN SAGE
BOOK 2

W. MICHAEL GEAR

WOLFPACK
PUBLISHING
—— EST 2013 ——

Wolfpack Publishing
9850 S. Maryland Parkway, Suite A-5 #323
Las Vegas, Nevada 89183

wolfpackpublishing.com

Paperback ISBN 978-1-63977-141-7
eBook ISBN 978-1-63977-140-0

AUTHOR'S NOTE

This is a work of historically based fiction set on the American frontier in 1825 and reflects the morals and values of the time. Some modern readers will find some dialog, words, terms, and cultural practices disturbing.

WHITE MIST DOG

CHAPTER ONE

 Over the years, the military post now called Fort Atkinson had had plenty of names, and been located in two places. Travis had seen both. The first name had been Camp Missouri, located about a mile north of its current location on the Council Bluffs. The army changed the name to Cantonment Missouri and expanded the post; then—with their usual wilderness prescience—had watched their fledgling fort wash away in the spring flood. After the engineers had relocated to the top of the bluff, the place was known as Cantonment Council Bluffs, and then, finally, Fort Atkinson, named after the commanding officer who was even now upriver pacifying the tribes for Dave Green's benefit.

Or so Travis sincerely hoped.

Fort Atkinson, perched on its bluff, was little more than could be expected for the American military's most distant outpost beyond the frontier. The fort had been laid out in a square, the buildings constructed of log, rock, and clay plaster. From its location more than one hundred and fifty feet above the river, it dominated the Missouri, and theoretically could sink anything that tried to sneak contraband upstream without the proper licenses.

The latter theory had always remained a point of curious conversation at the trading posts and among the fur parties. No one had ever been shot at, least of all fur hunters paddling downriver in bateaux loaded with pelts. In fact, Travis had once watched the artillerymen shoot at the river, practicing with their sights, levels, and trajectory tables. Several seconds after the squat howitzer belched gray smoke and rolled back on its carriage, a satisfying white plume spouted in the river. How close it would have been to an offending boat had, of course, remained academic. No one gave the artillery much thought, or respect, particularly after the army's less than sterling performance Leavenworth had demonstrated when shooting up the Ree village upriver. All the shot had been too high—and the Arikara had escaped.

Suffice it to say that military or not, the traders still made a stop here. This was the last toehold of the United States in the wilderness.

Letters could be sent from Atkinson, messages left, and news gathered. Here, too, final supplies could be had—for the most outrageous prices—from the military contractors who maintained their own trading establishments.

Travis slogged his way through the gravelly mud, his nose twitching at the septic smell of urine, garbage, night earth, manure, and rot. He carried his rifle over his shoulder, and a pack of deer hides on his back. Rounding the corner, he nodded at a vicious-looking Pawnee who squatted against the trading-post wall.

Travis kicked some of the mud off his feet, lifted the latch, and stepped into the smoky interior of the old Missouri Fur post. Tobacco, candle soot, and stale air added new insults to his nostrils.

The good Lord knows why it bothers me, he thought. I *reckon this child's done spent more'n one winter a-smelling smells just like this. T'aint never bothered me afore.*

"Travis Hartman!"

Travis cocked his head as he looked across the barrels and bales. A muscular black man sat lounging at a table behind the factor's bench. Travis grinned and said, "Baptiste de Bourgmont! I reckoned ye'd be dead afore now. Most likely the Ree would'a lifted yer topknot."

"Figgered they'd a-lifted yers," Baptiste replied, then he smiled. The Negro wore a long, fawn-colored leather jacket that dangled waves of carefully cut fringe. His canvas pants were tucked into tall moccasins dyed maroon and decorated with tin bells, bead-work, and silver conchos. The broad black belt snugged around his hips held knife, pistol, bullet pouch, and pipe bag.

Baptiste was tapping an empty tin cup on the table with the tip of a knife blade. The charcoal black of his skin contrasted with the bright white of his teeth. Like thick wool, his black hair had been pulled back into a severe ponytail.

"What brings you to Atkinson, old coon?"

"Same's always." Travis stepped behind the counter and threaded past barrels and tins, leaned the Hawken rifle against the wall, and unslung the tightly rolled deer hides from his back. Baptiste stood, then wrapped his arms around Travis in a bear hug, pounding him on the back. "It shore is good to see you, coon!"

Travis pushed him back, slapped him on the back, and

used a toe to snag out the bench opposite Baptiste's table. "Yer looking fit. Chopped off any heads of late?"

Baptiste shook his head as he sat down. "Lord God, Travis. I forgit just how ugly you are. I reckon as I always had the idea that time would make yor face look more like a man's."

"I could take my knife, whittle a bit on yers. Ye'd be surprised how them squaws take ter a man with a face like mine. Figger I'm chockful of medicine."

Baptiste chuckled and studied his knife. "You'd make my face look like my back, eh? The last man to scar me lies dead in a grave in Louisiana." He glanced up. "But I think I'd have my hands full killing you."

"Didn't do so well last time ye tried down ter Natchez —but I reckon we'd make a scrape of her, all right." Travis wiped his nose. "What's news?"

"Not much. Everyone is waiting to hear what Atkinson and O'Fallon accomplish upriver. Otoes, Omaha, and Sioux been picking on each other. The usual. Prices fo' plews are going up. People wonder if Ashley has fallen off the face of the earth."

"That would be some, it would. That Ashley, he's a canny old beaver if ever there was one. Maybe craftier than Manuel Lisa."

Baptiste shrugged. "Yor with Pilcher again this season?"

"Nope. Just roaming. Seeing whar my stick floats. Come up from Saint Loowee. Travel's a mess. These rains played hell."

Baptiste's eyes narrowed. "Uh-huh."

"You hunting for the fort?"

"Among other things. Like so many, I wait to see if the army can open the river. It'll take a heap big show to undo the damage Leavenworth did to the trade."

"Atkinson ain't Leavenworth."

Baptiste gave Travis a knowin look. "The gov'ment sent a new agent upriver. Fella name of Peter Wilson. Gov'ment thinks it's going to try and make treaties with the Kansas, Pawnee, Oto, and Ioway."

"Won't hold. Never does."

"Nope. Reckon not." Baptiste cocked his head. "You're up to yor neck in something. I can sense it...like a wolf around a weak buffalo."

"This child don't know nothing. If'n I did, I reckon I'd be plumb fat and sassy, sitting in Saint Loowee in a big house, with a fat woman tending my needs."

Baptiste leaned forward. "You? Don't feed me no poor dogmeat and tell me she be fat buffler, Travis. Not after what you and me been through."

"Ye never was much a one fer fancy palaver."

"They beat it out of me when I's a slave."

Travis glanced around. "Whar's the factor?"

"Probably asleep." Baptiste looked around the packed storehouse. His eyes rested on a keg of beads. "They's little trade now. Most of the tribes are planting, or out fo' spring buffalo."

Travis kicked the roll of deer hides. "Thar's eleven green deer, hides. Spring stuff with their hair slipping. Reckon that'd fetch me an outfit?"

"Such as?"

"Good pair of moccasins, set of good britches, a heavy shirt. Maybe a knife."

"I reckon. Yor particular about the moccasins? Want any tribe?"

"Got Crow?"

Baptiste studied him with half-closed eyes. "Mountain moccasins."

"They got ter have heavy soles. Made outta bull buffalo. Reckon yer figgering whar my stick floats."

"I think they gots a pair. Your size?"

"Smaller."

"A woman's?"

"Not that small. Let's say, wal, about the size of yer foot thar, maybe a tad smaller, but not much."

"Mountain moccasins, not fo' a woman but fo' a medium-size man. They got a pair in the storeroom. Good Crow work. And you expect such fo' green spring deer hides?"

"Reckon so." Travis grinned. "Maybe fer the time I kept the Sioux from lifting that curly black hair of yern."

Baptiste gave Travis a crooked smile. "Or fo' the days on the river, or the time in Louisiana when I hid in the tree. Or the time you got me that job. Or the time—"

"Reckon I'd be right obliged if'n ye didn't go a-palavering all about the fort with yer ideas, coon. Reckon maybe ye seed me, done some swapping, and old Travis Hartman just up and left."

"I reckon that might happen."

"Waugh!" Travis took Baptiste's hand and shook. He glanced around, and then added, "Reckon a boat'll arrive a couple of days from now. Dave Green's hauling supplies for Pilcher. Carrying them upriver. Pilcher's business, understand?"

Baptiste's interest visibly sharpened.

"Now, I reckon this hyar's just atwixt the two of us. Don't need to be nothing said."

Baptiste fingered his chin, thinking. "I work fo' the Company. Not many people would ask me what yor asking."

Travis shrugged.

Baptiste grinned then. "But then, yor not just anybody."

"Thanks, friend. Reckon I'll owe ye one."

Baptiste shook his head. "No. You took a big chance fo' a runaway slave. They'd a hung this child. Fed my carcass to the dogs as a lesson to the others. If'n they caught us, they'd a hung you, too. Baptiste don't forget."

"That's some, it is." Travis chuckled. "Saw something in ye, I did. Figgered ye was worth the risk."

"Perhaps they gonna hang you this time if they catches you? And maybe Green?"

Travis studied the tip of his thumb as if he'd just found something fascinating there. "Wal, ye knows Davey and me. Just hauling a load upriver fer Pilcher. But ye wouldn't know whar a feller might hire a string of hosses, do ye? Say seven or eight? Maybe fer a week?"

Baptiste pursed his lips. "They'd be questions. But..." His eyes narrowed. "No, wait. There's this Pawnee. Half Man. Last I seed, he was hanging around out front. He has hosses. No questions—but a passel of trouble."

"Half Man? Reckon I heard of him. Runs whiskey, hosses, and plews back and forth atwixt the Pawnee and the Omaha? Likes to play heap big man with the chiefs?"

"That's him. Now, let's say a man wanted to sneak whiskey past the army inspection. He'd help. And he'd kill you fust time you turned yor back on him."

Travis frowned, remembering the mean Pawnee leaning against the logs. "Thar's times a coon's got ter take a chance."

Baptiste reached out, powerful hand grasping Travis's shoulder. "Watch yor back, coon. If'n ye don't, yor gone beaver."

CHAPTER TWO

For in absolute freedom there was no reciprocal interaction either between an external world and consciousness, which is absorbed in the manifold existence, or sets itself determinate purposes and ideas, or between consciousness and an external objective world, be it a world of reality or thought. What that freedom encompassed was the world totally in the form of consciousness, as a universal will, and along with that, self-consciousness gathered out of all the dispersions and manifoldness of existence, or all the manifold ends and judgments of mind concentrated into the naked and simple self.

—Georg Friedrich Wilhelm Hegel, *Phenomenology of Mind*

 Fort Atkinson. The name had mingled itself with Richard's dreams to become the promised land, and the Platte his River Jordan. He splashed through the shallows, slipping in mud, back breaking. Despite the cool day, sweat trickled down his face to

sting his eyes and drip from his nose. The endless weight of the cordelle lay like the great earth on Atlas's shoulders.

"*Sacré!* Careful!" the cry came. "Hold on! Don't let it slip!" Behind them, coursing like a huge fish on a line, the *Maria* curved out from the shore, driven along the arc of the cordelle line by laboring polers as the boat passed wide of the sandbar she'd grounded on earlier that day.

What a Herculean labor to free her that had been. Now she had to swing wide around the sandbar at the mouth of the Platte—that or drop back downriver, cross to the far bank, and recross once the boat had passed the confluence.

Dear Lord God, all they did was pole and cordelle. Didn't the wind ever blow from the south in this wretched land?

A signal came from the patroon.

"Go!" Trudeau cried. "Run! No slack in the cordelle, or she slip right back on the sand!"

They stumbled forward, sloshing through the shallows, scrambling for footing in the quicksand. Breath rasped in Richard's throat.

At the end of the cordelle, the mast bent under the stress. But *Maria* held her place. Brown water curled white at her bow, and the grunts of the polers could be heard as they braced their bare feet and leaned into their poles.

The mouth of the Platte was a terrible place, shoaled with sandbars, dotted with small islands of willow, for the Platte spilled into the Missouri in interwoven ribbons of water. But beyond the Platte, up there where the bluffs rose above the tree line, lay Fort Atkinson. There lay all of Richard's hopes for escape.

He'd never paid the slightest attention to men in uniform. The only interest he'd had was a philosopher's: lofty and abstract. The military, as Hegel had noted, was for the protection and furthering of the state's interest *vis-a-vis* other states. The pomp, pretty dress, and regulations had appeared rather ridiculous. Those officers he'd met had been possessed of an arrogance unbecoming their lack of either the education or ability to discuss complicated subjects. Philosophy, for instance.

Richard now chafed to see a soldier; the first uniform would mean deliverance from his living nightmare.

I'll throw myself at the first brightly dressed mannequin, clasp his knees, and plead that he take me to his commanding officer.

That would work, wouldn't it? Or could Green come up with a reasonable explanation for his *engagé*'s odd behavior? Claim he was crazy, driven mad by fever, or maybe drunk.

No. I'll hit him. Ball my fist, and whack him right in the face. They'll have to arrest me. No amount of Green's excuses will keep them from dragging me away. Then, at the inquiry, I'll tell my story.

That was it. Foolproof.

Green would try and keep him on the boat, of course; but Richard had heard the talk. The army searched all of the boats, turned them inside out looking for whiskey. It was against the law to trade whiskey to the Indians, and —in addition to the kegs allotted for crew ration—*Maria* was chock full of curious triangular tins of the stuff. Way more than the half-gill per man per day allowed by law.

This time you won't stop me, Mr. Green. Once I hit that soldier, I'm free!

And then? Well, no matter what he thought about the men in the army, the system was rational. A man didn't become an officer without some sense and training that set him above his comrades. When Richard told his tale to the commander, they'd drop charges. He'd be placed on the first boat back to Saint Louis. From there, he could find the means to buy passage back to Boston.

I'm coming, Laura. You'll see. It won't be long now, and I'll be knocking on your door.

Boston! In defiance of his weary labor, he smiled dreamily. He could hear his boot heels striking the cobblestones as he and Laura walked down Washington Street. Her arm was tucked tightly in his. He touched his felt hat, tipping it to each passer-by, no matter how lowly. A silk cloak was swirling around his shoulders as he looked up at the familiar buildings. Just for good measure, he studied their reflection in the windows of a tobacconist, and straightened his cravat. Laura looked dashing in her long velveteen dress with a ribbon bow at the waist. The royal blue set off her long blond hair with its gathered ringlets.

Home. Boston. The cultured tones of intelligent people like music on his ears.

I will be a gentleman again.

"*Merde!*" Trudeau shouted. "Pull, you women! She is backing water!"

Richard threw himself against the cordelle, just one more grunting animal in a line of beasts. Tendons burning in his hands, he tightened his grip on the unforgiving hemp. *Heave! Heave! Come on, damn it!*

Maria skated forward, rounding the head of the sandbar. To avoid an abatis of wicked snags that thrust up from the water like the splintered ribs of a water monster, Henri leaned on the steering oar, sending her in toward shore.

"Too much slack! Hurry! *Run!*" Trudeau cried, and

they scampered forward like trained rats, churning muddy water with booted feet. They raced to take up the slack, diving into the willows on the Platte's north bank, clutching the slippery stems with one hand as they manhandled the heavy rope with the other.

Richard panted and gasped, humping forward under the swaying cordelle. Ragged breath sawed at his throat. Every muscle in his legs and back cramped and ached. Off balance, the cordelle pulled him sideways through the willows. With the last of his strength, he caught himself before falling. Springy stems tangled his feet so that he crashed forward instead of stepped. He fixed his attention on Toussaint's broad back. Whiplike branches slapped at him, smacking wetly.

Pull! Come on, Richard. Each step is closer to Fort Atkinson. Each step is closer to Boston. Boston...Boston....

"We 'ave her!" Trudeau called from ahead. "We've crossed the Platte!"

Their screams and shouts sounded more like an Indian massacre than a celebration. Someone began singing "*A La Claire Fontaine*," and Richard joined in between pants for breath. He didn't sing at first, not really, just hummed along.

They beat their way through the willows, cutting back toward the river through muck that sucked at their feet. Mosquitoes hummed up in clouds as they waded. Brain-numb, the *engagés* slogged their way out of the marsh like weary beads on the cordelle's string.

Richard, along with Toussaint and Robert, bellowed and roared as they dragged the thick wet cordelle through the marsh, crushing the long green leaves of cattails and flattening the round tubes of bulrush.

They could see the river here. *Maria* bobbed at the end of the cordelle, cutting water.

"Hand-over-hand!" Trudeau called, and like triumphant fishermen, they reeled in their prize.

Richard grinned happily. Let the *engagés* have their "*Fontaine*," his reward would be Boston. A summer eve's stroll around the Commons, just to enjoy the yellow squares of candlelit windowpanes.

Distant thunder rolled down from the plains to the west, and far off over the eastern bank, lightning flickered in the clouds.

"We've crossed the Platte!" *Engagés* pounded each other on the back, capered and jeered, whooping and leaping, taking turns as they pulled the *Maria* in and coiled the cordelle into a big black ring.

Richard watched the keelboat ride in across the choppy brown water. Normally ungainly, she moved with a grace he'd never seen before. Almost beautiful.

"Whiskey!" Green cried, coming to stand on the deck. "A good day's work, lads!"

Men jumped, shrieked, and waved their red wool hats.

Richard looked down at his hands as the *Maria's* hull whispered on the bank. The palms were caked with wet sand and grime, the skin reddened and callused.

His once white shirt hung in tatters about his shoulders. The duck brown pants—the envy of Boston gentlemen—were tied on with rope. Gaps hung in what had been the knees. The heel was missing from his right boot—and that was the good one. The upper had come loose from the sole of his left; the nails had rusted out, and the leather was rotten and torn.

He slapped at a mosquito and waded out into the river, washing the worst of the grime from his face and hands. He was the last to have a tin of whiskey handed down. He stared at it, fond memories in his mind of fine brandies, aromatic bourbons, sweet sherries. He could taste them, smooth, rich, and flavorful on the tongue. But that...that was Boston.

The clear liquid in the cup revealed sand floating in the bottom of the tin. A glob of fat, probably from last night's supper, clung to the rim. Nevertheless, he gulped the grain alcohol straight down, winced, and tried not to cough. The draught snaked fire all the way to his gut.

Stooping, he scooped up the muddy riverwater, and drank down all that his thirsting body could hold. The full flavor of the river no longer annoyed him; neither did the grit that stuck in his teeth.

"Line out, lads!" Green called. "We've an hour yet to reach a decent camp, but when we get there, double rations for all!"

Richard tossed his cup up on deck, combed his matted hair with his fingers, and waded back onto the beach. The cordelle had been coiled cunningly so the end could be unspooled from the inside out.

Richard took his place behind Toussaint, and shouldered the heavy rope.

Across the Platte. But this time, I'm going home. Each step is one closer to freedom.

Without further incident, they brought the *Maria* into the camp Green had insisted that they reach. True to his word, the rations were doubled, and more whiskey was given out.

Richard strung up his shelter the way Travis had taught him, collapsed inside, and fell asleep to the humming of mosquitoes around his blanket-covered ears.

The dreams were so pristine and clear: Boston, gleaming in the morning sun as he and Laura ate their breakfast before an open window. She was laughing at one of his stories as she sipped tea from a delicate china cup.

"Oh, Richard," she said softly, her other hand reaching for his. "You've made me so happy…"

―――

"Hyar! Dick! C'mon, coon. Git yer possibles together," Travis's rasping voice intruded. "*Leve!* Dick, we ain't got all day."

"Huh?" Richard shifted, pulled his blanket back, and peered out into pitch blackness. "Laura? I mean…Travis?"

"I ain't no Laura, coon. Best rustle, now. Got breakfast cooking. Tend ter yer needs and roll up yer outfit. I'll be over to the fire."

Richard rubbed his head, splinters of the dream clinging to him, fading…fading… Well, so be it. By sunset, they should be within sight of Fort Atkinson.

He climbed to his feet and fumbled with the ties. He rolled his blanket carefully and wandered over to the fire. Hartman squatted over the low coals, his horrible face illuminated by the red glow. The scars made him look like something straight out of Hell.

"It's the middle of the night, Travis!"

"Be coming on light soon, Dick. Hyar, I done boilt up some coffee. Side pork's cooked and pone's crackling in the grease. Figgered I'd dip into stores fer the occasion. Dig in and eat up." Travis glanced curiously at Richard. "They didn't shave ye? Didn't pull no funning on ye?"

"Funning?"

"Pranks. Fer making passage past the Platte. Reckon it's like when sailors cross the equator. Means ye ain't a pilgrim no more."

"I'm not?"

"Hell, no. 'Course, given yer queer ways, ye'll be a damn Yankee Doodle till ye dies. Some things cain't be overcome through travel, no matter how much a feller could wish."

"I didn't see any pranks, Travis. Unless you getting me up when I ought to be sleeping is one."

Hartman seemed to be thinking. "I reckon it's 'cause they's all been upriver. Every last man of 'em. Reckon, too, that yer not one of 'em. Yer no *engagé*. To their eyes, yer more like a tick: A...what do they call 'em? Partsite?"

"The word is parasite."

"If'n ye says so."

"Listen, Travis, I didn't want to be here in the first place. If you didn't wake me up as a prank, I'm going to go right back to sleep. It's a long pull into Fort Atkinson tomorrow."

"Who's Laura?"

"Nobody. Just a dream. That's all."

"Uh-huh. Drink yer coffee, Dick. Then eat yer fill. Soon's ye finish, I'll be needing ye ter give me a hand with the whiskey tins."

"Whiskey tins?"

"Wal, coon, it's like this. Cain't take whiskey upriver. It's agin' the law. 'Course the Injun trade works on whiskey. No whiskey, no trade. Now, Green don't want no more questions asked than need be when he reaches the fort. He'll have just enough over the limit on board to look normal, whilst the two of us packs the whiskey out around the fort."

"That many cases? On our backs?"

Travis looked up with mild irritation. "Tarnal Hell, Dick. I done fetched hosses, and a sneaking Pawnee ter go with 'em."

"Horses? An Indian?"

Hartman handed him a cup of coffee. "Ye fixing ter repeat every word I says?"

Richard dropped to his haunches and stared into the coals. He sipped the hot coffee, and glanced sideways at Hartman. This wasn't the watery brew the boatmen got on special occasions, but thick and black. Real coffee.

"Now, pay special attention, hoss," Travis said in a low voice. "This Pawnee—Half Man. Don't trust him, hear? Don't never turn yer back on him. Yer a gonna have ter be cat-quick, and watchful as a hawk. If'n ye see him do anything odd, tell me, right fast."

"If you don't trust him, why travel with him?"

"'Cause he's got hosses. I need hosses ter pack the whiskey. Now, I'd rather borrow 'em from Colonel Atkinson, but he's up-river. Reckon the only other choice is ter take my chances with Half Man, and hope I can keep the red devil buffler'd. Now, eat."

Richard needed no second invitation, but stuffed himself with the hot venison and corn meal. These days he shoveled his meals into his belly, constantly looking for more.

"Yer full?" Hartman asked, throwing out the grounds in the bottom of his cup. "Wal, come on. Let's unpack them tins."

Birds were singing by the time they carried the last of the heavy tins into the dawn-grayed trees beyond the camp. The musty smell of the river lay heavy on the damp air. Trees, like humped monsters, made a black silhouette against the glowing eastern horizon. A line of horses—scrubby-looking ponies for the most part—stood at their picket.

"That's the Pawnee," Travis said, pointing at a dark form rolled in a blanket. "Reckon the coon's getting all the sleep he can. All right, Yankee, come watch me. This hyar be how ye packs a hoss. Ye ever packed afore?"

"No."

"Wal, watch then."

One by one, they lashed the heavy tins onto the horses, and Richard suddenly understood why they were triangular—just right to be lashed to a horse with a complicated knot Hartman called a diamond hitch.

"And thar she be," Travis concluded as the last animal was loaded. "Whoa, there, hoss. Easy now. Dick, take up that slack on the rope. That's it. Now, bend down and look at that lash cinch. Setting pert, is it?"

"Looks so."

"Wal, then, I reckon I'll go kick that lazy Pawnee awake." Hartman half turned. "Huh, almost fergot." He pointed to a roll of tan hide. "Best put them on, Dick, whilst I roust out this hyar mangy half-breed. We got tracks ter make."

Richard bent over the roll, pulling out a pair of beautiful white leather moccasins, a heavy cloth shirt, and fringed leather pants. He cast an uncertain glance at Hartman, who was crouched several feet away from the Pawnee, talking in a strange tongue and gesturing with his hands.

How did they tan leather to be this soft? Richard stripped and slid into the pants, then pulled on the moccasins after stopping to feel the hard, thick soles. The shirt fit loosely, but how wonderful to wear something that didn't have a hole in it.

Travis walked up, rifle in hand. "Pawnee's up. Let's get a move on."

"Just a moment. I need to take my old clothes back to the boat."

"Reckon not. Wrap 'em up and tie 'em with a thong. A feller can always use rags."

"I...I'll pay you back, Travis. For the clothes, I mean."

"Fergit it, lad. It's on the jawbone."

"Travis?"

"What now?"

"You and I, we won't be going by the fort, will we?"

Travis stared around, as if to see if he'd forgotten anything. "Reckon not."

The deep sinking sensation hollowed Richard's gut. "Damn you. Damn you all."

Hartman's gaze went winter-hard. "Pay attention ter the Pawnee, Dick."

"Why? Maybe I'll help him steal your whiskey. That's what you're afraid of, isn't it?"

"Yep. 'Course, ye need ter be mindful, Dick. Ter lift our whiskey, he's gotta kill me first. Then, after he lifts my hair, he'll be fixing to lift yers, too."

"*Kill* us?"

"Reckon so. Keep yer eyes open."

———

Heals Like A Willow sat stiffly on her horse, her blanket over her head for protection. A low bank of gray clouds sprinkled her and Packrat with a gentle spring rain. They trotted down a trail, winding through a copse of trees.

After two months of hard riding, she'd grown somewhat fond of the mare. After all, it wasn't the animal's fault that she'd been captured. The stolid pony had carried her resolutely across desert, plain, and prairie.

Willow winced and tried to shift her position. If only her hands weren't always tied; but then, after two moons of practice, she'd learned to do a great many things despite bound wrists.

Riding through the rain, they crossed hilly country covered with tall grasses and interminable patches of brush. The trees were of a kind Willow had never seen

before, black-barked, with twisting branches. The wood
was heavy, and burned into better coals than even sagebrush produced. And how hard it was! A digging stick
made of such would last a woman all of her life.

"Here!" Packrat told her. "We are close now."

As they broke through the spring green trees, Willow
gasped. There, before them, lay the *La-chi-kuts'* fort. She'd
never seen the like of it. The White men had built their
soldier village in a square—and such lodges, like giant
baskets made of logs. And slanting roofs! A strong man
couldn't shoot an arrow across the place in three shots!

She rode in silence, trying to comprehend what her
eyes saw, remembering White Hail's claim that the
White men were magical. Perhaps they were.

As they rode up to a big lodge, she saw her first
White men. She could only stare as Packrat jumped off
his horse. He bent down to hobble her animal, ordering,
"Stay where you are. Do not leave your horse, or the *La-
chi-kut* will catch you. They do terrible things to women."

She waited until Packrat had stepped inside the log
lodge, swallowed hard to nerve herself, and carefully
slipped off her horse. The White men were watching,
their weird pale eyes gleaming, but no one shouted a
warning, or even took a step in her direction. She hadn't
made three steps when Packrat emerged from the black
doorway and came flying after her.

He bellowed in rage, leaping to tackle her and slam
her into the ground. "I told you!"

"What do you expect?" she hissed back.

"Get up! Get up, or I will beat you."

Laughter made her look up. More White men had
gathered at the door of the log lodge. Packrat noticed,
and colored. He cuffed her hard on the side of the head,
to regain some of his shattered honor.

Willow stood with reluctance, and allowed Packrat to lead her back to her horse.

"Where is Half Man?" she asked.

"Not here," Packrat growled angrily. "Gone. Working for a *La-chi-kut*. Now we have to find him."

Willow leapt, caught the mane of her horse, and kicked onto its back. She stared down into Packrat's burning eyes. Hatred sparkled there, fueled by frustration. He blamed his bad luck on her, on her polluting woman's blood.

"Whoa!" came a cry.

Willow turned her head to see a *La-chi-kut* step out of the opening of the log lodge. Her breath caught. He had hair the color of the sun on winter grass. And such eyes! Blue, like a clear sky. By Wolf, the stories were true! His skin was as pale as hide bleached with white clay. And, yes, hair grew on his face! A dog face, like the stories said.

Packrat turned, watching the *La-chi-kut* warily.

"Your woman?" the *La-chi-kut* asked in crude Pawnee.

"My captive," Packrat replied cautiously.

The *La-chi-kut* studied Willow with calculating eyes. "Snake?" He repeated the word, "Snake?" Then he pointed at Willow, eyes inquiring. With his hands he made the sign of her people.

Willow jerked a curt nod. Her heart had begun to pound. A *La-chi-kut*! No telling what he might do to her. Even slavery among the Pawnee would be better.

"Make trade?" the *La-chi-kut* asked Packrat.

Packrat bit his lip, glanced nervously at Willow, and shook his head.

"A rifle," the *La-chi-kut* said.

Packrat shook his head.

"Two rifles."

Packrat's face betrayed a man in pain. In desperation, he signed, "The woman is not for trade.It is finished."

He glanced around, and gathered up the lead rope for Willow's beast. Laughter broke out again as Willow's horse hopped, the hobbles forgotten in Packrat's hurry.

She'd never seen him so, the facial veins standing out as he slid down, soothed her mare, and worked the hobbles loose. The hoots and jeers might have been cactus thorns the way they stung him.

This time, they left at a run, Willow clinging to her mount, wind whipping at her, tearing her blanket from her shoulders. So desperate was the pace that she couldn't reach back for it, but had to let it vanish in the grass behind them.

They bolted across the flats, and up through the trees, before Packrat slowed, shoulders slumped, head drooping. From the heights, Willow could see the mighty Missouri River loop around to the south to meet the line of trees marking the confluence of the Flat River, and the route that would take her back west to her people. To the north, the big Missouri wound its way into the distance, water like a silver thread in the green land.

"Where is Half Man?" she asked, aware that any words might incite Packrat to violence.

"Somewhere. He said he would be back in four days, with whiskey to trade for guns, powder, and shot. He told them that then he would go back to the Pawnee. A rich man."

"I am sorry I ran. The *La-chi-kuts* frightened me."

Packrat glanced up, eyes smoldering. He sidestepped his horse close. Gripping the head of his war club, he cracked her on the side of the head with the handle.

She cried out in pain. Her mare shied at the sound and Willow's flinch.

"Next time, I use the head of the club, Weasel Woman. I won't kill you, but I will hurt you so badly that you will never be right again. Do you understand? I am *tired* of you! You are *evil.*" Tears glistened in his eyes. "You have ruined me!"

You have ruined yourself, fool!

But she only bowed her head, squinting at the sting of his blow.

No, you only started it. I have driven you to this. Goaded you, driven poison barbs into your soul. Whatever kind of man you might, have been, I have broken your Power, Packrat. You will never be able to trust yourself again. In the words of the Pawnee, you will always be pira-paru.

"This way. They said he had horses, probably to carry something for the *La-chi-kut.* We will cut for sign. Do not blind me with your magic. If you do, I will take you back. Give you to the *La-chi-kut,* and be happy to be rid of you."

Behind his tormented eyes she could see crazy violence brewing. She swallowed hard, aware that the time for threats was over. Like a man climbing rimrock, he hung by his fingers. Were she to make his grip the least bit slippery, he'd fall into the darkness that had grown in his soul, and she would suffer for it.

Late that afternoon, Packrat cried out in anticipation, "It is here! I know his sign. Look! Half Man walked here. And here you see where one *La-chi-kut* walked. And here, another, wearing new moccasins!"

She glanced at the tracks, interspersed with those of heavily loaded horses.

"Come!" Packrat cried. "I will succeed after all! And, who knows, perhaps I can take this whiskey. Wealth enough to pay for a complete cleansing by the Doctors!"

She fingered the bruise on the side of her head, and remained passive. If an opportunity was to present itself, it had better be quick. If Half Man surmised just what his son was doing to him, he might well kill her outright.

She cocked her head.

What has changed? Two moons ago, I would just as soon have died.

Deep within her soul, the will to live had been rekindled—or, perhaps, it had been smoldering all along.

CHAPTER THREE

If I strip this human being, thus constituted, of all the supernatural gifts which he may have received, and of all the artificial faculties, which he could not have acquired but by slow degrees; if I consider him, in a word, such as he must have originated from the hands of nature; I see an animal not so strong as some, and less agile than others, but, upon the whole, the most advantageously organized of any: I see him sating his hunger under an oak tree, and his thirst at the first brook; I see him laying himself down to sleep at the foot of the same tree that afforded him his meal; and there are all his wants, completely provided.

—Jean-Jacques Rousseau, *Discourse on the Origin and*
Foundation of Inequality Among Mankind

 Richard studied the Pawnee. He didn't look like much. Skinny, dark-skinned, with a protruding belly, he wore greasy black skins, a filthy blanket, and shabby moccasins with little metal bells on the tops.

The Pawnee's face might have been cast of weathered bronze, and appeared just as unforgiving as the metal. Those eyes were black, and hard as river pebbles, the nose hooked over thin lips. Half Man looked at Richard and Travis with a natural arrogance, as if he deigned to glance upon inferiors. But when they paused for a rest, Richard caught the crafty look as he appraised the whiskey.

Now they walked, single-file, each leading a string of horses, the animals tail-hitched. The Pawnee went first, then Richard, and finally Travis bringing up the rear. Richard had noticed that neither Travis nor the Pawnee went anywhere without his rifle in hand. Each might have been hunting a tiger, so alert were they to each other's movements.

They had passed beyond the trees and now crossed lush meadows of bluestem and wildflowers of every color. In the drainages, stands of mixed oak and ash were leafed out in a brilliant green that contrasted to the plum, hazel, and raspberry bushes.

A free wind tugged at the fringes on Richard's pants, playing with the wispy beard on his cheeks. After months of not shaving, he had come to resemble all the others. It wasn't a beard like the older *engagés'*, but it was good enough for the river.

Patchy white clouds scuttled across the sky, promising more showers. But how blue the sky was beyond them, how vast the distances. Down in the river bottom, a man didn't have this sense of eternity. Something deep inside him shivered at that. How easy it would be to get lost out there, naked to the eye of God.

"Ouch!" Richard hopped sideways, causing the horse he was leading to throw its head.

"Prickly pear," Travis noted from behind. "Told ye,

Dick. Watch whar ye puts yer feet. Don't stop now. Walk on it fer a while. It'll sure larn ye where ter put yer feet."

Richard whirled around, glaring. "Damn you, Travis. You knew I'd be free by now. You and Green. You plotted this! Took away my chance! I ought to...to..."

The hunter stepped up to him, a hardening glint in his eyes. "Easy, hoss. Yer not up ter taking this coon. Not by a damn sight. Now, settle down—less'n I fetch ye up good."

Sudden fear, like a cool wind, blew through Richard's hot guts. He swallowed to still the runny feeling down inside.

"Glad ter see ye got sense, Dick." Travis nodded his head toward the Pawnee. "Reckon he'd be plumb happy ter see us take a go at each other. After I kilt ye, he'd only have me to worry about."

"Killed me?" Richard glanced uneasily at the Pawnee.

"Oh, reckon not. Yer not that dangerous. I'd just have to slap ye around a bit. A feller's good sense creeps right back inta his head when he's getting whacked around and the lights start a-popping behind his eyes."

Richard rubbed the back of his neck, turned, and started off again. The Pawnee had been watching him as if he were a piece of meat. The Indian resumed his pace, rifle in his right hand, the lead rope for the horse in his left. Along with the rifle, the Pawnee carried a tomahawk and a knife.

"What about him?" Richard asked. "Why would he just kill us? I mean, he doesn't know us."

"What's to know? We got whiskey—he wants it."

"It's not rational, Travis. Look at him. A man raised in nature. How does he get tainted by the corruption of civilization? He's free! A free man doesn't kill others. It defies any philosophical dictum I've ever read."

"Philos'phy!" Travis snorted. "Ye thinks a man needs ter be civilized ter kill? Rot and hogwash!"

"That's not what Rousseau says. And I dare say, Travis, he's a great deal more thoroughly read than you are on the subject. In his *Discourse on the Origin of Inequality,* he makes a point that primitive man—and I assume our Pawnee is exactly that—keeps his dissensions to a minimum. Without the chains of property, or belongings, to bind him, he needs not resort to violence. What need does he have to strike another, when he can avoid the first blow? An insult can be easily repaired in a primitive society. A man need not seek revenge."

Travis blinked, his head cocked, mouth open. "Of all the foolish...Tarnal Hell! These Injuns war with each other just ter keep in practice! Don't ye know how they counts coup? By striking an enemy. The more the better! If'n ye wants ter start a war, just walk up and strike an Injun warrior. Afore ye can take yer next breath, he's a gonna lift yer hair, slit yer throat, and open yer belly so yer guts fall out fer the dogs to eat!"

"But that doesn't make sense. Rousseau—"

"Hang Roosoo with a rawhide rope!" Travis gestured his frustration by shaking his rifle. Then he glared—all the more terrible for the hideous scars. "Dick...Dick, listen. Please, now. I'm a-begging ye. That Pawnee up thar, he's a warrior, half-breed or no. They's proud people. Honor and coup mean everything to 'em. Now, ye can't go around judging them by the likes of yer Mister Roosoo, or by the Bible, or nothing else. Understand? If'n ye do, I reckon you'll be dead right quick."

Richard studied the Pawnee, trying to read the mind behind those obsidian eyes. "That isn't rational!"

"Hell! 'Course it's rational, so long's ye looks at it through their eyes. Strength, pride, honor. Hyar's how ye deals with Injuns, Dick. Foller these rules, and God willing, ye might see next fall roll around with yer topknot on yer head. Show 'em respect. Respect is just that. Don't never be weak. Not when they can see. They value strength and bravery. Last, keep yer word, coon. Injuns is getting used to whites breaking their word, but if'n ye keeps yers, they won't fergit. Now, that means yer not ter be making promises ye cain't keep. Think on that. Right now the Sioux'll spit on a white as soon as look at him, after what Leavenworth did up ter the Ree villages. Reckon ye don't promise nothing lessen ye can back her to the hilt."

"But how is that rational?"

"Wal, how's it rational that a man can shoot another man fer fooling with his wife? That's ter say he didn't force her. Reckon if'n she says yes, and her lover says yes, they both want to be with each other. What right's the husband got to shoot 'em? Ain't no court'll convict a husband that shoots his wife, or her lover. Is that rational?"

"That fact is, it is indeed rational. The tranquility of the hearth—"

"Horse crap! Rees, Kansa, Pawnee, lots of people let their wives sleep with lovers. So long as she's willing, and he's willing, thar ain't no upscuttle. They got rules, Dick. Just like we do. By their rules, if'n ye acts with honor, shows respect, and ain't weak, yer a gonna do all right. But ye've got ter use yer noodle." Travis hawked and spit. "Hell, I git along a heap better with Injuns than I ever did with white men. And Injuns comes in all kinds."

"So, Rousseau is right? The savages are carefree in love, unlike civilized man, whose passions lead him to entanglements. Savages make love, then part. Satisfied to allow anyone to mate with whomever they choose?"

Travis screwed his ruined face into a disgusted look. "Wal, among the Rees, maybe. But I'll tell ye, child. Don't ye never go fooling around with a Cheyenne woman, lessen ye wants ter marry her. They's worse than white men. Drive yer pizzle inta one of their young women, and her folks is gonna kill ye dead. But most peoples out hyar, they figger a man laying with a woman is plumb natural."

A huge rabbit, bigger than any Richard had ever seen, broke cover and went bounding and sailing over the grass. "What's that?"

"Jackrabbit," Travis said.

"How come they don't get cactus thorns in their feet?" The burning spine still made Richard hobble, but after the altercation with Travis, he'd be damned if he'd stop to dig it out.

"They ain't got feet, exactly. Just gobs of hair between their toes. Turns the cactus, I guess."

"So these women lie with anyone they and their husbands agree on. What about the bastard children?"

"Bastards? Hell, that's another way I don't cotton ter white ways. A child's a child. Given the number that dies young, who's to say? Injuns generally welcome a kid—lessen it comes from another tribe. Take that Pawnee, yonder—Half Man. Half Pawnee, half Omaha. He slips back and forth atwixt and atween. Home in both places—trusted by none. Talk among the Pawnee is that his mother'd have been better off to leave him out in the winter, let him die since he was planted by an Omaha when Half Man's mother was a slave."

"Slave?"

Travis squinted at Half Man walking several paces ahead of them. The Pawnee seemed oblivious to them, as if he were just out for a morning walk. "Reckon so. Most tribes out hyar, they takes slaves right regular. Used to be the Comanche stole Pawnee to sell to the Spaniards down south. Then the Comanche'd steal Lipan and Jicarilla kids and women, and sell 'em to the Pawnee."

"Morally reprehensible."

"Perhaps, lad. But watch yer tongue. Specially when we get up among the Crow. They steal anyone they can get their hands on. Kids especially. They love 'em, and raise 'em up to be good Crows."

"It doesn't sound like any slavery I've ever heard of."

"Reckon not, but then, ye ain't seen what the Osage do to an Iowa woman when they capture her, neither."

Richard skipped wide of a patch of prickly pear hidden down in the tall grass. "Rousseau can't be this wrong. Travis, we're missing something important. These people, they've been corrupted. That's got to be the answer. Like Half Man, here. He's been around whites for too long. Picked up too many of our vices: liquor, slavery, the drive to possess objects. I need to see someone who hasn't lived around whites, hasn't been affected by the traders with their guns and whiskey."

Hartman grinned amusedly. "Ye do take all, Dick. Ain't no such folks. Tarnal Hell, I seen 'em, from yer Boston to the Blackfeet. Folks has different customs, Dick. But they's all the same down deep. Some's good, some's bad, according to their lights. That's all."

"It's not rational!" Richard threw up his hands in protest, and to the horse's unease. "Whoa, boy." With restrained gestures, Richard said, "The closer to a state of nature, the closer man is to a state of innocence. Neither good nor bad, but like your Pawnee—"

"They ain't *my* Pawnee."

"—without binding morals. Morals are the result of ensuing stages of civilization placing ever more restrictive concepts of good and evil upon people. These Black-feet, they don't have any sense of evil, do they?"

Travis made a sour face. "Yankee, yer gonna be dead within the month. I can feel it in my bones. Why on God's green earth did I ever stick my neck out fer an idiot? Listen up, Doodle, the Black-foot will kill ye dead just because yer white. We call 'em Bug's Boys. They use that term in Boston?"

"The Devil's boys."

"And rightly so."

Richard tried to split his concentration between the argument and the patches of grassy prairie that gave way to groves of trees. But what was he supposed to see? With grass this tall, if Indians were crawling up on their bellies, they'd be invisible until the last minute.

Richard gave it up for a lost cause and said, "Then, well, name another people, even farther away."

"Wal, thar's the Snakes. Generally good folk. With the exception of old Left Hand, if'n he ain't gone under by now."

"Are they more innocent?"

"Naw, they damn near wiped out the Blackfoot a couple of generations back. Did such a damn good job of it, the Blackfoot ain't fergot. Them two tribes is in a fight ter the death. No treaties, no mercy. Just a fight till every last one's dead. And ye've got ter keep an eye on a Snake. He's a right smart trader, right up there with the Mandan. The story is that the Snakes used to trade with the Mandan before the Sioux, Cheyennes, and Arapaho cut the trade routes."

"Trade? I mean, Rousseau...Didn't any of these people ever just sit under an oak tree? Didn't any of them live off the bounty of the land? Aren't any of them innocent?"

Travis chuckled. "Yes, wal, as innocent as any other

folks ye can think of. At least as innocent as that Yankee captain what stole me off on his ship from Boston." He looked at Richard. "Which might be one of the reasons I stuck my neck out fer ye. Hell, if'n I'd a stayed in the States, I'd been hung or jailed by now."

"You don't seem like a criminal."

"I ain't, not much, if'n ye judges me by the rules out hyar. Back in that civilization ye harps so on, I'd be a handful. Reckon I like the rules better hyar."

Richard glanced at the Pawnee. "Some rules. According to you, he'll kill us to possess this whiskey."

"Reckon so."

"It's irrational."

"Tell it to him."

"I intend to."

"Speak Pawnee?" Travis asked, raising an eyebrow and changing the lines of scars on his face.

"No, I guess not. You'll translate?"

Travis chuckled. "I'd better. Maybe I can keep ye alive after Half Man decides yer an idiot. I wouldn't try and philos'phy him. Half Man ain't noted fer his elocution."

"Oh, what's he noted for?"

"Stabbing people in the back."

———

"Travis?"

Hartman came awake in an instant, hands tightening on his rifle. "What's up, coon?"

"I can't stay awake any longer." Hamilton yawned as he spoke.

"Reckon ye done fine." Travis sat up, kicked out of his blankets, and studied the dark camp. Half Man lay rolled in his blanket, no doubt hearing every word. Hell, that

Pawnee son of a bitch might be as good as his word. The dicker had been five gallons of whiskey for the use of the horses. Five gallons would allow Half Man to trade for a heap of hides. Maybe the red bastard wouldn't try and raise hair after all.

And all them book ideas the lad's been spouting have made mush outa my brain, too.

Travis walked out from the smoldering fire, sniffing the night air, damp and green-smelling after the rains. The land had needed that. Insect sounds carried to him as he checked the horses on their pickets.

All quiet.

Travis opened his senses, becoming one with the night. The sounds, the smells, the feel of the breeze on his skin. Overhead, stars made patterns against the black patches of clouds. The world had come alive again.

Travis made his careful way back to the fire, checking to see that the Pawnee was still in his blanket. The attack would come without warning. When?

Morning, most likely.

How?

Knife or tomahawk. He'll try and whack me, silent like. Maybe cut my throat. Then he can deal with Dick any way he sees fit.

The Pawnee would know Hamilton for a pilgrim.

So, how do I fox Half Man?

Don't give him a chance.

Travis tugged at his beard, and ran his fingers over the smooth ridges of scar tissue. That was the other thing about ever going back to the United States. He couldn't stand the way they'd look at him, like a monster. Out here, among the Indians, they understood what had happened and honored him for it. In the East, they'd stare, loathing on their faces, and they'd back away from him in horror.

Reckon I couldn't take it. Worst of all would be the women. The look in their eyes, like they done seed a serpent.

Better for him to stay here, where he knew the rules, was good at them, in fact. Like Baptiste, he could never go back. The planter had put the scars on Baptiste's back with a whip. The wilderness had scarred Travis's face, marking him as its own. *Each of us branded by his master.*

Travis settled by the low fire, warming his hands as he watched the darkness. Satisfied, he turned his attention on Richard.

Am I just stringing him along? Setting him up for some disaster he ain't prepared for?

A wrong word, an insolent act, and some Sioux, Ree, or Crow would smack the boy's brains out. And why? Just because he'd read a book written by some damn fool who'd never been shot at—or seen what a Blackfoot did to a dying man.

Innocent—in this country? Travis shook his head.

Sorry, Dick. Reckon ye be the only innocent out hyar.

He scratched his head. How in Tarnal Hell was he gonna give Hamilton an even break when every deck on earth was stacked against him?

For hours Travis thought on it, and finally made his decision. Wal, she'd be Katy bar the door, but he'd do 'er. Sunup was coming. Half Man might be waiting, figuring to make his play just at dawn when reactions were the slowest.

Still, it never hurt to make the first move in a cat-and-mouse game.

"Dick? *Leve!* Daylight's a-coming. Half Man, come on, ye Pawnee devil. Let's get a move on."

"In God's name, Travis," Hamilton moaned. "Let me finish the dream. Pastries, and a fine claret..."

"Sun's nigh to breaking forth, coon. Let's get on with her. Sooner we reach the river, the sooner we're all on our way."

Half Man hadn't moved, but Travis could see the glint of his slitted eyes.

We're a pair, you and me.

Richard was up. "Dick, rustle up them hosses. Let's get our likker tied on."

They ate jerked meat washed down with cold coffee. By the time the sky had turned pink, Travis had the pack string moving, never allowing the Pawnee the opportunity to act.

That's it. Keep him off balance. Don't let him have time to get the drop.

As the sun rose and shot glowing red rays across the cloud bottoms, Travis moved up beside Richard.

"These prickly pear, come fall they make a red fruit. A feller can eat 'em. Right sweet they are. The flowers, a feller can eat them, too. Takes a lot to fill a man's belly, but food's food, and can make the difference atwixt living and dying."

Richard stared quizzically at the cactus.

"Meat's meat. Ye got ter remember that. Don't make no matter what the critter. Mule or mouse. Fat cow buffler is about the best eating on the plains, but ye get into the mountains, and elk is some, it is. Better than these hyar plains elk."

"Any meat?" Richard asked. "Who'd eat a mouse?"

"Wal, if'n ye were starving, I reckon ye'd eat all ye could catch. Remember, lad. Meat's meat. Even lizards and buzzworms."

"What's a buzzworm?"

"Rattlesnake, coon. And they's good eating. Flaky white meat. Now the Shoshoni, way out west, they even eat ants. Collect 'em and grind 'em up on their slabs. Makes a kind of paste. I've heard coons tell it ain't bad eating, so long's ye don't dwell on it being ants. Grasshoppers, they's good, too."

"Travis, you're making me sick."

"Listen, coon. I ain't talking to hear my jaw flap." Travis pointed out at the grassy plains. "Thar's a whole big land out there. Reckon a feller that didn't know better, specially one full of book larning, wal, he might starve ter death surrounded by all the food in the world. He needs to use his noodle to think about the world a mite different."

"But ants? Grasshoppers?"

"Whar's an egg come from?"

Richard stared at him thoughtfully. "A chicken. They lay them."

"How?"

"Uh, well, I don't—"

"Right outa their assholes, coon. I hear they's rich folks what eat fish eggs. And didn't them Pharaohs eat birds' tongues?"

"I think that was Roman emperors."

Travis waved it away. "One's as good as t'other. Thing is, when it gets down to cat scratch, yer gonna do whatever it takes ter keep yerself alive. Remember that. Meat's meat. If it comes off a critter, ye can eat it. 'Course, meat ain't everything."

Travis pointed eastward. "Over thar, to Cantonment Missouri.

Reckon they had three hunnert soldiers billeted through the winter about five years back. Most of 'em ketched the scurvy. Reckon they had plenty of meat. Fact is, they didn't eat the lights."

"Lights?" Richard frowned. "What are the lights?"

"The guts, coon. Heart, liver, kidneys, boudins. Remember that, if'n yer ever getting poor in spite of eating all the meat ye can hold. Injuns, they know. If'n the lights don't fix ye, ye need plants. I've even seed Injuns boiling grass to make tea. Balances a man's blood, I'm told."

"I've heard that lemons are carried on ships for scurvy. Do lemons grow out here?"

"Don't reckon so. Plants, now, they take a little larning. Reckon it's early, and we're a bit north fer finding *pommes de terre,* but they's other things. Sunflowers, fer one. Prairie turnips, a feller can make a meal of them. Sego lily, Yampa root, blue-flower camas. I've et 'em all. Like a cross between potato and carrot. Wild onions is everywhere. Look, reckon that's one."

Travis led his horse over, and used his belt knife to lever a bulb out of the ground. He handed it to Richard, resuming his pace. "Smell her. Onion, ain't it? Thar now. Knock the dirt off'n it and eat it. Ye'll know onion from death camas. She's always got that smell. And did ye see how quick it was to dig that out? A feller can eat on the run."

"We didn't get killed by the Pawnee this morning." Richard ate the onion thoughtfully. "Maybe you're worried about nothing."

"Maybe." Travis slung his lead rope over his shoulder and lifted his rifle, checking the priming in the pan. "This morning, notice how I loaded the packs? Always kept a hoss atwixt me and the Pawnee? He didn't have a clear target."

"You always make him walk first," Richard noted. "Is that so that you won't get shot in the back?"

"Yer larning, coon."

"Travis, I don't know. He's strange. But how can you be so sure he's a bad man?"

"Maybe he ain't. But this hyar ain't a Christian land. Reckon old Half Man, he ain't heard of no Good Samaritan. Now, pay attention. If'n he makes a play, I want ye ter grab the hosses. Understand? I'll raise the Injun, you just make sure the hosses don't bolt."

"Raise the Injun? I don't understand."

"Kill him dead."

"Oh. Is that a Christian reference, as in resurrect?"

"Reckon not." Travis reached in his possibles for a twist of tobacco and cut a chew. After he had it juicing, he asked, "What's yer job if'n the Pawnee makes trouble?"

"I grab the horses...but what if he gets the best of you?"

Travis placed his twist back into his possibles. "Then, I reckon ye'd best hope he's been a-reading that philos'phy of yern."

CHAPTER FOUR

This appears to me as clear as daylight, and I cannot conceive from whence
our philosophers can derive all the passions they endow to natural man.
Except for the basic physical necessities, which nature herself requires, all
our other needs are merely the result of habit, before which they were not
needs or of our cravings; and we don't crave that which we are not in a
circumstance to know. Therefore it follows that as savage man yearns for
nothing but what he knows, and knows nothing but what he actually
possesses or can easily acquire, nothing can be so tranquil as his soul, or so
restricted as his understanding.

—Jean-Jacques Rousseau, *Discourse on the Origin and
Foundation of Inequality Among Mankind*

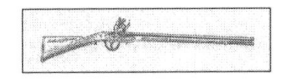 After so many days of rain, the
sun beat down hot and bright.
Travis might have found that a
welcome change, but for the muggy air that made a man's
sweat just about useless. The trilling of a meadowlark,
the chirping of the finches, and the colorful wild-flowers
helped to make up for the humid heat.

"Warm enough fer ye?" he asked Hamilton.

"I guess. After freezing for days, now I'd give anything for a couple of clouds."

"Later this afternoon. Reckon the thunderheads will come rolling in."

Travis never let his attention waver from where Half Man walked ahead of them. An Indian walked differently, planted his feet in a softer manner than a galomping, booted white man. Half Man didn't look like much, skinny, his eyes soulless. Made a coon figger he didn't have a thought in his head. But a man didn't skip atwixt and atween the Omaha and the Pawnee—mortal enemies —without having a heap of savvy locked in his noodle.

He's planning something. Knows we're smuggling, and if n we don't show up, thar ain't gonna be no questions asked. At least, not by the gov'ment. If'n I's in his moccasins, I'd be thinking to raise Dick and me, skip off to the Pawnee, and make like a king. Pile up a heap of buffler and beaver, and trade it while prices are high. Probably down to Fort Osage.

"What are you thinking?" Hamilton asked.

"'Bout the Pawnee. I got him figgered as far as the whiskey's concerned. What I ain't got figgered is when he's a gonna strike."

Richard made a face.

"Still don't believe this child, do ye?"

Richard's thin face looked pensive. "Travis, I can understand him wanting to steal our things. But unless we give him cause, he doesn't have any reason to kill us."

"Coup, Dick. I explained that to ye. Honor as a warrior."

"Such concepts of honor are irrational."

"Tell them soldiers they pin all them medals on."

Richard frowned as he walked, eyes on the grass.

"Best larn to watch around, Dick. Feller's got ter see

everything. Front and back, up and down. Trouble can come on ye from any direction. Thar's times that seeing a danger first means ye can avoid it altogether."

"I was just thinking." Richard wiped sweat from his forehead. The distant trees were shimmering in the light, and delicate butterflies fluttered in the hot air. The sweet smell of grass seemed to grow stronger with the heat.

"Yep, locked in yer Doodle noodle. Last thing ye'll be wondering about is how that arrow come ter be sticking through yer guts."

"They just shoot people. Without any warning?"

Travis gave the young man a twinkling grin. "Reckon they's plumb rational about it."

They walked along in silence, and to Travis's relief, Hamilton had started to look around.

"See the deer over ter the trees? Two does, still as can be."

"Nope."

"Right yonder, down under the branches of that hazel. Just ahint that patch of daisy flowers."

"No, I don't...Wait. Yes! I see them—or I think I do. How in God's name did you see them over there?"

"Got ter train yer eye, Dick. It's in the outlines, the way the light sits. Work at her, and ye'll larn."

Finally Richard asked, "What happened to your face? The scars, I mean. A fight? Indians?"

"Old Ephraim. He done it."

"You've talked about him before. Is he an Indian?"

"Waugh! He be the white bear. The grizzly." Travis pointed at his face. "Time this happened, we's working our way west, outa Fort Benton. Made her clear ter the Great Falls of the Missouri. I was walking up ahead, scouting like, ye see. That's Blackfoot country, so a child's got ter be slick, see them red bastards afore they can sneak up on ye.

"Wal, thar I be, a-sneaking through these sarvisberry bushes, and lo, Old Ephraim just rared up outa a hole and whacked my rifle away. He grabbed aholt of me, and it was Katy bar the door! Pressed down like I was in them bushes, I couldn't hardly move. He bounced on me, but the bushes gave, ye see. Didn't crush my lights out. Then he took a swipe with his paw. That's what took my cheek and nose, and made these hyar scars that run round me ear. At the smell of blood, he started ter chew my head up. That's what made these hyar scars running up through my hair. Pilgrim, I reckon ye've never lived till ye hears bear teeth a-sliding along yer skull."

Richard blinked as if in disbelief. "How...how did you survive? I mean...Good Lord!"

"Davey Green heard my screams and come a-running. He saw the bear, but couldn't see me. Davey, he ups his shooter and drives a galena pill inter Old Ephraim's lights. Then Davey dives in with his knife.

"At the sound of the shot, Old Ephraim turns, and swats Davey half across the berry patch. Plumb knocked him cold, and woulda busted him up, but for the bushes breaking his fall. Then Keemle, Immel, and Jones runs up. Wal, Old Ephraim, he sees all this and roars. He's still a-standing on me, mind. Keemle up and shoots." Travis chuckled. "Funny thing. I was looking up at that bear's head. Big as world, it was. I saw that pill hit him. Took him square in the nose. I felt that bear jerk and damn me if'n it ain't true, but I knew what he's a-thinking."

"You did?"

"Yep. Don't know the why of it, but we might a been a-sharing minds. He knew he's hit plumb center. That ball had busted up his nose and cracked his skull. And way down deep in that bear's soul, I felt the rage as he charged out to take old Keemle down with him. 'Course, afore he got thar, Jones shot him through the shoulder, and busted him down. Then Immel busted his neck with another shot."

"What about you?"

"Ain't much ter tell after that. Reckon all the excitement was over, and the real hurting started. They put me in a pirogue and sent me back down ter the fort. Dave Green went along, took care of me. Sewed up all the loose pieces he could find. Reckon Old Ephraim woulda kilt me but for Green running up ter give him something else ter think of."

"And Keemle, Immel, and Jones?"

"Ah, Keemle's printing the paper down ter Saint Loowee. Immel and Jones...they gone under. Blackfoots caught 'em a couple of years back." Travis smiled sadly, voice dropping. "And I'da been with 'em that day. They's under a bluff on the Yellerstone. Blackfoots wiped out the whole shitaree."

The old wound in his soul opened again.

"Makes a coon wonder, Dick. I was the scout—the keen devil ter slip on ahead. Now, if'n I'd a been thar—instead of a-laying flat on me back in Fort Benton—would I a smelt out that Blackfoot trap? Would I a saved them coons? Or would I be a-laying up thar, topknot gone, and all turned to bones?"

Hamilton had a funny depth to his eyes as he said, "Perhaps God saved you for a reason. If Isaac Newton is right, the universe is predetermined. Maybe God used the bear to save you for the express purpose of torturing me." A faint smile bent his boyish lips.

Travis chuckled. "Hell, Doodle, ye ain't worth the

torturing. Now, skin yer eyes and keep a watch on that sneaky Pawnee fer a while. Hyar, notice the way he walks, how his feet mashes the grass. See? From the pattern, ye can figger which direction he's a-going."

"What did Immel and Jones do to make the Blackfeet so mad, Travis?"

"Nothing. Blackfoots is just poison, coon. That's all thar is to it. They done declared war on whites, and by God, they'll fight her out."

"Well, were Immel and Jones going up to fight them?"

"Tarnation, no! Child, ain't none of us interested in fighting. Wal, 'cept maybe fer some fools like the British. Ye cain't never trust a Britisher no more than a Blackfoot, or a Ree. No, it was like this. Manuel Lisa died of the fever down to Saint Loowee. Joshua Pilcher, he took over the Missouri Fur Company. He and Lisa had been palavering about setting up a post to trade with the Blackfoot. Figgered, just like yer a-doing, that with the right presents, and a peaceful delegation, they could open that country up. Hell, we didn't want no war with the Blackfoots! A feller cain't trade fer plews when he's being shot at. Rational, eh?"

"Maybe."

"Wal, Immel and Jones, they met up with one band of Blackfoot, and sure enough, had 'em a peace talk. It was later that them Blackfoot all got together with the others and decided to wipe out the whites. And they done her."

An eerie feeling of danger had drifted over Richard like a miasma. He gave the Pawnee's back an unsure look. Was he like the Blackfeet? "But why? Travis, I'm looking for the reason. War is not the natural human state. I can't believe that. They must have had a reason."

"Who knows? They's just devils. Maybe their spirits told 'em to. Maybe it's because we're friendly with the

Snakes, and Blackfoot hate Snakes as much as they hate anybody. Dick, listen close now. Out hyar, a feller don't need a reason. These Injuns don't think the same as ye. Larn their rules, or they'll kill ye. Get that philos'phy mush outa yer head."

"It just doesn't make sense. Man is rational. Man *must be* rational. Otherwise, what's the difference between us and the animals?"

Travis scratched at the sweat running down his cheeks and into his beard. "Wal, now. That's the first smart question ye've asked all day. So far as old Travis Hartman's concerned, thar ain't a whole lot."

———

If nothing else could be said for him, Richard Hamilton had a quick and agile mind. "Coneflower," he said, pointing.

"Good. Yer a-larning."

White fluffy clouds drifted across the endless blue vault of sky. Richard had never seen such blue. The warm breeze skipped across the grass, moving it like waves on Boston Harbor. Butterflies flitted past in dots of spectacular color. Insects were chirring in the grass.

"Seems like the whole land is alive." He wiped his sweaty face. "But I'd sure like a drink."

"Spring up ahead." Travis said. "Pawnee's been making fer it."

"You know this country pretty well."

"Reckon so. Worked out of the Council Bluffs fer Lisa, then fer the Company."

The Pawnee started down into a brush-and-oak-filled draw where water had cut through the caprock. Deer trails led through the trees to a little brook.

"Water them hosses downstream, Dick. Reckon we'll let them drink, then us."

When the horses had watered and began grazing along the trickle of creek, Richard dropped to his knees to drink his fill of cool water. Oak boughs dappled the ground with shade, relief from the heat of the day.

Half Man sat a short distance away, crouched on his haunches, rifle across his lap. He watched Richard with expressionless black eyes.

Richard asked, "Do you speak any English?"

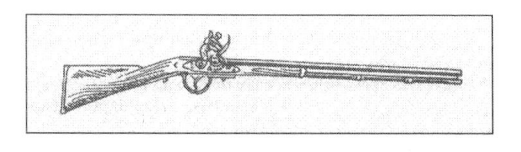

Half Man continued to stare at him for a moment, then spoke, the language incomprehensible. At the same time, those brown hands formed different patterns.

"He says he wants to trade." Travis tied his lead horse to a tree, and walked over to squat several paces from Half Man.

Richard shook his head. "I don't have anything to trade. I just want to ask questions."

Travis spoke slowly, haltingly, his hands tracing patterns in the air. When Half Man answered, Travis looked up and said, "He says he ain't got no reason to waste his time if'n ye ain't gonna trade. Says he's got better things to do with his day than jabber with a *La-chi-kut*."

Richard chewed at his lip for a moment, then slapped at a mosquito. "Tell him I'll trade ideas."

"Ideas? Hell." But Travis spoke, gesturing with his hands the whole time.

Half Man narrowed his eyes as he looked at Richard.

When he spoke, the tone ridiculed. Travis translated: "Words are empty air. I want whiskey, tobacco, gunpowder, mirrors. You are poor, you are nothing."

"I'm not nothing," Richard said. "I'm a student of philosophy, of ideas. The things you speak of are meaningless. Truth, the nature of God, the way in which you perceive the world, those things are all that mean anything."

Travis glanced warily at Richard, then made the signs, adding the Pawnee words he knew.

The Pawnee spoke in mocking tones. Travis translated: "He wants to know if ye'll trade them fine moccasins. He says if ye gives him yer moccasins, he'll find a reason ter be bothered by yer questions. And, which God are ye interested in? Evening Star or Wakonda? First is Pawnee, second's Omaha."

"My moccasins?" Richard cried. "They're the only shoes I've got!"

Half Man made a hissing sound, barked a couple of words, and spit in emphasis.

"He says yer a fool, Dick. And I reckon we'd better call her quits, afore he gets riled."

"A fool? I've at least the decency to have an interest in his beliefs. What does he think? That men have only things—tobacco, whiskey—to tie them together? Damn him, he..."

Richard started as the Pawnee rose, expression turning into a snarl. With the quickness of a striking cat, the Pawnee feinted at Richard, pivoted on his foot, and swung the butt of his rifle at Travis's head.

Travis ducked the whistling rifle, lost his balance, and fell against the Pawnee's knees. In that instant, Half Man dropped his rifle, whipped out his knife, and leapt on Travis, who blocked the slashing blade, growling like a wild animal. Half Man screamed like a panther.

Heart pounding, Richard backed away. The sudden fury of the attack stunned him. Terrified, his hands clutched spasmodically at nothingness.

On the leaf-matted ground, Travis and Half Man kicked and bit and gouged. Grunting now, straining against each other, their faces contorted. Travis got a knee into Half Man's belly and levered the Indian off.

Half Man landed on his side, but struck out with his blade. Travis rolled away, rising. Half Man knocked Travis off his feet. Before the hunter could recover, Half Man leapt. Travis shot his elbow forward, partially deflecting the vicious blade that sliced at his side. At the same time, he jabbed his other hand into Half Man's face, the fingers clawing the Indian's eyes.

Richard gasped for breath, slowly shaking his head. Travis howled with an unearthly fury that drowned Half Man's screams. The Pawnee jerked frantically at the hand clamped to his face, Travis's fingers digging ever deeper into his eyes.

At the same time, Travis jacked his knee into the Pawnee's crotch, again and again and again. Half Man's body jerked from the impact. In desperation, Half Man broke the hunter's grip, flinging himself backward. Cat-quick, Travis was on him, an insane moan breaking his scarred lips, gray-white hair flying. Travis tightened his hold on the knife hand, while his other caught the Pawnee's throat; they were face-to-face, panting, spitting in effort. Travis's strength slowly bent the knife arm until the blade hovered over Half Man. The Pawnee gave a last heave, letting the knife slip out of his fingers. At that moment, Travis butted the Pawnee with his head, battering the Indian's already bloody face.

Richard staggered forward as Travis grabbed a rock and hammered the Indian's head. The rock made a hollow thump like a stick on a melon.

"Travis, no! He's beaten!" Richard cried as he rushed forward. But again and again Travis slammed the rock home, using two hands.

When it was over, Travis rolled off the limp body and flopped on his back. He coughed, blinked at the sky, and closed his eyes.

Richard stood, numb. Blood welled in the ragged red holes where the Indian's eyes had been. The skull had been pounded to pulp from which streams of red leaked. What had been a man was now nothing more than meat. A big black fly landed on the dead man's ruined face.

"Travis?" Richard whispered.

"Dick? Come hyar. I reckon ye'd better take a look." Travis pulled up his shirt, the slice in the crimson-stained leather clearly visible. Blood ran in a bright red sheet from the cut in Travis's side.

"Come on, coon," Travis called. "Ye gots ter look at it. Tell me how bad. Stings like unholy Hell."

Richard stumbled forward, dropping to his knees. So much blood! He'd never seen anything like it before. "It's...Oh, my God, Travis!"

"Is there—is there guts hanging out, boy?"

"N...No. I...I don't...well, see any."

Travis gasped, lying back. With shaking fingers, he prodded at the long wound.

Richard watched those fingers as they worked carefully through the blood.

"Shit!" Travis growled. "Might not be guts out, Dick, but she's sliced clean through the side." He swallowed hard. "All right, coon. Ye gots ter sew her up. Savvy? If'n ye don't, old Travis is gone under."

"Sew?" Richard mewed.

This wasn't happening!

"God, Travis...I *can't!*"

"Reckon so, coon. Needle and thread's in my possibles." Travis felt around. "Must a busted the strap. Find 'em, Dick."

Richard crawled over to the leather bag where it lay in the trampled grass. He grabbed it up with shaking hands. "Got it."

"Come on, then. Let's get her done quick."

"Travis, I...I..."

Travis ground his teeth and swallowed hard. "Wal, now, Dick. If'n ye don't, who in hell do ye see around hyar to do her? The damn hosses?"

Richard closed his eyes, shaking. His soul went cold. "Can't we go to the fort?"

Travis propped himself on one elbow. "Dick... Richard. Look at me. That's it. Now, yer scairt plumb silly. But hyar's how it is, son. I got a slice in me side. It ain't a long one, or else my guts woulda spilled all over the ground whilst I's raising that red Pawnee son of a bitch. I checked the blood. Thar ain't no gut juice in it, so he didn't nick me boudins. If'n ye can sew me up, I'll be all right. It's on me right side, Richard. I cain't sew it myself, not without stretching. It's up ter you. So, fer God's sake, stop shaking like a puppy and dig around in my possibles. Ye'll find a needle all wrapped up with strong thread. I'll talk ye through it."

"Travis, I don't—"

"Thar *ain't* no choice, Richard. It's gotta be done. If'n ye cain't, step over thar, pick up my rifle, and shoot me through the head. I don't want ter die slow with my guts leaking out. It's up ter you, now. Yer gonna kill me, one way or the other, if'n ye don't dig out that needle."

Richard opened the bag, finding a bullet mold, a couple of lead bars, pipe, tobacco, rolls of leather thongs, a pouch full of small springs and screws, gun flints, several glass bottles with waxed stoppers—and the needle with its winding of thread.

He looked up, meeting Travis's sober blue eyes.

"Ye can do it, Dick. I got faith in ye."

Richard wanted to throw up, to run screaming from this horrible place. "My hands are shaking."

"So're mine," Travis said with a grin. "Wal, coon, we'll be plumb scairt together. Hell of a good scrape, warn't it? That old Half Man, he's some. Sure foxed me."

"You sound like you admire him."

Richard closed his eyes, and took a deep breath. He flexed his muscles, burning up the energy that pumped through him. Exhaling, he bent down, unwrapping the thread from the needle.

Travis watched him levelly, taking his measure. Richard drew strength from that cool look.

"Yep. I figgered he's a gonna raise ye, Dick. I's halfway to my feet when he took that swipe at me head. Cunning old coon. Crafty as a fox. Now, yer a gonna have ter tie a big knot in the end of that thread. That's it. Now, another. Cain't have that slipping through my hide."

Richard fumbled the knot, then got it right. The mending he'd been doing on his clothes might stand him in good stead. But mending on a person?

"Now, I'm a gonna lay on my side. Just like this. Ye got ter take the tip of the needle and run it right through the skin, not getting so deep as ter take any gut with it. Ye follow?"

"I think so." Richard held his breath and bent over Travis's bloody side. He lowered the point of the needle. "God, I'm scared, Travis."

"I reckon ye don't need ter tell me that, Dick. It ain't fixing ter make a body feel particularly at ease."

The needle dimpled Travis's bloody skin.

———

The long trail was finally coming to an end. Packrat nodded with satisfaction as he studied the horse droppings. They were so close, the manure hadn't even crusted.

He glanced at Heals Like A Willow—saw the tension in her eyes.

You know the end is near, don't you?

He raised his hands to the sun, saying, "I swear, before the sun sets on this day, I will be *rid* of this witch woman! One way...or another."

He glanced back to read how his words affected her. That mask had fallen into place again, and she remained aloof, as coldly beautiful as ever.

Half Man was close. As soon as they found him, Packrat would be free of her. He could begin the long process of purification. The air would taste sweeter to his lungs. His muscles would work with greater energy. He could feel his wounded soul chafing to finally escape the darkness. He could cure his manhood—for not even in dreams had his penis stiffened since that horrible day when she'd polluted him.

And how will you ever trust yourself to lie with another woman?

He drove the thought from his mind, looking back at Willow to say, "You'd like that, wouldn't you? To think you could make me afraid forever. Well, you've made a mistake, Weasel Woman."

She gave him the briefest hint of a smile—and that

maddening, knowing look. The anger rose, barely controlled. She could see inside his soul, know what he was thinking. By the Morning Star, he had to finish this now.

He kicked his horse to a trot, dragging her along behind. He could lie with a woman again, couldn't he? And what if he tried? What if he had the chance, and his penis remained forever limp?

His skin went hot at the thought. Among the Pawnee there were no secrets. They'd laugh at him behind his back. Some day, a woman would offer herself.

I'll say no. Walk away.

And when it came time to marry? How long could he put it off? His mother would make an alliance. And when he moved into his wife's house, into her bed, what then?

The hatred festered.

He jerked around and called, "What if I just kill you?"

"I be with you forever," she told him with complete sincerity. "Inside your soul. You can only be free when I am."

He bit his lip, straightened, and longed for Half Man as he'd never done.

The tracks led down into a tree-filled drainage lined with brush. As his mount stepped down the trail, he could see other horses tethered to the trees along what looked like a small stream.

"Half Man! It is Packrat! I come to bring you a gift." His heart leapt. Here, at last, was freedom from the witch. He could begin healing now. The other problems could be solved one at a time.

"Half Man?" He cocked his head, reaching for his bow as a skinny *La-chi-kut* stepped out from among the trees. He looked pale, and very scared. He held no weapon.

Packrat glanced around. Several of the horses

belonged to Half Man. Better yet, the tins they carried were whiskey tins.

All the wealth I will ever need to pay for a cleansing!

He slipped his bow from his back and drew an arrow. Where was Half Man and the other *La-chi-kut?* He could sense that something was wrong, felt a dark intuition that he'd arrived in the nick of time.

The skinny White man was talking in the gobbling White man tongue. He looked terrified. So, not a warrior? Maybe one of the men who made black marks on paper?

Packrat cocked his head. "Where is Half Man? Where is the other *La-chi-kut?*"

"We here. Hurt," a second voice called from the brush in badly inflected Pawnee. "Horse kick! Give help."

Packrat glanced around, looking for any sign of ambush. The skinny White man swallowed hard. Warily, Packrat kneed his horse forward, bow ready. He could see the second *La-chi-kut* now. He lay on the ground, looked weak. Somehow broken. His shirt was bloody.

"Half Man?" Packrat asked.

"Gone fort," the wounded man croaked. "Give help."

Packrat counted the horses. Ten. Then he saw the bloody spot on the ground, the drag marks where a body had been hastily pulled into the brush.

Packrat drew his arrow, pointing it at the wounded *La-chi-kut.* "I think Half Man is dead."

The wounded man stared at him for a moment, eyes drained, then slowly nodded his head. That's when Packrat saw the scars on his face. The sign of the bear. This man had fought the grizzly—and lived.

"Tell me," Packrat rasped, a melting sensation in his guts.

"Tried to kill us. He wanted whiskey." The Bear Man

made a sign for truth. "I would not let him steal it. If you know Half Man, tell me if my words are false."

Packrat aimed for the soft spot just under the White man's ribs.

Dead? Half Man dead? This White man will die, and then the skinny one. After all of Packrat's suffering to...

Willow laughed, her mockery tearing something in his soul. Gone! Every plan ruined, as ruined as his life would be.

He spun his horse, seeing the victory in her eyes. No, an arrow would be too good for her. He wanted to beat her, to hear and feel the impact of his club as he broke her skull. Lowering the bow, he snatched up his war club.

Destroy her. Kill her! Strike her down as she has stricken you with her witchery.

As from a great distance, he heard himself shout: "You *killed* him! You *witched* him! You did this—you knew!"

In fury, he slashed downward with the war club, but she dodged enough to take a glancing blow on the back. The club, deflected, struck her mare on the kidneys. The horse bucked violently, throwing Heals Like A Willow from its back. She hit hard, bounced on her bottom, and blinked with dazed eyes.

Packrat leapt from his own shying mount.

Kill her first, then the White men. She seemed stunned, unable to focus. He swung at her, hissing his rage. She barely managed to duck the blow, scrambling awkwardly backward across the shade-dappled grass.

He skipped to one side, kicked her brutally in the ribs, and raised his club high.

No escape now, Willow.

Their eyes locked, and in that instant, he exulted in her terror.

"Now you *die,* witch!"

He'd just started his club on its downward arc when the concussion knocked him sideways. He staggered, dazed, the ground twisting up to hit him. He blinked, thoughts gone muzzy. A ringing sounded in his ears, and his chest felt odd, sharp with unsensed pain.

He coughed, raising his hand to the wetness at his mouth, surprised by the blood. So much...blood. He blinked again, seeking to drive the grayness from his vision.

Heals Like A Willow was watching him, drinking his soul with her eyes.

Witch, you won't win. I'll beat you...in the end...

The ringing in his ears, the growing gray mist before his eyes, they seemed to fade. If he could just remember... what he'd...

CHAPTER FIVE

To this war of every man, against every man, this also is consequent; that nothing can be unjust. The notions of right and wrong, justice and injustice have there no place. Where there is no common power, there is no law; where no law, no injustice. Force, and fraud, are in war the two cardinal virtues. Justice, and injustice are none of the faculties of neither the body, nor mind.... It is consequent also to the same condition that there be no propriety, no dominion, no *mine* and *thine* distinct; but only that to be every man's, that he can get; and for so long as he can keep it.

—Thomas Hobbes, *Leviathan*

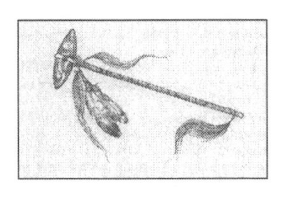 Reckon that was plumb center!" Travis called from where he lay.

The musket fell from Richard's numb hands as the last echoes of the shot died away. He walked through the curling blue smoke, smelling the odor of sulfur from the burned powder. The horses snorted and stamped, panicked by the scent of blood and the sounds of human violence.

Richard stared at the macabre scene.

What have I done? The young Pawnee's body—the chest torn open—dear Lord God, so much blood! How did the human body hold it all?

The young man's eyes were wide in the penny-brown face, staring and glassy, the black pupils large. Clots of frothy red blood still leaked from his mouth, soaking into the moldy leaves beneath his cheek.

Young. So very young.

The woman moaned and moved in a slow writhe.

Richard turned, backing away from the dead man, watching her uncertainly. She winced in pain.

The Indian hit her.

Richard remembered that twisted fury when the young warrior turned on her. Why? Because she'd laughed. Right there in the middle of the nightmare, she'd laughed. And the warrior had gone berserk.

The war club whistling down; the woman twisting desperately away; the war club bouncing off her back to hit the horse; the animal rearing. Her body had slammed the ground like a sack of onions. Still, she'd struggled to escape as the warrior pursued on foot. But her hands were tied...tied...

And then I grabbed up Half Man's musket. Lifted it as the war club was raised.

Had he sighted down the barrel, or just pulled the cock back and triggered?

Don't remember.

But the echoes of the shot remained—along with the image of the young warrior jerking from the bullet's impact. Frozen forever in Richard's mind.

He blinked at the woman. Mute misery reflected in

her face, and with it, fear. A young woman, beautiful in a wild sort of way. Her glossy black hair was loose, spilling over her shoulders. Had he ever seen hair that black, that lustrous before? Her skin had a smooth radiance, a vitality he didn't understand.

She had such slender hands, the fingers long and delicate. Then he saw her wrists, the red welts, and the rawhide thong that had cut and chafed them.

"You're safe now," he told her gently, and tried to smile. He reached out to her, to reassure her. But his guts felt suddenly queer. The trembling in his fingers moving into the hand he'd offered her, and on to all of the muscles in his body. Shaking uncontrollably, he sat down to cradle his head in his hands.

"Oh, God, what did I do?"

"Dick?" Travis called. "Ye all right, coon?"

Richard rubbed his face with shivering hands. "I'm alive, Travis. I guess I'm...alive. Dear sweet Jesus. I'm alive."

"Easy, coon," Travis soothed. "It comes on a body sometimes. It'll pass."

I killed a man. Shot him dead.

He didn't need to look again. Those empty staring eyes, the blood, would be with him whenever he closed his eyes. But for the wound and blood, the young Pawnee would have looked peaceful, as in repose for a nap, his arm outstretched.

Richard glanced at the woman; she watched him intently with fathomless dark eyes.

The trembling receded, leaving hollow weakness in its wake. He stood, again offering his hands. For an eternal moment her eyes bored into his, and then she reached out to him.

Her hands were cool, firm in his. As he pulled her to her feet, Richard saw the pain in her face.

"You're tougher than I am," he told her. "After what you've been through, I'd be screaming."

He held her hands up. The knots had pulled so tightly that he couldn't undo them.

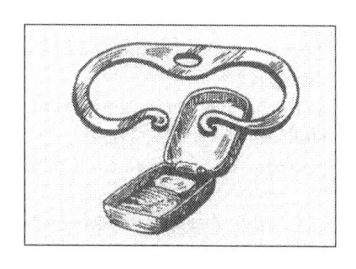

Her eyes fluttered, expression going slack. She swayed on her feet then, head lolling. Richard caught her as she wobbled and collapsed.

"*What the hell?*"

Travis laughed from where he lay. "Reckon she took a hell of a wallop when she hit that ground. This child would guess she stood up a mite too quick. Pack her over hyar, lad. Let's see what ye ketched."

Richard got a good grip, and dragged more than carried her. She should have been heavier. Then he was shockingly aware of her soft breasts against his arms. He laid her down gently, awed that he'd touched her so.

Travis studied her with quizzical eyes. "Snake, by damn! What in hell's she doing clear out hyar?" Then, "Slave, by God."

"Slave? But she's Indian."

Travis gave him a disgusted glance. "And I reckon yer Roosoo don't figger 'man in nature' takes slaves?"

"It's Rousseau. And no, he didn't."

"Wal, lad, a Pawnee don't tie up his wife with bindings like this. Let's see—roll her moccasins down."

Richard tried not to touch her warm skin as he pulled the soft tops of her moccasins down to her ankles. The welts there had mostly healed.

"Slave, all right." Travis cocked his head, curious blue eyes on Richard. "Reckon she's yern."

"*What?*"

Travis scratched at his beard with blood-caked fingers. "Wal, hoss. Ye raised that Pawnee what had her. She's yers now by mountain law. Reckon she's worth keeping, too. She's right pert. Do ye a good day's work. Warm yer bed at night, if'n she don't drive a knife atwixt yer ribs while yer on her."

"*Travis!* She's—she's a human being. I *won't* own another human being. It's...beastly."

"Wal, fine, Dick. Reckon ye won't mind if'n I take her?"

"You take...Hell, no! She's free, Travis."

The hunter chuckled. "Ye takes some, ye does, Dick. You and yer Yankee ideas."

Richard sighed wearily, absently stroking the woman's hair. How incredibly soft. He'd imagined Indian hair to be bristly. But then, he'd never touched a woman's hair like this—or a woman's breast, for that matter. She was so unlike his Laura.

Travis winced. "Now, why don't ye take my strike-a-light and build us a fire. I reckon we ain't a-going nowhere soon."

"I don't know how to make a fire, Travis."

"Wal, coon, it appears t' be yer day fer larning."

———

Heals Like A Willow slept late into the night. She blinked, coming awake slowly. The pain wasn't just part of her dreams. She cataloged the sounds as she tried to gather her muzzy thoughts: the distant hoot of an owl; horses cropped grass nearby; and water was trickling as though from a spring. A fire popped. Someone grunted in pain.

Pain? She reached up to rub her face. Her head ached as if she'd been clubbed half to death...and the memories of the afternoon came back in vivid clarity.

White men! Packrat was dead.

Willow sat up and gasped. The ache in her head left her sick and reeling. Agony shot up through her hips and back.

A blanket had been placed over her against the chill of the night, and when she looked down, her wrists were free. When had that happened? How long had she been out?

Short flames licked up periodically around a chunk of firewood lying in a round bed of glowing coals. In the firelight, she could see one of the White men, the old one. Those odd, pale eyes watched her with interest. His face was drawn in pain. It looked wrong, somehow misshapen, but she knew little of White men and how they ought to look.

He made the sign for her people: "Snake?"

She nodded, then signed: "What are you going to do with me?"

He smiled crookedly. "Free."

She cocked her head. A trap hid in this. But where? Why would the White man at the fort offer two guns for her, when these White men would turn her loose?

The man's hands continued, "The young warrior

killed the Pawnee who kept you. The young warrior says you are free."

She glanced at the third set of blankets. The young White man was rolled up like a papoose. He hadn't seemed much of a warrior. She remembered the soft look in his eyes as he'd reached out to her. Then he'd been betrayed by the shakes. What had she seen in those brown eyes? Confusion, relief, excitement, all mixed together?

She gazed down at her hands. She'd seen that look before—in the eyes of her husband.

Was that why I took the White man's hand? Or was it the fall that addled me?

Willow rubbed her flushed face, recalling the way she'd gone dizzy and fallen into the White man's arms.

How long ago? What did they do when I was senseless?

What men did with any woman, no doubt. She reached down under her skirt, but found no indication that a man had taken her. Maybe White men didn't— but, no, that wasn't what the *Ku'chendikani* claimed. According to the people who knew Whites, they were as bad as, if not worse than, anyone when it came to coupling.

She flushed at the old White man's knowing eyes as she pulled her hands into view. "Free?"

He nodded, signing, "Free. But I would ask the Snake woman to stay for several days. I will be very sick. Fevered. The young warrior knows nothing of wounds, or fever. If you help him to help me, we will give you horses. We will take you to your people."

Take her to her people? Was this where the trap...?

She stifled a cry as she shifted and white-hot pain lanced through her.

Tam Apo help me, my back isn't broken, is it?

Drawing deep breaths helped, and she shifted to a different position that eased her back.

At that moment the fire flared; she got a good look at the White man's face. She'd seen scars like that before. He'd fought the white bear—and survived. A powerful warrior, White man though he might be. But why free her? Brave or not, it didn't make sense to turn a good captive loose.

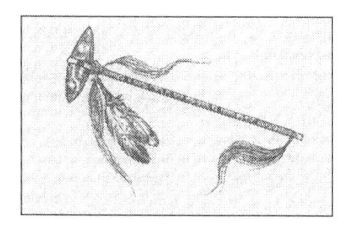

She signed, "My people live many moons to the west."

"In the Shining Mountains," he returned. "I know where the Snake live. I have seen their land. We are headed close to there. We will take you home. I speak straight."

"Why?"

"Maybe trade with your people."

Ah! Now I begin to understand.

"What makes you think we want trade?"

"Everyone wants trade."

Her fingers flashed angrily. "Trade not good. Trade for rifle, must trade for powder, trade for bullet. This is good?"

He watched her with thoughtful eyes. "Trade makes people wealthy and strong. Snakes need guns to fight the Blackfoot. Blackfoot enemy to Whites as well as Snake people."

"Is it not better that Whites kill Blackfeet?" She

glanced at the metal tins. "Is it not better that you trade medicine water to Blackfeet? Make them crazy and weak? Then *you* can kill them."

He smiled at her, and signed: "You are too much like Young Warrior. Many questions. Answer one question, and he asks two more."

She started to stand, got dizzy, and sank back.

"Hurt?" he signed.

She ignored him, heart racing, senses going blurry.

"Bad fall," he signed, then pointed to his side and added, "Bad cut. Young Warrior sew."

She made the signs: "Half Man cut you?"

He nodded. "Tried to steal whiskey."

"I heard," she grunted in Pawnee.

How free am I?

She nerved herself, rising slowly to her feet. Squinting against the horrible headache, she made her way, step by step, into the brush. Holding onto a tree, she relieved herself, half expecting a cry of pursuit. When none came, she stepped carefully to the creek and scooped up water. She relished the water's cool touch on her hot skin. She drank all she could hold.

Go, now. Escape!

She glanced out into the darkness, wincing at her pain and blurring vision. How far could she make it before she collapsed? Her stomach tickled with the urge to vomit. Like it or not, she needed rest.

But she would do one thing before hobbling back to her blankets. She picked her way to where Packrat lay, almost falling over him in the darkness. With questing fingers she found his war club and picked it up.

She gasped as she stood again, vision swimming. Her skull must be cracked to ache this badly. She waited out the nausea, and carefully picked her way back to the White man's camp.

The Bear Man sat as she'd left him.

"Where are you from?" she signed.

"All over."

"And Young Warrior?"

Bear Man said the word aloud: "Boston." In signs he added, "Young Warrior will tell you about Boston until you are sick of hearing it."

She grunted noncommittally. Her vision was spinning —the headache shredded her thoughts. *Rest a while.* Then, after a couple of hours' sleep, she'd slip away, find her mare, and be on her way before sunup.

"Name?" Bear Man asked.

In *Dukurika* she said, "Heals Like A Willow." Then made the signs for it.

"Travis," he said, then pointed at the Young Warrior all wrapped up in his blankets. "Dick."

She grimaced against the headache. "Trawis. Dik."

"Please," he signed. "Help the Young Warrior."

She closed her eyes, sinking back. Not even bearing her son had been this painful.

————

The soft light of morning bathed the land when Richard folded back his blanket. In the half-light the brush had taken on a grayish tint, the dark trees like mysterious spirits suddenly frozen while waving armlike branches.

Richard yawned, reassured by the lilting trill of the meadowlarks and the long call of the robins. Then he remembered the previous day and sat up. Travis Hartman hadn't moved a hair. Blessed God, he hadn't died in the night, had he?

Had yesterday really happened? Or was it all a dream? Across the stream, the Pawnee youth still sprawled, the blood turned black. Damnation, it wasn't a dream.

I killed him. And what does that make me?

Richard stood, rubbed his eyes with a knuckle, and walked down to wash his face in the clear water. His reflection—little more than a dark silhouette against the morning sky—stared back at him.

What have I become?

The dark shadow on the water returned no answers.

The fire had burned down to white ash. Richard stirred it and added the last of the branches he'd collected. Bending down, he blew the embers to life. Stomach growling, he sat and stared at the flames through vacant eyes while the previous day replayed over and over again.

"Yer up?" Travis asked hoarsely.

"Yes." Was life like firelight? An instant of wavering brilliance, snuffed so quickly?

"Reckon I could use a drink, Dick."

Richard fetched Travis's tin cup and filled it at the spring before crouching at Travis's side.

"Travis, what happened yesterday? None of it makes sense. Half Man going berserk, trying to kill you because I asked questions. The two of you fought like animals. What you did to him...ripping his eyes out...beating him to death..."

Travis looked ashen, eyes sunken in a drawn face. "A feller's gotta fight like a banshee out hyar. Ain't no way around it. Now, don't go a-blaming yerself for Half Man making his play. He was a-looking fer an excuse. Thought he had me off balance, and took his chance. Come right close ter working, too, Dick. "

He paused. "Now, afore ye gets all carried away with

yer philos'phy, think hard on this: Reckon he's a-laying out there, all stiff and gone under. If'n I hadn't a kilt him, you and me, we'd both be laying hyar dead. Green's whiskey'd be plumb gone, and that Pawnee coon would be one rich red son of a bitch."

"And the young man? I don't understand that. Where did he come from? What did he want?"

"I ain't figgered that meself." Travis resettled himself, wincing as he eased his side. "But, coon, no matter what, we was dead men again. The only thing what saved us was Heals Like A Willow, the Snake woman. I was looking inta that Pawnee kid's eyes. He was gonna kill us dead with that bow and take the whiskey. That light was a-burning in his eyes as he looked at them tins. And right then, Willow up and laughed. Saw the expression in his face, didn't ye?"

"Yes. His face screwed up like something wild. It scared me, Travis. I saw she was tied. I just couldn't watch him kill her like that."

Travis chuckled—and winced. He lifted a hand to his side. "Reckon I didn't bet wrong on ye, Dick. I saw it in yer eyes on the river that day."

"Travis, please. I'm not the kind of man you think I am. I could never be. My roots are different from yours, not of this wilderness. My only wish is to go home and take up my life again."

"With this Laura? Want ter tell me about her?"

"No."

"Wal, then, best check yer stitching, coon."

Richard lifted Travis's shirt. The sliced leather was blood-crusted now. "I've got to get this off you, wash it. Then I'll stitch it back up again."

"I'd be obliged."

Richard squinted uneasily at the curving wound in

the hunter's side. It looked terrible. The skin was puckered and red; blackened blood had soaked into the thread and dried. Here and there, where the sewing was uneven, meat could be seen, and yellow crusts of pus had risen.

How on earth did I ever do this?

Even now Richard felt faint.

"Is the stitches pulling?" Travis asked, looking down. "Nope? Well, that's some, it is. If'n she don't tear, I reckon I'll heal up pert."

"How do you feel?"

"How do I feel? What sort of idiot Doodle question is that? I feel like if I laugh or sneeze, my guts is gonna fall out on the ground."

"I mean, besides that."

"Hot. A little giddy and girlish. Sort of floaty. Reckon the fever's a gonna start."

"I'll get you more water."

"I'd take that right kindly." Travis closed his eyes. "Hyar's things ye need ter do. Go strip them Pawnee corpses. Half Man had powder, bullets, and makings in his possibles. Reckon we'll take that kid's bow and arrers, and any outfit he's got. Pull them moccasins, and wrap the whole keeboodle in their blankets. Ye savvy this, Dick?"

Loot the dead?

Richard's stomach turned. "Yes. I'll do it, Travis."

"Roll up all the plunder—inter a pack, understand?"

"Yes."

"Keep watch, Dick. Check the priming in my rifle. If'n ye needs ter shoot, pull the cock back, pull the back trigger first, then the front one. She won't shoot like that Injun trade gun did. This one's a Hawken. Back trigger first."

"You think there will be more trouble?"

"Hell, I never counted on that second Pawnee yesterday. He caught us nigh dead to rights. Be careful, Dick. Oh, and one other thing. I asked Willow ter stay and help ye. Maybe she will, maybe she won't. Keep in mind, boy. She's Injun. Aboot as trustworthy as a buzzworm."

"She's a woman, for God's sake!"

"She ain't no *white woman,* Dick. She's Snake...and she picked up that Pawnee kid's war club and went ter sleep with it last night. Don't turn yer back on her."

But she was so pretty! Richard glanced over his shoulder. She lay under the blanket he'd draped over her last night. When he looked her way he could see her eyes glint, narrowed slits, watching his every move.

———

Even the wary vigilance of a wounded and hunted animal finally ebbs. Heals Like A Willow lay under her blanket, hurt and exhausted. The fear of the White men, despite their assurances, goaded her to watchfulness—as if she could defend herself, groggy and swimming as her senses were. Her punished flesh, however, demanded respite, no matter what the consequences.

Willow never realized when she crossed the divide from consciousness to sleep....

I remain hidden beneath my blanket the way a grouse tucks herself under a log when coyote is hunting the black timber. The scent of danger lingers on the wind, something acrid, like the stench of rot mixed with smoke.

I hear a stick crack in the trees behind me. A foot crackles dry needles as weight shifts in the darkness.

Who? I peer out at the shadowed forest with new alarm, but see nothing in the shifting shadows.

When I look back at the White man's camp, a giant bear

now sleeps where the wounded White man was. The fierce head rests on large paws, the claws gleaming in the fragile moonlight that penetrates the dense canopy of the trees. He is an old animal, his silver-tipped hair giving him a frosted look.

Out in the forest, buckskin rasps against bark as the enemy creeps closer. The sound is loud enough, close enough, to stop my heart—but the giant bear doesn't hear. He sleeps on, and only now do I notice the beast's breathing is labored and weak.

He's dying. The voice repeats over and over within me: The bear couldn't protect me if he wanted to.

I tense under my blanket as stealthy feet come closer, ever closer.

Run! I throw off my blanket and dash for the timber like a frightened rabbit. I know I am hurt but fear gives my legs new power. So long as I don't think, don't accept my weakness, I can run forever.

I duck between the trees and into the dark protection of the forest. I know this place, understand how the elk trails run— well defined as they leave the clearing, but fading into nothing back in the black timber. I duck shadowy branches, leap deadfall in my desperate haste.

He is still chasing me, crashing through the forest, his steps pounding the ground, shaking the very earth. I charge ahead, heart hammering, arms pumping, full-tilt through the jumble of interlacing branches, deadfall, and duff.

Sticks snag my dress, and I have to bat branches aside as the forest closes in. Where a huge tree has fallen across the trail, I drop to my belly and squirm under, only to plunge ahead into a virtual net of splintered dead wood.

In the end I have to wiggle through the deadfall like a bull snake through a serviceberry thicket.

Upon reaching the other side and regaining my feet, I stagger into a grassy, moonlit clearing. From the trees, an owl hoots; coyotes yip and wail in the distance. I circle, panting for breath, while my body shakes with fatigue. No matter where I turn, an impenetrable mass of forest blocks any escape.

The owl hoots again, and the coyotes sound like they are laughing.

He's coming; dry wood crackles as he pushes through the deadfall.

The moonlight shines eerily in Packrat's crazy eyes. He smiles at me, and throws his head back to scream his triumph at the stars. As the ululation echoes, the forest turns silent.

Packrat grins, moonlight sparkling on his teeth, and speaks to me from the Land of the Dead: "Your souls, Willow. This time, I want your souls...forever..."

He opens his arms and steps forward, his moccasins sinking into the brittle grass.

How do I defeat the dead? I back away, the chill certainty of defeat shivering through my exhausted body.

So much pain, so much hurt, is it worth it? Why continue to fight when the only result is more suffering?

A voice inside me says, Give up, Willow. The world belongs to Coyote, full of tricks and pain: Drop to your knees. Let Packrat take your souls. Accept it. Misery is inevitable.

Packrat cocks his head in anticipation, his shadowed eyes like black pits in his smooth face.

At that moment, the white mist dog dances into the clearing, twisting and leaping. He cavorts like milkweed down on the wind, flitting this way and that, twirling and rising, then rushing down to skim the surface of the grass.

Packrat's expression strains with shock and disbelief. The mist white dog dances past him and blood begins to drain from Packrat's mouth. He falls, sprawling in the grass. His mouth opens and closes, making bubbles of frothy black blood.

Panic drives me thrashing through the forest. I must find a way out.

The pale mist dog dances before me, teasing, then leaps, curls in the air, and beckons. Fear burns bright within me, but I follow the spirit dog. The way leads down a winding maze of trails that crisscross through the dark forest.

At the foot of a mountain, the way turns steep and rocky. I climb with the mist dog cavorting above me like a spark from a fire. From rock to rock, grasping for purchase with fingers and toes, I lever myself up the mountain. Finally, I pull myself onto a high pinnacle.

There the mist white dog sits, his tail wagging. As if irritated, he barks. When I do nothing, he whines insistently.

"What are you?" I ask, reaching out to pet the animal.

I barely touch him when, in a flash, he strikes savagely, sinking teeth into my hand.

I cry out, tear my hand away, and stagger back. The mist dog shoots up, spinning in the air. This time, instead of barking, he howls with Coyote's keen voice. The misty hair hardens, and the pale color darkens. I cannot mistake that pointed muzzle, or the pricked triangular ears.

For one eternal instant, I stare into Coyote's blazing yellow eyes. Then, in a snap of the fingers, he turns and races off, his bushy tall bobbing behind him as he skips across the landscape.

I grind my teeth against the pain. Settling onto the rock, I tuck my bitten hand in my lap. I fight the desire to weep.

CHAPTER SIX

The passions that incline men to peace, are fear of death; desire of such things as are necessary to commodious living; and a hope by their industry to obtain them. And reason suggested convenient articles of peace, upon which men may be drawn to agreement. These articles, are they, which otherwise are called the Laws of Nature: whereof I speak.

—Thomas Hobbes, *Leviathan*

 The morning grew hot. Slanting yellow rays of sunlight penetrated the new leaves, fresh burst from the bud, to dapple the ground with shadows. Flies buzzed in a wavering column over the two dead Pawnee. Birdsong, light and melodic, mingled with the tinkle of spring water.

Willow lay still, recruiting her strength as the Young Warrior, the one called Dik, cared for the Bear Man. He kept glancing shyly in her direction, unsure of her.

The feeling is shared, White man.

That wretched headache had dissipated to a dull

throb that only bothered her when she moved too quickly. She stretched, feeling each muscle and its attendant aches. Better. But how far could she push herself? Had she healed sufficiently? Or, if something went amiss, would she leap to her feet only to topple into a pile again?

The Bear Man moaned. Willow watched Dik lay a hand on his forehead. He mumbled nervously in White tongue and shook his head.

Willow sat up noiselessly. So far, so good. The headache still throbbed, but her senses weren't swimming. Her bones ached, but she gambled that that would go away with movement. She clutched her war club and stood, waiting for the dizziness. When it didn't come, she took a careful step. Then, to her relief, another.

Dik never heard her, but jumped aside with surprise when she crouched beside him.

She met his startled eyes and smiled innocently, saying in Shoshoni, "If I'd wanted to kill you, Dik, you'd have never known until the instant I broke your skull."

He bobbed a happy nod and smiled his reassurance, then turned thoughtful brown eyes on Trawis.

Willow placed a hand to Trawis's cheek. "Hot. Fever."

She took a deep breath. Her fingers had looked just like that as they lay against her husband's cheek. Then, too, she'd felt the heat that had burned him to death from the inside out.

I couldn't save him. I failed.

And this hair-faced White man?

She studied him in the daylight—especially those scars. The bear had torn off half his face. From the scars' look, he must have been pus-fevered then, too. "Are you strong enough, Trawis? Can you beat the fever again?"

Dik was talking, the words as meaningless as wind over the rocks.

With her hands, she asked: "What medicines do you have?"

Vacant eyes watched her signs, then he slowly shook his head. In reply he spoke White babble.

She leaned back, elbows on knees, and inspected him. "So, you can't even make signs. Are all Whites ignorant of the most basic of things?"

Maybe he didn't know anything about medicine, either.

But, do I? Or am I only fooling myself?

A familiar desperation, one she hadn't felt since Packrat captured her, slipped around her guts.

What if I fail? What if my Power to heal is truly broken?

Dik rose and walked to a bundle of cloth by his blanket. He ripped off a piece, stepped to the creek, and dipped it in water. When he returned, he used the cloth to wipe Trawis's sweaty head.

Willow lifted the leather hunting shirt to study the wound. Pus had begun to leak from some of the stitches, but other parts had scabbed over nicely. The stitching itself was rough, inexpertly done, but effective.

Dik was babbling again, and Willow ignored it. She looked around, recognizing few of the plants she needed. In her country, she could have found phlox, the first shoots of gumweed, and... Well, here, at least, was willow. That would help with Trawis's fever and her own headache. She pulled Trawis's steel knife from his belt.

Dik went silent, unease in his wide brown eyes.

"You think I'd take his knife to kill you? When I have the war club in my other hand?" She snorted derisively, before winding her way down to the patch of willows beyond the spring.

When she had her cuttings, she located a small metal pot in the packs, scoured it with sand, filled it with water, and put it on to boil. With the war club and a flat slab of limestone, she pounded the willow to loosen the bark. Her deft fingers stripped off the bruised bark and placed it in the water to boil.

As she worked, her stiffness eased. From the tenderness, a horrible bruise must have marked her where the war club had glanced off her back—and the rest of her trouble came from the fall from the mare. Thank *Tam Apo,* no bones had broken.

Where the earth had slumped at the edge of the caprock, she located green shoots of goosefoot. The other flowers defied her. This country produced no shooting star, no biscuit root or desert parsley. No balsam root sent up shoots, to mark its location. In the soggy ground below the willows, she found mint and added that to her collection.

"Who'd live here?" she wondered. But certainly most of the plants she saw must be edible or medicinal.

By the time she returned to the camp, the willow bark had boiled down to a murky paste. With sticks Willow plucked the pot from the fire and cooled it in the spring. When she could hold the pot, she tasted the bitter contents. Some she drank for her own aches, and then walked up to where Trawis lay.

He was awake, watching her through glittering eyes. Sweat continued to bead on his forehead before slipping down his scarred face in rivulets that disappeared into his beard. She made the sign: "Drink."

Trawis choked down the bitter brew without complaint and gasped.

Dik came to kneel beside her as she lifted the shirt again. Pus not only leaked from the stitches but had begun to swell the flesh. "If only I knew the plants, knew what spirits live in this land."

She glanced sideways at the big triangular tins. "Spirit water? Medicine water? They call it many names." But would it work? What had White Hail said? That he'd seen visions?

Willow tapped Dik on the shoulder and pointed at the tins.

"Whiskey," he said.

"Whiskey," she replied. Then she reached for the tin cup Dik used to get water for Trawis. "Whiskey," she said, pointing inside the cup.

Dik frowned, then nodded hesitantly before taking the cup. She watched, seeing how he untwisted the lid and poured the clear liquid. No doubt about it, these White men were very clever. Among her people, the best container was still a gut bag. The pottery they made was brittle, primarily for the storage of winter foodstuffs.

When Dik brought her the spirit water, she did not take it at once. She leaned forward, smelling its tang, and cautiously looked into the liquid. She didn't quite know what to expect, maybe some amorphous form swirling like fog, faces, or tiny shapes. But only clear fluid lay between the surface and the bottom of the cup.

She had been around Spirit Bundles, fetishes, and medicine before. Most could be felt—a sense of Power in the air. Now, she felt nothing, no sense of threat. Nerving herself, she took the cup and studied the wound.

"White man's spirit water," she mused. "White man's wound." Her mind made up, she poured the spirit water along the puckered cut.

Trawis grunted, eyes popping open as he tried to sit up.

"Shssh!" she told him, placing her fingers to his lips and easing him back. "Do not fight."

Dik was speaking in low tones, talking to Trawis. She caught the word "whiskey" a time or two.

Trawis blinked, then stared into Willow's eyes. He signed: "That will cure or kill me."

She nodded, then scrutinized the wound to see if anything happened. Would it smoke? Perhaps little demons would come wriggling out like worms. She'd seen some of the *Dukurika puhagans* suck bloody feathers, bear claws, and other objects from the sick. Would such things pop out of Trawis?

The pus pockets would be a problem. She'd seen Dik digging in the leather bag that lay beside Trawis. She pulled it over, found an awl made of metal, and raised the sharp point to the light.

"What you do?" Trawis signed.

Dik was looking nervous again. Did neither of them have a brain in their heads?

"Your wound must be drained." She made the signs, then bent over his stitched side. Unlike her knowledge of plants in strange country, when it came to draining wounds, she had plenty of practice. The metal awl worked much better than the sharpened rabbit bones she was used to. She lanced the puffy flesh, twirling the awl at the same time.

Trawis grunted and hissed as she worked. Mostly he kept his eyes closed, pale features even whiter, if that were possible.

"You'd think I was working on a ghost," she muttered to herself. Then looked up to meet Dik's eyes. She handed him the cup and pointed at the whiskey again.

He nodded hesitantly and left.

Willow lanced the last of the pockets, very gently

squeezing the wound. To her satisfaction, the pus mostly ran clear. She dribbled whiskey on the oozing sections, and bent down to squint at the flesh while Trawis made suffering sounds. To her disappointment, nothing like bloody feathers or bear claws popped out.

She sighed and sat back, thankful that the willow-bark extract had killed most of her headache. To the uncomprehending Dik, she said, "I can do no more for now. Let him rest. In the meantime, I will boil the goose-foot and mint for something to eat."

Dik smiled at her then, soft lights in his brown eyes touching her soul. He took her hand, raised it, and pressed his lips to the skin on the back. In clear tones he said, "Thank you."

In return, she lifted his hand, brushing her lips on the back of the pale skin. "Thank you." Some curious custom of the Whites?

He laughed, shaking his head and jabbering away in White talk.

"Excuse me," she said. "If we are to eat, I had better do something about it. From the looks of things, you Whites would starve to death."

As she bent to the task of boiling the goosefoot and mint, the thought crossed her soul: *If the Whites are so helpless, why haven t they starved to death before this?*

————

Travis hissed, teeth clenched, as Richard poured whiskey on the stitches in his side. It took several seconds for the sting to drain away and the world to come back into focus.

"Waugh! That's some, it is. Damn, I'd like ter give ye a dose of that!"

"You did," Richard said, bending over him. "Back on the boat, remember? When I had the scours? You were the one made me eat that gall. I think it was you who said that the worse the taste, the better the cure."

"Wal, ye better go easy on that whiskey. Tarnal Hell, whiskey's supposed ter go in a feller, not on him."

Richard shrugged. "Perhaps. The pus isn't as bad today. Fever's broken, too. I think Willow was right about pouring it on you."

Travis bit his lip as the inflamed skin on his side cooled in the air. "Spirit water," she'd signed, making a motion for Richard to pour it on the suppurative wound. And damned if it didn't seem to help. The scab was tight and dry on his side, whereas pus had leaked out of his bear cuts for weeks.

Travis looked down at the curving scar. Half Man had come damned close to killing him.

Green would be at the rendezvous today, or tomorrow at the latest. Tarnal damnation, they were a hard day's walk from the river. Time was running out.

"I been laying hyar two days now." Travis made his decision. "Real slow, Dick. Take my hand. Help me up."

"You can't get up! You'll kill yourself!"

"Dave's gonna be waiting. Worrying himself sick." Travis reached out. "Come on! Hell, child, I'm half-healed already. This hyar's a scratch."

Heals Like A Willow came up behind Richard. In her sibilant speech, she said something that Travis could tell was unkind. Richard reluctantly held out his hand and helped pull Travis upright. His weight tugged at the stitches. "Damn!" Cold sweat popped out, the pain building. "Whew! Hang onto my hand, Dick. Reckon I'm just a hair stiffened up. Need ter move a little, warm my joints."

"Crazy damn bastard!" Richard scowled his disapproval.

"What? Ye larning ter talk like an American?" Travis blinked as he looked around the shaded bottoms. Over there, where Richard had dragged them, lay the Pawnee corpses. They'd be stinking something fierce real soon.

Willow, still muttering to herself, took Travis's other arm. He set his jaw, and took a step, hating the premonition that his guts were about to spill out on the ground.

"I'm just going to walk a little. Nothing tricky like."

And by Hob, don't let me fall down and bust open like a rotten melon.

For several minutes, he hobbled around, and sure enough, his side seemed to soften. He dared not turn, reach, or bend, but he could walk.

"Now, Dick, I reckon ye might pack them hosses fer me."

"You *can't* travel!"

Travis looked at Willow, his hands making signs. "You would help me get to the river? Help with the horses?"

A curious respect grew in her eyes, then she nodded slowly, almost grudgingly.

"Why did you stay?" Travis asked.

She smiled crookedly while her graceful hands told him, "I did not feel good, either. Head hurt until this morning. I also said I would help Young Warrior."

"You are a good and brave woman."

She laughed cynically at that.

Travis indicated Richard, and asked, "Will you help him with the whiskey?"

After a thoughtful glance, she walked off to bring in the horses. Travis hobbled over to the two dead Pawnee. Glancing back, he saw that Hamilton and the squaw were out of sight. Gingerly, he bent his knees, easing down.

The bloated corpses reeked of death. Flies had blown the wounds, and the little maggots were wiggling and feasting under the caked blood. Funny how maggots made rot smell worse.

Travis took his knife from his belt, and did what he needed to. Placing his prizes in his possibles, he straightened, ever careful of the stitches in his side.

One slow step at a time, he walked back to the horses. Richard had learned the basics of packing, and was doing tolerably well at hoisting the tins, tying the knots, and checking the balance.

"Watch that lash cinch," Travis warned. "Yer a bit far back 'round the belly. If'n that nag were ter throw a fit, ye'd have a hellacious wreck—whiskey all over Tarnation."

When the last of the horses was packed, Travis gritted his teeth and hobbled up the winding deer trail, moving as carefully as possible. How far to the river? Six, seven miles?

And I'm racing along at maybe a mile an hour.

"Travis?" Richard asked, head down.

"Huh?"

"Those men...the Pawnee...well..."

"Well, what, fer God's sake?"

"We ought to give them a decent burial, don't you think?" Richard scuffed his toe on the grass.

"Tarnation! What's a coyote ever done ter ye? Anything?"

"Why, er, no. Nothing."

"Then let 'em eat, Doodle. Coyotes, wolves, buzzards, worms, hell, they all got ter make do out hyar, too, don't they?"

Richard's mouth had dropped open.

"I ain't saying no more about it." And God alone

knew, he'd better save his breath for the climb out of this little valley. Those gentle slopes now looked for all the world like the highest of the Shining Mountains.

He was panting when he made it to the caprock, eased over the lip, and looked onto the flats. A sea of grass led eastward to the bluffs above the river. He stepped aside as Dick led the horses past.

"You're a fool, don't you know?" Richard called. "You'll be dead before nightfall!"

Travis squinted up at the sky. "Too much buffler meat in my blood, coon. I'll swear ye this! If'n I up and decides ter die, today, I'll do'er at the river. Hyar's fer the moun-tains, Dick. This child'll race ye ter the water!"

Heals Like A Willow was saying something in her tongue. Telling him how stupid he was, no doubt.

"Wal, hell," he said, whether they heard or not, "Hugh Glass crawlt this country after Old Ephraim tore him up. Afore that, old John Colter outrun the Black-foots plumb naked. He crossed half the Plains without a stitch on his hide. Me, I got, oh, maybe a hunnert or so. I reckon I'm way ahead o' Colter. And I done been bear-chewed long back. If'n that didn't kill me, well, by God, I'll make her."

An hour later, he was wondering if maybe he shouldn't have had his lips sewed shut along with his side.

Anything ter keep ye from a-spouting off like a jackass!

A terrible weariness had settled on him, making each step an agony. Had he ever been this tired?

Yep. And in a hell of a fix worse'n the one I'm in now.

"Travis?" Richard asked, pacing alongside, lead rope in hand.

"Yep."

"Are you all right?"

"Hell, no! As smart as yer always claiming ter be, I'd

reckon ye'd be right mindful of what old Half Man done ter this beaver with that knife of his."

"We could rest."

Travis slowed to a stop, staring around at the waving bluestem and the puffy clouds that had built to the west. How far had they gone? Maybe a mile.

Feels like I've crossed half the world.

"All right, Dick. Ease me down. Reckon I could rest a bit, get my puff back."

Richard helped him down. The grass prickled against him, smelling of spring. Damn! Why did it have to be so cussed hot?

What I'd do fer a cup of water.

Heals Like A Willow leaned down, studying him. By God, she was a smart-looking woman. Travis allowed his imagination to play as he watched her full breasts sway while she checked his wound. He'd been too long without a sits-beside woman. The whores in Saint Louis were just relief for a man's pizzle. Maybe if this trip didn't kill him...

But he'd had his one great love: Calf in the Moonlight. A young Crow. Her gaze, so like Willow's, haunted him from the past. She smiled at him, that dancing twinkle in her eyes. How they'd loved through that too short period. His heart twisted with the old familiar sorrow.

Hell, stop it. She's dead, damn ye. Ye damned well knows ye cain't live with no woman. Not after her.

Willow hunched down beside him, making signs. "I must find medicine. Then I will be gone"—she held her hand to the sky, making the sign—"two hands."

Two hands? Not long. The sun traveled that in a couple of hours.

He closed his eyes, head spinning. So very weary. The

world had gone floaty, shimmery. Travis smiled, falling back into the dream, seeing Calf in the Moonlight. That year had been like magic. Everything had been new, heady as foam on cool ale. A man could come to like living like that, his robes warm each night. And, unlike white women, she was always willing to open herself to his need. How they'd loved, and shared, and merged two lives into one.

And to think he'd always dreamed of having a white wife. But why? White women were nothing but trouble.

Stupid coon, how come ye never understood that afore?

"Because us fools always bought the notion that white women was fer successful men. Injun women, hell, they's fer the mountains and plains."

But a white woman, she had to be cared for, a stay-at-home woman who lived in a cabin, baked bread, and raised children.

He could see Moonlight so clearly. He was walking toward her, and she looked up, laughing at him. Her white teeth gleamed, that soft black hair streaming over her shoulder... Gone. Dead, lost in the hazy past.

Voices. He knew them, coming from the haze that had wrapped around him.

Someone leaned over him, blocking the sunlight. He frowned up at Michael Immel. Tall and lanky, and so young. Yes, that had to be Immel bending over him.

Travis chuckled hollowly. "Reckon ye had her wrong, old coon. Thought ye'd be headed back ter Saint Loowee a rich man. Figgered ye'd get yourself some fancy lady, all decked in rustling silks. Stick ter the Crows, or maybe the Sioux. If'n ye wants ter do it up right, I'd say find ye a Cheyenne wife. She'll stick with ye through thick and thin."

"Travis?"

"Stay away from the Yellerstone, hoss. I had me a dream that you and Jones went under. Dreamed ye were ketched by the Blackfoot and kilt."

"Travis! Wake up!" A hand reached but of the shimmering past and grabbed his beard. Shook his head back and forth.

"Huh?" He blinked and asked, "Dick? Whar'd Immel go? He's just hyar."

"Travis, listen. You're sick. Wounded. This is Richard Hamilton. Willow brought in some cactus and peeled it. She tied it onto your wound. Then she got on her horse and rode away. Travis? *Travis!* Listen to me! What do I do?"

He frowned, mouth dry. "I got a terrible dry on, Dick. Fetch me a tin of water, will ye?"

"Do you hear me?" Dick bent down, eyes wide. "Willow took her mare and left! *What do I do?*"

"Serves ye right fer setting her free, pilgrim. She's some woman, did ye know? Be a sight better fer ye than some white gal who only wants to sit around a house and live on a feller's labor. An Injun woman, Dick, she's more. Work side by side with ye, she will."

"I don't want a woman. I want you to tell me what to do. You're raving, Travis. Out of your head. You just had to push yourself, didn't you? Well, if you die out here, what am I going to do?"

"Foller the rivers, Dick. A feller cain't get lost. Clear out to the Black Hills, all the rivers run east to the Missouri. Beyond the Black Hills, the rivers run north to the Missouri. Any creek will take ye ter the Missouri. Foller the Missouri downstream to Fort Atkinson."

"What about the whiskey?"

"We gotta get that t' Davey. Reckon he'll go bust without her. We owe him, Dick. Kept us alive he did, nursed us after Old Ephraim tried ter put us under. Davey's a good man. Got grit whar it counts. That's all that matters in life—if'n a feller's got...grit."

Richard shook his head. "I've got to figure out a way to move you. We can't just stay here. There's nothing to tie the horses to."

"Back," Travis whispered. "She'll be back—in two hands. How long?"

"What?"

"Willow. She'll be back."

"Maybe. If she comes, it will be a miracle. I sure wouldn't."

"Reckon ye would, Dick. It's in ye. Yer not the kind ter up and quit." Damn, when did it get so hot? "Reckon I'd do fer a mite of water, Dick."

"I don't have any, Travis. The closest is back at the spring."

"Wal, I reckon I done without water afore. This child's just plumb tuckered, that's all." He swallowed hard. "Let me close my eyes. Just fer a while."

In the hot blackness, he floated, hearing voices from far away. Firelight flickered, and the sparks formed into faces: Immel, Jones, Keemle, Joshua Pilcher, Manuel Lisa. They sat joking, smoking long-stemmed clay pipes. Four heavy log posts gleamed golden in the background, upright to support a square smokehole. Mandan lodge. The fire popped and sparked.

Someone was singing "Yankee Doodle," while a squeeze box wheezed and tooted the notes. Along the southeast wall, where the horses were sometimes stabled, *engagés* danced and cavorted in their heavy white canvas clothing. The red hats bobbed and swung with each merry dancer's pirouetting steps.

"She is dying, Travis," Manuel Lisa said. The long-faced

Spaniard watched him through those brooding dark eyes. *"The river, she will never be the same. Perhaps the Omaha chief, Blackbird, poisoned it like he did all of his rivals. We had but a moment, a shining time. The river is going to die soon, choked in steam and smoke. But I have suspicions about the mountains beyond. They, too, will die. But for a time, the freedom will be there."*

"The mountains?" Travis asked. "We're a-headed thar. Me and Davey Green."

"Watch out fer the Blackfeet, coon," Immel warned. *"Watch yer topknot, Travis. They'll hit ye when yer not ready."*

Jones puffed at his pipe, cheeks sucking in. He lifted a lip in disgust, then broke off an inch of the stem, the white clay discolored from the smoke. He puffed again, and smiled, saying, *"Much better. She smokes a mite sweeter now."* Jones raised his eyes. *"Yer stars has always been lucky, Travis. Bug's Boys ain't whar ye expects 'em. Light out south. They'll seek ye all along the river, a-figgering ye'll double back fer the Mandans."*

"Ain't no Blackfoot down here near Fort Atkinson." He wished the fire wasn't so hot. Lord God, he was hotter than a Doodle in a sweat lodge.

"Travis?"

"Huh?"

"Travis! Wake up!"

He felt something cool—water—passing his lips in dribbles. He blinked, dazzled by the bright light of afternoon. A gut water bag was placed to his lips. He sucked down more of the refreshing liquid. Not Immel and Jones, not Lisa. He squinted up at Dick Hamilton and the Snake woman, Heals Like A Willow.

"Travis," Dick told him, "we've got to get you up. Willow made a...well, a thing. We can get you to the river."

Travis took a deep breath, hating the lightheaded floating.

Fever! It's still got ahold of me.

Willow on one side, Hamilton on the other, they eased him to his feet. He stood on weak legs, the wound stinging and pulling. The scrubby little mare waited, head down, a travois tied onto her withers. Travis hobbled to the woven mat of willow and hazel branches. Then he settled back, feeling the springy wood give under his weight.

Willow lifted his shirt then, and checked the split cactus on his wounds. She made the signs: "Cactus will keep the wound from drying and cracking. At the river we will poke the wound, make it flow. Then more spirit water."

"Whyn't ye just up and kill me?"

Tarnal Hell, that whiskey stung like rattlesnake poison.

He winced when the mare started forward. He eased his side as best he could given the jolting and watched the trails of bent grass made by the travois legs. The sky was clear this afternoon, cloudless and wonderfully blue. The water had helped, but he felt so terribly weak.

He reached into his possibles and brought out the scalp he'd carved from the young Pawnee's head that morning. With his patch knife, he began to carefully scrape the bloody tissue from the skull side of the hardening skin. As the knife scraped, dreams of Moonlight flitted through his head like cottonwood down on warm morning breezes.

CHAPTER SEVEN

We must not confuse selfishness with self-love; they are two very discrete passions both in their nature and in their effects. Self-love is a natural sentiment, which inclines every animal to look to his own preservation, and which, directed in man by reason, and tempered by pity, is productive of virtue and humanity. Selfishness is nothing more than a relative and factitious sentiment, engendered in society, which disposes every individual to set a greater value upon himself than upon any other person, which inspires men to all the mischief they commit upon each other, and is the true source of what we call honor.

—Jean-Jacques Rousseau, *Discourse on the Origin and Foundation of Inequality Among Mankind*

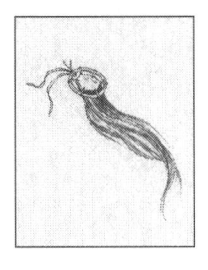 High clouds burned with a salmon-pink radiance in the peaceful dusk. Richard made a final inspection of the night's camp. Through gaps in the trees, he could see the evening-silvered waters of the Missouri flow past. The surface looked so smooth,

polished pewter marred only by the shimmering columns of insects that hummed over the water.

He checked—then double-checked—the picket line that held the horses. The knots were tight on the rope that stretched between two cottonwoods. Willow had helped him with the work, surprising him with her strength as she carried the heavy tins of whiskey to the pile. She'd watched him warily as they watered the horses, and studied him with those large dark eyes when they tied the lead ropes to the picket line.

What was it about her? Why did he keep sneaking glances at her? He shook his head, irritated with himself, with the attraction he felt, and concentrated on his duties.

Everything looked sound. Even the fire that he'd made—luck riding his shoulders with this, his second-ever fire from a strike-a-light.

His first smoldering spark had caught in the char-cloth and blown to flame in the dry grass he'd used for a starter.

Travis lay on his blankets beside the firepit. His eyes had cleared and his color was better. Tongue stuck out the side of his mouth, he worked on a small patch of hide with his little patch knife. Long black hair streamed from the pale leather. Horse mane? No, the hair looked finer than that.

Richard dropped to a squat. "You feeling all right?"

"Heap better, coon." Travis looked up, mild curiosity in his eyes. "Reckon I caught a tetch of fever today."

"Shouldn't have tried to leave before you were healed."

Travis waved his piece of hide toward the river. "We beat Green hyar, didn't we?"

"They might have poled past here—or been on the far bank."

"Yep, or even sailed if they got wind. But they didn't."

Richard followed Travis's gaze. Willow sat on a downed cottonwood at the water's edge. Since they'd finished chores, she'd stared in silence at the river. At this point it had to be over two hundred yards across. What thoughts were in her head?

Richard said, "I never thought she'd be back. She saved us."

"Yep. I reckon she did." Travis smoothed the glistening black hair with his callused fingers. "Hunt around in my possibles. Build us a smoke, coon."

Richard did so, lighting a twig to start the bowl. He puffed and passed the pipe to Travis.

The hunter pulled and exhaled the blue smoke through his nostrils. "I reckon tomorrow morning ye might want ter take that gnarly-looking brown gelding. I'd backtrack, oh, maybe a mile or two, then cut straight south. Follow along the flats where the bluffs break down toward the river. Yer two days' hard ride from Fort Atkinson."

"What are you talking about? You mean to go get help? Willow says you're going to be all right."

Travis fixed those hard blue eyes on him. "If'n yer not dumber than a Kentucky fence post, I don't know what is. The *fort's* two days *south*. Reckon I'd take that Injun trade gun. Being smooth bore, she ain't fer long shots, but she'll raise anything up close...even Pawnee."

Richard took the pipe, staring. "You mean, you want me to ride off?"

"Wal, yer game, Dick. Reckon I'll just up and tell Dave ye got the slip on me, and I kilt ye when I finally run ye down. Reckon that'll give them *engagés* something ter think about. Davey, wal, I reckon he'll weasel it outa me by the time we make the Mandan villages."

Richard drew on the pipe, staring down at the crackling fire. Free? Just like that?

He glanced at the brown gelding standing head down, eyes half closed on the picket line. The evening deepened, faint rays of light spreading amber across the sky while shadows grew among the trees. On the eastern bluffs, several miles away, the hilltops looked golden.

A mourning dove cooed out in the trees.

"What about you? What if Green's really upriver? Do you think Willow is going to stay? She could leave, too."

"Reckon I'm about healed, Dick." Travis lifted his shirt, staring down at the ugly wound. "Ye done right fine. Hell, ye otta seen the job they did on old Louis de Grotte. Looked like chickens danced on his gut."

"I was scared to death."

"So's I. Don't know which of us was shaking worst."

"I was," Richard said softly and vividly recalled his tacky red fingers, the needle dimpling the blood-slick skin, and the sodden pull of Travis's flesh on the thread.

How did I ever do that?

He looked down at his hands. The sun had burned them dark brown, the skin rough and callused; dirt made dark arcs under his nails. They looked like a man's hands. That thought startled him. *Are they really mine?*

Heals Like A Willow rose and walked slowly toward them, head bowed, her long glossy black hair slipping around her shoulders. Her leather dress was worn, but it clung to her in a way that accented her broad shoulders, full breasts, narrow waist, and the provocative curve of her hips. The tattered hem ended just below her knees. Richard had never seen a woman's legs before; unabashed, he kept staring. Her skin seemed so smooth and silky. The way the soft leather outlined her thighs and flat abdomen brought thoughts to Richard's mind that he'd never encountered before.

"Reckon ye'd best close yer mouth," Travis observed. "Yer like to start drooling."

Richard threw his tormentor an irritated glance, but by then Willow had arrived. She shook out her blanket, gave Travis a solicitous inspection, then settled herself. Expressionless, she stared into the fire.

"Willow, why do you look so sad?" Richard asked.

She cocked her head, listening intently to his words as she studied him. Were her lustrous eyes larger than a white woman's? Was that why they seemed to engulf him? Could they swallow a man's soul?

She made signs to Travis, and he made signs back.

"She says she's sad because her husband and son are dead. They died of a fever this last winter. She was supposed to save them. She's a healer—uh, medicine woman. They died anyway. They were Meat-Eater Snakes, *Ku'chendikani.* She's with the high mountain Snakes, the *Dukurika,* Sheepeaters. She was on her way home when Packrat—that Pawnee kid ye sent under—captured her."

"How'd she get here?"

Travis made more signs, and Willow's hands traced out the shapes of a response. "She says Packrat was Half Man's son. Packrat was bringing her to Half Man as a sort of Pawnee insult—a way to shame his father for having shamed his mother. Packrat hoped to gain power and prestige among his people."

Richard scratched at his bristly chin. "Let me get this straight. Packrat was going to give her to his father, and by doing so, shame him?"

Travis puffed on the pipe. "Wal, the Pawnee, they got

their own ways of doing things. Like clever jokes. For instance, let's say a warrior says another Pawnee is a miser, selfish when other people are in need. Such a thing can destroy a man's reputation among the Pawnee. To stop any such nonsense, the feller accused of hoarding, he up and gives everything he's got to the feller that shot off his mouth. Ye can damn well bet it would put the gabber in his place fer good."

"I see. Aesop would have liked a story like that."

"He one of yer perfessors?"

"No. He was a Greek. Wrote fables. Like the dog in the manger? Ever heard of that?"

"I reckon."

"Stories with a moral message...and the Pawnee put the stories into practice?"

"Reckon they do. And, when ye think about it, it makes a sight more sense than throwing a coon inta jail."

Willow's slender fingers danced.

"What did she say?" Richard longed to reach out and touch her long hair where the firelight played in it.

"Wants to know about us, coon. Yer not married, are ye?"

"No."

Travis's hands molded the response. Willow continued her inspection of Richard, then she signed again.

"She wants to know why you keep staring at her that way. She says it's a lost-puppy look."

Richard blushed and avoided her eyes. Good God, what would Laura think? "Tell her...Tell her I..."

But Willow's hands were in motion again.

Travis chuckled. "She says that I look at her with lust, but you look at her with a different eye, the soul's eye."

Richard glared hotly at Travis. "Stop looking at her that way!"

Travis laughed out loud, winced, and placed a hand tenderly to his side. Willow glanced curiously between them.

"What about this soul's eye?" Richard asked. "The soul doesn't have an eye."

Travis made his signs. Willow started a response, then made a cutoff sign. She stood, walked over to Richard, and settled herself immediately in front of him. She placed cool hands on either side of his head. Then, her face inches from his, she looked deeply into his eyes.

Richard fell into those endless pools. Brown, limpid, they expanded and engulfed the world with their soft strength. She probed, challenged, and waited for a reaction.

It's as if our souls are touching.

Richard's heart leapt, rising to the challenge. He reached up, cupping her face with his own hands, meeting her challenge and searching as she did. The blood had begun to pulse in his veins.

How long were they locked like that? An eternal moment.

She nodded then, lowered her hands, and backed away.

Richard sat like a statue, hands frozen in the air, still caressing the memory of her soft warm cheeks. His heart slowed its hammering beat, the blood cooling in his veins.

Her hands formed graceful signs, and Travis said, "The soul's eye."

Richard nodded and took a deep breath as the tingling surge slowly boiled out of his blood. She continued to watch him, her full lips pursed pensively.

When her hands moved again, Travis translated: "What did you see?"

Richard answered, awed, "I saw your soul, Willow."

"She wants to know if you were afraid."

"No. Not at all. Why should I be?"

Travis made signs. "She says most men fear women's Power. Men fear her in particular. She does not act as men think proper. She seeks medicine Power. With it, she destroyed Packrat."

"Willow"—Richard reached out, desperate to keep that link—"I do not fear you. I am a philosopher, a seeker of truth."

"Ain't no sign fer philos'pher," Travis growled. "Hell, I'll just make this up."

"Don't!" Richard cried. "This is important. I've been looking for her! Don't you see? She's proof!"

"Proof?" Travis screwed his face up. "Proof of what?"

"Man in nature, Travis!" Richard beamed in his excitement, Willow watching him with glowing eyes.

"Wal, hoss, if'n ye think's she's a man, yer not only an ignerant Yankee, but tarnal blind to boot!"

Richard grinned triumphantly. "Tell her I have hoped to meet someone like her. I want to...to talk to her. Ask her questions."

Travis translated. Willow watched curiously, then responded: "What questions?"

"About God. About perception and the nature of mankind, the epistemological basis of reality that dictates—"

"Whoa, now! Damn it, Dick! I ain't got no signs for none of that hoss crap but God!"

"Dik," she said, then her hand made a sign.

Travis translated: "Learn...Talk...White man."

"It takes a long time," Richard told her.

She gave him her challenging stare and said, "Willow learn talk White man."

"I'll be damned," Travis muttered. He put his pipe back in his possibles and retrieved the hairy piece of hide. He fingered the long black hair and studied Willow thoughtfully.

Richard grinned. "I'll teach you."

Travis lifted an eyebrow and signed.

"What's that?" Richard asked.

"I asked if she was going with us up the river."

Her fingers flew.

Travis related: "I will travel with you for a while. It would be wise to know more about the White men. You have not been what I expected." In English she ended, "I will learn. Eye of the soul."

"Eye of the soul," Richard agreed. "One day we will talk about God, and nature, and man's place within it."

Travis scraped his piece of hide. "Careful, coon. I gotta hunch she ain't just any old squaw."

"How's that?"

"I believe that bit she said about Packrat. She said she destroyed him. Watch yer topknot, coon. See that she don't destroy yer soul whilst she's a-looking at it."

"What do you mean?"

Travis studied Willow thoughtfully. "When she walked up and looked ye in the eyes, didn't ye feel it?"

"I did indeed."

"Power, coon. Heap big medicine. I felt it afore, at Okipa and Sundance, but never from no woman. I reckon she kilt Packrat, all right. And saved our bacon in the process. Reckon she knew what she's about the whole time."

Richard gave Travis a quizzical glance. "How could

magic kill? It's irrational. Ask her, Travis. Willow, how did you kill Packrat?"

Travis made the signs, and read Willow's answer: "I drove his soul from his body and made him insane."

———

Why am I doing this?

Heals Like A Willow walked barefoot along the muddy bank of the Missouri, as the Whites called it. The golden morning had dawned cool, with a light mist rising above the water.

Throughout the long night, she'd dreamed of Dik, of the way his soul had reached out to touch hers. She had never dreamed that a man would look at her with such fearlessness. What kind of man was Dik? She'd seen him shaking after killing Packrat, and yet he had no fear of her. Even the Bear Man now looked at her with reservation. Deep in his soul, Trawis understood what she'd done to Packrat, if not the exact way of it.

She crossed her arms, wisps of hair blowing around her like a cloak.

I used my puha*. I didn't hesitate, didn't worry about acting correctly, or as other people expected me to. I used all of my* puha*, and Packrat is dead. I might have been* Pa-waip *herself.*

Pap-waip. Water Ghost Woman. The enchanting siren who lived in rivers and springs. Beautiful, she enticed men into her embrace. And once they had lost their senses and lifted her dress, she' allow them to couple with her. At that magic moment when they convulsed, she would roll them into the water, drown them, and devour their souls.

The parallels between what she'd done, and *Pa-waip* were unsettling. But Water Ghost Woman didn't use her *puba* to heal, though she did grant it to women seeking fertility.

If I had used all of my puha, *instead of being so cautious, would my husband and baby be alive today?*

Willo drew a deep breath to counter the bitter ache within. Her husband's face hovered at the edge of her thoughts—but she dared not reach out to him, fearful of what the attempt would do to his souls on their journey to the afterlife.

If only I had allowed myself to use all of my Power.

But she had been frightened of where that would lead, and what would happen to her.

And if there is a next time?

She knotted her fist, refusing to consider the possibility.

The roiling water flowed past—an incredible moving sheet of brown that shaded into gleaming silver before it met the far wooded shore. Behind her, the new cotton-wood leaves rattled in the breeze from the blufftops. With it came the smells of grass, wildflowers, and dry earth.

Far out in the river, a giant cottonwood rolled with the current, the branches yellow and pointed, scrubbed bare of bark. Two great blue herons flapped slowly upriver, their needle beaks and trailing feet thin against the sky.

Trawis said that a huge canoe was being pulled upriver, that it would meet them here. She tried to comprehend what he'd told her. A canoe longer than fifteen men. She couldn't form the image of such a thing in her mind.

I will ride this big canoe, and learn more.

She stopped, toes in the lapping water, and looked up. An eagle soared in easy circles against the morning sky.

Is that you, husband? Are you still watching out for me?

No answer came to the aching loneliness inside. What would he say at the sight of so much moving water?

Dry-eyed, she blinked, clearing her soul's vision of his smiling face. Killing the desire in her heart for his gentle touch.

Perhaps getting captured hadn't been such a bad thing. She'd had no time for grief. During that long ride with Packrat, her concentration had centered on endurance, and the battle of wills with her captor. Like two otters on an ice floe, they'd teetered back and forth, but in the end she'd worn him down. Right down to the moment when he drew an arrow to kill Trawis.

The moment I laughed, I won, Packrat.

She curled her toes in the muddy sand. Her only hope at the moment had been to lose him the whiskey, to thwart his little victory. But Power worked in mysterious ways, and Dik had killed Packrat.

Why?

Because Packrat was beating her. What Indian man would kill another because he was beating a slave?

Strange beings, these White men. Trawis, she could understand. He was just a man, possessed of all the normal things a man was possessed of—and of some things more so. Courage, for one. No one could doubt his courage, or the strength of his soul. Not only had he insisted on traveling to the river when he should have stayed flat, but he had insisted on healing on the way.

And he hasn't died.

Dik had played a big part in keeping Bear Man alive, but Dik didn't seem to realize his Power. Had no one trained him, taught him to open his soul? What a curious man. He didn't shrink back from a woman using her medicine skills. Didn't he fear the loss of his manhood? That she would somehow weaken him?

She wondered what Water Ghost Woman would do if she ever encountered Dik beside a creek.

Behind her, a rifle made a *pop-boom* as Richard practiced.

"Keep yer eye open, coon! Ye gotta keep yer aim after the flash in the pan!"

She cocked her head, trying to follow the words. "Eye," she knew, and "yer," "ye," and "keep." Dik had worked with her all evening, until she went to sleep, her souls spinning with new words.

Today Dik was learning to shoot, a fact confusing to her, since he'd shot Packrat dead.

She bent down to touch her fingertips to the water and let the crystalline drops run down her hand.

What brought me here, so far from my people? Where is Power taking me?

A person could ask the questions, and the answers always came, but only after a long time.

She caught one of the drips of water on the tip of her tongue. The important thing was to ask the questions. Two Half Moons might have had a glimmer of that truth when she climbed up under the rim to save Willow from freezing to death.

Perhaps Slim Pole had been part of the pattern, aware of her shaken belief in her Power, and frightened of the consequences among his people.

Red Calf knew and rightly feared me. I would have destroyed her.

And to what purpose? Justice? The Pawnee showed a great deal more sense than the *Ku'chendikani* when it came to settling disputes.

Pop-boom!

"Reckon that's a mite better, coon! Ye hit the tree," came Trawis's reedy cry.

"Reckon," that meant to think, but there were other words for the process. "Tree," she'd learned that word, too.

So, you will go upriver with them? Why, Willow? The smart woman you used to be would take a horse and race straight back to the Powder River Mountains.

Her gaze played over the huge river. Like clouds, the water never made exactly the same pattern twice.

"And how," she asked herself, "will you act when a White man crawls into your blankets at night? You are a lone woman traveling with men. Men are no more than they are."

As women are no more than they are. But are we so different? Yes, we are. A man seeks to plant his seed in as many women as he can. The more women, the better his chances of making a child. A woman seeks a man who will keep her secure and help to raise the child. Because of this, we are always pitted against each other.

"That doesn't answer your question, Willow. What will you do when one crawls into your blankets?" She made a face at the notion of ghost white skin against hers. It would be the same as coupling with a corpse.

She might not be Water Ghost Woman, but *Dukurika* woman knew ways of keeping men off. Her hand slid down to the smooth handle of the war club she'd tied to the rope around her waist. With it, Packrat had subdued her.

But I will subdue any man who threatens me.

Similarly, she would claim Pack-rat's bow and arrows. She hadn't practiced with the bow since girlhood. Perhaps the time had come to grow proficient again.

Dik will protect me.

The thought surfaced in her soul.

"And you are a fool, Heals Like A Willow. Only you can protect yourself. Anything else is a lie."

She entered camp and found the bow and arrows rolled in Packrat's blankets. Stringing the hardwood bow took all of her strength. Most of the arrows were headed with soft-iron trade points, the kind that cut cleanly but bent upon impact with bone. She'd seen the effect they had on a man. Those she would have to save, but the blunt-headed bird points could be used for practice.

Pop-boom! At the shot, the horses started, then relaxed.

She headed toward the shooting, testing the pull on the bow. "Are you ready, Dik? I am coming to shoot against you. You with your White man's rifle and I with my Pawnee bow."

———

The Indian pony that Richard rode had the roughest gait he'd ever felt. The little animal hammered each stiff-legged step down the grassy slope, following the travois tracks. Richard held the reins in his left hand, the Pawnee trade gun in the right. To his annoyance, he wasn't a good enough rider to keep from bouncing on the animal's back like a corn kernel on a tin lid.

The horse snuffled and shook its head.

"Whoa, now. Damn you, keep your head up. Travis told me about you. If you get your head down, you're going to buck me right off."

The afternoon sun cast golden light into the hazel-skirted grove of oak and ash that lined the bluffs descending to the river; it blazed in the high tops of the cottonwoods on the floodplain. Beyond, in shadow, the river had a bluish-brown sheen broken by the sinuous lenticular shapes of sandbars on the far side.

The wiry pony picked his way down a deer trail and onto the grass-rich Cottonwood bottoms. Richard booted him, and the little horse pounded his way forward in that bone-jarring trot.

Camp was right where Richard had left it, spirals of blue smoke rising from behind the circular fortification of whiskey tins. Their feet had beaten the grass flat, and trails led down to the water's edge. The other horses whinnied from their pickets.

"Hello, Dick!" Travis called from where he was propped comfortably on the packs. "See anything?"

Richard reined the pony to a stop and gratefully slid off the animal. It took a moment for his rubbery legs to hold him. The muscles quivered like violin strings from gripping the horse's barrel. "Can't these Indians use stirrups?"

"Reckon not. They figger it's only fer white men what can't ride."

Richard led the horse down to water, Travis hobbling along behind. "I saw the *Maria*. She's coming, Travis."

The hunter sighed, then grinned. "Been a sight worried, coon. Hell, now wouldn't it just figger? We make her all the way around that cussed fort, and they catch Davey with them forged papers and confiscate the boat?"

"Well, rest assured, she's coming. I'd say she'll be here by noon tomorrow." Richard watched the horse drink. Each swallow of water could be seen as it traveled up the throat. "Willow's still around?"

"She's gone hunting. I reckon she'll be back." Travis gave him a sideways look. "Yer not sounding happy."

Richard kicked idly at the sand, then stared out over the silver sheet of river. "I guess by noon tomorrow, I'll be breaking my back on the cordelle, that or wearing a hole in my shoulder with the pole."

"Reckon so." Travis was silent for a moment. "Why didn't ye run? Ye could have kept right on going—straight south into the fort."

"It was tempting. To be honest, I thought about it. I thought about a lot of things. But I have an obligation, Travis. You were wounded on my account. I gave the Pawnee the opportunity. If I'd kept my mouth shut, he'd be alive, you would be healthy, and I wouldn't have killed a man."

"That bothers ye? That ye sent that Pawnee under?" Travis lifted a grizzled eyebrow.

"I keep thinking about his body, the way it bloated. How it was covered with flies. I have nightmares at night, shooting him over and over. All that blood...the look in those glassy eyes... He was a young man, Travis. Barely more than a child. I still don't believe I killed— murdered him like that."

Travis scuffed his moccasined toe in the soft sand. The horse had raised his head, muzzle dripping, ears pricked, to look out over the river.

"Thought ye was the one wanted ter be so damned rational? Wal, if'n ye'd not shot him, Willow'd be dead. I'd be dead. And, why, tarnal hell! Ye'd be dead, too!"

"It's not a matter of rationality. It's...it's how I *feel*, Travis."

The hunter said, "Wal, Dick, I ain't got the words fer it, not to palaver with a philos'pher. Maybe it's God, maybe it's plumb chance, but there's times when a body's headed fer a mess. Half Man and me, we both knew that first day on the trail that one of us would kill t'other. He figgered he'd walk away, I figgered I would. That was the only real question. What's that word? The one for when something's just bound ter happen? Ain't no way around it?"

"Inevitable."

"Inevitable. That's it, Dick. What's yer philos'phers say about that?"

"They say that human behavior can be changed by reason."

"Wal, maybe so, given enough time, and given men of like minds, but do ye reckon ye could have reasoned that kid outa killing Willow? Or Half Man outa not trying me?"

Richard fingered the lead rope. "I don't know. So many of the answers that were once crystal clear are turning fuzzy and fading now."

"Reckon that happens when a man starts growing. This child suspects that any fool can write a book when he's sitting in a room in a city with folks around ter keep his arse safe, a fire in his stove, and his belly full. A feller can justify anything he wants...so long as it's rational, and there ain't no consequences if'n he's wrong. But out hyar, wal, it plumb ain't real."

Richard scratched his neck and said nothing, his gut churning.

Travis reached out to Richard's side and tied the piece of hide to his belt so that the long black hair hung down along his leg. "Wear that, coon. It'll bring ye luck."

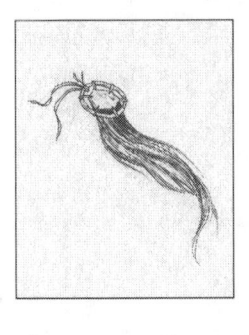

"What is it? What animal did you take it off of?"

"A kind of skunk that lives out hyar."

Richard fingered the long hair. "Is it a fetish?"

"What in hell's a...sure, yep. Reckon so. That's what she be." Travis had a funny look in his eye. "Wal, now, Dick, I got me an idea. Seems we got us eleven hosses, twelve if'n ye counts Willow's. Ain't much above here but trouble. The Omaha country is a couple of days' journey north, but beyond there, yer not going ter find nobody but Sioux, Rees, and Cheyenne until we reach the Mandan. Ain't none of 'em but would lift them hosses plumb quick."

Richard fingered the glossy skunk hair. "What do we do?"

Travis reached for his possibles and pulled out his pipe, gesturing with it as he talked, "Wal, the way I'm thinking, a coon needs to have help a-guarding these hosses. Now, if'n ye'd be of a mind not to escape, perhaps I could use ye."

"Promise not to escape?" Richard frowned, then shook his head. "I can't, Travis. What was done to me was wrong. I have ethical values, and I must stick to them."

Travis pursed his lips, the effect pulling the scars tight

across his ruined face. "Yep. A man's gotta do what he's gotta do. I keep forgetting that."

"Why do I always get the feeling that you're mocking me?"

"Mock ye? Wal now, Dick, that's about the silliest idea I've heard since flying buffler chips. Reckon ye'd never catch me a-funning ye, not with all them philos'phy ideas in yer head."

A twinkle filled Travis's eye as he turned and made his way carefully back to the fire.

Richard's horse jerked him away from the river; he led the animal to the picket line instead of letting it crop. After he'd tied the horse, he stopped and fingered the fetish. He lifted the long hair and sniffed. It didn't smell like skunk.

He was still studying it when he got to the fire. "You said this would bring me luck?"

"Yep." Travis seemed suddenly fascinated by his stained-leather knee. "It's a sign of respect in these parts, Dick. Reckon ye could say it's a sign of a man, one ter be listened ter, and looked up ter."

Richard frowned and sat cross-legged in front of the fire. "Respect? Why? I mean, why me?"

Travis puffed on his pipe and handed it over to Richard. "Ye done a man's job this hyar trip. Ye saved me...saved the whiskey. Saved Willow, fer that matter. Made us rich on hosses—and they'd have cost a heap of goods about the time we made 'er to the Mandans. Yer a man, Dick. By all the rules of this country, red and white. That thar, what did ye call her, fetish? That fetish ain't nothing more than the proof of it."

Richard glanced skeptically at Travis. "But I'm still a slave?"

"Man's a slave only so long's he allows himself ter be.

Reckon that Packrat, he larned that lesson and did her the hard way."

"He was going to kill Willow."

"Of course. She'd beat him at his own game. When a man's got no choice but ter kill his slaves, he's plumb licked. At least by that particular slave. See whar my stick floats, Dick?"

"Not exactly." Richard puffed on the pipe. The tobacco was welcome—even if it wasn't up to Bostonian standards. "What good is freedom if you're dead?"

"Ye ever figger what would happen if all the slaves in the world said no ter their masters? Reckon they'd be beat the first day, whipped the second, starved from then on, maybe even all kilt. Wal, all right, so let's say all the slaves was dead all over the world. Now, do ye reckon thar'd be any more slaves?"

"Someone will always turn another person into a slave," Richard pointed with the pipe stem. "Plato wrote in his—"

"Plato? Another philos'pher in a room?"

"He was. And my point still stands."

Travis pulled at the fringes on his sleeve. "I reckon so, but a slave can only stay a slave if'n he sets more store on his life than on his freedom. I got the story outa Willow. That's how she drove that Packrat coon plumb crazy. Ain't the first time I heard that story. Come upriver with Baptiste. Now thar be a man what wouldn't be a slave."

"Life is a pretty powerful argument...especially when it's yours."

"Hand me my pipe back! Ye gonna smoke her dry?"

"Sorry. I'm sort of used to arguing with a pipe in my hand, but with much better tobacco."

"Life, ye say." Travis studied the tendrils of smoke rising from the stained bowl. "Ever hear tell of them

Spartans? The ones back in Rome what fought off that Egyptian king and died fer it?"

"That's a Persian king. At Thermopylae, in Greece. No Romans were involved. What's your point?"

"They died t'save a heap of others, Dick. Reckon yer no different, not down deep. Reckon if'n it was Katy bar the door, ye'd be just as quick jumping inta the breach. Figger this"—Travis waved his pipe in emphasis—"yer house is on fire. Now, yer whole family is in thar a-screaming, and all ye've got ter do is jump inta the fire, burn yerself, and hold the door open to let 'em out. Ye'd do her, wouldn't ye?"

"Using my family for an example isn't very smart, Travis. If it was my father in there, I'd be throwing oil on the blaze by the bucketful."

Travis raised an eyebrow. "No wonder he kicked ye outa Boston. But, anyhow, ye get my meaning."

"Yes, yes, the examples are necessary. Just not sufficient."

"Huh?"

Richard grinned. "Philosophical standards—but, yes, people do risk their lives and lose them to save others. That's not at issue here. Slavery is."

"Reckon so, coon. And my point is that no slave needs ter be a slave if'n he's willing ter give up his life ter save himself and all the others. Now, tell me, ain't it damned peculiar—illogical, in yer words—that all the slaves don't just up and quit? Take their chances just like folks do all the time to save their friends and kin. Hell, even strangers! No one would have to be a slave again...ever."

Richard reached for the pipe, puffing as he frowned. "Mass civil disobedience."

"Yep."

"It would never work. It is the nature of the slave to value vain hope for the future over almost certain death and potential greater good."

"Plumb irrational, wouldn't ye say?"

"I see what you're getting at. Sure, people are irrational all the time. But, don't you see, it's only through rational action that we can improve our lot."

"Uh-huh. And if'n ye was rational, ye'd give me yer word that ye'd stick her out to the mouth of the Yellerstone, and help me with the hosses."

"Why do you care so much?"

Travis stared moodily at the fire. "Just a cussed streak I got in me. I reckon the bear's outa the cage. Maybe I want ter see him become a real bear."

CHAPTER EIGHT

Then again, on the other hand, the unsophisticated mind takes under its guardianship, the good and the noble (that is, what retains its state of meaning in being objectively stated), and protects it in the only way possible here—that is to say, the good does not lose its value because it may be linked with what is bad, or mingled with it, for to be thus associated with badness is both its condition and necessity, and the wisdom of nature is found in this fact.

—Georg Friedrich Wilhelm Hegel, *Phenomenology of Mind*

Travis grinned as he watched Willow. She stood frozen, stunned as a surprised deer, mouth ajar, eyes wide with astonishment. Her disbelief tickled him clear down to his roots. In the end, she could only shake her head and mutter softly. The *Maria* was being poled upriver, momentum carrying the boat forward against the current before the next set of the poles. The keelboat might have been some giant water insect, propelled by multitudes of legs across the roiling brown water.

Travis hitched his way down the muddy bank to stand between Willow and Richard. He raised his rifle, firing a shot into the air. Willow jumped at the concussion.

"Sorry, gal," Travis mumbled.

"All right," she whispered absently. Shots answered from the boat, puffs of blue smoke rising over the cargo box. In incredulous tones she rattled away in her Snake tongue.

Travis pressed a gentle hand to his side. Still damned tender. "Dick. Like her or not, yer on hoss duty fer a couple of days."

Richard gave him an uneasy glance. "Why me?"

Travis chewed at his lip and squinted into the midday sun. "Wal, reckon it's like this, coon. This hyar beaver's got a cut in him bigger and uglier than Hob's smile. Reckon I cain't go a-traipsing after the hosses. I plumb sure ain't gonna turn Trudeau nor any of them other French lard eaters out to guard 'em. That leaves ye, Mister Hamilton."

"I told you I'd escape."

"Hoss crap! If'n ye'd a wanted ter, ye'd be gone."

"I told you, it's ethically untenable. I had a responsibility to ensure that you made it back to the boat. That you were injured was partially my fault. Here's the boat. When they drop the plank, I will have fulfilled that obligation."

"Nope. Nothing's changed. I ain't up ter hunting and hoss keeping. Not fer another week at best. Reckon ye can do yer duty, then escape when I get all healed."

"Travis Hartman," Richard whispered, "you are a black bastard at heart."

"I reckon so."

Maria turned gracefully, coasting in toward the bank. Travis had picked this place precisely because the bottom dropped off, and the river didn't carry much current. The perfect spot for on-loading the whiskey.

"How do, coon!" came a familiar cry, and Travis shaded his eyes to study the brawny black man at the bow. He stood like a sassy pirate, his dark face shadowed by a large-brimmed felt hat.

"Baptiste? Tarnal Hell! What are ye doing aboard?"

"Ha! I be yoah new partner, coon!" The ebony face split with a smile. "Life at the fort…wal, 'tain't nothing but poor bull. I reckoned I'd come along and hunt down that Pawnee what kilt you, but I see yor topknot's still on!"

"Reckon so, but she was Katy bar the door! Don't ye come a flying off ter give me no bar hug, neither. Ye'll squeeze me guts clean out!"

"You hurt?" Green called from the cargo box as the *Maria* swung up against the shore. *Engagés* were craning their necks, eyes wide as they whispered back and forth.

"Sliced nigh in two. But old Dick, hyar, he done sewed me up."

"Got a squaw, too?" Green studied Willow with a cocked look. "Hell! That's the Snake woman I saw at Fort Atkinson. Where's that Pawnee kid she was running with?"

"Dick raised him. Shot him plumb center."

Green gave Hamilton a sidelong glance. "Do tell."

The plank came out and Willow backed slowly away, looking like a rabbit about to break for the tall sage.

"Easy, gal." Travis made the signs. "You are safe. No one will hurt you, I promise."

She gave him an uncertain look and signed: "Yellow-haired White man tried to buy me for two guns at fort."

"Why, I'd a fetched five fer ye." Travis winked to reassure her, then in a loud voice hollered: "Hey, Dave! This hyar's Heals Like A Willow. I don't want no harm t' come ter her. She's with me." Travis narrowed an eye to glare wickedly at the *engagés* who stared down with appraising eyes. "Y'all hear that, coons? If'n she don't kill yer arse fer trying ter fool with her, I'll do it! Or maybe Dick, hyar."

Laughter rose at that.

"The woman is to be left alone!" Green ordered.

Henri was leaning on his steering oar, and rubbed his blunt jaw as he glanced dubiously back and forth between Willow and the *engagés*. He finally muttered, "*Chercher des ennuis! Beaucoup troubles.*"

Travis patted Willow on the shoulder. "Ain't nobody gonna bother ye none."

Engagés trotted down the plank, headed for the trees and the tins of whiskey. They leered at Willow with hawkish eyes; and she glared right back at them; her grip on the war club tightened.

Baptiste strode down like a lord, his long buckskin shirt swaying at mid-thigh. Leggings and high moccasins rustled with long fringe. A man might have danced on those broad, muscular shoulders. White teeth flashed in his face as he looked Travis up and down.

Willow uttered an amazed sound as Baptiste stopped before them. She made signs, and Baptiste laughed, signing back. Timidly, Willow reached up to rub at his face, and then his hands.

"What's this?" Richard whispered, leaning toward Travis.

"Trying to see if the soot will rub off," Travis told him. "Dick, this hyar black cutthroat is my old friend,

Baptiste. He goes by Baptiste because he's afraid some coon might recognize his real name."

"I reckon there be a death warrant fo' me in the United States," Baptiste said easily. He withdrew his hand from Willow's and offered it to Hamilton. The Yankee swallowed hard, but shook, the grip strong.

Good work, Dick. That'll set ye right with Baptiste.

Baptiste turned to Travis. "Yor looking a mite peaked, coon. I done warned you about that snaky Pawnee."

"Wal, I fetched him in the end." Travis cocked his head. "But I thought certain ye had more sense than to sign on ter a crazy venture like this. Ye've always had a fondness fer that topknot of yern."

Baptiste leaned his head back, the sun's rays bathing his face. "A man can't live shy all his life, *mon ami.* I smelled a possibility."

Green came bouncing down the plank issuing orders to the *engagés* as they filed out of the trees, heavy tins perched on bent shoulders. He looked at Travis, worry in that bulldog face. "How badly are you hurt, Travis?"

Travis grinned, and lifted his shirt.

Green let out a low whistle. "How long ago did this happen?"

"About three days. Dick, hyar, he done a mite of sewing on this old coon. Reckon I'd let him darn my socks now. He's plumb practiced."

Green, muttering, gave Richard another skeptical glance.

Baptiste bent down and scowled at the wound. "Stay at it, Hartman. Another five or six years on the river and you'll use up all the hide you got left."

"Huh! Wal, come the day my pizzle gets sliced up, this child's callin' 'er quits."

Baptiste gave Willow an amused inspection, adding, "Then steer clear of this'un, coon. She's pizen."

Richard stiffened, but Travis reached back with a hand to cut him off. "Baptiste, I want ye and Dick hyar ta see ter the hosses. Reckon I'm gonna take my leisure like a booshway, and ride like a king up on the cargo box."

"Travis!" Richard cried.

Travis ignored him. "Now, Baptiste, Dick hyar, he's a mite of a greenhorn yet. Reckon I can recall when ye were of a same mind, all piss and vinegar and damn little sense. Dick's got savvy and larns right quick, but ye needs ter explain things in simple words and with a lot of detail. Like I say, he's a-larning. That being so, I'd take it as a favor if'n ye didn't cut his throat fer a couple of days, lessen, of course, he really riles ye."

Baptiste snorted, his dark stare pinning the sputtering Richard. "I'll see. Come on, pilgrim. Show me what you've got."

Travis gestured for Richard to follow the black man toward the picket. Willow hesitated, then trotted after them, sticking close to Richard.

Green squinted, then pointed. "Hanging on his belt... that's not what I think it is?"

Travis chuckled. "Reckon so. Our Boston Yankee thinks it's a...what in Hob, uh, 'fetish.' That's what he calls her."

"What's a fetish?"

"Beats hell outa me. But pass the word. We don't want none of the crew a-telling him he's wearing that Pawnee's topknot on his side."

"Civilized, my ass!" Green fingered his chin.

"Whar ye been?" Travis asked, turning toward the boat. "Take my hand, Dave. Reckon I cain't afford ter fall off'n the damn plank. Thanks."

Green helped him balance as they crossed to the deck. "Had no trouble at all. Seems as if the Company factor was down sick."

Green slapped a hand to his leg. "That Baptiste, he's a sly one. Showed up just as we landed at the fort. He was standing on the bank cursing like a sailor. Gave me all kinds of hell for being late. Said we were due in a week ago, and how in hell could the Company expect to keep the upriver trade if the supplies were late."

"Do tell?" Travis settled himself against the corner of the cargo box and slid down onto his butt.

"You put him up to that?" Green asked.

"Nope. Reckon he figgered this was his chance ter head back upriver. Baptiste, he's a clever coon. He's figgered there's a chance fer him with us. One he ain't never gonna get with the Company. Treat him square, and he'll back ye to the hilt."

Green watched the last of the whiskey being toted aboard and stowed. Henri was shouting orders as the plank was drawn in. "After that cocky captain signed our papers and had his boys search the boat, Baptiste walked up as plucky as a strutting cock and hired on. Asked for ten percent."

"Ten?"

"Yep, and I gave it to him. He's another American—black though he might be. He'll stick...if you will."

The *Maria* was swinging out from the bank as the polers drove her into the current. "He'll do. Half cat scratch and all fury. But he's just looking fer the same things the rest of us is. Wants ter be treated like a man, and willing to fess up ter the consequences."

"He's got it." Green watched the trees passing by on the bank. Through the trunks, the horses could be seen, Baptiste, Richard, and Willow riding along. "Since we weren't under suspicion, I took an extra day and signed on three more *engagés*. The gamble is they'll more than make up the time. Now, what's between you and that damned Yankee?"

Travis leaned back and told the story. When he finished, he cocked a grizzled eyebrow. "And that's the whole of it. That Packrat had us dead ter rights. Woulda kilt us all, and lifted the whiskey. Willow suckered him, and Dick kilt him. We end up with fat cow instead of poor bull."

"Is he going to run?"

"Hell, I don't know. He don't even know. He's all knotted up inside over this philos'phy. Got all these high and mighty notions of ethics and responsibility. Reckon the trouble is, folks can spout what they will, but that coon's never mixed his idears with real life. It's a-playing Hob with him. Shoulda seen him trying ter talk me inta burying them damn Pawnee."

"So, you sent him out with Baptiste?"

"Yep. Poor Dick. Fer a feller full of worries about being a slave, I reckon old Baptiste is a gonna fetch him up right smart."

CHAPTER NINE

As an unbroken courser raises its mane, paws the ground, and rages at the sight of the naked bit, while a trained horse patiently suffers both whip and spur, in a like manner the barbarian will never extend his neck into the yoke which a civilized man bears without murmuring, but prefers the most stormy liberty to a peaceful slavery.

—Jean-Jacques Rousseau, *Discourse on the Origin and Foundation of Inequality Among Mankind*

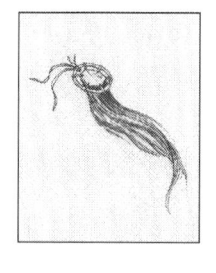 Richard studied Baptiste surreptitiously. With his swinging fringe, heavy rifle, knife, and a pistol jammed into his belt, the hunter fit every image of a swashbuckling brigand. He sat his horse as if he were a centaur. The blacks Richard had known were mostly house servants, like Jeffry, waspish, elegant, and mannered.

Baptiste rode to Richard's left, Willow to his right. For once she wasn't asking for words in her headlong charge to learn English. Rather, those beautiful eyes reflected a pensive struggle. Reprising the morning's events, no doubt.

He longed to reach out, to pat her arm reassuringly. Anything to see that warm glow in her eyes. His gaze kept slipping in her direction, fastening on the curve of cheek and nose, the fullness of her lips, those high breasts pressed against the soft leather of her dress.

"Known Travis long?" Baptiste asked. He rode with his polished rifle held easily across the horse's withers.

"No. Only since they dumped me on the deck one night."

"Reckon yoah not gonna find a better coon nowhere."

"Indeed?"

Baptiste examined him with veiled eyes before returning his attention to the countryside. Richard had noted the same habit in Travis: constant vigilance.

Richard cleared his throat. "Look. I'm not here of my free will. I was robbed, tied up, and sold to Green. I'm a man, not a chattel!"

Baptiste used a finger to push his hat up on his head. "Then why're you heah? I'd a run by now, hoss."

Richard slumped, wishing he had stirrups. "It's a little complicated. It's partly my fault that Travis got hurt. You heard him. I'll stick it out until he's well. Then I'll do what I have to to gain my freedom."

Baptiste laughed sourly. "Freedom, coon? Look around. Where on God's green earth is you gonna be more free than heah?"

"Boston."

"Shit!"

"Have you ever been there?"

"City, ain't it?"

"Perhaps the grandest in the world."

"They got slaves there?"

"There are...some." *Like Jeffry, God forbid.*

"Ain't no freedom in no city, coon." Baptiste's smile rode crookedly on his face. "Ain't no freedom nowhere there's men. Freedom only comes of a wilderness."

"Then you don't know the meaning of freedom. Freedom is born in the mind, in the ability to think and question. It is reason that raises man above the beasts."

"Do tell."

"Indeed I do! Can there be any vocation greater than the search for absolute truth? I think not. And how, the question is asked, can we, as mere mortals, search for the ineffable and sublime? Our only course is through reason, Baptiste. Absolute truth is attainable, and our minds are the levers by which we shall lift ourselves to that lofty goal. There, sir, is the only meaningful freedom."

Baptiste was looking at him as if he were some kind of unusual new insect. "What did you just say?"

"We agree that rationality, the ability to reason, is what sets us apart from the rest of the animals, don't we?"

"The ability to figger."

"Exactly."

Baptiste scanned their surroundings, then frowned. "Reckon so. And yor saying that the ability to figger is what makes men free?"

"Absolutely."

"That's a passel of nonsense, Dick."

"My name is Richard. And if you don't think reason sets us free, what does?"

"Wal, Richard from Boston, fo' me, it was a doublebitted ax."

"I don't understand."

Baptiste made a slicing gesture with his hand.

"Whacked off my massa's head. Cut her right clean, I did. Shoulda seen his eyes a-blinking when his head bounced on the ground. A feller don't die right off when his head's cut off, you see. It takes a couple of seconds afo' the blood drains out."

Richard grimaced. "I thought we were talking about freedom, not murder."

Baptiste chuckled. "Reckon it can be the same thing."

"Why'd you kill him?"

"I wanted to be free, boy. I runned off twice. Got ketched both times—and whupped like a damned dog both times. Reckoned I warn't gonna live like that. No, suh. So, I whacked the planter son of a bitch what owned me, and I runned again." Baptiste gave Richard a hard glance. "Now, yor not a slaveowner, are you?"

"N—No, I'm not. I don't believe in it. One human being shouldn't own another human being."

Baptiste jerked a nod. "Reckon I'll tolerate you."

They passed the next minutes in silence.

Rather than contemplate the fact that he rode beside an ax murderer, Richard turned his attention to the country. The plants seemed greener in the bright sunlight. Three buzzards spiraled in the hot air. Wildflowers of all colors swayed at the passage of the horses' feet through the tall grass. Birdsong rose and fell.

Richard finally nerved himself and asked, "Is that why you're out here? You can't go back because of, uh, having dispatched your owner?"

Baptiste tilted his head, making another inspection of Richard. "Aw, that's right, I forgit you ain't got no idea of freedom. I'm out heah to be free, coon. It ain't like yor Boston. Ain't no folks out heah to be shackling a man's legs in iron." He jerked a thumb back toward the river where the *Maria* now moved under sail, the wind finally having turned to the north. "I got ten percent share. Why? 'Cause I can be who I is. It don't matter if'n I be a nigger. Dave Green sees a man when he looks at Baptiste. He don't see no runned-away slave. So, tell me, what's all this head-shit about reason and freedom?"

Richard frowned. *God in Heaven, what do I say to that?*

Baptiste went on, "Reckon fo' this coon, I done found all the freedom I can stand. Tarnal hell, I hated that fort. All them so'jers looking at me like I was some kind of animal instead of a man. Listen well, Mister Dick. So long's you can stay ahead o' them folks from back East, you'll be a free man. It's only when they shows up with their army, and churches, and solid folk that a man's got to bow his head 'cause he's a nigger."

"That isn't what—"

"Now, I reckon you can chaw on that fo' a while. It ain't no easy thing to larn, and old Travis, he said you needed a mite of larning. So, I'm larning ye, Doodle."

Richard sighed. "All right, I'll think about it. I'm not a boy." He glanced at Willow, but she'd obviously been unable to follow the conversation.

Good! She doesn't know I'm sounding like an idiot.

"Huh, wal, that's notional."

"You don't talk like I'd expect a man raised in slavery to talk."

"How so, massa? Sho 'nuff, I's a-gwine talk like dis from now on? Make yo all feels right at home now, chile?" Baptiste threw his head back and laughed. "Tarnal hell, coon. Folks judge a man by how he talks. Old Travis, he done larned me that right off. Told me, 'Now, ye needs ter talk like a white man. Do her, hoss, and ain't no sheriff a gonna figger yer no 'scaped slave.' So I larnt it."

"How long have you known Travis?"

"Since the day he saved my sorry hide down to New

Orleans. Reckon that's back in eighteen and eleven. They plumb near had me, hounds closing in, folks swarming the country with rifles, shotguns, and knives a-looking fo' me, I's about as dangerous a nigger as had been loose in them parts in years. That's when I run acrost old Travis. He skins me up an old live oak and I hides up there in the moss. Meantime, Travis scrapes this gouge in the mud next to the bayou. When that posse shows up, he's a cussing and stamping, swearing some buck nigger just done stole his pirogue.

"Me, I lays up there on that limb, still as an old gray squirrel. That posse, they ask some questions, and finally turn right around and head back south. Travis, why, he scouts around, sees thar ain't nobody watching, and waves me down. From there, we lit a shuck north. Follered the river right up."

As Baptiste talked, Richard measured those powerful shoulders and swelling biceps. Dear God. Richard absently fingered his neck. How soft and fragile it felt.

"Why did you kill your master?"

"Man can beat another man," Baptiste said simply. "Reckon that ain't so much. Reckon it was justice, Dick. That planter, he's just plumb cruel. Now, I run, and I got beat fo' it. Fair's fair. But he beat hosses, and wimmen, and every slave he had, good, bad, or innocent. I's running again. I knew he knew it. He's waiting, see? Gonna beat me to death in front of my woman and childrens. Make me an example. Shouldn't otta drive a man to desperation. I's desperate, and one day he turned his back when he shouldn't."

"Is cruelty worth a man's life?"

"Ask yerself, Dick. Way I hear it, you done kilt that Pawnee what was beating Willow."

Richard exhaled slowly.

How do I judge him when I'm no better?

He said, "Then I suppose you understand better than anyone why I have to get away."

Baptiste's hard brown eyes displayed no emotion. "Travis beating on you? Green?"

"No. But they took advantage of me. I was robbed—tied up! They made me sign that contract. Held a knife to my throat!"

"Who did?"

"Francois and August."

Baptiste betrayed the first surprise Richard had seen. "Francois? And yor *still* alive?"

"If that's what you call this."

Baptiste shook his head. "Waugh! That's some, it is. That Francois, he's as mean a snake as you'll find. Pilgrim, yor just plumb lucky. Be right happy to see each sunrise. Francois don't let many of his victims live."

"But they've turned me into a slave here!"

Baptiste turned his head long enough to give Richard a narrow-eyed stare. "Never should'o promised Travis I wouldn't cut yoah throat, boy." A pause. "Reckon I'm scouting ahead, boy."

Richard licked his lips as Baptiste trotted his horse ahead, the long fringes waving with each step the animal made.

"What that?" Willow asked, breaking her silence and gesturing at Baptiste.

Richard rubbed the back of his suddenly too-hot neck. "I guess I just made a fool of myself."

"'Guess'? 'Fool'? Dik?" Her eyes probed his, questioning.

Dear Lord God, how did a woman get to be so beautiful?

"Yes, you could say that. Dik a fool."

———

What kind of people are these? The question hung in Willow's souls like thin blue smoke on a cold day. She walked through the evening encampment, winding between the fires. Men sprawled about the crackling blazes, staying close to sparks and heat in an effort to avoid the humming columns of mosquitoes.

As she passed, the *engagés* looked up at her with lust gleaming in their eyes—just like yellow-eyed bobcats when they inspected a covey of sage grouse.

I am not prey for the likes of you, she mocked from within. *Not unless you want your head split.*

She'd heard White men called "dog-faces," and how true it was. They all had hair growing out of their faces. At first, she'd been startled. Men shouldn't grow hair on their faces. It made them look peculiar. But then, the Pawnee, Oto, and Omaha shaved their heads, and that looked just as peculiar to her as hair on the face.

Wolf-men. Even to the light-colored eyes. Wolf-men who traveled on a floating lodge bigger than any council lodge she'd ever seen. Their spirit water had healed the wound in Trawis's side. She'd seen her reflection, so clear, in one of their mirrors. Their metal pots could be dropped without shattering the way ceramic ones did.

Their heavy rifles killed the small whitetail deer at distances that defied a bow.

Perhaps, like Wolf, they really were powerful.

But what do I think of them?

That question lurked in her thoughts and dreams. She'd searched for evil, and found none. Nor had she found anything other than the ways of men: laughter, lust, hunger, kindness, and cruelty.

When they watched her, it was as men watch a

woman; not with suspicion like *Dukurika* would watch a Crow woman, even if she came among them as a friend and not a captive.

Baptiste had become oddly protective when he learned that she'd been a captive. His skin was not painted, but naturally black. He'd patiently allowed her to feel his soft kinky hair so like a buffalo's.

The White men ranked themselves in an interesting way. The booshway was chief. Trawis and Baptiste were like war leaders, and the patroon was in charge of the boat. Finally came the *engagés,* French, a different tribe of White men who spoke a separate language. She still hadn't placed Dik in the system of rank. He seemed high, yet low. He could speak to Trawis or Green at any time. The *engagés,* however, despised him.

Did no one understand his Power? Didn't they see that he was a seeker of visions?

"Willow!" Trawis called from Green's curious cloth lodge. "Reckon we could use ye."

She'd picked up most of the easy phrases. Now she crossed to Green's lodge. She stepped through the flap to see Trawis being settled on a blanket. Two small fires wavered on the wax sticks they called candles. Dik was shifting nervously while Green saw to Trawis's comfort.

"What happens?" Willow asked.

"Stitches have to come out," Dik told her. He looked nervous, licking his lips, and lookimg paler than usual.

"Wal, come on, coon," Trawis muttered.

"Travis, don't you think someone with a little more—"

"Hell, ye sewed 'em in, ye can yank 'em out!"

Dik made a face, then leaned down. Green was saying something Willow couldn't understand. Dik lifted a small metal tool from a wooden box. She watched with interest as he inserted his fingers in the little loops opposite the points.

"What?" she asked, pointing.

"Scissors," Dik muttered. Then he grunted uneasily and dropped to his knees.

"Easy, hoss," Trawis said. "Snip, and then ye gots ter jerk."

Willow craned her neck to watch. Dik slipped the sharp tip under a puckered thread and the scissors clicked and cut it as cleanly as an obsidian flake.

"Losing yer nerve?" Trawis asked.

"Be quiet," Dik growled back. He said some other things Willow couldn't understand.

When Dik finally finished, Trawis was blotting at little beads of blood where Dik had pulled the threads out. Dik wiped sweat from his forehead and took a deep breath. What a curious man, so fragile, but at the same time so incredibly strong. Of all the men she'd ever known, only her husband had ever engaged so much of her souls.

Willow signed to Trawis. "Why is Dik so worried?"

"He's never pulled strings out before." Then Trawis barked a laugh. Green slapped Trawis on the shoulder and ducked outside.

Willow seated herself and inspected Trawis's scar before signing, "It will heal fine."

Dik slumped, head down, hands on his knees. Willow took that opportunity to examine the scissors.

"Careful," Trawis signed. "Sharp. Don't cut yourself."

She plucked up one of the bloody stitches from the floor and experimentally snipped it in two. What a marvelous thing this was.

She signed, "White men are very clever with things."

"Clever any way you look at us," Trawis responded, talking in time to his signs.

"People can be clever with things, but not with God or spirits." She snapped the scissors open and shut.

"How so?" Dik asked after Trawis translated.

"When do you talk to spirits? When do you take *Tam Apo* into your heart?"

"God must be examined by the mind, by thought." A strange gleam had come to Dik's eyes. "How do Shoshoni think of God?"

She shook her head, signing and filling in the White words she knew. "This is too hard for us now. I must learn more talk to discuss this."

What an odd idea, that *Tam Apo* could be known by thoughts. Didn't these White men understand that Our Father could only be felt in the soul?

Later. You must learn their tongue; then you will understand.

She settled herself and studied Dik from the corner of her eye. Did he have a woman waiting for him? And if so, what was she like? To Trawis, she signed: "Where are the White women? Or are there only men?"

Trawis chuckled. "White women are all back East. They do not come here."

"Why don't they come?"

Trawis pulled at his beard. "It wouldn't be right. Not out hyar. This country is too hard on them. Too dangerous. They couldn't stand the hardships."

Willow glanced around at the snug tent—warm, light, and waterproof. Then she thought about the huge boat with all of its space and goods. Too hard on their women? These men traveled in unheard-of luxury. No packs to carry. No lodges to pack on a travois and then unpack. What sort of women were these?

She said, "I do not understand."

Trawis and Dik talked for a moment, then Trawis replied, "It would not be proper to have white women here. It ain't their place."

"And what is their place?"

Trawis glanced uneasily at Dik and the two of them muttered back and forth. Willow caught the word "lady" several times and asked, "What is 'lady'?"

"A woman. No, I mean, well, special woman."

"And what is her place?"

"Uh...in a house."

"What is house?"

"Wal...like a lodge."

"Ah!" Willow nodded. "Lady's place is in lodge." But that didn't make any sense, either. By words and signs, she noted the tent. "This is lodge. Very fine lodge. Warm, dry, easy to move. Why is this not lady place?"

"Aw, hell!" Trawis threw his hands up.

Dik said, "Lady is gentle. To be...to be prized. Very special. Do you understand?"

"Who works?" Willow wondered. "Men?"

"Yes, men." Dik nodded happily.

"White women keep the lodge," Trawis signed. "Take care of children for men. Cook, clean, make clothing."

"But not travel," Willow mused. "Why?"

"Too dangerous," Trawis asserted. "Woman might get killed."

Willow snorted irritation, fingers flying. "Indian women get killed all the time. That is part of life. Part of war, of bad luck—lightning, snow, starvation. Anything can kill. Why are White women not to be killed?"

Trawis signed, "White men do not think white women should be killed by these things. White women are too precious."

"A man protects a lady," Dik said solemnly. "Very

precious. A lady is delicate. Understand? Like a flower, to be cherished."

Willow's eyes narrowed. "You mean weak?"

Trawis shot a wary glance at Dik, but signed, "It's not the same."

Willow's lips twitched. "Is that why you come here? You seek strong women? Like horse breeders, you wish to strengthen your blood?"

Trawis made a face, lowering his voice as he talked to Dik. Dik's expression betrayed mystification.

"No," Trawis muttered. "I know." His hands made the signs, "White women are prized. Very special."

Willow considered. Both men had begun to fidget. She asked: "Lady does what man tells, yes?"

"Yes."

She didn't have all the words, so she signed, "White woman is very special to White man. She is to be taken, then kept safe in the lodge to have children. Man works to take food to her, because man works and White woman doesn't. She is a prize, not to be risked. I understand this."

Trawis translated, and Dik grinned.

Willow continued. "I understand this because *Ku'chendikani* do the same. They treat special buffalo horses this way. They take food to them in the winter and always guard them. So, White men treat women like horses."

Trawis's face fell.

Willow puzzled on the idea. What kind of woman would a White woman be? Like some helpless child? Who'd want a woman like that? Worse, what would it be like to *be* a woman like that? Locked in a lodge, fed by someone else, and doing nothing but bearing children?

"No, no," Trawis was muttering. "White women are..."

"Weak," Willow muttered.

"No."

"Like coup? Won from other men?"

"Yes!" Dik cried.

"Shut up, coon," Trawis muttered. "It ain't the same. Courting ain't winning."

"Courting?" Willow asked.

Trawis made the sign, and added, "We don't fight over our... Hell, that's a tarnal lie!"

"Prize," Willow supplied. What was that other word? "Trophy?"

Trawis stared at Dik. Neither looked happy.

Willow clapped her hands. "You come here, find Indian women. Not prize. What is the word? 'Partner'?" She lifted an eyebrow.

Trawis finally shrugged and grinned. "Reckon so."

Willow gave them a sly smile and signed, "But where are you going to find an Indian woman who would want to lie with a man with such white skin? She'd shiver so hard at the idea of that ghost skin against hers that she'd clamp too tight to enter. And if she did, when she looked up at you—saw all that hair on your face, she'd think she was coupling with her dog!" And at that, she squealed with laughter.

After Trawis translated, Dik's face turned a violent red, and he slipped silently out into the night.

Willow gazed thoughtfully at the swaying tent flap, then asked, "Dik have woman?"

"Nope." Travis raised an eyebrow. "Ye interested?"

"No," she said much too quickly.

Travis nodded solicitously, but she could see the twinkle in his eye.

CHAPTER TEN

Savage man and civilized man differ so greatly in the depths of their hearts and in their inclinations, that what constitutes the supreme happiness of the one would reduce the other to despair. The first longs for nothing more than repose and liberty; he desires only to live, and to be immune from labor; nay, the ataraxy of the most confirmed Stoic falls short of his deep indifference to every other object. Civilized man, on the other hand, is always in action, perpetually sweating and toiling, and racking his brains to discover occupations still more laborious; he continues a drudge to the last minute; nay, he courts death in order to live, or renounces life to obtain immortality.

—Jean-Jacques Rousseau, *Discourse on the Origin and Foundation of Inequality Among Mankind*

Richard, Baptiste, and Willow were driving the horses along the west bank. They followed dim trails through groves of ash, elm, and oak that gave way to grassy meadows. A hot wind blew from the prairie to the west and added to the bright sun's heat.

Richard tried to concentrate on Laura, but he couldn't stop glancing at Willow, catching that speculative look in her brown eyes. In the sunlight her copper skin seemed to glow with a new radiance. In spite of himself, he kept smiling at her, almost wishing that Baptiste were somewhere else. But what would he say to her?

She's a savage, Richard. Not your kind of woman. If you must think of a woman, think of Laura.

He concentrated on Laura's blue eyes, her golden hair, and charming smile. Yes, that was it. Think about her thin waist, and the way her skirts rustled when...

"That tall bluff"—Baptiste's voice intruded—"yonder, with the mound of dirt. That's the Blackbird's grave." Baptiste pointed, the long fringes hanging down from his arm.

"The Blackbird?" Richard studied the high point. Laura Templeton had vanished into nothingness.

"Heap big Omaha chief. Some years back the Mahas controlled the river. And Blackbird controlled the Mahas. Nothing passed this part of the river 'thout old Blackbird's approval."

The wind switched to gust down from the north, thrashing tree branches and bending grass in rippling waves. Willow tucked her hair back where the wind had pulled long strands loose. She gave Richard a shy smile, attentive to Baptiste's words and the hand signs he used as he spoke.

The high bluff to the north dominated the skyline, piercing the tree-crowned heights. Beyond, the clouds raced southward in puffy mounds of white.

Richard peered at Baptiste. "Tell me about this Black-bird." Anything to take his mind off Willow.

"Traders give him arsenic, hoss. He was a canny one, old Blackbird was. Anybody challenged his power, sho' 'nuff, he'd slip poison into their food, then foretell their deaths. Got so that nobody among the Mahas would cross him. Smallpox finally kilt him. His last wish was to be buried up on that hill, a-sitting on his warhorse. The old coon said he wanted to be up thar high so he could see the white traders coming up the river."

As he spoke, Baptiste's dark hands made signs for Willow. She stared up at the knob. "I heard of him," she said. "Strong chief."

Richard ground his teeth, forcing his gaze away. The wind had pressed her dress against her like a second skin, outlining her perfect breasts and thin waist. Damn it, he was a gentleman, and a gentleman didn't look at a woman that way.

"Reckon," Baptiste agreed. "Story is that once he had a trader brought up to the main village. Had all the trader's plunder—all his goods—brought in. Old Blackbird, he took half, called it a gift. Now, that trader figgered he was just about to go bust, when Blackbird up and says, 'My friend, you may trade the rest to my people...fo' whatever price you wants.' That coon made his fortune, 'cause t'warnt a one of Blackbird's people would say no to the trader."

"That's piracy!" Richard manfully fastened his gaze on the high point. "Blackbird. Now, there's a man my father would really like."

Baptiste gave Richard a thoughtful inspection as the horses wound through the trees. "Travis done told this child a mite of that story. Yer pap, now, he done sent you out heah?"

"Yes, he did. But for him I'd still be studying philosophy in Boston." Richard ducked a low branch. "He cut me off. From my studies, that is. I was supposed to deliver money to a booshway, to outfit a Santa Fe expedition. So, what happens? Francois steals the money. That French brigand is headed back to civilization to live rich all the rest of his life, and I'm on a fur expedition. What kind of justice is that?"

"Beats being dead, Dick."

"My name is Richard."

"Rhitshard," Willow said softly, her soft brown eyes meeting his for one glorious moment.

"Richard."

"Ritshard."

"Willer, yor a quick one." Baptiste made a smacking sound with his lips. "Never knew an Injun to pick up talk as fast as she's a-doing." Baptiste gave the country another of his careful scrutinies. "Wal, Dick, I reckon yor pap figgered to make a man of you."

"Maybe. Looks like he made me a slave, instead."

"Boy." Baptiste's voice hardened. "You don't know shit. Yor no more than a damned planter's boy. They's times you makes me want to puke with yor whining. A slave? Shit! You don' know the fust thing 'bout it."

Richard returned hot glare for glare.

Baptiste lifted a lip in disgust. "Do tell, what's this? You reckon you can kill me with a mean look like that? Care to back her up, coon? Want to try and whip it outa this sassy child?"

For a second Richard held that gaze; then cold shivers wound through his guts. He dropped his eyes and reddened in humiliation. The worst was, he couldn't hold his own in Willow's presence.

"Good. Last man what tried to whip me's a-laying dead in the grave."

"Perhaps slavery was a bad analogy."

"Reckon so, coon." Baptiste turned his gaze ahead. "If'n yer keen to larn, I'll be happy to show you what a slave's life is all about."

"I can guess."

Baptiste's expression sharpened. "Do tell?"

"Maybe I can't. Oh, I don't know. I don't seem to know much of anything anymore."

For the first time that day, Baptiste smiled. "Wal, coon, I reckon that's when yor ready to larn. Cain't larn a damn thing when you knows all the answers already."

"You sound like Travis now."

"Yep." Baptiste resettled his rifle. "I come outa Louisiana ready to whip old Hob hisself. I's mad, boy. Plumb clean killer mad. They done took my pap and sold him off to Tennessee. Had me a woman. They wanted a strong buck like me to make young 'uns. So I had me a woman. Sold her off to Cuba after I run the fust time."

Baptiste spit off the side of his horse. "Shit. Lost everything I had. Old friends wouldn't even talk to me. 'Fraid they'd be beat, too. So I's mad." He grinned. "Hell, even tried to slice up old Travis just afo' we made Memphis. That coon, he's some, he is. Took my knife away and boxed my ears till I couldn't stand up fo' the ringing. And, hell, I figgered I knowed how to fight right fierce."

"You tried to knife Travis?"

"I done told you, Doodle. I's a rough buck in them days. Had the fight on. Wal, old Travis he done taken it right outa me. That's when he set me down, all bunged up and bleeding, and we had us a parley. That coon talked sense inta me. Understand? He told me just what I's doing, and why, and asked this child when I's gonna straighten out, 'cause he wasn't about to waste his time on no nigger bound ta get hisself hung fo' being a stupid ass!"

Baptiste slapped his leg. "Hell, Dick. I didn't know shit neither."

"What if they'd caught you?"

"A murdering slave? And a runaway to boot?" Baptiste lifted an eyebrow. "They'd a kilt me on the spot. Reckon Travis, too. It don't do fo' no white man to go ferrying 'scaped slaves north."

"Why do you think he did it?"

"No telling. Not with Travis Hartman. Says he saw something in my eyes that day when I run inta his camp. Hell, he mighta done her fo' the hell of it. Why, catch that coon in the right mood, he'd spit in old Hob's right eye."

"You like him, don't you?"

"Reckon so. Now, he asked me ta larn you, so scrape the wax outa yor ears, Dick, 'cause old Baptiste's a gonna do just that." He held up a black finger. "Don't never go agin' yer pap. Don't matter what's ahind you, I reckon it can be patched. If'n not, I reckon I'll trade you, 'cause you got a pap and I don't."

At Baptiste's cutthroat glare, Richard kept his peace. Willow was listening intently, struggling for the words.

"I mean 'er, Dick. If'n ye lives, make peace with yer pap. T'aint a small thing, having a pap. White folk think everybody's got one, just like a right hand. Black folk can tell y'all different."

Richard chewed at his lip, remembering Phillip's hard face, the fleshy nose and pinched-on glasses.

How can there be any reconciliation? We might as well live in different worlds.

Richard asked, "What do you think my chances of living through this are?"

"Depends, coon. How bad you want to live? If'n yor of a mind to go under, I figger you'll be maggot meat afore the Yellerstone."

"Thanks for the confidence."

Baptiste turned to Willow, ebony hands flying. For a long moment she studied Richard with those large dark eyes, then made signs in return.

"What's all that?" Richard demanded.

Baptiste sucked at his lips, dark eyes burning under the wide brim of his hat. "I asked her if'n she thought you'd live. She says she thinks so. She says yor a medicine man, but you don't know it yet. She says that none of us knows yor Power. That such medicine is a gift not many people have. She says you carry the answer down inside. If'n you wants to live, you'll do her, but the only one can call it up is you. She says she don't understand why the spirits would give such Power to a young white man."

"Medicine? Power?" He let his gaze follow the smooth curve of her cheek, remembering the soaring sense when they'd looked into each other's eyes that day in camp. Was that what had touched his soul?

Willow's fingers were moving again, dancing gracefully.

Baptiste continued, "She says that you need to sweat, to purify yourself. That yor confused. Power's pulling you lots of different ways. To larn yor Power, you gotta be cleansed of the White man's confusion. Become pure, and seek yor vision."

"Vision? My only vision is of Boston."

At that, Willow laughed and said, "Ritshard not think his way to God." She tapped her chest. "God hyar. Souls know *Tam Apo,* not thoughts."

Power? Spirits? It was nothing more than the superstitious nonsense of the savage mind. No matter how he might be attracted to Willow, that gulf between the savage and the civilized would always separate them.

So, Richard, think of something else. He cleared his mind and turned his eyes back to Blackbird's grave. A river pirate. Red instead of white. *You weren't any different from my father. Maximize your investment, even if it took poisoning your competition.*

And what did that imply about the state of man in nature?

I just haven't found it yet. I need to look a little further, beyond the influence of the traders.

But that meant going farther upriver. Ever farther from Boston, and civilized society.

Remember, I'm only stuck here until Travis is well. Then, I'm off for those pleasant streets. Pick a goal? Why, Boston, of course, and Laura, and the life we'll have together. That's it. My spirit quest.

And when he returned, there would be no compromise with Phillip Hamilton. Some things, like shattered crystal goblets, could never be put back together again.

"Got an answer fo' Willow?" Baptiste asked. "About God?"

"Whose answer do you want? Hegel's? Anselm's? Augustine's? Voltaire's? How about Montaigne's observation that while men create gods by the dozen, they can't breathe life into a lowly worm?"

"Want truth, Dik," Willow said simply.

"Truth flies like a bird," Richard whispered, staring up at the windy point.

"Like eagle," Willow said softly. "Or hummingbird who brings the thunder. Or Magic Owl. Truth flies high."

Richard ignored her, lost in thought. What if he went

beyond the reach of the traders and still found men willing to pay any price for goods?

Blackbird, just how different were you from my father?

And if men should all prove to be the same, no matter what their origins or circumstance?

No, that thought was too grisly to entertain.

Just make it home...to Boston, Richard. Nothing else matters.

His fingers absently caressed the long silken hair on the fetish Travis had tied to his belt.

———

Morning bathed the land with new light; mist drifted across the smooth river and through the trees lining the bank. Smoke hung in blue smudges over the fires as the men in the messes finished their corn and venison. Over-head, the heart-shaped cottonwood leaves hung silently, waiting for the dawn. Occasional coughs and the metallic clank of pots and tin cups accented the *engagés"* low voices.

Richard sipped at his steaming coffee as he sat on a weather-silvered cottonwood log. He glanced across the fire at Willow, then quickly averted his eyes. She and Laura were like night and day.

Dreams of Willow had tortured him all night long, of her smile and the straightforward way she looked at him with those incredible eyes.

That knowledge plagued him, as if he'd been somehow disloyal to Laura's faith in him.

It's not that I'm in love with Willow, just fascinated. As a scholar. It's my business to investigate her thoughts, to learn about her and her ways.

But Willow kept creeping into his thoughts in the

most unscholarly ways. With the exception of Laura, he'd never bothered with women. They frightened him even more than they fascinated him. Those he'd met in Boston —gentle ladies, every last one—either stared right through him as if he weren't there, or they gave him a gushy, airy-eyed look of false worship. And in no instance had he carried on a conversation of importance with a woman. They just dithered on about the weather, or was the coffee prepared correctly? Always trite.

And now Willow fills my imagination—an Indian *woman, who barely speaks English, has never held a book, and carries a war club, bow, and arrows.*

Yet they'd conversed about God, and souls, and he'd barely touched the rind of her knowledge about life. And that slight touch had enthralled him.

She's an illiterate savage!

But what fed the glow that filled her eyes when she looked at him? He shook his head, biting his lip.

His coffee was bitter, watery, laced with the now familiar taste of riverwater. Dear God, what he'd give to be in a coffee shop in Boston, tasting the rich brews— dark and steaming. The aroma filled the nose. He'd add a dollop of cream and fine Jamaica sugar. Just right... *Someday.*

He glanced at Willow. What would she make of Boston? He could imagine her laughing, eyes shining as she raised a porcelain teacup to her lips. No, impossible! The vision burst like a ruptured bladder.

His blankets were rolled and tied, ready to be packed. Across the fire from him, Willow was working the snarls out of her raven hair with a comb Travis had given her, the teeth sliding through that glossy wealth.

Travis ducked out of Green's tent and walked through the camp to hunker down beside Richard. Through squinted eyes, the hunter watched Willow. "Purty, ain't she?"

"Indeed she is," Richard admitted. To his embarrassment, Willow glanced at him from the corner of her eye. "And I think she's learning English much too quickly."

"Do tell, coon?" she asked. "I reckon I don't know shit yet."

Richard took a deep breath. "Willow, that's..." But, what? She was learning the speech of these frontiersmen, not the cultured language of the civilized East. "I mean, well, there are different ways of speaking. Some are proper, and some aren't. Ladies don't say words like that."

"Like what?"

He colored. "Like...'shit.' It isn't polite for a lady to use."

She lifted the corner of her lip, then said, "White lady is no better than horse to White man. Willow is no trophy, Ritshard."

Travis laughed, reached across, and took Richard's coffee. He sipped, swished the liquid around his mouth, and swallowed. "That's some, it is. Gonna philos'phy her to death?"

Richard ignored him, concentrating on Willow. "Do you want to learn the proper way?"

"Hell!" Travis growled, giving the tin cup back. "She ain't never a-going to no Boston. Leave the child be."

"Proper?" Willow studied him thoughtfully, her long fingers caressing the comb.

"Formal. Like the way I speak. You've been learning the way Travis and Baptiste talk, that's fine for here, on the river, but not for civilized places."

Travis snorted disgust.

"I learn," Willow told him, and gave Travis a challenging glance.

"Good!" Richard cried. "We'll begin at once."

"Reckon not, coon," Travis interrupted. "Daylight's a-wasting. Fetch up the hosses, Dick. I'm a-riding today. Old Baptiste, he done snuck off with his rifle a couple of hours afore daylight. Now that we're past the Omahas, we otta cut buffler sign."

Richard looked the hunter up and down. "Do you really think you're fit?"

"Hell! I been a-loafing on that damn boat." He pulled up his shirt to expose the wound. Scabs had fallen off to leave shiny red scars on Travis's white hide. "If'n that ain't healed, I'm a sorry pilgrim."

Willow glanced at the wound, nodded, and rose to her feet. She walked off toward the river, long hair swaying. As she passed through the camp, the *engagés* went silent. Heads turned; gleaming eyes followed her.

Richard stiffened unaccountably.

"Finally started ter notice, have ye?"

"Notice what?"

Travis lowered his voice. "Ye seen Trudeau?"

Richard glanced around. "No. But then, I haven't been looking for him."

"Uh-huh. Wal, I run up on his sorry carcass last night. Caught him slipping through the brush ahind Willow." Travis paused. "Thought fer a second that French varmint was a gonna try me."

"Following Willow? Try you? I don't understand."

Travis gave him a disgusted look. "Dick, why's a man foller a woman inta the brush? What's he after? Now, ye don't see a whole lot of wimmen fer these coons ter go a-bedding, do ye? Trudeau's gonna be a mite of trouble fer Willow. He's pulled his horns in fer now, but ye mind that coon close, hear?"

Richard's gut tickled. "Is that why they've started looking at her that way?"

"Reckon so, coon. Man gets ter missing woman flesh against his own. She's a heap of woman. Reckon they'll be trouble over her."

"Trudeau?"

"He's the ringleader. And he's got the glint in his eye. Heard tell he signed on because a feller from Kaskaskia was a-looking fer him. Something about a daughter. Trudeau's supposed ter have lifted her skirts against her will."

"You mean rape?"

"I warn't thar, coon. Reckon in this country, a feller don't just up and point a finger. Ain't got no proof, Dick. 'Sides, we got a boat ter get upriver."

"That justifies anything, doesn't it?" Richard threw out the last of his coffee, picked up his bedroll, and tramped to the boat. He tossed his gear onto the deck and headed through the tall grass for the horses.

Lugging the *Maria* northward outweighed any morality these human beasts had.

The time has come. I've got to run, escape. Find a way back to Saint Louis...and then to Boston.

At least there he could find a decent cup of coffee. And conversation worthy of a man of letters. In Boston, Laura's mere presence would drive away plaguing thoughts about Willow.

———

Travis slumped in the saddle as he rode into the clearing. Not much had changed since the last time he'd camped here. How many years ago had that been? Nigh to five, now. Old Manuel Lisa was still head of the Fur Company. That was back when...

He pulled his horse up and tightened his grip on his rifle. That little tickle of wrongness was playing with his guts. The wily Pawnee gelding he rode pricked its ears, attentive on a thicket of hazel across the clearing. Overhead, the cottonwood and ash leaves rustled with the breeze.

"What is it?" Richard asked from behind.

"Hush!" Travis kneed his horse forward, half-raising his rifle. Nervous as a cat on a floating log, he eared the hammer on the Hawken back, the click loud in the still clearing. There, behind that thicket. "Come on out!"

"I don't...who's there?" Richard asked from behind. The horses snorted and stamped, aware of the sudden tension.

Travis raised his rifle, sighting toward the hazel, ready for a snap shot.

Willow had ridden her horse off to one side, hurriedly stringing her bow and nocking an arrow.

The evening sun slanted through the leaves to dapple the clearing. Off to the right, fifty yards away, high grass screened the Missouri's muddy bank.

A man stood up behind the brush—a whip-thin Indian. His hair was worn loose except for a long braided scalp lock rising from the center of his head. Two wary black eyes stared out from a flat face with a straight nose. Despite the heat, he was dressed in tight skins that covered most of his body. Behind him, a woman half-crouched in the brush with a little boy at her side.

"Omaha," Travis muttered to himself. Then, in a louder voice, he added, "Banished, by God."

"Banished?" Richard asked.

"Yep. That's the only reason an Omaha buck would

wear a full set of skins in this weather. And he's Omaha, all right. It's in the cut of his clothes and that scalp lock. Where his hair is parted, it's painted red. A mite faded, but red it is."

The Omaha stepped out of the hazel and spread his hands wide. He walked forward, smiled, and waited nervously.

Travis signed: "What do you want?"

In return the Omaha signed: "We friends. Hungry. Make trade."

"Trade for what?" Travis asked in signs.

"Whiskey."

"What's he saying?" Richard asked.

"Wants ter trade." Travis squinted. "Keep yer eyes peeled, coon. He might be banished, but there could be others."

In signs, Travis asked, "What would a banished man have to trade with?"

The Omaha turned and called out. The woman walked forward, leaving the child partially hidden. No expression betrayed itself on her round face. A dirty stroud dress hung on her like an old tent. She'd parted her hair in the middle, two braids falling down her back.

The Omaha glanced uneasily at Willow, and then asked in signs, "You have woman?"

Travis nodded. "We have woman."

The Omaha sagged, then signed. "I can only trade woman. I am poor. White men are powerful and rich. They will take pity on me."

Willow exhaled her disgust. The faint calls of the *engagés* could be heard as they pulled for the meadow and the night's camp.

"Boat come?" the Omaha signed.

"Yep. Boat come."

"Have whiskey?" The Omaha's eyes lit with a crazy anticipation.

"What's he want?" Richard asked again.

"Wants to use his woman for trade."

"He...What?" Richard sounded genuinely puzzled.

"Wal, coon, yer about ter come face to face with that philos'phy of yern." Travis cut off any further questions with a slashing of his hand. Eyeing the Omaha, he signed: "You are banished for murder. Tell me the story."

The Omaha's eyes dulled and reluctantly he began to make signs.

———

Travis could barely make out Richard's shadow. The lad had done exactly as Travis had instructed: He hunkered in the darker shadows of the cottonwood trunks, a thick tree to his back so that no one could sneak up on him from behind.

Travis cocked his head to listen: distant coyotes, leaves whispering with the breeze; crickets and night insects.

"Dick? It's me, Travis." He started forward. "Seen anything?"

Richard straightened, the Pawnee trade gun in his hand. "Nothing here, Travis. Just horses farting and chomping grass."

Travis checked the picket line, found it tight, and leaned against one of the cottonwoods. His eyes and ears probed the night. "Seems quiet."

"Yes."

"Yer sounding a tad sour, Dick."

"You should have chased him away."

"Uh-huh, and he'd be out in the dark somewhars with

all kind of idears about our hosses. As it is, he's nigh ter stumbling drunk and fit ter fall flat on his face and snore the rest of the night away."

"We're no better than he is. We're accomplices."

Travis plucked a stem of grass and chewed the sweet end. "Immoral as all Hell, ain't we? Plumb gone ta Hob hisself with sin the likes of which ain't been seen since Sodom and Gomorrah. Wal, I'll tell ye, it ain't up ter Green and me ter tell the men they can't dally with no squaw. Not when she's been offered right fair."

Richard snorted derisively. "It's pure prostitution! What kind of people are these Omaha?"

"Folks like most other folks, only a sight more virtuous than a lot of 'em out hyar."

"Virtuous? That...that *beast* is using his wife for a whore, Travis. That's hardly what I call moral rectitude!"

Travis squatted next to the fuming Richard. "Tell me, why is it that you figger that every man otta be measured by yer plumb line and level? One book of laws fits 'em all? Hell, it don't matter, white, red, or black, every man's gotta live up ter Dick Hamilton's ten commandments of philos'phy, or by God, he ain't even dirt! Must make life pure-hell, such a damn set of notions ter live up ter."

"There are universal criteria of proper behavior, Mr. Hartman. Ethical rules by which men in society mutually govern their behavior. It's not just my beliefs that are—"

"Wal, good. I'm glad ye thinks so. So do most other folks."

"Evidently not the Omaha or they wouldn't—"

"Damn right they would! Tarnal Hell, Dick, ye drives me ter the point of cutting my own throat so I don't gotta listen to yer jaw flap! Now, shut up, or I'll fetch ye one."

"You don't have to get mad." Richard scowled into the night, both hands gripping the trade rifle.

"Don't I? Yer more bullheaded than Adam's off ox! Since ye got all the answers already, tell me about the Omaha. Go on, do her."

"Well, I..."

"Uh-huh. I'm waiting."

"Travis, I don't need to know about the Omaha to know that what he's doing—"

"Is plumb wrong. Son of a bitch. Imagine that. Now, listen up, coon. Hyar's the way of it. Omaha is about the strictest Injuns out hyar, except maybe fer the Cheyenne. They got their ways, and most is plumb persnickety 'bout who flirts with who. They take pride in giving their word. A man don't lay with another man's wife. He don't steal from his people. They take friendship all the way to death...a heap further than most white men I know. Ye wants ter talk morals, wal, Omaha have got 'em by the barrelful."

"What about Blackbird?"

"What about him?"

"He was a despot, a tyrant. He used poison to make himself rich."

"So'd King George. So'd Napoleon. Hell, he's a chief, and a black-hearted one ter boot. And that makes my point. Folks always got one or two bad apples in their barrel." Travis paused. "If'n I was ye, I'd wonder what in hell this Omaha's doing out hyar when all the rest of his people are out hunting buffalo."

"All right, what's he doing here?"

"Banished for murder. That's why he's all dressed up in them hides. It's punishment. He's been cast out fer four years. Seems he got drunk and killed his father-in-law when the old boy caught him beating his wife."

"And she went into exile with him?"

"Hell, no, she divorced his sorry arse. No, this woman that's with him, she run away fer committing adultery. Her husband caught her with a feller, and she took to the brush before they could beat her. The way the Omaha tells it, it ain't the first time, so her family was like to whup her good, and she didn't want no part of it."

"Good God." Richard cocked his head as a nighthawk's wings buzzed in the night.

"Yep, wal, I figgered ye'd need the whole story lest ye get in a foaming philos'phy mood and start preaching Roosoo or something."

"But how do people get to be like them?"

"Oh, just 'cause they's people, I suspect. Why, I reckon thar be folks ye wouldn't be right proud of in Boston, neither." Travis stood, patting him on the shoulder. "Now, keep yer eyes skinned, Dick."

"Who...who's he been trading her to?"

"Trudeau mostly. Right after the boat tied off, he started swapping fer whiskey. I reckon Trudeau's promised his daily ration fer two months by now."

"It just makes me sick," Richard said miserably. "A human being should be worth more."

"Should be. But most ain't, son. And that's just the way the wind blows and the water flows."

———

"I think we got trouble," Travis told Green as he ducked out of the evening shadows and through the hatch into the cargo box.

They'd crossed the Niobrara earlier that day, and a freak wind from the south had allowed them to make fifteen miles up the twisting Missouri. Now, after having satisfied himself with the establishment of the camp, posted guard, and lined out the messes, Travis had the opportunity to talk with Dave Green.

Green hunched over the flour barrels, a candle in his burly right hand. The oaken-plank roof wavered in the candlelight, flickers chasing shadows behind the bales, packs, and tins.

Green had been squinting in the dimness, inspecting his goods, searching for any water that might have pooled in the bilge. Seepage could turn trade goods into disaster.

Green turned his eyes to Travis. "Trouble how?"

"Trudeau's getting ideas about Willow."

"Tell him to leave her alone. What's the matter? Didn't he get his fill of that Maha squaw?"

Travis pulled on his beard, tugging the scars tight. "Some men just got themselves a passion, Dave. Fer some it's the bottle, fer others a game of monte. Reckon fer Trudeau it's wimmen."

Green gazed at him thoughtfully. "You know, I'm counting on that girl. She's a Snake. Seeing her home safely might make for real good trade with her tribe."

"Reckon so." Travis lowered himself to sit on the steps. "I warned Trudeau off. Don't know that it'll take. Might have ter kill him."

"I suppose." Green leaned over stacked kegs of gunpowder and reached out with the candle to stare down into the blackness beyond. "And how'd your day's ride treat you?"

"I'm a mite stove up yet. A couple more days and I'll have vigor back in my blood again."

"Enough to take Trudeau down?"

"Him and four others."

Green turned, his face sallow in the candlelight. "You getting killed won't do me any good."

"He ain't gonna do nothing yet." Travis braced his elbows on his knees. "I'm just a-warning ye, it's coming. 'Sides, I reckon Trudeau'll tie into Hamilton first. They had words this morning. The kid was grousing about the Omaha selling his woman, and Trudeau, he was a-bragging about how good she was. Sort of prickled old Dick's hide, I tell ye."

"And Trudeau didn't kill him?"

"I was too close. And, wal, I reckon Willow would'a drove an arrow through old Trudeau if'n he hurt Dick. She's plumb smart with that bow, you know. But, yep, it's a-coming between Dick and Trudeau. Matter of time."

"Well, it won't be much trouble burying Hamilton."

Travis cocked his head. "Trudeau sent a shiver down Dick's back, all right. That Yankee pilgrim looked fer all the world like he's a headed straight ter Hell."

"How come he hasn't jumped ship yet? He's still figuring on that, isn't he?"

Travis chuckled. "So he claims. Just as soon's I'm all healed. Reckon it'll be one thing after another. He ain't going, Dave. He just don't know it yet."

Green set his candle on a crate before dropping down to feel about under the plank decking. *"Sonuvabitch!"* Green jerked back, banging his head on a whiskey tin in the process. Something scampered in the darkness.

"What the hell?" Travis demanded.

Green shivered, rolled back, and stared owlishly into the dark hole he'd just pulled his hand from. "Grabbed a damn rat in there!" In the candlelight, he studied his hand and then rubbed the side of his head. "I *hate* rats. Did I ever tell you that?"

"Time or two. Find any leaks?"

"Nope. We're still tight, Travis. After we grounded so

many times the last couple of weeks, I was getting worried. Damn rats! I hate 'em."

"Comes with the country, coon." Travis fingered the worn oak steps. "We've done right fine, Davey. No serious trouble."

Green retrieved his candle and picked his way carefully through the cargo. "I don't call you getting gutted no trouble."

"Ain't nobody dead yet. Nobody drowned. No holes in the boat. Nobody arrested at Fort Atkinson. We're plumb chipper."

"We're just reaching the frontier, Travis." Green blew out his candle, and Travis rose and climbed out onto the deck.

"You find anything?" Henri asked as he stepped around the *passe avant*.

"She's dry." Green thrust thumbs into his belt, staring out at the river. For a time the three of them stood there, watching the gathering darkness over the water.

The evening was cool, the air still, and the river had taken on a silvered sheen in the sky's fading glow. As the current tugged at it, the long steering oar canted to the starboard. Travis slapped a mosquito that had been humming around his left ear. Swallows swooped low over the water to skim a drink.

"Think we'll make it?" Green asked as he watched the dark river swirl below them.

Travis shrugged. "Sioux country is up ahead. Never can tell about Sioux. Since Leavenworth made such a fool outa himself, it's hard ter say how they'll react. Then we got the Rees up near the Mandans now. Probably still madder than hell. Tarnation, Dave, we're on the upper river now. Who knows? The game changes past Blackbird's grave and the Mahas. Downriver, yer more likely to drown. Upriver, yer more likely to get shot, scalped, starved, or froze. If'n 'tain't water, it's fire."

"I take water every time," Henri said as he flexed his powerful hands. "If there is one law on the river, it is that God lets no man die old, *non?*"

Green nodded thoughtfully. "Makes you wonder what sort of fools we are, doesn't it? So many things could go wrong. A sawyer could rip the bottom out of the *Maria*. We could run into a band of Sioux with the prod on. The Rees could figure us for a lone boat and ambush us."

"And I might get ate by a bear. Reckon there ain't no gain if'n a body don't take no risk. What the hell, Henri is right. This coon's done figgered he'll lose his hair afore he dies of old age, Life's fer living, Dave. It's fer taking a gamble and seeing where yer stick floats. Hell, yer not figgering on dying in a bed in Saint Loowee, are ye?"

"No, I suppose not."

"Then stop yer cussed worrying. Each day takes care of itself."

They could hear the *engagés* singing softly as their supper cooked on the bank. Travis batted futilely at a swarm of mosquitoes humming above him in a wavering column.

"These mosquitoes," Henri growled. "Like the plague, they come to a man most just when he wants to rest. *Nusibles!* Ah, well, I got to check the painter before I see you at zee tent, *bourgeois.*" The patroon slapped at the humming air and disappeared around the corner of the cargo box.

"He's a good man," Green noted. "I got lucky."

"Yep. And we'd best hope that luck holds, coon."

"I hope all night and most of the day. Come on, I'm half starved." Green started for the *passe avant.* "Baptiste cut any buffalo sign today?"

"Yep. Old, but still sign." Travis followed Green down the bouncing plank.

"River's up." Green pointed to where the water had risen. "Must be a flood somewhere upriver." He hesitated. "Travis?"

"Huh?"

"Thanks."

"What fer?"

"For being here."

Travis patted Green on the back. "C'mon. Let's fill our bellies and get shy of these skeeters afore they suck a man dry."

———

Heals Like A Willow sat at the fire, a blanket over her head as protection from the mosquitoes. This night, camp had been pitched on a high bank, the keelboat tied off to gnarled old cottonwoods. She'd placed their fire off to one side, away from the other *engagés*. These White men ate and camped in little groups called "messes." She shared hers with Trawis, Dik, and Baptiste. Dave Green and Henri camped right in the center of the messes, the two of them generally eating alone before the square-walled tent.

The flames danced happily around the wood. Unlike the White men who chopped logs in two with their axes, she'd used the tried-and-true Indian method of breaking them into lengths, often wedging them between two tree trunks to get the leverage. She didn't need as much fire as the Whites who built bonfires and sat back away from them. Her people built small fires and sat right on top of them.

Baptiste lounged on the flattened grass, idly slapping

at mosquitoes and scratching itches. In her country, she would have used a mixture of larkspur and fir sap to keep the bugs off. Here, among these strange plants, she didn't know what to use except smoke and the blanket.

From the protection of her blanket, she watched Ritshard—seeing past his blank face to the unease he tried to hide within. From across the camp, she could sense Trudeau's hungry interest.

And when the two finally faced off over her? It didn't take much imagination to visualize Trudeau beating Ritshard into unconsciousness.

And when he does, I'll split the Frenchman's skull with my war club.

The deadly maternal urge to protect rose within her until her eyes slitted, and she briefly considered rising, stalking across the camp, and killing Trudeau before he had the chance to cause real trouble.

No. Doing so would shame Ritshard.

And from that, he might never recover. But why did she even care? A smart woman would let them sort it out between themselves.

Why Ritshard? She ground her teeth, knowing full well what attracted her. Power hovered around his soul like mist around a warm pond, and it drew her relentlessly toward him.

And do you really think he could follow in the place of your husband? He doesn't know the simplest of things. Do you think he's a warrior? He nearly threw up after facing Trudeau!

No, it would be impossible. He couldn't speak a word of the People's tongue. The *Dukurika* would eventually laugh him out of camp. And worst of all, what would her father say? It had been bad enough when she married a *Ku'chendikani.*

The gentle strains of a song rose on the night air as

the men finished their suppers and lit pipes full of fragrant tobacco. So peaceful now, but Trudeau would be trouble—as inevitable as winter on the heels of a late fall wind. Up to now, she'd been able to avoid him, using her skills to slip away when he prowled after her.

From the corner of her eye, she watched Ritshard.

I should leave. Take the trouble away before I get him killed.

But she stayed, watching, seeking to find that link of understanding within herself. Who were these ghost-skinned men from so far away? Their talk of giant villages, of boats larger than *Maria* that crossed oceans, the fascinating things they manufactured from metal, wood, and cloth, all drew her to know more.

And to think I ridiculed White Hail for wanting White man's things.

The Whites took wealth so casually. The day before, Trawis had given her a looking glass, one that portrayed her with such clarity that she might have been seeing another world rather than a reflection of this one. Among the *Dukurika* the looking glass would have been a source of awe for the entire band, passed from hand to hand with cries of amazement. Trawis had handed the magical glass to her with no more ceremony than he might have used to give her a rabbit-bone bead.

The fire popped, and sparks twined into the night sky. In the trees, an owl hooted, the mournful note interwoven with the voices of coyotes out in the bluffs.

Rich in things, yes. That was the White man's way. But of their souls she could detect little if anything. Some of the *engagés* knelt in the morning, mumbling to themselves, eyes closed, and finished with a motion of the hand, touching forehead, stomach, and each breast. Praying, Ritshard had said. Sending a message to God, as they called *Tam Apo*.

But on their knees like children? And with their eyes closed? How could a man find God with his eyes closed? And if he mumbled, how could God hear? Among her people, praying was done standing or dancing, arms upraised, eyes open to allow the soul to embrace Creation. When calling out to God, one sang, rejoicing and raising one's voice so that *Tam Apo* or the spirit helpers could hear clearly.

And perhaps that is the key. The White men keep Tam Apo *locked up like a little thing inside them.*

If so, how did God feel, to be treated thus?

When she questioned Ritshard about it, he used words far beyond her. Trawis would make signs, but they, too, ran out of meaning. Talking in signs was for trade and the interactions of peoples having different languages, not for such things as the nature of God.

Ritshard had told her that Whites kept a special "lodge" for God. A place called "church." Was it the nature of Whites to enclose things? That they did so with their women was understandable if one thought of a woman like a good horse—but the idea that anyone would try such a thing with God confounded her.

Trawis stepped out of Green's tent. His pipe was in hand, and he puffed at it as he walked over to the fire and settled himself cross-legged beside Ritshard.

"How do, coon?"

"I'm fine," Ritshard responded.

Baptiste spoke up, "Reckon tomorrow I'll scout northwest, see if I cut buffler sign."

"Ought to. We're close." Trawis stared at the end of his pipe stem. "This child's froze fer buffler."

Willow kept her head down as Trudeau walked past, then beyond into the darkness. She could hear him urinating just beyond the halo of firelight.

When he returned, he stopped long enough to nod at Trawis and give her that toothy leer she'd come to dislike.

After he'd left, Trawis said quietly, "Willow, you stay close ter me, hear? Reckon ye'd best not be walking off by yerself."

Baptiste nodded as he reached for his belt knife and began fingering the shining blade. "Reckon that's a heap of sense. Old Trudeau, he's on the prod."

"I avoid him," Willow replied. A small ache touched her soul at Ritshard's expression—strained, shamefaced.

"Yep, well, that's good," Trawis added. "He's some at moving a boat. Be a shame ter have to send him under."

"Always the boat," Richard muttered wearily.

"Boat's all we got," Trawis answered in that lazy voice he used sometimes.

Ritshard slapped a mosquito, but remained silent, his eyes on the fire. What did he see that was so far away? What did he long for with such yearning in his eyes?

"Ritshard? You have woman in Boston?" Willow asked.

"No."

"Family?"

He laughed sharply. "Yes, but none who would miss me."

"What is in Boston?"

He closed his eyes and whispered softly, "*Everything.*"

CHAPTER ELEVEN

Thus the distinct boundaries and offices of *reason* and of *taste* are easily ascertained. The former conveys the knowledge of truth and falsehood: the latter gives the sentiment of beauty and deformity, vice and virtue. The one discovers objects as they really stand in nature, without addition or diminution: the other has a productive faculty, and gilding or staining all the natural objects with colors, borrowed from internal sentiment, raises in a manner, new creation. Reason being cool and disengaged, is no motive to action, and directs only the impulse received from an appetite or inclination, by showing us the means of attaining happiness or avoiding misery. Taste, as it gives pleasure or pain, and thereby constitutes happiness or misery, becomes a motive to action, and is the first spring or impulse to desire and volition.

—David Hume, *An Enquiry Concerning the Principles of Morals*

"Easy, coon," Travis whispered as they crept along a brush-choked drainage. Richard paid careful attention to his feet, making sure that each step was placed so as to avoid rustling the green grass. His heart was pounding with excitement. This was the hunt!

The drainage cut like a twisting wound through the flats. Buffaloberry, currants, and spears of cedar lined the slopes, while a trickle of water fed rushes and cattails in the bottom. Sunflowers and daisies sprinkled color through the grass. Overhead, the sun's white intensity flushed water from every pore in Richard's body.

"Close," Willow whispered behind him. "Wind is right Waugh!"

Travis throttled a chuckle.

"Waugh is not proper English," Richard reminded, but he grinned and winked at her. To his delight, she winked back and gave him a smile that melted his heart.

"Shhh!" Travis raised a finger to his lips. The hunter dropped to his belly and snaked into a dry gulch that branched off from the cut. Richard dropped to follow, the green smell of crushed vegetation filling his nostrils. His blood began to quicken.

Digging in with his elbows, he followed Travis's moccasined feet. A hole had worn into the grass-polished right heel.

Travis slipped sideways past a patch of grass-bound prickly pear.

In a matter of moments, Richard's muscles started to protest from the awkward position. This mode of travel was ordained for snakes and salamanders—not human beings. He bit his lip and squirmed along in Travis's wake, aware of skittering insects, blades of grass, and the sun's heat boring into his back.

How far were they going? He tried to lift his head to see, but Willow slapped his foot. When he shot a glance over his shoulder, she shook her head emphatically.

He grumbled under his breath and dragged himself onward.

Travis had wriggled up to a patch of thorn-bristling rosebushes that clung to the side of the now shallow depression. Heedless of the vicious stems, the hunter eased up to the edge of the draw, parting the plants carefully to slide the long Hawken through the leaves.

Richard winced as he scratched himself and eased into place beside the hunter.

"Careful, coon," Travis whispered.

Richard peered through the screen of small serrated leaves and thorns. Blooms had already opened in puffs of pink that delighted the nose. But where had...? Yes, there!

The shaggy hump of the animal was no more than fifty paces away. Willow appeared as immune to thorns as Travis as she crawled up beside Richard.

The metallic click of the hammer might have sundered the world, but the buffalo remained oblivious. Time passed interminably.

"So, why don't you shoot?" Richard barely mouthed the words.

"Poor bull," Travis hissed. "We'll wait. Fat cow'll step up in a minute."

The minute turned into an hour under the relentless sun. The first fly was almost bearable as it buzzed around Richard's head. The rest who came—no doubt at some inaudible fly call from the first—drove him to distraction. The best he could do was flip his head to discourage the beasts, but all that earned him was a disgusted look from Travis, whom the flies seemed to ignore.

The bull had moved away, but a second animal, smaller, almost tan in color, was grazing closer with an agonizing slowness.

"Fat cow," Travis said under his breath, slowly lifting the heavy rifle.

The long wait continued.

Step by step, the buffalo moved into range. Rosebushes and grass screened most of the animal. All Richard could see was the humped back nearly seventy paces away. The stubby tail flipped and swished with a manic passion.

"We'll die of starvation," he muttered as he twitched to unseat the flies.

"Hold still, coon," Travis warned. "Ye'll have every critter from hyar ter the Yellerstone a-running."

Richard barely noticed when the cow turned sideways.

Pffft-boom! At. the report, blue smoke obscured everything ahead.

"Hit her in the lights," Travis chortled.

Richard started to rise, only to have a strong hand pull him down.

"Yer a damned Yankee pilgrim, Dick. Hold tarnal still and listen."

Richard glared in hot reply, but cocked his head. "I don't hear anything."

"Uh-huh." Travis slipped the rifle down beside him and rolled onto his back as he fiddled for his powder horn. The sunlight accented the white lines of scar tissue crisscrossing his face. As he poured powder into his measure horn, he gave Richard a sideways glance. "And if'n they's a-running, ye'd hear 'em, eh?"

Richard grabbed fruitlessly at the fly. "You mean you shot one...and the rest are just standing there?"

"What's a buffler ter be a-feared of? Maybe a griz, but no bear's a gonna take a full-grown buff on fer the fun of it. Nope, men's about the onliest thing they's a-feared of.

We don't stand up, they'll figger it's just thunder or some such. Buffler don't savvy gun shots."

Richard swiped at the flies and ran his dry tongue around his mouth. "They'll just stand there and let us shoot them?"

"Reckon so." Travis extracted a ball from his bullet pouch and placed it on a patch. He short-seated the bullet and used the keen blade of his patch knife to trim the cloth. With careful motions, he pulled the ramrod and sent the load home before priming the pan and snapping the frisson shut.

"Hyar now, coon," he handed the heavy rifle to Richard. "Crawl up aside me. Slowly, now. Oh, don't mind the damn rosebushes, them little scratches will heal. Hell, look at my face and tell me about scratches!"

Nevertheless, Richard winced as the tiny thorns scored his skin. He inched forward until he could see more humped backs. The buffalo remained unconcerned.

Travis continued to whisper in his ear, "Slow, pilgrim. Now, pull yer rifle up. That's it. Get a good brace and set the stock in yer shoulder. Thar ye be. Now, put yer hand under the forestock; that's it. Ye want solid bone under the gun. Don't wobble that way."

Richard settled in and nestled his cheek against the stock so he could squint down the sights.

"Hold up, now. We'll wait her out."

Richard waited, his left arm slowly going numb under the weight of the rifle. He blinked to clear his right eye.

"Don't sight all the time, coon. Keep both yer eyes open till yer ready to shoot. What damn fool larned ye to close yer eye?"

"You did."

"Eh? Oh well, guess we never got this far."

"Shoot good," Willow whispered from behind.

Shoot good? Richard took a deep breath. What if he missed? This was his first buffalo, his first hunt.

Don t bungle it, Richard.

He could imagine the disgusted look in Travis's eye. Worse, Willow would think he was a complete doof. Anything but that.

"Cow's coming up," Travis hissed. "On yer right. Now, don't shift. She'll come ter ye."

Richard swiveled his head, seeing the animal through the masking grass. Close...so close. What? Forty paces?

If I miss from forty paces...

He'd never survive Willow's disdain.

Please, God. Just this once, let me do it right!

And then his heart began to pound with a terrible vengeance; excited blood boiled bright in his veins. Never in his life had he experienced this heady rush. Each nerve tingled, breaths coming in quick succession.

"Easy, coon. That's the fever a-coming on ye. Breathe easy, now. That's it, slow and careful. Relax, hoss. Take yer time and think."

Richard swallowed hard and watched the buffalo. His electric heart refused to still its pounding. The cow took a step, lowered her head, and continued grazing. Richard could hear the grass tearing, the grinding of her jaws, and the puffing of her breath.

Another step, and another, and he could see most of her above the mat of grass and flowers.

"Cock the hammer," Travis whispered.

The click should have deafened God.

"Take aim," Travis continued. "Set yer sights right ahind the shoulder joint. Low down...way down. Buffler hearts sit low in the body."

Sweat trickled down Richard's flushed face. The heavy rifle seemed to waver like a snake in his grasp.

"Shoot!"

Richard flinched and jerked the trigger.

Nothing happened.

"Figgered that," Travis grunted. "Now that ye got all the foolishness outa ye, pull the back trigger to set the front one. And remember, when ye gets yer shot, she'll flash in yer face. Don't move a breath. Recoil ain't gonna hurt ye, and it all comes after the bullet's been shot."

Richard settled himself, watching the front sight blade in the V of the rear. It settled behind the cow's shoulder. There, right there...

Pfft! Fire erupted in his face. *Boom!* The Hawken butted his shoulder. *Spat!* He heard the bullet hit home.

"Don't move!" Travis growled, his heavy hand already on Richard's shoulder.

"Are they running?"

"Nope. But ye hit her high, Dick. Lung shot."

"Lung shot?"

Travis reached out and slipped the Hawken back from Richard's grasp, then slowly raised himself, heedless of the vicious prairie rose.

Richard eased up, barely aware of the needling thorns tracing angry patterns across his flesh. Travis was reloading, a crooked grin on his face. Several calves who were close grunted and turned to look at them. Willow reached out to pat Richard's leg, the action more rewarding than a chorus of huzzahs.

The buffalo cow trotted off a few paces and stopped, head down, the short tail up.

"I didn't kill her?" Richard asked frantically.

"Reckon ye did, coon. But listen close, Dick. Larn this. If'n ye shoots a critter and she don't drop dead, ye settles down fer a second shot. The last thing ye do is go a-charging down there like a runaway stallion, 'cause if'n that animal gets its blood up, it'll run halfway to Mexico afore it falls over."

"So you wait?"

"Yep. Let the critter lay down and stiffen up. Hell, I seen a feller chase a gut-shot antelope nigh onto five miles once. And if'n he'd just set tight for a short spell, that prairie goat would a been dead in minutes."

"So we're waiting?"

"Yep. Not long, Dick. Ye hit her plumb solid."

The other buffalo switched their tails and watched the wounded cow for several minutes before dropping their heads to graze. From where he sat, Richard could see bright red blood draining from the cow's nose. She grunted, took another wobbling step, and dropped to her knees before sinking onto the grass.

"Good shot," Willow whispered happily, and took Richard's hand. "First buffalo?"

"The first." And Richard watched, torn with remorse and an unquenchable pride. "But, Travis, shouldn't we shoot her again?"

"What? And waste the powder? Dick, she's dead. Ye gotta larn, thar ain't no store around hyar no place. Use only as much as ye needs ter get the job done. There's times a mite of powder has to last a coon fer a long spell."

The cow lifted her head, then dropped it.

"She's nigh gone under, Dick. Ye done made meat."

The fever had drained away to leave him oddly empty.

The cow's last hoarse gasp carried to his ears; then she was still.

Travis rose to his feet, and as Richard and Willow stood, the other buffalo turned to stare, some raising their tails and defecating.

"That's a warning," Travis said. "Watch their tails.

The more nervous a buffalo gets, the higher it puts its tail. Like a warning flag that there's trouble."

As Travis spoke, the animals whirled, charging away with a pounding of hooves. How many were there? Seventy? A hundred?

Richard followed Travis forward. To one side lay the mounded shape of Travis's buffalo. It had pitched forward and fallen on its side.

Reverently, he walked up to his cow.

"Careful, coon," Travis warned. "Foller me. Cain't never tell when a critter's dead. I remember old Jonas Farb. Why, he walked up and grabbed ahold of a bull's head that he'd shot. That bull come to, flipped his head, and old Jonas, he had no place to go so he jumped right a-straddle that bull's back. Let me tell ye, that bull stood up and took off lickety-split fer parts unknown...and there was old Jonas, a-hanging on that hump fer all he's worth. By the time he got shut of that bull, he's five days' walk from camp."

Richard nodded soberly, failing to see the twinkle in Travis's eyes.

The cow lay dead, eyes wide, her nose planted in a pool of foamy blood.

"My God, look how *big* she is!" Richard spread his arms and gaped.

"Reckon yer a gonna find out just how big she is, all right. Now the work starts." Travis poked the cow in the side with his rifle. "Let's get her guts out. Hump roast and boudins fer dinner tonight."

Willow placed a caressing hand on the buffalo's back, then raised her arms to the sky and sang softly, the Shoshoni words lilting in the air. When she finished, she walked over to Travis's animal and repeated the gesture.

"What's she doing?" Richard asked.

"Praying fer the buff, or this child don't know sign. Injuns figger that critters got souls. They thank 'em for the gift of meat."

"I guess there's something to that."

Travis gave him a sidelong look. "Rational, huh?"

Richard grinned and looked away. But inside, he, too, said a prayer for the animal.

"Now what?"

Travis handed Richard his knife. "Slit her around the neck just back of the ears and horns. Then cut her right down the back to the tail. No, not that way. Yer just a-cutting hair. The edge has to be under the skin, that, or ye'll dull yer blade till it won't cut a dry fart."

Willow had already begun work on the cow Travis had shot. Glancing over, Richard couldn't help but admire the way she used a knife, so practiced and efficient. Bent like that, her buckskin dress emphasized the roundness of her hips and the slender lines of her back.

"Uh, reckon ye wouldn't mind watching what yer a-doing? She's a right smart woman, I'll agree, but I'd rather ye kept yer eyes on what yer cutting...my fingers being so close to that blade, Dick." Travis pulled the thick hide down while Richard blushed and severed the tissue.

"Easy, coon. Cut along the hide, not into the meat like a Yankee would."

"I've never done this before." The exposed flesh was hot against his skin, the muscles still quivering. White patterns of fat contrasted to the warm red of the meat.

When they had peeled the hide down, Travis took the knife and began slicing cuts of meat. These he placed on the grass until only strips of meat hung on the bloody bones.

"I'm gonna fetch the hosses and a hatchet," Travis said before he turned and trotted away.

Richard picked at the clotted blood drying on his hands. The flies buzzed in excitement around the carcass. How ephemeral life was, the scavengers drawn so quickly to the dead.

He walked over to Willow, who still labored on the other cow.

She gave him a radiant smile, and he noticed blood on her lips. "Meat!" she cried. "You are a hunter now, Ritshard. You have killed a buffalo. Today is a special day for you."

"Special?"

"Special among my people." She sliced another thin strip of meat and handed it to him.

He shook his head, and she shrugged before popping the treat into her mouth. He watched her jaw muscles working under smooth brown skin. The sparkle in her eyes, the happiness reflected in the set of her mouth, made his soul sing. "You don't cook it?"

"Of course." With a dainty pink tongue, she licked a bloody morsel from her finger. "But for now, it is food."

He bent down to help her. Unlike Travis, who cut across the grain, she severed each muscle individually, cutting it loose from the bone. Her deft abilities had already stripped the backstrap, hump, and ribs.

She glanced at him, a curious smile playing along her lips. "Do you always help women butcher?"

"No...I mean, this is the first time."

"Why?"

"Why not? I like to help you." He fidgeted, oddly uneasy. "You prayed for the animals. Sang to their souls."

The wind teased her long black hair. "White men do not?"

"Most don't. But, well—I did."

She paused, the bloody knife hanging. "I do not understand. White men do not thank the animals who die to give them life? Ritshard, are White men without respect? Do they not understand that everything is related?" She shook her head. "I think your people are rich in many things...like knives and guns and pots. But in your souls, I think you are all empty."

He took a deep breath, meeting her dark eyes and the certainty expressed there. The memory of the woman on the steamboat surfaced, her voice shrill as she smacked her child. "Many are, I guess. But not all. Some men spend their entire lives seeking to understand the soul."

"Some men?"

"Anselm, Augustine, Meister Eckhardt. We have many men in our history who have sought God and the soul. It's an old quest in our society."

"What is quest?"

"The search."

"Men again? Women do not seek?"

"Not very many. Some do. It has been suggested that women do not have the same capacity for understanding the infinite that men do."

She lifted an eyebrow, then bent to her work. "In some ways, White men and Snake people may not be so different."

"For every Heloïse there are twenty Abelards."

"I don't understand."

"No, you wouldn't. But it's—"

"I quest," she told him as she sliced another thick slab of muscle from the buffalo. "Does that bother you?"

He reached down, pulling on a rubbery muscle as she severed it from the bone. "What do you hope to find?"

She glanced up at him. "In your words—understanding. Of everything. You did not answer. Does that bother you?"

Richard glanced up at the sky, aware of the spiraling wings of a hawk far overhead. "No. I mean, after all, that's what I've spent my life studying."

"Studying?"

"Uh...larning."

She nodded, that secret smile on her lips. "Isn't that all anyone can do? Try to larn?"

He looked into her gorgeous eyes, and his soul floated. Her lips parted, and he reached for her, barely conscious of taking her hand. At the sound of approaching hooves she lowered her eyes, the connection severed.

Richard turned away, self-conscious, as Travis rode up out of the drainage, sitting his horse like a lord. On a lead rope, the tail-hitched cavvy followed with heads up and manes flying. At the smell of blood, the horses snorted, backing and pawing. Travis handled his animal with a firm hand until the mare settled down. He landed lightly on his feet, soothing the horses.

The hunter dragged the mare forward, tying her off on the last of the man-sized cedars at the edge of the gully. He pulled a hatchet from his possibles and stalked across the grass. Richard pushed to his feet, ears burning redly, but Travis seemed oblivious.

"Now, what's left?" Travis asked absently before using the hatchet to separate the ribs from the gut cavity. Richard dodged flying chips of bone and stared at the organs as Travis and Willow cut the last of the muscles loose and lifted the ribs off.

Travis chortled as he reached into the wet mass to tug out the heavy liver. From this he sliced long strips and handed them around. Willow immediately sank white teeth into the bloody stuff. Richard stared as Travis asked, "Ye gonna eat? First meat, coon."

"It's not cooked."

"Yer a Yankee Doodle if'n I ever saw one. Eat'er, child, or I'll whack ye one."

A quest? A search for understanding?

Richard made a face and bit into the rich, hot liver. He tried to ignore the hot blood dripping down his chin.

———

Travis hunched over his horse's neck as the toiling line of men leaned into the cordelle. Like some curious caterpillar, they splashed through the rippling shallows in the river below him. Willow sat placidly on her horse, fingers tracing the handle of the Pawnee war club. The horses stamped at the few flies brave enough to dare the weather.

Gray clouds had settled in; drizzle fell in fits and spits, coupled with gusts of cold wind. Thunder growled out of a mass of black clouds rolling in from the western plains.

The river had a sullen look, as if resentful of the progress the line of men made as they pulled the *Maria* into the strengthening current. Travis picked out Richard Hamilton as he struggled along, sloshing and wet, the heavy cordelle over his shoulder. Farther up the line, Baptiste bent his powerful body to the thick rope, his black skin contrasting with that of the white *engagés*.

This particular passage was deadly, the worst they'd encountered yet. Richard hadn't wanted to go back to the cordelle, but here they needed every hand to pull the boat through the fast water.

"So much work," Willow said. "In all the world, only White men and ants work like that."

"Reckon so," Travis agreed. "It's a bad spot, Willow." He pointed to the embarras of twisted logs and splintered branches that had dammed half the river. Water spilled around the end of the obstacle, but against that rush *Maria* was hauled inexorably forward, white-water foaming at her bow, the cordelle pulled tight enough to bead droplets. Under that weight, the mast bowed perilously. On the cargo box, Green raced back and forth like a desperate mouse, shouting orders, watching fearfully as disaster loomed. Face twisted, Henri braced his feet and leaned against the protesting steering oar to keep *Maria* out of the tangled wood.

"If anything goes wrong, there'll be hell ter pay," Travis said softly. "Painter crap, I otta be down there with 'em."

Maria gained a few feet against the rush of the water, each inch made at the expense of tearing muscles and straining joints.

"Ritshard did not want to pull the boat."

Travis grinned. "Reckon he still figgers he's a gentleman."

"Jentl...What is that?"

"Gentleman, uh, like a sort of chief. Not like a worker. Whites have these differences among them."

"So do Pawnee." A frown marred her brow. "Ritshard is a chief?"

Travis reached into his possibles and found what remained of his tobacco twist. He cut a length and chewed it until it juiced. After spitting a brown streak, he said, "Not a chief, exactly, but I'd guess you'd say a respected man. One looked up to by most people."

"But not the *engagés.*

"Now, Willow, ye got ter understand. Dick's got ter earn his way." He waved his hand. "This hyar ain't Boston. It's the river, and rules is different wherever ye goes. Dick ain't larned that yet."

"Tell me of this Boston."

"It's a city. Cold in winter. Good taverns...but a mite hard on coons deep in their cups. Not the kind of place a feller wants ter go a-sleeping in the street, that's plumb certain."

"Ritshard wishes for a place like this?"

"Wal, ye see, he figgers it a bit different than this child. 'Course, every feller's got the right ter his own brand of hydrophobia."

"Hydro...?"

"Foaming mouth—like the critters get. White bubbly spit leaking from the mouth? Won't get near water. Crazy mean—bites everything in sight. You know the sickness I mean?"

"I know it. You think Ritshard wanting Boston is a sickness? Crazy?"

"Yep."

"Why do you not let him go, Trawis?"

He reached up and scratched his ear. "In the beginning we needed men, Willow. Just like ye see down there, each one pulling as hard as he can. Times is, just one body can make the difference atwixt living and dying."

"Green took on men at Fort Atkinson."

"Yep."

At that moment, Richard stumbled on the cordelle, dragging two more men down after him. Another fell, and then another. Shouts carried up to them as the men floundered, battling the rippling brown current and the weight of the cordelle. The river's grip pulled *Maria* back, and the scrambling men with her. Some were dragged through the water, floundering as they sought their feet.

"Come on. Come *on*." Travis knotted his fists, moved his quid from cheek to cheek, and prayed fervently.

Baptiste let out a bellow, bracing himself and gripping the cordelle. Trudeau cursed and shouted, plunging along the thick rope. The men who'd fallen had scrambled for a hold, slowing the retreat, stopping it just as the *Maria* swung like a pendulum toward the end of the embarras with its foaming Whitewater and pointed logs.

"*Pull!*" Green's scream carried from the river. "One more slip and we're dead!"

Henri battled the steering oar while *Maria* edged closer to death on the jutting logs. If she hit, they'd tear through her like teeth.

The *engagés* bellowed and pulled, Trudeau motioning them onward.

"Come on," Travis prayed. "Hold her, boys."

For long minutes they watched silently as the misty rain picked up. The boat inched forward against the surging water.

Willow pulled her blanket over her head, and Travis noted the strain in her face. Richard had been dragged through the mud. He coughed, soaked and bedraggled, as he leaned into the cordelle.

Maria crept away from destruction.

"Close one." Travis rubbed his face. "Mighty close."

Maria pulled clear of the current. The weary *engagés* toiled toward the sandbar. At the lead, Lalemont staggered out onto the land, feet pocking the muddy sand.

Henri steered wide of the shallows to keep draft. Green was rocking from foot to foot, still tense with fear.

"What if the boat sank?" Willow glanced at Travis.

"We'd be in a mess. If'n we lose that boat, she's a long

walk ter Saint Loowee. Green would have lost everything he's worked for. All them years...gone."

"You White men are hydro...hydro—"

"Hydrophobied."

"Crazy."

"Reckon so, gal. Ain't no worse than some, I'd say."

"Some?"

"Folks. Guess we're all a little crazy. Maybe yer *Tam Apo* made us that way."

"Not in the beginning, Trawis. But after the Creation, when Coyote was making trouble, that's when the world got crazy."

The *engagés* had all reached the thin spit of sand. They lined out now, holding their places on the cordelle, catching their breath.

Trudeau walked down the line to Richard, waving his arms, shouting angrily. Richard stood stoop-shouldered, chest heaving as water trickled down his face.

Travis couldn't hear the words over the distance, but Trudeau balled a fist and drove it deep into Richard's gut. The Yankee doubled under the impact and dropped flat onto the mud.

"Son of a bitch," Travis growled, eyes narrowing. "The kid couldn't help falling."

Baptiste had left his place, running down to pull Trudeau off. The other *engagés* watched silently. Trudeau and Baptiste stood toe-to-toe, and finally Trudeau shook his head with disgust and tramped off to take up the cordelle again.

Baptiste had bent over Richard, then pulled him to his feet.

"*Levez!*" came Trudeau's cry. And the *engagés* threw themselves into the endless pulling.

Richard stood bent over, head hanging as the *engagés* pulled past him, none daring to look him in the eye.

Willow sat in stony silence, a hardness in her delicate face.

"Wal, I'd reckon thar's more coming from Trudeau."

"Ritshard should kill him," Willow said woodenly.

Travis allowed himself to slump in the saddle again. "Ye care fer that Yankee, don't ye?"

She glanced at Travis with smoldering eyes. "Power... how do you say? The medicine is strong in Ritshard. He has a fire in his soul, one that he does not know yet. Green has his boat. The *engagés* their work. Ritshard looks for more. I understand that quest."

"Quest?"

"The search, Trawis. One day, Ritshard will find it, and when he does, he will be a great man."

Travis ground on his quid for a moment, spat the juice, and crossed his arms. "Maybe. 'Course, we gotta keep him alive long enough."

CHAPTER TWELVE

It may seem strange to some man, that has not well weighed these things; that nature should thus dissociate, and render men apt to invade, and destroy one another: and he may therefore, not trusting to this inference, made from the passions, desire perhaps to have the same confirmed by experience. Let him therefore consider with himself when taking a journey, he arms himself, and seeks to go well accompanied; when going to sleep, he locks his doors; when even in his house he locks his chests; and this is when he knows there be laws, and public officers, armed, to revenge all injuries shall be done him; what opinion has he of his fellow-subjects, when he rides armed; of his fellow citizens, when he locks his doors; and of his children, and servants, when he locks his chests. Does he not there as much as accuse mankind by his actions, as I do by my words?

—Thomas Hobbes, *Leviathan*

 Sheets of rain slanted down from the night sky to spatter steam from the smoking remains of Richard's fire. He shivered in his blanket, wet to

the bone. Water dripped through the soaked tarp he'd tied overhead.

His belly hurt where Trudeau had hit him. Dear Lord God, how low could a man sink? To be abused by brutes, tormented and cold, and somehow ashamed that he'd only been able to lie in the sand while Baptiste rescued him.

Trudeau wants to kill me.

Numb from the cold, Richard fingered the soggy fetish on his belt. Lightning flashed whitely in the sky, illuminating the slanted blanket shelters, shiny-wet against the backdrop of the dripping cottonwoods. Several seconds later, the bang of thunder hammered the air.

Richard closed his eyes.

Why haven't I run? I could have been back to Fort Atkinson by now. Or on my way to Saint Louis by pirogue or bateau.

But he hadn't taken any of the opportunities. Instead, he'd promised himself it would be the next day, or the next, when he made his break, stole a horse, and galloped south.

"I'm a coward," he whispered, and wrung water from a twist of his blanket. Perhaps Laura did deserve Thomas Hanson more than him.

Trudeau. Damn Trudeau! If only he could have blocked that blow, given the boatman back measure for measure.

And degenerate into what? Another human beast like Trudeau?

"Coon?" Like some hunched night creature, Travis ducked out of the dark into the shelter. He grunted, pulling off his hat and wringing it out. "I reckon they's frogs what will drown in this."

"Go away."

"Ain't much of anywhere to go. Hell, even the hosses won't get stole in weather like this. River'll be up another couple of feet in the morning. Creeks is all flooded."

"Then maybe we'll be lucky and all drown."

"Yer not sounding so pert, coon. This beaver figgered ye'd be keen ter philos'phy me half ter death with yer Roossoo."

"He can drown, too—except he's already dead."

"How's yer gut?"

"Sore."

"It warn't yer fault. Fellers slip in the mud. Could'a been Trudeau as likely as ye."

"But it wasn't, Travis. Let's face it, I'm not fit for this. It's not my place. I should be back in Boston, working on the docks if nothing else. I had that chance once... Patrick Bonnisen was hiring."

Damn you, Father. Maybe I should have taken him up. You'd appreciate that, wouldn't you? A son who worked as a dockhand?

Travis had seated himself cross-legged. A flash of lightning illuminated his terrible face, the scars water-slick. "I worked docks before. Men there is the same as Trudeau."

"How cheery. Something to look forward to when I get back to Boston."

"Don't have to be that way."

"Indeed? Perhaps you know something about my father that I don't? I'm a failure, Travis. All I wanted was to continue my studies, stay at the university. I lost my father's money. Was kidnapped to this hell. Killed a boy... almost wrecked everything today. All I'll ever be is a failure."

Travis's face twisted. "Ye ain't no failure—lessen ye wants ter be."

"Oh?"

"Hell, coon, ye knows a sight more than old Travis. All them fellers ye talk about. Roossoo, Haggle, Kant. And a passel more I been hearing ye tell of."

"A great deal of good it does me here."

"Yep, wal, yer not seeing things with a skinned eye, coon. Willow's free of that rascal Packrat. I ain't wolfmeat 'cause ye sewed me up."

Richard pushed his wet hair back. "I didn't have any choice."

"Reckon ye did. What of all that free will yer so fond of spouting up?"

"Do I look free, Travis?"

"Yep."

Richard stared silently at the fire's steaming ashes. Rain pattered in the darkness, accented by louder spats of water falling from the trees. The smell of smoke carried from the half-drowned fires to mingle with the wet scents of trees, grass, and ground.

"Dick, a feller's only as free as he makes hisself. Ask Baptiste. Hell, ask me. I done been in a sight worse mess than yer in. On a brig in the middle of the ocean, ye can only dance the jig while the fiddler plays the tune."

"I'm not convinced."

"Lord God A'mighty, Dick. Yer problem is that ye've got to thinking ye've all this high and mighty truth tucked away inside, but ye don't. I ain't read all them books. I don't know what them fellers said, but I know about living, and freedom, and going whar my stick floats. And that, coon, is why I'm a heap smarter than ye —and all yer book larning to boot."

"Aristotle would be pleased to hear that."

"I'll tell him next time I see his sorry arse. But tell me this: If'n a philos'pher's got all this truth, it sure otta stand up ter living, ottn't it? I don't know what's in them books, but I do know this: If'n ye've got all the larning in the world, it's poor bull ter fat cow if'n yer not willing ter be wrong. Ye might as well be a turtle as a man."

Richard studied Travis's dark silhouette. "What are you saying?"

"I'm saying yer right. Yer a failure. And ye'll always be one unless yer a-willing ter look life straight in the eye. The way I figgers it, ye've growed up thinking it's all easy. Even yer philos'phy. Read a couple of books, and ye knows it all. No sweat and blood, no pain and misery. Wal, coon, philos'pher or not, yer gonna be a failure lessen ye stands up like a man. Maybe ye'll get shot straight through the lights...and maybe ye won't. But ye'll know yerself. And die like a man instead of a boy."

Lightning arced in the sky, flashing weird shadows over the sodden camp.

"Yer pretty damn silent fer once."

"I was just thinking of Socrates," Richard said uneasily.

"I knew a slave by that name once. On a plantation in South Carolina."

"A slave...no, Travis. This is the real Socrates. A Greek philosopher who lived two thousand years ago."

"And he wrote one of these books?"

"No. But he taught the men who did. Any student of philosophy has heard his immortal teaching: 'The unexamined life is not worth living.'"

"Did he get that out of a book?"

"No. As you would say, he stood up and looked life straight in the eye. He was an orator, and a soldier. When Athens went to war, he picked up his shield and sword and fought. When he encountered a wise man, he questioned him, regardless of the consequences. In the end, it cost him his life." Richard stroked the fetish. "You'd have liked him."

"Real cat-scratch scrapper, huh?"

"Yes." Richard took a deep breath. "So, what do I do?"

"Take life as she comes. Why, ye've an opportunity most men'd kill fer. Yer on the river, Dick. Headed fer the Shining Mountains. Stop trying ter see everything from outside, and see it from inside fer once."

What was it about Travis Hartman? Where did that fearless self-assurance come from?

The same place as Socrates', the internal voice told him. *From having tested the truths in the crucible of life.*

"I've been a fool, Travis." He rubbed his stomach. "The lesson's a little painful, is all."

"Them's the best ones."

"I guess Trudeau was right to hit me."

"Nope. Warn't yer fault. Reckon that Frenchie's gonna be a thorn in everybody's butt lessen I take him down."

"Why you?"

"Running the men is my job."

"It's me he's after...and Willow."

"Yer not up ter Trudeau. He'll make wolf meat outa ye."

"I could learn, couldn't I?"

"Might mean taking a couple of lumps, Dick."

Richard stared out into the night rain and swallowed hard as he made his decision. "Trade you."

"How's that?"

"You teach me how to whip Trudeau, and I'll teach you how to read and write."

"I cain't larn that!"

"Painter crap, as you would say. Or...are you afraid of failing?"

Thunder blasted the night.

"I...uh... *Me?* Larning ter read?" Travis snorted in final defeat, then smiled. "Yer a damned Yankee bastard, Dick."

Yes, but then, when it comes to being a damn bastard, I've had good teachers.

———

The experience was magical. Heals Like A Willow sat on the front of the cargo box and looked down over the bow of the boat. In the lee of the storm, the wind blew strongly from the south, and *Maria's* bulging sail drove her upriver.

Muddy water sparkled in the sunlight as the boat raced the waves. The sensation of such movement lifted Willow's soul as if born on the wings of a mighty eagle. She couldn't see enough of the bank passing, of the wake left behind, or the current sliding under the pointed prow—and without muscles to do it! The boat seemed alive, a sentient being instead of a human creation.

And in that lay another puzzle. Did White men have the ability to create beings?

High overhead the last of the delicate clouds raced them northward, contrasting to the deep blue of the rain-fresh sky and the aching green of the trees and grass. So clean compared to the muddy river with its flotsam.

Dave Green came to sit beside her, resplendent in a jade shirt and fawn-colored pants. His blond hair caught glints of golden sunlight, and his blue eyes sparkled. Eyes she still hadn't grown used to seeing; they simply shouldn't be that pale and curious-looking.

"A good day," Green told her, clasping his hands in his lap. "After yesterday, I can use a day like this. Sailing, by God. What a relief. But help me watch for floating logs. The banks will be washing out and toppling trees."

"The boat moves," she said. "Strong medicine."

"You've seen the wind push a leaf across a pond? Same thing, but bigger. I've come upriver many times, and the wind is always a chancy thing. I was starting to believe it had deserted us altogether."

Willow tucked a long strand of black hair behind her ear. "I never would have figgered such a thing."

Green's expression betrayed his delight with the day. "If we could have a couple of weeks of this, we could ride up to the Yellowstone in complete comfort."

She glanced up at the curving sail. Canvas, they called it. Such an incredibly strong and light fabric. Even the finest scraped buffalo hide could not match it for strength.

"You have many marvels, Green. I had heard the stories told by some of my people. I did not believe them." She touched the looking glass she wore on a thong around her neck.

"I hope all of your people share your enthusiasm." Green rubbed his hands together. "I've been thinking, Willow. This first year we'll set up at the mouth of the Big Horn. Trade with the Crows. If that goes well, maybe we'll move up the Big Horn, put a post in Snake country. Maybe around the Hot Spring."

She knew the place of which he spoke: *Pa'goshowener,* Hot Water Stand. The huge hot springs where the Big River ran through the canyon in the Owl River Mountains.

"Why would you go there?"

"Your people could come to trade. They would have their own post, Willow. As it is, the Snakes must travel a great distance, through many enemies, to trade hides for white goods."

She shook her head slowly. "You call these things 'goods.' I am not sure they are good. Marvelous, yes. Good? That is a word I worry about. Ritshard and Trawis have taught me the word 'medicine.'" She made the hand sign for "Power." "Among my people, medicine can be good or bad. It depends on how people use it. A healer can use medicine for good. A sorcerer can use it to kill. These things you Whites would trade, they, too, have medicine. Tell me, Green, are they really all good?"

His blue eyes probed hers. "Travis told me you were a smart squaw, and that I'd best not underestimate you. Well, Willow, I'll tell you the truth as far as I know it, all right?"

"All right."

"I don't know if all the things White men make are good for them, or not. I guess it depends on how you use them. A gun kills more efficiently than a bow. A man can defend his home better with a bullet than an arrow."

"But you must trade for powder and bullets. And if your gun breaks, you must get a White Man to fix it."

"That's true. But in the meantime, an Indian can make him a new bow and arrows until he runs into a trader with gun parts."

"A gun is heavy thing to pack around while looking for a trader."

"Not if you have a post at the Hot Springs. The parts would be there whenever you needed them."

"And if this trader wants as much for the gun—what did you say? Parts? Those are the pieces?"

"That's right. A gun is made of parts."

"But if one part breaks, the gun is worth as much as the broken part. What then, Green? I heard the story about Blackbird. He let the trader charge what he wanted. And the people had to pay."

The booshway frowned. "Happens. On my honor, Willow, if I am your trader, I will never charge as much for the part as I would for the whole gun."

"But you might charge a lot."

He gestured at the boat and the *engagés* riding along the *passe avant*. "This costs a great deal, Willow. I had to pay a heap for the boat, and the men don't work for free. You understand about money?"

"Yes. Trawis explained. Like trading plews. So many for a certain thing."

"Well, it's a bit more complicated than that, but yes. I still have to make more on trade than I give out. You understand that? I must make enough more so that I can get the things I want for myself."

She lifted an inquisitive eyebrow. "And what do you want, Green? I think you would be a hard man to satisfy. You remind me of my..." How do I say brother-in-law? What is their word? "Of a man I know. He always wants more, and will risk himself to get it. One day it will kill him. You are such a man, Green. I can see your soul. It will never be full."

Green stared out at the river, the waves breaking in white-caps. "You can see my soul?"

"Medicine has given me certain ways of seeing. Your soul is a lot like Ritshard's. He is driven to know. You are driven to have things. Neither one of you will ever have enough of what you want, but Ritshard will try to share what he seeks. Will you try to share your things, Green?"

He took a deep breath and laughed. "Damn, woman, do you always ask so many questions?"

"Ever since I was a little girl. It is said that I'm nothing but trouble. Better for you that Ritshard shot

Packrat and freed me. Think how you would have felt if you'd traded two rifles for me back at the fort. You'd want your rifles back."

A twinkle filled Green's eyes. "I doubt it, Willow."

"We have not solved the problem of your 'goods.' They can be bad, can't they? Like the whiskey you carry. People will want more and more of them."

"If they didn't, I couldn't trade for very long. Willow, many things the whites have make life easier. A metal pot lasts forever. An iron ax is sharper than one made of stone. It takes less labor to chop down a tree."

"Gunpowder runs out. Whiskey is all drunk up."

"Iron needles are better than bone ones. Blankets are lighter than buffalo hides—and just as warm."

She placed her palms together, rubbing her hands. "The *Ku'chendikani* believe that horses are good for them, too. Now they move camp all winter long looking for grass for the horses. I think they work harder for the horses than the horses work for the people. Would trade be this way? If all the bands want White things, will they be working all winter to hunt enough beaver to pay for gunpowder, needles, pots, and whiskey? Are these things you bring just something else to take my people away from their old life? From the familiar ways of doing things?"

Green made a face. "Hell, Willow, I don't...I mean... Look, I can't *make* them trade for things. It's up to them, isn't it? You've got to understand how trade works. I've got to bring things people want. If I haul a boatload of blankets all the way upriver and no one wants a single one, I'm broke. I sure can't make a man trade for a blanket he don't *want*. Follow my stick?"

She nodded. "Plumb center, Green. My people *wanted* horses. They still do. More than anything else in the world. I fear they will want the White man's goods with the same—is the word 'passion'?"

"It is."

"Then your goods may be very bad, Green."

He fingered his chin. "Blackfeet and Crow will have these things. Guns give warriors a big advantage in a fight."

"The *A'ni* and *Pa'kiani* seek out the *Ku'chendikani* just to take their horses. The *Dukurika* high in the mountains are mostly left alone. The *A'ni* and *Pa'kiani* don't like to ride their horses up the mountains. And the *Dukurika* have nothing they want to steal."

"Sheepeater," Green said, understanding in his eyes. "You're not a Snake? Which tribe do you belong to?"

She shrugged. "We are just 'the People.' Some live far to the west and call themselves the *Agaidika,* the Fish-eaters. Some are the *Po'hogan'hite,* the Sage-people. It depends on where the People are and what they do."

Green ran thick fingers through his hair. "Willow, it's going to happen. If I don't set up a post and trade, someone else will. You and your people have to understand. The white traders will go any place they must to find hides. They'll fight for trade just as hard as the Blackfeet and Crows fight with each other. If the river can be made safe, many traders will race for your country. Take my word, they'll come. Just as winter follows summer."

Just as winter follows summer? The words settled in her soul. She couldn't help but stiffen at the thought.

"This place you will make, it will be like Fort Atkinson?"

"No, not that big. Just a small post. A couple of houses, a storehouse, and the trading house."

"And what if it isn't good for us, for my people, Green?"

"You've seen the things we have. Wouldn't life be easier with them? A copper pot doesn't wear out like a buffalo gut. Glass beads are brighter than porcupine quills. A good steel knife works a heap better than a stone one. That can't be bad."

Water slapped at the bow, splashing whitely against the brown water. Despite the magic of a huge boat that moved with the wind, she couldn't shake the sense of worry.

Someday my people will regret the coming of the White men.

And she couldn't help but think of Coyote, who promised wonderful things—and brought disaster.

———

"That wasn't fair!" Richard picked himself up off the grass and wiped his bloody nose. Every muscle ached, and his nose stung. The only saving grace was that Willow was on the boat and didn't have to see him look a simple fool.

They stood out in the open on the bluffs west of the river. The horses watched them with pricked ears, then lowered their heads to crop at the fresh grass and challenge the limits of their ground picket. A brisk south wind tugged at Richard's shirt and ruffled his sweaty hair. Out in the grass a meadowlark trilled the most peaceful of songs. Beyond wave after wave of grassy hills, the horizon lost itself in the distance. Patches of white fluffy cloud contrasted to the crystal blue heavens.

Travis stood with feet planted, thumbs in his belt. The insolent wind teased the long fringes of his tawny hunting jacket. "Dick, the thing about fighting is that yer supposed to win."

Baptiste laughed and added, "Boy, you gotta figger that Trudeau ain't a gonna worry about fair, neither. He ain't no gentleman. And, Dick, you gotta savvy this: Out heah, winning means living."

Richard stared at the bright blood on his fingers. "So what am I doing wrong?"

"Yer holding back. Now, try her again. Give her all ye've got. Fight with yer heart. C'mon. Try me." Travis gestured him onward.

Richard tasted blood and spit. "This is just practice. Do I have to bleed?"

"Hell, yes! Fighting ain't painless, coon. That nose ain't shit ter what Trudeau'll do ter ye. Here I come."

Richard squared his shoulders, knotted his fists, and Travis closed. This time, Richard blocked two of Travis's blows before a third landed in his gut. Richard doubled, thumped into the ground, and wheezed fer breath.

"C'mon, ye silly girl!" Travis cried, bounding from foot to foot. "Get up, ye stinking Yankee. Yer dog shit, boy! Farting philos'pher! Ye've got the guts of a buzzard!"

The mocking tone goaded him. The humiliation of that last blow, the indignity of his dripping nose, all broke loose at once, and he threw himself at Travis, a red rage burning free inside.

Clawing and scratching, Richard kicked and gouged, heedless of the blows that rained down on him. But Travis slipped inside, backheeled him, and dropped him to the ground.

"That's it!" Travis leapt back, a grin on his ruined face. "Ye turned yerself loose!"

"You son of a bitch!" Richard staggered to his feet.

"Them's fighting words!" Baptiste crowed.

"Whoa, now!" Travis held his hands wide. "That's just the first step. When yer a-fighting, rage is half of it. T'other half is in yer head. That's what we gotta work on next."

Richard glared, fists knotted.

"All right, coon. Come over hyar. Now, grab a-holt of me. What I just did was wrap my leg around ahind yers and push. Give her a try."

Richard did, while Baptiste pointed out the proper place to put his feet.

"Gonna have you all fit to whup Old Ephraim hisself," Baptiste declared. "Ain't nobody on the river knows knuckle and skull like ol' Travis Hartman."

Richard threw the hunter, surprised at what he'd done.

"Now, coon," Travis told him from flat on his back. "Jump plumb in the middle of my lights, and I'll show ye how ter gouge a man's eye out. Ain't gonna do her fer real, mind. I got lots ter see afore I goes under."

"Gouge a man's—"

"When ye fights, coon, ye fights fer yer life."

"But, Travis, a man's *eyes?* My God, that's—"

Baptiste stepped close, his black face grim. "Make yor choice now, white boy. Life ain't fair. It ain't just. Fighting ain't nothing more than two animals going at it to see who wins. Ain't no rules out heah. You win, yor alive. You lose..." Baptiste ran a suggestive finger across Richard's throat.

Reluctantly, Richard nodded. "All right, Travis, how do I gouge a man's eye out?"

Hours later, Richard picked at his blood-crusted nose as they waited by the side of the river for the *Maria.*

Travis sat cross-legged, peering intently at the ABCs scratched into the dirt. Baptiste lounged on his side, watching with amused interest. Laboriously Travis scratched out: T-R-A-V-I-S. Then wiped it out and started again.

"Gives a coon a curious feeling, a-wiping out his name like that. Injuns, they figger words got power, heap of medicine in 'em. Most like a-stepping on a grave."

Richard winced as he shifted his abused body. "Well, think of it this way. As long as you can write it again, you're still alive. And unlike the spoken word, the written one can last forever. Like those of Socrates, who spoke two thousand years ago. Were it not for writing, his thoughts would be long gone. All that wisdom, vanished forever."

"Tee. Are. Ay. Uh—"

"Vee."

"Yep. Vee. Eye. Snake. That's what it is."

"Ess."

"Wal, she looks like a snake ter me, coon. Them letter sign, wal, it's some harder ter cipher than this poor child ever figgered on."

Baptiste chimed in. "Where I comes from, it's agin' the law fo' niggers to larn to read."

"It's an immoral law," Richard replied. "They're afraid of what slaves would learn if they started to read. You might pick up a copy of Rousseau, or Hegel, and get ideas that might cause dissent."

"What?"

"Unrest. Rebellion. As long as the slaves are ignorant, they can be oppressed. In Boston, there are abolitionist factions who would change that."

Baptiste gave him a blank look.

"Abolitionists," Richard repeated. "People who want to abolish, do away with, slavery. It's quite fashionable among the intellectuals."

Baptiste picked a twig from the ground, cocked his jaw, and one by one, began to trace out the letters Richard had drawn. "Reckon I could larn, too. If'n it's agin' the law, this coon's fo' it."

Richard moved his sore arm, watching both men make letters in the sand.

Here I am, a prime candidate to die by violence, learning to fight like a ruffian, and teaching an escaped slave to read.

But the memory of Trudeau, of the triumphant look in his eyes, had burned into Richard's soul.

One day, Trudeau, you're going to regret that punch to the belly. So help me, God.

The anger of that promise sobered him enough to wonder, *What am I becoming?*

Richard climbed slowly to his feet, walking out into the trees. One nostril was still plugged with blood. Had that been him, clawing and kicking in red fury?

I was a wild man. The antithesis of everything I've ever believed.

He stopped to watch a squirrel dashing through the cottonwood branches overhead. Beyond the belt of trees lining the river, the plains stretched endlessly toward the western horizon. A man stood alone out there, naked to the eye of God. And from what Travis had told him, the plains stretched on for weeks, months—endless grass, caressed by the sun and wind, home of the buffalo and the Indian.

"*You can't lock* Tam Apo *into a lodge, Ritshard. He is everywhere...and can only be known here.*" And Willow had pointed to her heart. For the first time he fully understood the truth she'd taught.

The Power of raw God overwhelmed him; his sense of smallness crushed him. "How do we know what we know?" Professor Ames had asked as an introduction to the works of David Hume. "How does the mind perceive?"

In far-off England, safe amid the tame and fertile fields and the cozy, brick-paved streets, Hume could ponder such weighty questions. Here, in the wilderness, perception was pressed on a man. It wasn't to be examined, but experienced.

And where was Richard Hamilton to find rationality so close to raw God? He gazed out at the ocean of grass, and remembered waves marching endlessly across Boston Harbor.

So far away.

For long moments, he lost himself in the distance, seeking...what?

He walked on, struggling to fit together the changes within himself. In breaks through the trees, he could see the river, brown water chapped by the wind. In defiance of rationality, he'd come to sense the river's soul. Power, Willow would have told him. All things having a soul. An idea discarded millennia ago by Western civilization.

Or have we just disassociated ourself from the natural world?

That strange awareness of land and water, wind, storm, and sun, had fingered his soul, heedless of his rational mind. Yes, Power, a sort of spiritual essence, uncaring of men or their concerns. A force to be accepted, but never denied. This face of God cared not for the desires, prayers, and wants of men.

How silly to think God was only an internal experience. No wonder Willow dismissed the idea that God could be encompassed by a cathedral. What a silly thing a man was, how insignificant when abandoned in such a wilderness. Was that the revelation experienced by

Moses in the desert? Had such a forge tempered Augustine's soul in the isolated caves of Egypt?

Richard took a deep breath, trying to sort through his confusion.

I am learning to fight, to kill. Where is my purpose in this land of quick death?

Did God even care?

Richard stared down at his hands, those hands that had held the fusee that blew Packrat's life out of his body. No divine wrath had descended from the heavens. The Pawnee youth's red blood had drained out of his body, and the birds had continued to sing. Richard Hamilton had continued to breathe, eat, see, and feel. Only the flies had taken note of the fact that a life had been terminated —with little more effort than Travis wiping out his name.

"What kind of world is this?" Richard threw his head back, eyes closed, listening to the cottonwood leaves rattling overhead. The air moved against his skin. Nothing changed with death. Life was only meaningful for the living.

He shook his head, and when he opened his eyes, it took several seconds for the sight to sink in. The men walking slowly toward him carried half-lifted rifles and bows. They wore breechcloths, leather leggings, and feathers stuck into their gleaming black hair. No expression crossed their hard faces. Keen black eyes watched him warily as they spread out to surround him.

Richard filled his lungs and shouted: *"Travis!"*

CHAPTER THIRTEEN

As everything is useful for man, so, too, is man himself useful, and his singular characteristic function consists in making himself a member of the human herd, to be utilized for the common good, and serviceable to all. The extent to which he looks after his own interests is the measure to which he must also serve the interests of others, and so far as he serves their needs, he is taking care of himself: the one hand washes the other.

—Georg Friedrich Wilhelm Hegel, *Phenomenology of Mind*

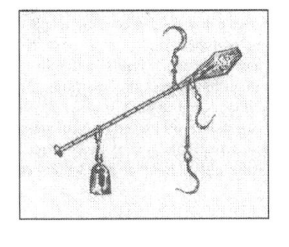

Travis dodged from tree to tree, his Hawken in hand. There! He caught sight of movement, signaled Baptiste, and ducked low as he scuttled behind one of the thick cotton-woods.

Hamilton stood surrounded by six warriors. They'd cornered the Yankee fair, and the leader was fingering Richard's clothing, paying particular attention to the coup at his belt.

Travis filled his lungs and bellowed, *"Waugh!"*

At the call, the Sioux whirled, weapons ready. To the side, Baptiste had wriggled up behind a log, slipping his Hawken over the scaling bark.

"Dakota!" Travis cried, walking out and making the hand sign for good. *"Wash-te!"*

Richard threw him a terrified but grateful glance. Travis chuckled, and called out, "Dick, if'n ye gets any more scairt, yer eyes is gonna pop plumb outa yer body and ye'll be blinder than a cussed gopher!"

The Sioux shuffled uncertainly, staring about, worried that there might be more Whites.

"Stand up, Baptiste," Travis called. "Let 'em know they got a shooter on them."

Baptiste raised himself to a sitting position, his Hawken braced for a shot.

In signs, Travis gestured, "We are friends. Traders. A boat is just downriver with many men. You have something to trade?"

This was the part that puckered a man's string. The Sioux glanced back and forth, evaluating their chances. Travis held his breath; then the leader smiled, signing, "It is good to see our White brothers. Traders are always welcome among the Water Spirit's people."

Water Spirit, *Wah-Menitu;* so that's who the tall coon was. A Teton Sioux chief, Water Spirit, could go either way depending on how his medicine played out. Maybe he'd lift hair, or maybe he'd be a man's best friend.

"Wah-Menitu" Travis called out loud. *"Wash-te!* It is good."

At a command from Wah-Menitu, the other Sioux lowered their weapons.

"C'mon out, Baptiste, but keep yer iron ready."

"Got that right," Baptiste agreed, rising slowly.

Wah-Menitu made the sign for "It is good." He was a lodgepole of a man, thin of frame and tall. Scars puckered the skin on his breasts. When he smiled, his projecting upper lip exposed worn yellow teeth. The aquiline nose hooked like a bird of prey's. Copper bracelets, tarnished as dark as the flesh beneath, decorated his sinewy arms. Tin cones held the horsehair tassels on his moccasins.

He pointed to the coup on Richard's belt. "Whose?" he signed.

"Pawnee," Travis signed back. "A warrior named Packrat."

At that, the Sioux yipped and began to leap about in enthusiastic joy. Richard had begun to sweat, his balled fists pressed desperately to his sides. If he stood any stiffer, his joints were going to snap like dry sassafras sticks.

"Easy, Dick. Ye ain't dead yet. Stay calm, coon. They's just glad ter see ye."

Wah-Menitu touched the scalp reverently, then threw his arms around Richard in a bear hug that nigh to squeezed the grease out of the Yankee. The rest of the Sioux continued to leap and yip their shrill calls.

"What...what's happening?" Richard gasped.

"Made friends, coon." Travis laughed in spite of himself.

And ifn old Dick ever figgers out what that "fetish" is, he's gonna come plumb unstuck.

"Now, Dick. Whoop and holler a little yerself. C'mon, coon. Dance and shout! Join 'em. Or, yer wolf meat!"

His back rigid as a keel, Richard jerked into step. Had his voice not been cracking, the whoops would have sounded a little more enthusiastic. The way Richard pirouetted reminded Travis of a stick figure on a string.

The Sioux didn't seem to mind. They leapt and shrieked, nimble as hunting cats.

"What am I doing, Travis?" Richard shot him a frightened glance.

"Why, making friends, Dick."

"Am I gonna die?"

"Reckon. But ifn ye'll dance a little harder, it won't be hyar and now."

Richard jumped and bucked like a spring foal.

Baptiste sidled up to Travis, whispering, "Now, don't that beat all?"

"Reckon so. Ifn his perfessers could just see him."

Travis stepped forward, grinning, and as the dance wore down, offered his hand around, smiling and shaking. Baptiste did the same, one hand still gripping his rifle.

"Smoke," Wah-Menitu said in English.

"Waugh!" Travis made a gesture and seated himself, digging his pipe and fixings out of his possibles. With flint and steel, one of the young warriors conjured a fire, and Travis used a twig to light his pipe.

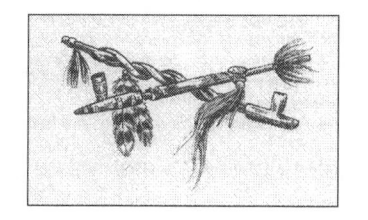

Travis glanced up at the nervous Hamilton. "Sit down, Dick. Right hyar next ter me. That's right. We's gonna have us a palaver." Travis puffed his pipe to seat the fire, offered it to the four directions, and handed it to Wah-Menitu. The Sioux made his offering to the four sacred ways, to sky and earth, then puffed before handing the pipe to the next man. In silence, it made the rounds to Dick.

"Do like they done," Travis coached. "Follow the directions sunwise, then up and down. In the beginning, White Buffalo Cow Woman taught the Sioux how to use the pipe. Tobacco's sacred. Takes prayers to *Wakantanka,* to God. All words spoken here will be spoken truthfully."

Richard did as he was told, but his fingers shook as he offered the pipe and took a puff.

In signs, Travis said, "You gave my young friend a start. He thought you might have been Pawnee."

The Sioux laughed uproariously.

"You have boat?" Wah-Menitu asked.

"Downriver a mite. Be hyar soon."

"Our village is one day's travel upriver."

"He talks," Richard whispered in surprise.

"Hell, he got a tongue and talker like everybody else," Travis chided. To Wah-Menitu, Travis said and signed, "I am Travis Hartman, this is Dick Hamilton, and hyar's Baptiste. We will come to your village." He lifted his foot to show the hole in his moccasin. "Reckon I'm right keen ter trade, hoss."

The Sioux laughed again.

Wah-Menitu was studying Travis with hard black eyes. He said, "I know of you, Trawis Hartman. It is said yer a great warrior and a man of yer word. You have wintered with the Dakota before. Helped with the hunt. Shared our lodges and fires."

"Time or two, I reckon."

Wah-Menitu gestured to indicate the scars on Travis's face. "The bear left his sign. Only a strong man would keep his hair...and the bear lifted some of yers."

"Yep, wal, I reckon I got a sight more of his than he got of mine."

Wah-Menitu smiled. "It will be good to have you. Shining times for you, booshway. *Beaucoup* vittles." Wah-Menitu reached over to touch the coup on Hamilton's belt. "The Teton Dakota always have a welcome for warriors. We will dance...honor Dick for his courage and victory. Not all White coons are strong and brave."

"Damn that cussed Leavenworth anyway. Ye fought the Ree two years back?"

"Yer Leavenworth, and his soldiers, have water for blood."

Travis snorted. "Some do. Not all."

"But you, friends, are some. You are warriors. You come with yer boat, Trawis Hartman. Dance. Eat. *Wash-te.*"

Richard leaned close. "What's *wash-te?* They keep saying that."

"Means good."

They stood, everyone smiling, shaking hands, and Wah-Menitu called out, "*Hooka'hay!*"

The Sioux let out blood-curdling screams again, and danced away through the trees.

Travis replaced his pipe, and said, "C'mon. We'd best hustle and make sure we still got hosses. Be just like them red varmints ter have lifted 'em while we was a-palavering."

"But they said they were friends," Richard cried.

"Whar ye been all yer life, Yankee?" Baptiste muttered. "Among Injuns, even friends steal each other's hosses."

"I was someplace sane," Richard muttered as they trotted back toward the horses.

Travis grinned again. If the pilgrim thought today was a scare, he'd be plumb twisted come tomorrow night.

"Sioux." At mention of the word the assembled *engagés* peered fearfully out at trees turned so suddenly ominous in the twilight.

Heals Like A Willow shifted nervously as she, too, stared into the woods. She knew the Sioux as *Bambi-ji'mina,* the Cuts-Off-A-Head People. And their sign was the cut-throat sign. Among her people, only the *Pa'kiani* were more hated.

The entire attitude of the party had changed. The engagés, normally of cheerful countenance come the evening camp, now fidgeted. An unbidden shiver ran down her back.

Trawis, Ritshard, and Baptiste stood at the center of the knot of men. Behind them, *Maria* lay snugged tight to the bank by her painter. Green stood halfway up the plank, thumb thrust in his belt.

"All right," Green called out. "Before we eat, I want trees drug up. Let's fort up. Horses inside, and double guard tonight. Baptiste, take first watch. Dick, you're in charge of second, and Travis third. I don't want anybody wandering out into the dark, hear?"

As Willow studied the men's faces, she decided any such order was needless.

"How many Sioux?" Trudeau asked.

"Handful," Trawis stated. "But we ain't taking no chances, not with Sioux. Hell, after Dick hyar got ter dancing with 'em, I figger he wore them varmints plumb out."

"Dancing?" Green asked. Trudeau scowled his disbelief.

"Hell, yes! Jumping and screaming like a young buck back from his first hoss raid," Trawis cried. "Why, ye should have seen 'em! Dick had 'em bunched up in a circle by the time we got there. If'n they'd had a fight on, all Baptiste and me woulda had ter do would be plug them coons from the trees."

Green lifted an eyebrow.

Ritshard looked sheepish.

Trudeau snorted and stomped off in disgust.

"You heard me, now. Let's get forted up. Nobody eats until I'm satisfied." Green waved them away. "And I don't want nobody out there alone gathering logs. Groups of three, and sing out the second you see anything."

The *engagés* muttered among themselves as they started for the trees. Trudeau kept glancing back over his shoulder and swearing sourly.

Green turned. "Travis? What's your opinion?"

Trawis pulled thoughtfully at his beard as he walked up to the plank. "Reckon they won't try anything. That's just a hunch, Dave. The way I figger, they's been starved fer trade last few years. Might have a couple of kids sneak out just fer a try at the hosses. One of them 'Just ter show ye we could do her' raids. Mostly, I'd guess that Wah-Menitu would want 'em ter leave us alone."

Green glanced at Baptiste, who said, "I'd say the same, Booshway. Way I read it, Wah-Menitu's savvy enough to know he'll get more from happy traders than mad ones."

"And Dick had 'em circled up?"

Ritshard flushed red, glancing down at the toes of his moccasins.

"Just the way I told ye," Trawis said with a twinkle.

"Shore 'nuff," Baptiste added, straight-faced.

"Uh-huh." Green looked at Willow. "I want you on the boat. No sense in baiting the Sioux with a Snake woman. You'll be a heap safer aboard."

Willow reached down to the war club tied at her waist. "I am no *white* woman, Green."

"Oh, I know that, Willow. But I want you out of harm's way, hear?"

She glanced at Trawis, who nodded, fixing her with those knowing blue eyes. "It ain't a' gonna hurt nothing to stay on the boat fer a couple of days. These Sioux, they're a sneaky bunch."

Ritshard looked up. "Please, Willow?"

One by one, she read their souls. Green wanted her safe for his trade. Trawis worried that a friend might come to harm. And Ritshard? That look betrayed the ache in his heart should anything happen to her.

"I will do this. But if there is fighting, I will take my bow and arrows and fight like a *Dukurika"*

"It'd be a help," Trawis replied.

Ritshard kicked hesitantly at the dirt, then looked up with resignation. "Mr. Green? Just a moment." Ritshard walked up to the plank. He clenched his fists, face strained. "I...I'd like a rifle. Not that Pawnee's trade gun, but a Hawken. One like Travis's. And powder and ball."

Green glanced at Trawis and saw his scarred eyebrow raise. "You want a rifle?"

Ritshard shrugged. "Yes, sir. I do."

"Why?" Green cocked his head. "I thought you were going to run the first chance you got. Why should I take a risk on a rifle?"

Ritshard took a breath. "On my word as a gentleman, I won't run off with your rifle."

"But you might still run off."

Ritshard swallowed, struggling with himself. "I...I won't run off—at least, not yet. Not with the Sioux so close."

Willow noticed the barely suppressed smirk on Trawis's face. Baptiste's black eyes glinted as he leaned on his rifle.

Green cast another glance at Trawis, who nodded. "All right, Hamilton. It'll go against your wages. You understand?"

Ritshard now stood lodgepole-straight. "Yes, sir. I understand."

Green shrugged. "Come on, then. I'll fetch you a rifle. I just hope to God you're better at shooting Indians than you are at dancing with them."

As Ritshard walked past, Willow could see the gleam in his eyes, as if he'd just proven something to the world, and himself.

She turned to Trawis. "He did well today?"

Trawis grinned outright. "Wal, now, I reckon with a little work, he'll come around. He's a-fixing ter be more than he figgers he can. Just you be careful the next couple of days, Willow. Them Sioux, they might go fer the hosses, but they'd sure as hell make a try fer ye. If'n they do, it'll mean a fight to get ye back, understand?"

"Why fight for me?"

Trawis patted her shoulder. "'Cause yer one of us." Then he walked out to supervise the forting up.

Baptiste touched a finger to the brim of his hat before he followed the hunter.

One of them? She sighed as she began collecting wood, careful to stay within the bounds of the camp. Trudeau was watching her as he worked, stripping her with his eyes. She glared back at him, and spat contemptuously.

"No, Trawis. I am *Dukurika*. I can never be anything else." The day would come when she would leave them. She hoped that it would not hurt Ritshard or Trawis. But they would forget. Such was the nature of men: red or white.

In the meantime, she would stay on the boat. Given a choice, she'd take thieving Pawnee over cut-throat Sioux any day.

When the night skies finally darkened, and ominous silence settled on the camp, Ritshard walked over to her fire, his new rifle in hand. He seated himself on a blanket, staring wearily at the flames before inspecting the stew she'd set to boil over the coals.

"Long day," he said, a faint smile playing on his lips. He turned brown eyes on her. The intimate inquisitiveness of his look brought a tingle to her heart.

"You are lucky the Sioux didn't kill you and cut yer head off." Then she smiled, and for a long moment their eyes held.

"But they didn't. It's so different, Willow. Not Boston at all."

"Boston. Always Boston. Tell me of this place."

He rubbed his face, the tenuous intimacy gone. "Willow, sometimes things must be lived to be understood." He gestured around. "This is your country. Boston, well, it's like a completely different world. So many people, endless buildings and paved streets. Those words don't mean anything to you, do they? I can't explain it any more than you could have explained this to me a year ago."

She stirred the stew, glancing at him from the corner of her eye. "This is *not* my country. My land is high, what is the word—mountains? The trees are different, and air is clear and cool. The colors are brighter, even the dirt. From the mountains, I can see forever, the way *Tam Apo* and eagle see."

He rolled onto his stomach, gazing up at her. "What was it like, growing up in a place like that?"

She tasted the rich stew and laid the ladle to one side. "My father, High Wolf, he let me do things the other children couldn't. I like to think he saw something special in me, but it was probably just because I was his favorite. He let me hold his sacred things, and listen to their voices, even though I was a girl. Since he was a great *puhagan,* no one said anything."

"He wanted you to be a medicine man, too?"

"No. At least, he didn't really encourage me. But I wasn't strange, or anything."

"What do you mean, strange?"

"Sometimes, when Power lives in a person, he acts strangely. You can see it. A hollow look in the eyes. The head cocked, listening to spirit things other people can't hear. As a child, I was like the other children. I played among the rocks and trees, seeking out brother marmot and hunting rabbits. As children, we would build little mountain-sheep traps. The littlest children got to be the mountain sheep and the older children drove them into the trap and threw blankets over them. I was always hard to catch." She grinned at him, the memories so fresh in her souls.

His eyes twinkled, as if imagining her as a child. "It sounds like fun." He idly twisted the grass into knots. "I never played much. I didn't have many friends."

"Boston is not full of children?"

"Oh, yes, full of them. I just didn't get out to play much. Father was always so busy. Jeffry and the other slaves took care of me. Mostly I read books. They were my friends."

She wondered just what a book was, Ritshard talked

of them so much. "This way you lived, it doesn't sound good, Ritshard."

He shrugged. "It was all I knew. How about you? Did you see your father often?"

"Every night." She looked up at the trees, the branches lit by firelight. "After we ate, Father would play with us. Sometimes he was Coyote, and chased us around trying to eat us. But when he caught us, he just tickled us until our bellies hurt. He told us the stories about the beginning of the world, and how *Tam Apo* made things. Mother would nod at all of the important places. Then, when I started to fall asleep, Father would carry me to the robes and tuck me in."

"How lucky you were." He frowned, still toying with the grass. Finally he asked, "What did you want out of life?"

She lifted an eyebrow. "Want out of life?"

"What did you think you'd be doing? I mean, what did you dream of being?"

She paused. She'd only told High Wolf, and then, only once. A woman did not speak of such things. But Ritshard was different, and the honest interest in his eyes overcame her reserve. "I wanted to be *a puhagan,* just like my father. I wanted to know all the things he knew. To cure, to sing, and to seek *Tam Apo."* She hesitated, unsure of herself. "I do not talk of these things, Ritshard. They are between us and no one else."

"Why?" He cocked his head. "Your people wouldn't approve?"

She looked around, then bent down close to meet his eyes.

"Among my people, women do not seek *puha.* It is said to be dangerous, that a woman might not be strong enough, that she would damage the Power and use it for evil."

"Like a witch?"

"What is this word?"

"A woman who uses magic—uh, power—for evil. To kill and inflict disease."

"Witch." She sounded out the White word.

"Did your husband know you wanted power?"

"A little." She backed away then, averting her eyes.

"Did...did you love him?"

"Yes." The memory stung her.

And I couldn't save him in the end.

To avoid more hurt, she asked, "Did you ever love, Ritshard?"

He shrugged, lips parting as if to speak, hesitated, and said, "I didn't do well with girls. They just didn't...I couldn't talk to them. Do you understand? They weren't interested in philosophy, in ideas. They just wanted to be pretty and admired."

"White women," she said sourly.

He chuckled uneasily. "Yes, white women." Then his brow lined. "Oh, someday I'll have to marry, I suppose. Father always expected it of me. Later, you understand, after I'd proven myself, I'd be quite a catch, rich, capable of providing a good home. A friend of mine has a sister. A very attractive young lady."

"And this *lady* will be pretty...in her house...and admired?"

"Yes. Just that." He studied her pensively. "I could do a lot worse. Laura is a very charming girl."

Willow watched him. "Is that what you want, Ritshard? Charming? Or do you want Power, and truth, and all the pain it brings?"

He shrugged, looking away into the night so that she couldn't read his expression.

Willow dished out a bowl of stew and handed it to Ritshard before filling her own. She was becoming proficient in the use of the little metal spoon. Why did her fingers suddenly seem so clumsy?

She said, "My father was disappointed that I married a *Ku'chendikani*. I think he wanted me to stay with the *Dukurika*. But when I made my choice, he smiled and wished me well."

"How lucky you were." Richard blew to cool the stew. "By the time I return, Laura will no doubt be married to that irritating Tom Hanson, and I'll probably end up with some blithering shrew who faints all the time."

"I don't know all those words."

He waved it away as inconsequential.

"I think you have been lonely all of your life, Ritshard. It should not always be so."

"Maybe not, but in Boston there aren't many women like...." He glanced away, swallowing hard.

"Like me?" Her souls began to stir uneasily, like snakes twining around each other.

He started to nod, then shook himself. "Some things, Willow..."

She waited. "What is it, Ritshard?"

"Oh, life, the way people are. God, what a sorry mess we are! I think your people are a lot smarter than mine."

"People should be who they are."

He kept sneaking glances at her.

"Ritshard, your eyes have changed. Now, you look at me as a man looks at a woman."

He glanced down at his empty bowl. "I'm sorry."

"You do not have to be sorry."

"A gentleman does not look at a lady that way."

She bent down, staring into his eyes again. "I am not White, Ritshard. I am Heals Like A Willow, a *Dukurika* woman. I am not a lady."

His lips parted as he reached up to touch the side of her face. "Lord God, what you just said. If you only knew how I..."

Then he shook his head. Rising to his feet, he said, "Thank you for supper, Willow. Travis needs me. I...I've got to go." And he hurried away into the darkness.

Willow took a deep breath to settle her writhing souls, and exhaled wearily. In silence, she watched the fire burn down to glowing red coals.

———

"You been quiet all day," Baptiste noted. "Got the Injun shivers?"

"No." Richard shook his head as he led the string of horses. He'd had an odd dream the night before, as if he'd floated over the land, draped in a foggy white haze. He'd been seeking something, unable to find it in the mist. And there at the end, he'd felt someone watching, staring at him out of the mist.

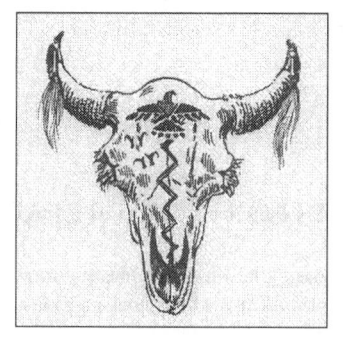

The whole day had been eerie. Walking along with Baptiste, he couldn't shake the uneasy feeling. Maybe Baptiste was right, and it was nothing more than a case of Sioux-induced nerves.

The abandoned Arikara village they'd passed that morning hadn't helped matters. The place consisted of nothing but big round depressions, as if God's finger had dimpled the flats. Timbers stuck out here and there, most of them charred and splintered. A thick carpet of grass had already reclaimed the town, but an occasional broken piece of clay pot, a scattering of burned bone and beads, could be found. Open storage pits were a hazard for man and beast.

Something about the old Ree town depressed the spirit and dampened any optimism the morning might have had. Who had those people been? Once, children had played and chased among the domed houses. Men and women had smiled at each other and built bright futures out of dreams.

The most unsettling sight for Richard had been the skull. Baptiste pointed out where a coyote had dug out a den in the side of a low earthen mound. Just inside the hole, half lodged in the soil, the skull had lain, watching with dirt-filled eye sockets.

To avoid his thoughts, he pointed at the engagés. "I can't believe the change in them."

The men struggled along the bank, dodging around cotton-woods that hung out over the water. Instead of gay songs, jokes, and good humor, they labored in silence, as if doom hung over their bobbing heads instead of the bright late-spring sky.

"They's worried 'bout Sioux," Baptiste told him.

Baptiste squinted up at the sun as they walked along, feet swishing the new grass. The horses followed reluctantly on their lead ropes; they wound their way around the gray boles of cottonwoods and paused only long enough to crop a mouthful of grass.

Richard and Baptiste paralleled the bank, staying close to the sweating men on the cordelle. Baptiste's gaze never rested as he scanned the grassy bottoms, the branches overhead, the tangles of deadfall and driftwood.

But what an odd dream. Not in his wildest imagination had he ever been a cloud before. And what had he been looking for?

What have I always been looking for? Truth, ultimate reality, an understanding of myself and the world around me.

"Want to talk about it?" Baptiste asked suddenly. "If'n you got a sense of something, you tell ol' Baptiste. In this country, a feller best heed his hunches."

"It's nothing. Honest. Just a dream I had last night."

"You wasn't scalped and dead, was you?"

"No. Nothing like that." And Richard laughed to relax. "Oh, all right. I dreamed I was a cloud."

Baptiste grunted, and renewed his wary inspection of the quiet trees around them.

Richard tightened his grip on the Hawken, reassured by the slim rifle's weight. He'd loaded it the night before, careful not to spill a single grain of powder. He could still feel the ramrod pushing the half-inch ball down the smooth rifling, seating it against the powder. Knowing his life might depend on it, he'd taken special care with that load.

He cast another glance at the *engagés*. "It doesn't make sense. I've seen them skip from log to log across a flooded embarras. I mean, the slightest misstep, and they'd fall into the torrent, be swept away before anyone could lend a hand. And they do it *singing!*"

"French is curious coons," Baptiste said with a shrug.

"Way I figgers it, men got different fears. These French... maybe it's something Catholic, about being scalped and cut up. Killed in blood. I ain't Catholic, so I don't know. But a boatman, he don't scare a hair over bad water that shivers my bones. Hunt up Injun sign, though, and he plum turns to quivers."

"They didn't seem so nervous when we crossed Osage, Kansa, and Maha country."

"Them's tame Injuns." Baptiste pulled his big black hat off and wiped a sleeve across his sweaty forehead.

"Tame?"

"I tell you, Dick, I been out heah nigh onta fourteen years now. River's changing, and it's white men what's doing it. Tame means broke, hear?"

"How's that?"

"Missouri, Oto, Omaha...they used to rule the river. Remember Blackbird? That Omaha chief buried up on the mountain? Why, he's like most was. These Injuns, they get their time with the coming of the whites. But it don't last. Think back. How many Injuns did you see on the way upriver? Reckon not more than a handful—and them in rags. Just like that drunk Omaha selling his squaw. The rest was all out fo' the spring buffler hunt. Used to be they'd hunt buffler within a couple of days' ride of the village. Now they be gone fo' months. Buffler's plumb scarce on the lower river, hoss. But so's the Injuns. I heard tales of the Kansa—the Wind People, they called themselves. Them and the Missouri, they controlled the lower river a while back. They's just a handful now."

"Why? The constant war?"

Baptiste squinted, a bitter twist on his lips. "Maybe. But I figger it's more. It's white men. They's like a plague rolling slow across the land. Like them locusts in Egypt. Look back, Dick. Ain't nothing atwixt us and the frontier but a dead zone—just like that village we passed this morning—and it's filling with whites. Farmers, you know. The great tribes, the Oto, Ioway, the Big Osages, the Mahas...hell, they ain't shit now. Disease kilt most of 'em. Why, I seen piles of bodies after that pox come through. Whole villages left standing empty—and nothing but dead bodies a-laying where they fell. Biblical, I tell you. Plumb biblical."

"You make it sound like the Apocalypse."

"Reckon you and I, we got different ideas about white folks."

"How's that?"

"You ain't never been no slave."

Richard considered as he scanned the country for lurking Sioux thieves. "Not all white people are bad. I told you about the abolitionists. Some of us believe that all men have the same potential."

"In Boston."

"Yes."

"Wal, Dick, I tell ye, that ain't normal fo' white folks. Most of 'em take, and take some more. Them farmers down to Saint Loowee? I don't go there. They look at me, and they sees a nigger, a man what otta be a slave. Hell, them coons live in them dinky log huts, scratching in the dirt, living in it. They don't know nothing but what's in their Bibles—if'n they can even read at all. And they looks down on me. *Me,* what's seen the Shining Mountains, taken a plew, and sat side by side with warriors. Them's yor white folks, Dick."

"But here you are, partnered up with white folks."

"Yep, but this is the wilderness. That's a heap different. Men be free heah. Larn this, Dick. Out heah, it's what you do, how you act, that gets you judged. Ain't no color of yor skin that counts a damn when the Rees come a-fogging down on you, or the cordelle breaks. Yes, sir, it's what's in a man's soul that makes him poor bull or fat beaver out heah."

Baptiste threw his head back, broad nostrils flared as if scenting the winds of freedom. "Won't last, though. Them farmers, they gonna come and kill all this land. You'll see. But afore that, this coon's gonna be gone under. That's some, it is. I reckon I'll go as a warrior. Proud. This child's gonna die like a man."

Richard walked wide around a pile of debris left by a long-past flood. He peered intently into the tangle of logs, branches, and old brush, seeking any sign of a lurking Sioux.

"Yor a-larning," Baptiste said with a smile. "Come cat scratch, a feller can hole up in a pile of junk like that. Old John Colter, he hid under a mess of embarras that time the Blackfoot cornered him. Always look to the holes come tough times. They can shore 'nuff save yor life."

Richard licked his lips. "But getting back to what you were saying. Whites don't ruin everything."

"Huh! Yor a white man what can go where you wants, do what you wants. Try 'er as a black man, or an Injun. White folk make things plumb shining fo' other white folk. But they sure as hell ruin everything fo' everyone else."

"That's not so. They bring civilization..." The words stuck in his throat.

"You was saying?"

Everything he'd said to Charles Eckhart on the journey down the Ohio came back to haunt him. Those bitter fights with his father about commerce defeating the higher callings of man, were they just words? The silly ideas of a spoiled young man living in the land of plenty?

"I was about to argue against everything I've come to believe about civilization."

Baptiste seemed not to hear as he continued, "I'll tell you about yor civilization. It's built on the ruin of others. I had me a squaw one winter. Shawnee, she was. Died of fever that next spring. She's the last of her family—a cousin to Tecumseh and the Prophet. Rest of her kin was killed of smallpox or shot dead by white soldiers."

Baptiste gripped his rifle in emphasis. "The Shawnee, they owned that whole Ohio country, boy. And now, they ain't but memories. I tell you, it'll be the same heah real soon. Nothing but memories of the Injuns...and farms as far as the eye can see. Nothing free then, not even the birds in the sky."

"And the Sioux? You think we'll destroy them, too?"

"Yep. And the Rees, Arapaho, and Blackfeet. Them and all the rest. Even the Mandan. Hell, probably the Mandan fust. They likes white men. White man always ruins his friends fust."

"What do Travis and Green say when you talk like that?"

"Travis, he agrees. Reckon Green does, too. They just figger a feller's gotta make what he can. You come cross country from yor Boston, what did you see? White folks everywhere. How're you gonna stop 'em, Dick? Spout a little philos'phy to them farmers? Whar they gonna go? Back to Virginia, maybe back to yor Boston? Ain't no room fo' 'em all.

"Naw, Dick, it's just the way things is. That said, all a coon can do is make his way whilst he can. That's what this beaver's a-doing. Anything else is like trying to stop the wind."

They'd reached a place where the Missouri curved out in a wide loop. *Maria* had pulled over to the shore, the *engagés* hauling in the long cordelle and coiling it on the deck before breaking out the poles. Richard could see Willow sitting cross-legged on the cargo box. She held her bow in one hand. Even from here she looked regal. Perhaps it was the way she held her head, proud and high.

"We'll slip across this neck"—Baptiste pointed—"and meet 'em when they comes around t'other side."

"You know, it would be a lot shorter trip if the river ran straight."

Baptiste gave him a grin. "Yep, but like I told ye, it's just the way things is."

"Do you think we'll make Wah-Menitu's village by dark?"

"Reckon. Old Travis, he'll have scouted the whole way."

"Think he's all right? Going up ahead like he did?"

"That coon could sneak up on old Hob hisself. If'n thar be an ambush up ahead, Travis'll sniff her out. He's hell on Injun sign, that coon is."

"What if it comes to a fight? What do I do?"

"Don't shoot till the last." Baptiste plodded ahead after making sure the horses were following. "You got one shot in that Hawken. Injuns generally don't charge lessen they knows they can take you. Why, I've seen one man hold off thirty Injuns with a loaded rifle. A band of warriors knows that whoever makes the first play, he's gonna get shot. I tell you, it settles a man's blood to stare down a rifle barrel."

Remembering the gaping maw of Green's pistol, Richard could agree.

"That's the secret—and it ain't no sure thing. Keep that shot till you needs 'er. That's the only thing a man's got going fo' him when he's outnumbered. The Injuns might know they can kill you, but yor taking more of them rascals with you than they're getting. If Injuns figger they'll get one scalp to the loss of three, most times they'll back off."

What would Kant or Hegel make of that?

Richard shook his head. "I hope I never have to find out."

As the sun slanted into the western sky, the *Maria* rounded yet another of the river's oxbows, and Travis walked out onto the riverbank to watch them approach. A number of Sioux warriors stepped out of the trees to stand behind him.

Richard and Baptiste checked the lead ropes one last time to ensure that none of the stock were loose. The horses approached the waiting men with pricked ears.

Richard swallowed hard, sweaty hand tightening on the rifle. Nothing in the world could have reassured him like the feel of that hard wood and steel. He yearned for his father's pistol—the one he'd so foolishly left behind in that other world. What a reassurance it would be. In that instance, at least, his father had been right.

Travis leaned on his rifle, a huge smile twisting the scars on his maimed face. "About time ye coons made her this far. Right up round the bend hyar, thar be a good place ter camp. Little creek runs out along a grassy flat. Dick, reckon you and Baptiste can make a picket fer the hosses."

"How far to Wah-Menitu's village?" Baptiste asked before striding forward to shake hands with the grinning warriors.

"'Bout a half mile. They's camped up on the bench above the river where the breeze keeps the skeeters off."

Richard forced a smile and ceremoniously shook hands with each of the warriors. They looked fierce enough—keen-eyed, with faces that could have been carved of dark walnut. Streaks of yellow, red, and black paint decorated cheeks and foreheads. Several had feathers stuck lopsided in greased hair. A small leather pouch—sometimes beaded or covered with quillwork—was suspended from each neck. Brightly painted bags with long fringe and beadwork hung from breechclouts. Fringed moccasins and colored blankets made up the rest of their apparel. Each carried a bow, a war club, or a trade gun. The latter exhibited polished brass tacks driven into the stocks in geometric patterns.

Maria had come into sight, the *engagés* poling her nervously onward. Trudeau shouted at those on cordelle to keep them moving. Green waved from his place on the cargo box beside Henri. Willow was conspicuously absent. Inside the boat, no doubt.

Travis led the way toward the campsite, walking in the midst of the warriors. He talked with the Sioux, hands making signs despite the rifle he carried. To Richard's eyes, it looked like the reunion of long lost friends.

Richard started at a rustling in the grass to his left. There, hidden so carefully, lay two young boys, big-eyed and excited at having sneaked so close to the White men.

Richard nodded at them. One gasped, while the other leapt to his feet and charged off, only to be outrun by his frightened companion.

"Kids is kids anywhere," Baptiste noted with a shake of the head.

More Sioux, Wah-Menitu in the forefront, waited silently in the clearing Travis had chosen for their camp. What thoughts were passing behind those black eyes? Richard could see women standing behind the men at the edge of the fringe of trees.

Travis stopped and spread his hands wide, shouting in Sioux. Wah-Menitu barked out an answer, and lifted his pipe. The Sioux surged forward.

"What do I do now?" Richard whispered. His nerves tightened.

"Smile and act glad ta see 'em." Baptiste grinned like it was a birthday.

Richard met grin with grin, bobbing his head, enduring the hugs and cries of amazement as fingers felt his fetish. The horses stamped and shied until it was all Richard could do to hold his string.

The camp Travis had located proved perfect. Four trees stood in a small clearing beside the slow stream. The river lay no more than a hundred yards away.

"Throw yer picket around them trees." Travis pointed out the four. "We'll pen the hosses thar. Reckon we can pitch the camps round the outside." He raised a grizzled eyebrow. "Get my drift, thar, Dick?"

"I do." Surrounded, the horses would be much harder to steal.

As *Maria* pulled up, the Sioux rushed down to watch, babbling in excitement as the wary *engagés* lowered the plank and tied off the painter. Even as Richard watched, more Indians appeared out of the trees, clustering around the boat.

"Green'll be needing help," Travis said softly. "I got ter go down and keep them red coons from swarming the boat. See ter yer hosses, Dick. Then come give me a hand. Baptiste?"

Together the two stalked off toward the growing crowd of Sioux. Richard hurried to stretch his pickets and crowd the horses into the enclosure. As he pulled hobbles and halters from the packs, Sioux women were picking their way toward the boat, backs bent under doubled hides. Squealing children and yapping dogs followed in their wake.

Richard checked and double-checked the picket, making sure each horse was secure.

Toussaint and Louis de Clerk trotted up, packing blankets and a rifle. To Richard, Toussaint said, "We take care of the horses. The booshway wants you at the boat."

Richard grabbed up his rifle and headed for the knot of Sioux crowded around the *Maria*.

He shouldered through the throng, surprised by the smoky smell of the Indians. The women watched him with wary black eyes while suddenly-quiet children clung to their leather skirts.

At the plank, Green had set up his table and taken a chair. A pile of buffalo hides was already laid out for inspection while Wah-Menitu stood with arms crossed, talking in mixed Sioux and English with Green. Travis and Baptiste stood to either side, guarding the plank that led to the boat.

Richard sidled up next to Travis. "What's happening?"

"Trade. Reckon it'll go on till about midnight. After that, we'll mosey up ter the village fer a feast."

Richard scanned the growing crowd of Sioux. "They'll clean us out."

"Yep, if'n they could." A gleam came to Travis's eye. "That's the art of trade, Dick: Give as little as ye can fer as much as ye can get—but don't rile the Sioux in the process. That's whar Davey shines. He's got the savvy fer it. This child don't."

Baptiste added, "That's why he's Booshway, and I ain't."

At the same time, Henri was carrying out blankets, hanks of beads, gun flints, mirrors, knives, lead, and other items. He spread several blankets on the ground and laid out the articles atop them.

"Injuns want ter see it all, make up their minds about what they want ter trade fer," Travis explained. Even as he spoke the Sioux crowded around, fingering needles, kettles, and iron arrowpoints. Bolts of colored cloth passed from hand to hand amidst muttering and some little shoving.

"Is that wise?" Richard asked, indicating a warrior who picked up an ax and walked away.

"He ain't a gonna steal it. See that mean-looking rascal yonder with the black stripe painted across his eyes? He's a soldier, like camp police. He's a-watching. Wah-Menitu don't want no trouble over this."

"But they'd take the horses."

"That ain't trade, that's stealing."

Richard scratched the back of his neck. "So, why steal a horse, but not the ax?"

"'Cause it's the rules, Dick. And if'n that coon did walk off with the ax, that soldier yonder would make him bring it back."

"Honor among thieves?"

"Listen up, Dick. Ye camps in a Sioux village, ye can leave yer possibles whar ye will. Nobody'll touch 'em. Or, if'n they do, they'll bring 'em right back after they done used 'em fer whatever. Ree and Crow, now, that's a sight different. They'll steal ye plumb blind given half a chance. Most folks, they don't steal from their own kind. It'd be... wal, it just don't happen."

"And if someone does?"

"They cast his arse out in the snow and let him freeze. Sort of like that Omaha. That, or the thief's relatives whack him in the back of the head some night rather than have the culprit bring down shame on the family."

"Some sense of justice."

"Yep. Wal, I reckon it works a sight better'n ours." Travis studied Richard from the corner of his eye. "Now, when we get up ter the village, ye be on yer uppers. Anything I asks ye ter do, ye do. And, tarnation, lad, do 'er with a smile. Ye don't know the rules, and they can kill ye dead. Savvy?"

Richard nodded. The warrior returned with the ax and muttered something to a woman who followed him with a bundle of furs on her back. Then he took the ax to Green, and commenced haggling.

Richard began practicing his smile.

CHAPTER FOURTEEN

All men in the state of nature have a desire and will to hurt, but not proceeding from the same cause, neither equally to be condemned. For one man, according to that natural equality which is among us, permits as much to others as he assumes to himself; which is an argument of the temperate man, and one that rightly values his power. Another, supposing himself above others, will have a license to do what he lists, and challenges respect and honor, as due him before others; which is an argument of a fiery spirit.

—Thomas Hobbes, *Leviathan*

As Richard followed the dark trail over the rim of the bench, Wah-Menitu's village greeted his eyes. It was a sight that he would never forget. The village covered the flat— a series of conical skin lodges, each three times the height of a man. Bonfires cast wavering light over the tipis. The rows of illuminated lodges against the star-filled night sky took his breath away.

Men and women stood around talking and laughing, some highlighted by the fires, others mere silhouettes. Camp dogs barked and growled while the trilling shrieks of happy children created a benign chaos.

"Let's do her up!" Travis chortled, a salt-glazed jug of whiskey riding on his shoulder.

Richard steeled himself, nodding resolutely, and strode forward across the trampled grass. He'd expected nothing like this, figuring the Sioux would be dour and stoic as Scotsmen. As he walked past the fires, looking into the faces, he couldn't shake the notion that they looked a great deal like ordinary people but for their barbaric dress. No one failed to call a greeting and flash them a smile.

"Wah-Menitu's lodge is up hyar." Travis bulled his way forward, heedless of whether Green, Baptiste, or Richard followed.

A roaring fire in the open space before the chief's lodge crackled and sent sparks wheeling up into the starry night. Around it were seated several rows of Sioux men, all older, all dignified. Wah-Menitu himself rose from where he sat in front of his large tipi. The hide walls had been painted with rude images of buffalo and horses, and with round dots. Several hand shadows decorated the doorway. For ventilation, the lodge skirts had been rolled up and tied on the poles. Richard caught glimpses of buffalo robes, blankets, and hard leather cases on the inside, as well as what appeared to be a backrest. A painted war shield stood on a tripod behind Wah-Menitu, along with a bow, quiver, and rifle.

"Greetings, coons!" Wah-Menitu cried, raising his hands. "Come, sit. We will smoke and say the blessings. Then ye can share the hospitality of Wah-Menitu!"

"Where'd he learn to talk like that?" Richard asked.

"Traders, Dick," Baptiste answered. "Ain't nobody else out heah."

Richard followed Travis and Green to a blanket spread beside Wah-Menitu. With great ceremony, the pipe was brought forth by a young warrior. In the meantime, Richard studied the faces of the Indians, who in turn studied him. Each man wore an elaborate headdress, finely worked buckskins with dangling fringe, and bead-covered moccasins. Some held fans in their hands, many made from the entire wing of an eagle. Others carried painted sticks, and still others sat before long poles from which feathers and bits of hair dangled in the wind.

They did indeed look noble, all except for one who'd lost an eye and left the gaping socket uncovered. That one fierce eye fixed on Richard with an unwavering intensity and filled his soul with ice and horror.

Richard jerked his gaze away, heart hammering.

But why? I've never seen him before. Who is he?

Wah-Menitu was holding a beautiful pipe up to the sky and had begun a singing chant. The others nodded their heads, as if in approbation.

"What's he saying?" Richard asked.

Travis leaned over to whisper, "Telling the story of White Buffalo Cow Woman, and how she gave the sacred pipe to old Standing Hollow Horn back in the beginning of time."

At last the pipe was offered to the east, south, west, and north, then to earth and sky. After Wah-Menitu puffed and exhaled, he passed the pipe to Green, who repeated the ritual.

Richard took his turn, surprised by the pipe's weight. As long as his arm, the bowl had been carved from some red stone and fitted to a wooden stem. Feathers hung from the carved and painted wood. Warily, Richard puffed, and exhaled. He could taste tobacco, but the other odors defied him.

Person by person, the pipe was passed around. When at last it had been returned to Wah-Menitu, he placed the pipe on its beaded bag before him, and smiled at Green. "We have missed our White brothers. Waugh, it is good to see you again. The trading was good, no?"

"Good, yes," Green replied, fingers dancing in signs as he spoke. "I am pleased to have made such good trades."

Wah-Menitu politely translated to the others as Green spoke. At the same time, women appeared bearing horns of stew, steaming joints of meat, and platters of roasted vegetables of a sort Richard had never seen. He smiled up at the young woman who laid a bark platter in front of him.

"What is this?" Richard poked at the small animal on the platter. The pink flesh had been cooked until it slipped from the bone, but what sort of...

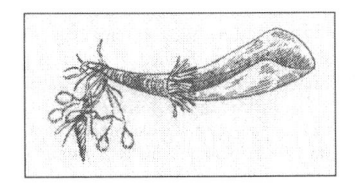

"Just eat it," Travis growled.

"But what...?"

"Eat!"

Richard twitched his nose and pulled a piece of the hot meat loose, blowing on his fingers to cool them. The tender meat melted in his mouth, curiously sweet and satisfying. "I've never had anything like it."

"Reckon not. Sioux delicacy, cooked just fer us. Eat 'er all, Dick. Then suck the bones clean. Make like it's real doings."

Following such instructions wasn't hard. His stomach had been growling for hours. When he sucked the last of the juice from the little bones, he sighed. "Excellent."

"Good, coon. Ye done ate yer first dog."

"I...*what?*"

"Dog. Puppy. Just special fer us. Good, ain't it?"

Richard's gut cramped, and he started to stand, only to have Travis fasten a hand like an iron shackle to his arm.

"Now, try this hyar," Travis insisted, handing Richard a horn of stew. "She's buffler tongue chopped ter bits and biled with onions and mint."

"Travis, I don't think I'd better eat any—"

The grip on his arm tightened.

"Eat 'er, Dick. They done this special fer us."

Under Travis's hard eye, Richard sipped at the stew, pronounced it tasty, and gulped down a swallow. The ugly one-eyed man watched, his good eye half-slitted. Richard did his best to avoid that vulture's gaze. Even the other Sioux seemed to shy from the old buzzard.

Green uncorked the whiskey jug, pouring the clear contents into another of the buffalo-horn bowls and passing it around. "For my friends, the Dakota!" Green cried.

Shouts of "*Wash-te!*" raised from all sides. The horn

bowl was passed around as yet another was filled.

"Time ter shine!" Travis whooped, and took a swig of the horn that passed his way. Richard sipped, made a face, and passed it on. Bad whiskey on top of dogmeat was too much to contemplate.

"Good friends!" Wah-Menitu cried, leaping to his feet. "Times is shining! The traders have come back!"

"Death ter the Rees!" Travis bellowed, jumping to his feet and hopping from foot to foot.

Raised whoops and screams erupted from all sides, men leaping up to cavort and whirl about.

"Get up!" Travis gestured to Richard, who was finishing his stew.

Richard clambered up and Travis shoved him, half stumbling, into the space before the fire. "Hyar's a coon what raised a Pawnee warrior! Hyar's ter Dick!"

A nervous hand at his stomach, Richard stared at the faces surrounding him. Wolfish eyes gleamed back at him in the firelight.

"Ter Dick!" Wah-Menitu cried, shaking a fist and ululating the most horrible of war cries. Then he barked out words in Sioux, and the others whooped and screamed ecstatically.

"Dance!" Travis hissed in Richard's ear. "And hold up that fetish."

Richard fumbled at his belt, only to find Travis's quick fingers had beaten him to it. The skunk hair was thrust into his hand as Travis shoved him forward. "Dance, coon. Dance smart, now!"

Richard started roughly, jumping and twirling as Travis began chanting, *"Hey-a hey-a-hey-hey"* The Sioux joined him.

"Hold 'er up!" Travis prompted. "So's everybody can see!"

Richard raised the fetish and skipped in the milling circle of warriors. A song rose on the lips of the Sioux, and a drum began a rhythmic beat. The excitement of it built in Richard's breast, a kind of exhilaration he'd never experienced before. His feet found the rhythm of the music, and he mimicked those around him: step-shuffle, step-shuffle, leap.

He leapt and ducked, pirouetted and jerked in time to the warriors around him. Electric energy seemed to pulse within him, flowing up from the ground, down from the sky, and through him so that his feet grew light. Time vanished in the exertion and wheeling bodies.

Free! I feel free!

An ecstasy bright as the Sioux fires burned in his breast. His feet skipped and leapt with the airy buoyancy of the sparks that flickered upward.

He wrapped himself in the singing of the Sioux, weaving himself within it. He let the music carry him, like moss in a gentle current. Men, women, and children had come to watch, all swaying with the chant. They were stepping and clapping in time with the lilting song.

As if we were all one, together, relatives instead of strangers from different worlds.

Richard threw his head back, whirling in time with the dance. His spirit soared, buoyed by the dance until his body had become remote, a leaf on the wind.

In the end, all that remained was a pure, shining bliss the likes of which he'd never experienced. Power rose within him, stretching, opening itself to the night and the rising harmony of Sioux voices.

How long did he dance? Winded, sweating, he slipped from the circle, in time for Travis to hand, him a hornful of alcohol. This time he choked a burning draught down his throat.

"Shining times," Travis cried, then crowed like a rooster.

"Shining times," Richard agreed, wiping his sweat-shiny face. "What next? God, for a drink of water!"

"That gut bag hanging yonder. That's water, coon. Haw! Lookit old Baptiste! He's a-prancing like a buck antelope come fall! And thar be Green. Lookee there! Reckon he'd outjump a buck mule deer in high sage!"

Richard grinned, watching the others cavort with the Sioux.

"Hell, Doodle, ye ain't done, are ye? Night's young! Fetch yer water and go gallivanting! I'd be a-dancing with 'em...specially afore they notice yer not out thar!"

Richard drank his fill from the musty-tasting gut, then charged back into the gyrating bodies.

When he staggered back to Wah-Menitu's-lodge, sweating and grinning, the ugly old man still sat in his place, single eye gleaming in that ruined face. Richard hesitated; the old man raised an age-callused finger, beckoning.

———

Willow lay in the darkness, aware of the rustling rodents scurrying behind the cargo. She'd lived most of her life with mice sneaking into the lodges. Mice were a necessary evil, the little creatures doing as *Tam Apo* willed, seeking to fill their bellies and raise their pups. Rats, too, had their place. The kind she knew best were the bushy-tailed packrats of the mountains: the ones who'd leave a rock in place of a shiny bead. Packrats chewed anything leather, or even the sweaty wooden handle of a hammer or the middle of a good bow. They raided food caches, and generally made life miserable for humans.

The old conflict favored neither side, for when times got hard and starvation rubbed a person's belly raw, the *Dukurika* set fire to packrat nests, ambushed the fleeing rodents, and roasted their little carcasses for their soft pink meat.

These dark gray rats, however, were different, with glinting eyes and naked scaly tails that gave her the shivers.

She resettled herself in the bedding Green and Henri had laid on the packs of blankets. Over the furtive scuttling of the rats, and the water slapping the hull, the faint beat of a pot drum, and the yip-yaiing snatches of song carried down from the Sioux village. The edges of her souls frayed with each distant scream.

Here I am, hidden away in a White man's boat while he trades with the Cuts-Off-A-Head People.

And what if the cut-throat Sioux turned on their guests? Murdered them all?

She could imagine Ritshard's headless body, white and naked in the sunlight, flies thick in the blood pooled beneath his severed neck. Those soft brown eyes would never sparkle again. He would never have the chance to seek the answers that lay just beyond the fingertips of his soul.

Trawis wouldn't go down without a fight. He'd shared his soul and blood with the white bear—the greater the honor for the Sioux who finally killed him.

This is ridiculous. I'm only doing this to torture myself. Trawis and Green know what they are doing.

Or did they? She tightened her grip on the war club that lay between her breasts.

I should leave as soon as I can. Sneak away into the night and find my way home.

It couldn't be that hard. Follow the rivers west. Eventually they'd rise to the mountains, and as a girl she'd walked most of them, or heard the stories about which rivers ran where.

So why don't I go?

The lie she had told herself, about learning more about White men, had worn as thin as last year's moccasins. She'd learned enough about the Whites.

She blinked at the dark roof over her head, images of Ritshard growing in her soul. What was it about him that drew her so? Had he cast some spell on her that day she'd looked into the eye of his soul?

That was it, wasn't it? He'd done what no man of the *Dukurika* would dare to do. And he'd done it without fear, without anything except curiosity.

And does that bother you, Heals Like A Willow? Is that what draws you to Ritshard? Is it because he didn't see you as a woman—or did he see you as a complete *woman?*

She shifted uneasily. The sounds from the Sioux camp grew louder.

"You're being an idiot," she told herself. *"Tam Apo* alone knows who these White fools will find next. Maybe the next people will just kill them...and you, too! You should run while you still can."

She nodded to herself. Yes, run. Now...tonight. Before anything else horrible happened to her.

Just as she'd made up her mind, the soft scuff of leather on wood reached her ear. Every muscle stiffened. Her soul pictured a wily Sioux creeping along the *passe avant,* intent on murder and theft.

A shadow darkened the doorway, but Willow had already lowered herself into a gap between two flour barrels. She clutched the war club in one hand, her knife in the other.

Step after careful step, the intruder eased down the

stair slats. Cloth rasped ever so softly, and a big man slipped over to her bedding.

Willow's skin crawled. He reached out cautiously to finger her blankets.

One of the rats scampered away, and the man jerked, stifling a curse.

Couldn't he hear the pounding of her heart, the fear pumping in her blood?

He grabbed at her bed now, searching frantically, then whirled to peer around the black interior of the cargo box.

If he reached into her hiding place, she'd strike with all her strength. Thrust up from below with the knife so that he had little chance to block it. Then she'd rise, braced against the barrels, and hammer him with the war club.

"Willow?" he whispered softly.

She strangled the cry within, recognizing the French accent. Not a Sioux—an *engagé*. Why?

Ritshard, Trawis, and Green were gone. Only Henri slept atop the cargo box.

Who? Trudeau, most likely, but it could have been any of the others. In the charcoal black, she couldn't be sure.

He stood in silence for what seemed an eternity, then carefully turned, easing back the way he'd come.

Only after the shadowy form ghosted back up through the doorway did she take a deep breath and wipe at the fear-sweat that had beaded on her upper lip.

———

The one-eyed Sioux continued to beckon with his crooked finger. In his other hand he clutched an eagle-feather fan as long as his withered arm. In desperation,

Richard looked around for Travis, Baptiste, or Green, but only Wah-Menitu remained seated, his pipe resting on the ground before him. Now the chief's feral eyes narrowed as he studied Richard. The beating of the drum, the eerie singing of the Sioux, and the tramping shuffle of feet filled the night, but the music had changed, turned ominous.

"Sit." Wah-Menitu pointed to a spot on a blanket in front of the old one-eyed demon.

Richard swallowed hard, and sank to his knees. His entire body was trembling from exertion and the sudden sense that something had gone very wrong.

"Who are you?" Wah-Menitu asked. "The *wechashawakan* wants to know."

Richard glanced at the one-eyed man, and fear chilled his guts. That single burning eye pinned him like a lance. "Richard. Richard Hamilton."

The old man spoke, his voice rising and falling, saying lots of *wh* and *che* and *sh* sounds. The gaping wound where his eye had been seemed to study Richard with a red-wealed, scar-tissue intensity that looked through Richard: saw all that he was, and was not.

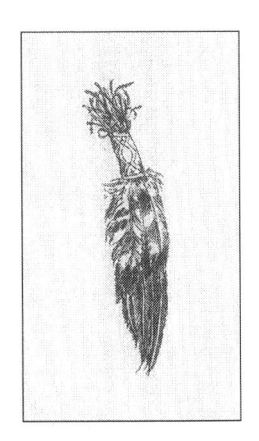

Blessed God, where's Travis?

The panic rose to pump as brightly as Richard's blood.

"He says he saw you," Wah-Menitu said. "He says that you came to him last night in a dream. You came as a cloud white dog, but when you looked at the *wechashawakan,* your eyes were those of a wolf, or maybe it was a coyote. Because of that, he has come to see you tonight. He wants to find out what you are."

Richard's throat had gone dry. "I...I'm Richard Hamilton. From Boston. That's all. I didn't have any choice when I came here. I was forced to. Honestly. I just haven't had a chance to escape yet."

Wah-Menitu drank some of his whiskey, then translated. The old man's eye gleamed, and he sucked his thin lips over peglike brown teeth. Richard's stomach turned as he realized that the dark patches in the eye socket weren't shadows, but crusted dirt lodged in the scar tissue.

The old man was talking again, his horn-dusky hands moving to form shapes and signs. Then he reached out and grasped Richard's hands in his. His skin was warm and dry, the grip powerful.

What should he do? Pull back? Shout for help? What was it Travis had said? Do as he was asked, or they might kill him?

The old man leaned forward and spat on the backs of Richard's hands. Richard flinched as the spittle cooled in the night air. Then the old man took his finger and rubbed the saliva on each hand around in circles. He closed his good eye, and bent down to inspect the damp spots with his gaping socket.

Richard fought the urge to vomit.

The old man straightened, opened his eye, and spoke again, his voice a low growl.

"He wants to know if your stomach hurts," Wah-Menitu translated.

"Yes."

One-Eye grinned evilly, and laughed before he chattered in Sioux. Wah-Menitu said: "He says the cannibal's stomach always hurts. It is hard to eat yer own kind."

"Cannibal? Eat my *what!*"

But the old man leaned so close that his single baleful eye filled the world. Richard couldn't break that sudden connection. From some corner of his mind, the words "eye of the soul" floated, then slipped away. One-Eye reached out with the eagle-wing fan. He used the tips of the feathers to trace the outline of Richard's head, chanting softly. Then he touched the feathers to Richard's forehead. A sensation like chilled mint extract flowed through Richard's head, and the world seemed to shimmer and fade.

What are you? The words came soundlessly. Richard shuddered as his insides went greasy with fear. *You called to me, came floating through the sky as I spread my wings in the night.*

"I did what?"

"*You came here, looking, searching. What do you want?*"

"To go home."

The horrible gaping socket was so close now, Richard could see the rippling folds of scar tissue, and what looked like eroded bone in the back. At the same time his soul stood naked, transparent as window glass.

Wowash'ake *fills you, White Cloud Dog, burning like a slow fire.*

From a great distance, Wah-Menitu's voice told him, "He says you are *wah'e'yuzepe,* confused. You have been fooled. Like *Inktomi,* the Spider Trickster, you have fooled yourself. Now, you must choose."

"What are my choices?"

Paralyzed, Richard gazed into the depths of that terrible empty eye, seeing flames reflected there. But as he watched, the flickers of firelight began to dance and shift, spiraling, falling, metamorphosing into snowflakes. The cold stole through him, driven by winter winds. His bones might have become ice, snow crystallized in his lungs.

Wah-Menitu's drunken voice said, "The *wechashawakan* says this is your future that you feel. This awaits you upriver. Snow, hunger, and cold. A dog curls up and freezes under the snow. He dies there without man to feed him.

"The *wechashawakan* says that four paths lie before you. You can take the red way, up the river. There, if you live, you will become a wolf...or maybe a coyote. Or, you can take the black way, and go east. There, you will always be a white dog—all hollow inside.

"What will you do, *Washichun?*"

Richard clutched himself, shivering in the reflected winter in the old man's eye. It seemed like an eternity before the old man backed away, and Richard gasped, breathless, at the warmth of the summer night that seeped into his frozen body. He panted for breath, exhaling air cold enough that he swore it frosted in the air.

"And if I go home, to Boston—I'll be hollow inside? Forever?"

The old man grunted then, and ran weathered fingers over his eagle fan. He spoke in a breathy voice, hesitating every now and then, nodding and gesturing with his hands. Then he stood, joints crackling, and walked off into the night.

"What did he say?" Richard rubbed his shaking hands on his leather pants.

Wah-Menitu made a face, as if the whiskey was bothering him. "He said he does not know if you will survive the snow on the red way. He does not see that far, so it is uncertain what will become of you. He only sees you starving in the snow, and no more. But truth lies there. An end to the confusion.

"If you take the black way, he said he saw you in a *Washichun* place where lodges are stacked on lodges and the streets are made of stones. He saw you there, lonely and sad—and your soul was empty, like a buffalo-gut bag with all the water drained out."

Richard shook his head, shivering from more than the chill in his bones. "But why did he spit on my hands?"

Wah-Menitu drank more of his whiskey and grinned foolishly. "When he spit, he tried to wash off your outside to see in. He wanted to know what kind of creature you were...if you were human at all, or some kind of monster who had come to harm the people. If you were a monster, he would have to kill you before you could do harm. When he looked inside you, he saw the white cloud dog looking back, terribly afraid. If you do not remain a dog, you can become a coyote, or a wolf. That's why you came here. Not to bring trouble to the *wechashawakan* or our people, but to choose what you will be—and how you will live."

"That's crazy. I didn't *come* here at all. Not of my..."

"The *wechashawakan* says you did." Wah-Menitu shrugged and belched, having trouble focusing his eyes. "Here. Drink this, White fool. I didn't want to waste whiskey on a man who might be dead soon." And he handed Richard the drinking horn.

Richard lifted it in shaking hands, drank deeply, and let the horrible stuff burn away the last of the bone-deep chill inside him.

They're drunk, that's all.

But what had that terrible cold been? Where had it come from? The old man thought he was a white dog? And he was supposed to choose to become a coyote or a wolf? Richard shook his head. "Superstitious nonsense."

Wah-Menitu was watching him though half-lidded eyes, looking very drunk. "I think ye'll stay a dog, *Washichun*. White men are naturally dogs. They do not have the Power inside them. Inside here"—he thumped his chest with a fist—"to become wolf."

"I don't think I understand."

Wah-Menitu grinned, his mouth falling crookedly open. "I speak of Power, of looking inside yourself...and seeing through what ye are." He wiped at a dribble of saliva that escaped his lips. "And I think yer a coward, White Cloud Dog. Go home. Die empty." At that, he laughed uproariously.

Travis let out a whoop and came stumbling into sight, a young woman under each arm.

———

Willow jerked awake at the sound of booted feet on the steps that led down into the cargo box. Slivers of pain lanced her cramped back. She sat crouched in her hiding hole, propped by the rounded sides of rough oak barrels. *Tam Apo,* when had she fallen asleep?

"Willow?" Henri called, squinting at the rumpled bedding on the blankets. "Morning is here. Willow?" He stepped forward to prod the empty blankets. "*Sacré! Non! Les Sioux diaboliques!*"

"Henri?" she called.

He whirled, a hand to his heart. A slow smile crossed his mustached lips. "Ah, *mon papillon,* you are safe. But what are you doing down there?"

Willow placed her war club atop one of the barrels and groaned as she pulled herself up. A gasp escaped her as blood ran into her numb legs. "A man came in the night." She indicated the narrow space. "He did not find me."

"Sioux?" Henri glanced warily about.

"*Engagé.*" Prickles like a thousand nibbling ants coursed down her legs, and she made a face.

"Who?"

Willow shook her head. "I do not know. It was dark."

Henri growled under his breath, then sighed. "This is not good, *ma petite femme.*" He paused, an eyebrow rising. "And this happens when the Sioux are near...and the booshway is gone? I do not like this. *Tres mal!*"

Willow took a hesitant step, and had to lock her knee to keep from falling. Henri, breaking from his dark musing, reached out and offered his arm. The surprising slabs of muscle in the patroon's arm felt like a thick, gnarled root.

Together they climbed out into the gray of the false dawn. The *engagés* were swarming around like bees. Normally, they lingered like lazy dogs over their coffee, waiting until the last moment to take up the cordelle.

As if he read her thoughts, Henri said, "The Sioux have put a fire in their hearts, eh? Today, *mon papillon,* we will make many miles, *prêter serment.*"

Having found her legs again, Willow made her way to the privacy on the other side of the boat to relieve herself. Below her, the restless waters roiled and stirred as if alive. A thin mist hung over the surface like a faint silver skein of spiderweb.

You must leave, Willow. Trouble is coming, and you are bringing it upon yourself.

She stood at the sound of feet on the deck. The *engagés* were filing onto *Maria* and pulling their poles from the top of the cargo box. She could hear the cordelle buzzing as it was pulled over the bow to the cordellers.

This day, too, she would ride inside the cargo box lest some Sioux see her. She nodded to Henri, who had taken his place at the steering oar on the cargo box. Then, reluctantly, she climbed down into the musty darkness.

Only for today, she insisted.

But how many more hostile tribes lay ahead? Did they expect her, a *Dukurika,* to ride the whole way inside this black box like a rabbit in a sack?

She ran her fingers over the line of rifles in the rack by the door. The wood was so smooth, the iron cool and remote to the touch. They had a menacing power all their own. Not the warm familiarity of a bow and good arrows, but a darker presence that might be understood only through time and familiarity.

There is nothing for me here.

She straightened, the decision made. She would leave, but not in a panic, like Coyote fulfilling some whim of the moment. No, instead, she would go like Wolf in his wisdom. From this day onward, she would prepare for the long journey home.

Henri barked out orders. She settled herself on the blankets and stretched her back to release the kinks from her cramped sleep. She would need food, extra moccasins, a good pack, netting, a stout thong for a snare, new arrows.

As she planned, she couldn't shake the memory of the shadowy hand reaching out of the darkness for her bedding.

———

Travis waved a final farewell as Wah-Menitu's warriors lifted lances and rifles. The Sioux wheeled their mounts with mechanical precision and raced away across the plains, southward, toward their village.

Travis ran a hand over his face and groaned aloud. The bright sunlight and warmth of the day did little to ease the splitting ache of his whiskey-head. God, he'd drunk half the river that morning to cure the terrible thirst.

Baptiste and Dick sat their horses, slumped over like the newly dead. Of the two, Richard certainly looked the worst off. His face was pasty, his mousy brown hair sticking out at all angles. Grease had matted his wispy beard on one cheek.

"I swear I got coyote piss running in my veins," Baptiste muttered, squinting after the disappearing riders.

"Nice of them boys ter see us this far," Travis mumbled, his gut trying to heave again. He fought it down.

"Yep," Baptiste agreed. "How in Tarnal Hell is we gonna mount a guard on these hosses tonight?"

"Just do 'er," Travis grunted. "Reckon one night of fun ain't gonna kill us...but I sure feel it might. How 'bout ye, Dick? Can ye stand guard all night?"

Hamilton, face green, gave him a bleary-eyed glare.

"C'mon," Travis heeled his horse around. "Let's make tracks. Them boatman'll probably make fifteen miles today."

As the horses plodded along, Hamilton asked dully, "What's a *wechashawakan?*"

"Ye mean old One-Eye?" Travis asked. At Richard's slight nod, he added, *"Wechashawakan* means holy man, a medicine man. And old One-Eye, he's a heap powerful medicine: The story is that he can see the future, turn hisself into an owl and fly around—and Sioux ain't too keen on owls." Travis struggled to keep from belching, fearing what might come up with it. "Why? He talk ter ye last night?"

"Yes." Richard's body swayed like a grain sack with each step his horse took. "Said I had to choose, that I was a white cloud dog."

"He didn't up and hex you, now?" Baptiste gave Richard a sidelong glance. "I ain't ridin' with no hexed man. No, suh, not this child. Why, hell, you could have lightning and all sorts of grief called down on you. And, if'n that's the way of things, I ain't gonna be no part of it."

Richard croaked, "Said I had to choose. Die like a dog, or turn into a coyote or wolf. Then he almost froze me."

"Huh?" Travis closed his eyes tight to make the spots go away. "Froze ye? That why ye drunk all that whiskey? Hell, I figgered ye fer a frog fer a while. Drinking and dancing."

"I was trying to forget," Richard declared.

"Old One-Eye put the scare into you, boy?" Baptiste asked.

Richard nodded his head carefully, as if afraid it might fall off. "Damn right, he did." Then a pause, as if to change the subject. "I can't believe I drank that much... and danced all night. And you, Travis, I can't believe you slipped away with that squaw."

Travis ran his tongue around his mouth and grimaced at the taste. The spots had come back. "Worked well for both of us...I think."

"You cain't remember?" Baptiste chided.

"Wal, of course I remember, ye damned fool! What in Tarnal Hell do ye think?" Travis lied, forcing his eyes to search the surroundings with their usual wariness.

"Then ye'll remember how cussed ugly she was. Older than Abraham's boot. Hell, couldn't ye dicker fer a pretty young one?"

Travis flipped up the pan on his Hawken, checking the priming. "Ye know, I could blow ye right off that Pawnee nag yer riding—'cept the sound of the shot might kill me."

Richard made a strangling sound, cheeks and eyeballs protruding. Then he belched, and groaned. "Thank the dear Lord God, I thought I was gonna throw up again."

Travis tried to grin, but it hurt too much. And damn it, his own stomach was none too easy.

They rode for a while longer, angling down into the bottoms with their lush cottonwoods. An eagle cut lazy circles in the hot sky, and puffy white clouds scuttled across the northern horizon far beyond the tree-banded river.

Richard was mumbling under his breath, saying, "Choose? Choose what? Die like a dog? I heard him... talking in my head. How'd he *do* that?"

A fly kept buzzing around Travis's sweaty face. Oh, to be able to kill the miserable creature. To crush the life right out of that tiny black buzzing...

"Fort Recovery," Baptiste pointed. "I thought this country looked familiar."

Richard perked up, staring across the meadow to the abandoned building, little more than ruins. "That's a fort?"

"Used ter be," Travis said. "Missouri Fur Company gave up on her last year. Forts in this country, they come and go. Reckon that'll change one of these days. Once ye get a real fort, most everything just up and dies."

Baptiste swatted a deerfly that lit on his arm, and said, "We're a day shy of Fort Kiowa."

"Another fort?" Richard gestured at the fallen timbers. "Like that one?"

"Yep." Travis rubbed his chin. "Pratte and Chouteau, that's the French Fur Company. Rivals of Josh Pilcher's. Let's see, old Joseph Brazeau built it. He's a cuss if ever they was one."

"Is he a friend of yours?" Richard asked.

Travis made a face. "Sort of."

"He went under last year," Baptiste said.

"The hell ye say! He did, huh?"

"Yep. Just up and died." Baptiste slouched in the saddle.

Travis spat off the side of his horse. "I'll miss that old coon. Just up and died? With his hair on? Reckon that's a wonder fit fer the second coming."

"Hell of a country," Baptiste said dryly. "People keep dying everywhere."

"Reckon it's the same all over." Travis glanced at Richard. "Even Boston. I hear tell folks die there, of occasion, too."

Richard seemed curiously attentive, a gleam fighting to establish itself in his glassy eyes.

Travis picked the most likely reason. "Figgering on slipping away come Fort Kiowa?"

Richard scowled and looked away.

"Maybe we'd best put the Doodle on the cordelle tomorrow," Baptiste offered.

"How 'bout it, Dick?"

"I ain't going nowhere." He sounded uncertain.

Travis patted his horse and squinted against the pain in his head. "Wouldn't do ye no good. The trader at Fort Kiowa ain't gonna give a care if'n ye's indentured or not."

Richard bit his lip and stared at the collapsed timbers across the meadow. "If that's the only kind of fort they've got up here..."

"Reckon so." Travis made the "It is finished" sign with his hand. "Dick, I figgered after last night, ye'd come ter enjoy our company."

"Maybe we don't dance nigh enough," Baptiste said. "Tarnal Hell, Dick, I'll dance with yor sorry arse. Reckon you gots to tie a rag on yor arm first, but I'll shake a leg with you."

"Why a rag?"

"Well, these coons up heah, when they ain't got no women to dance with, they up and ties a rag on. The ones with rags is the women."

"Charming," Richard growled.

"Maybe we should o' traded foofawraw fer a woman fer Dick last night?" Baptiste offered. "Yes, sir, we needs to get his pizzle squeezed by some pert young squaw. That'd take some of the rough off him."

Travis rubbed his sore eyes, then blinked hard before squinting at a mirage to see if it were real. Or had his vision gone blurry again? It wasn't real. "Naw, he's a-saving hisself fer Willow."

"Travis!" Richard warned, glaring.

"Got a rise outa the coon, shore 'nuff," Baptiste observed, grinning.

Richard quickly asked, "Will the Sioux really come steal the horses? I mean, after last night? We shared their hearth, ate their food. Danced with them."

"Toss a coin," Travis growled. "Like as not they will."

"But it wouldn't be fair. We're their friends."

"Yesterday, Dick. Today's a different day. Hell, hosses is hosses, white or red. Them what can take 'em, takes 'em."

"But you said they wouldn't steal from people that had been in their village."

"Nope. I told ye they wouldn't steal from ye while ye was *in* their village."

"Then, correct me if I'm wrong, but I get the feeling that out here all ethics are situational."

"What'd he say?" Baptiste wondered.

"Cuss me if I know." Travis blinked his eyes to clear the bleary image. "But if'n words could kill, Dick'd be right deadly."

"My name is Richard."

"He keeps saying that," Baptiste remarked.

"Coon's gotta flap his lips about something. I reckon Dick figgers that's as good as anything around us ignoramuses that don't savvy philos'phy."

"Ignoramuses?" Baptiste asked. "I don't know no word like that."

Travis pulled at his beard. "Wal, by God, Baptiste, yer hellacious living proof of that. Ain't that so, Dick?...Dick?"

Sounds of retching came from behind.

They wound down to the river, letting the horses drink. Richard slid off his mare and doused his head in

the murky water. Travis noted that the *engagés* had stip-
pled the shore here. The boat was upstream.

Richard stayed on all fours, his hands in the water,
head down. "The one-eyed *wechashawakan*...do you think
he really knows anything? I mean, do you believe any of
this power talk?"

Travis squinted up at the hot sun. "Reckon so. I seen
some things, Dick. Old One-Eye, the Sioux call him *Wah-
Kinyahdonwonpe Konhe*, the Lightning Raven. They say he
can see things other folks can't. Chase souls into the
Happy Hunting Grounds. It sort of surprised me ter see
his lights around a whiskey doings. He don't hold with
drinking whiskey."

"What happened to his eye?" Dick sloshed a little
farther out into the water and drank deeply.

"Story is that he fought a monster once—like a big
rattlesnake, and it bit him in the eye. To kill the critter,
Lightning Raven plucked out his own eye and fed it ter
the monster, and why, sure 'nuff, it died on its own pizen."

"Damn!" Richard cried suddenly, smacking the water
with a fist.

"What's wrong, coon?" Travis immediately went wary,
eyes on the peaceful trees around them.

"I don't believe it!"

"Believe what?" Baptiste had also stiffened, thumb
going to the cock on his gun.

"There I was, right in the middle of a Sioux camp!
Surrounded by them!"

Travis shot Baptiste a wary glance. "Yep. So?"

"I didn't ask a single one about how they perceive the
world! About their concept of good and evil, about God,
or principle, or the nature of reality!"

Travis took a deep breath.

Baptiste slumped in the saddle. "Tarnal Hell, fo' a minute I thought we's dead. And it's 'cause of what? What didn't you do, Dick?"

"He didn't drive them coons half mad trying ter figger out why the world's the world." Travis yawned.

"And I ate dog!"

"And liked it."

"Don't remind me."

Travis grinned to himself. *And ye'd go a mite crazy ifn ye knew ye done a scalp dance last night.*

"Then they called me a dog!"

"A what?"

"Oh, they were drunk, Travis. I just forgot about it until now. Cannibals, dogs, coyotes, wolves—and I could have asked about God, and truth, and reality."

"Life's like that." Travis glanced suspiciously at Baptiste. "That squaw, she *warn't* bad-looking."

"Wal, fer being nigh onta sixty years old, and fer as few teeth as she had left, I'd say she's right pert, Travis."

From the lift of Baptiste's eyebrow, Travis could tell he might even be saying that kindly.

———

Go home. Die empty.

Richard sat in the thick green grass on a low bluff overlooking the river. In the twilight, the water gleamed silver. Birds filled the trees with their lilting evening songs. Around him, the grass waved beneath the breeze blowing in from the west. Grasshoppers hung on gossamer wings. He could hear occasional voices and the periodic clank of metal as the *engagés* set up camp in the trees below.

What are you? the voice whispered inside.

Surely, not a monster.

When he looked inside me, he saw a frightened white cloud dog looking back.

Confused, tricked by myself. Am I a dog or a wolf? What the hell did that mean?

No matter what he'd told himself, Lightning Raven's empty eye socket and his haunting words remained sharp as splintered glass in Richard's memory. That eerie voice whispered in his mind; the terrible chill lingered in his bones.

Richard rubbed his arm, stiff from where Travis had thrown him in one of their "larning ter fight" sessions. The pain jarred in contrast to a mourning dove cooing in the trees.

How peaceful this was, the sun setting behind him, its light burning yellow on the bluffs across the river. Just to the north, he could see what they called the Grand Detour. A loop of the river twenty-five miles around that would leave *Maria* within a half mile of her starting place.

Richard caught movement to his right, and watched as a pair of buffalo wolves—disturbed by the arrival of the humans—headed up out of the trees and trotted westward toward the setting sun and a night's hunt.

So, why didn't I slip away to Fort Kiowa?

He could have just sneaked off and ridden hell-for-leather back to the log post. A French Fur Company boat would have been along in a couple of weeks. Any boat would take a strong back in this country.

And to think, I now have a trade with which I can sell myself.

He smiled, remembering the twinkle in Will Templeton's eyes. He'd find the joke a grand one, indeed.

Boston, and Laura, seemed farther away than ever—and each step took him ever more distant from the lodestone of his dreams. Already they were well into June, the days long and hot.

Were it not for Francois, he'd be home now. Back in Boston, safely investigating the intricacies of Hegel and Kant.

I'd be spending my evenings with you, Laura, instead of learning how to break an assailant's hold and cut his throat in the process.

But fate and perfidy had brought him here, to this low bluff above a silver ribbon of winding river and beneath an eternal dome of gold-lashed sky. To a place where all he could do was remember Boston, and ask himself why he hadn't escaped when every opportunity in the world had presented itself.

The wechashawakan *said that I'd be empty, like a buffalo-gut bag with all the water poured out.*

It's because you don't have any of the answers anymore. Nothing works the way you thought it did.

Maybe it didn't, not here in the wilderness. But in Boston, that was a different story. There, he could stroll into Samuel Armstrong's bookshop on Bullfinch Street to search for the latest volumes from Europe. Armstrong kept all the new titles as well as the translations of older works. From there, he could cross to John Putney's fine clothes emporium at 51 Newbury, or the even finer clothes at Henry Lienow's over at 3 Roe-buck Passage. A far cry from the worn and stained moccasins and the already tattered leather coat he now wore.

And afterward, decked in new finery, what a delight it would be to step into John Atkins's tobacco shop on Cross Street for a tin of his latest find and a bit of polite conversation while he smoked a good bowl.

You could leave any time you wanted. Just take a horse and ride south.

But here he sat, staring out at the smoothly deceptive river. He took a deep breath, allowing tranquility to soak into his churning soul. To the river, he said, "Perhaps I'm afraid."

Was that it? Fear of the look in his father's eyes when he reported the theft of more than a year's profit? Thirty thousand dollars: more money than most people saw in a lifetime. Lost.

Until the river, he hadn't understood the real value of that incredible sum. Money had simply been an abstract. *Engagés,* solid men like Toussaint, would labor for two years, their lives in peril, for a total of two or three hundred dollars. To them, thirty thousand dollars was a fantasy.

And I lost it through stupidity. He winced, rubbing his bruised knees. *How could I ever have been that naive?*

On one thing Lightning Raven had been correct. The time had come to choose. Richard smacked a mosquito and asked himself: "So, what are you going to do, Richard? Head upriver to freeze to death, or slip away and ride off to Fort Kiowa and wait for a boat?"

At that moment, Travis and Willow stepped out of the trees and began climbing the steep slope. From Travis's posture, something was wrong.

Willow had a hard look on her face, too. But, now that he thought about it, she'd been looking a bit grim ever since the night they'd camped with Wah-Menitu's Sioux.

"Seen any Injun sign, coon?" Travis called up. "Ain't no ambush atop the hill?"

"Just ten thousand cussed Blackfeet waiting to lift yer hair, pilgrim."

Travis and Willow continued their climb.

When they crested the bluff and walked over, Richard asked, "What's the trouble?"

Travis settled on his haunches. "That night we were with the Sioux? Wal, Green hid Willow in the cargo box. I'd sort of figgered she's been a mite tight-jawed the last couple of days, and I finally got it out of her. Some coon snuck in in the middle of the night."

"What?" Richard shot an uneasy look at Willow.

"An *engagé*," she said, face expressionless. "I heard him coming. I hid between the...how you say?"

"Barrels," Travis supplied.

"Barrels. I hid there, in a small place. Very dark. He couldn't see me—or the knife and war club that would have killed him when he found me."

"Why didn't you scream?" Richard asked.

"Why scream? He'd find me sure." She continued to watch him with those probing dark eyes.

"Well, because it's..." He shrugged. "Someone would have done something about it."

"And give myself away to Sioux?"

Richard frowned and turned to Travis. "Who'd sneak after Willow?"

"Reckon any of 'em. Willow's a pretty woman." Travis shook his head. "I didn't hire no saints fer this trip, Dick. I took men, no questions asked. Hell, I'd a taken Francois and August given half the chance. Even if'n I had ter kill 'em afore Fort Osage, that would a been that much farther they pulled the boat."

"The boat, the boat...yes, I know." Richard sighed. "So, what now?"

"We keep Willow close."

"I take care of myself," she said firmly, and patted the war club. "I come close that night."

"But ye shouldn't have ter," Travis said softly. "Not on our boat, as our guest."

A faint smile curled her lip. "Trawis, the time has come. I should go back to my people. I have been hyar too long."

"Don't." Richard laid a hand on her arm. "We haven't even had the time to talk. I—I don't..." He lowered his head, surprised at his sudden panic.

"You don't? Don't what?"

"Want you to go," he finished lamely. In his mind's eye he could see Laura's eyes narrowing, her lips hardening.

Travis pulled a grass stem from its sheath. "Wal, I reckon that's some fer elocution. Couldn't a done better meself, and me without a lick of philos'phy."

Richard felt himself redden and growled, "I'll bet it was Trudeau. Was it him, Willow?"

"Don't know. Couldn't see. Very dark." She shrugged.

Richard fingered the wood on his rifle, glancing down at the camp hidden in the trees. "If this happens again, I'll beat the hell out of whoever's doing it."

She gave him that enigmatic smile, dimples forming in her sleek bronzed skin. "So, Ritshard is a warrior now? And a seeker as well?"

He shrugged. And to think he'd just been drowning in memories of Boston, and gentler days when men didn't sneak around in the dark after women.

From the very beginning, Trudeau had tormented him, right up to the moment he drove that fist into Richard's gut. A lot of payback was owed to Trudeau.

But, if it comes down to it, can I take him? Or will he just kill me like swatting a fly?

CHAPTER FIFTEEN

Man's initial feeling was of his very existence, his first care that of preserving it. The earth's produce yielded him all the necessities he required, instinct prompted him to make use of them. Hunger, and other appetites, made him at different times experience different manners of existence; one of these excited him to perpetuate his species; and this blind propensity, quite void of anything like pure love or affection, produced an act that was nothing but animalistic. Once they had gratified their needs, the sexes took no further notice of each other.

—Jean-Jacques Rousseau, *Discourse on the Origin and Foundation of Inequality Among Mankind*

 Heals Like A Willow planted her moccasined feet carefully on the trail, alert to the sights and sounds of the hot afternoon. A woman couldn't be too careful in uncertain country like this. Cuts-Off-A-Head warriors might be lurking, ready to take an unwary captive. Ritshard's tracks had already imprinted the soft deer trail she followed down from the flat ridge

that made the narrow neck of the Grand Detour. The way led through the green plum, hazel, and raspberry bushes to the sandy shore below. Lazy cottonwoods stood just up from the sand, the leaves waxy in the heat.

The day was stifling, cloudless, and perfect for a bath. The *Maria* was far away, struggling around the far bend of the Grand Detour. On the narrow neck of land above, Travis and Baptiste were processing buffalo meat. She had left them telling stories, waving lazily at flies, and feeding wood to drying fires as the smoke and sun cured long bloody strips of buffalo. They'd shot a young cow that morning.

Birds sang in the cottonwoods, and she caught the gentle musk of the river on the breeze.

Willow stepped out of the rushes and onto the packed sand, seeing the pile of Ritshard's clothes. His rifle, bullet pouch, and powder horn lay propped on a piece of driftwood. He floated in a riffle of current, no more than twenty paces out, lost in his thoughts, looking downstream.

A crystal brook emptied into the river here. The whims of current had left a sand spit separating the Missouri's muddy water from the clear mouth of the creek. The pure water looked so inviting. For the first time in days, she could really feel clean.

Willow unlaced her moccasins and slipped her dress over her head before taking one last look around. Placing her war club on the folded leather, she waded slowly out into the water. She was within a body length before he looked up, stunned. His mouth dropped open, but no words formed.

"What a good day," she said by way of greeting, stepping off into the deeper water and seating herself on the gravelly bottom. She splashed water over her hot skin, then used sand to scrub under her arms.

"What...What..." Ritshard had huddled into a protective ball. His tanned neck and hands contrasted with the stark white of the rest of him. How could skin be that glaringly pale? Ritshard's chest wasn't covered by the dense mat of black hair she'd seen on some of the *engagés,* but rather with a mist of brown curls that gleamed in the sunlight.

"Bath," she told him. "Doesn't it feel good?" She used a thumbnail to chisel dried buffalo blood from her cuticles.

His agonized expression betrayed growing horror. What could possibly be causing him to panic so?

Willow dipped her head in the water to wet her hair before she lifted her face to the sun and wrung the water out. *Tam Apo!* He hadn't been bitten by something poisonous, had he? "Are you all right?"

"You...you're naked!"

"Naked. I don't know this word."

"B—Bare! No clothes!"

Her brown knees bobbed up as she lay back in the water and gave him a curious glance. "Yes. Take off clothes for bath. You did."

"But—I mean—you're a *woman!*"

She thought for a moment. "Ah! I see. White women take bath with clothes on? How do they do that? I think it would be hard to wash all over through clothes."

He swallowed hard. "Willow. Men and women...they don't bathe together!"

She used a wet finger to clean out her ear, then splashed her face, rubbing it vigorously. "They bath with clothes on?"

He closed his eyes, took a deep breath, and said,

"Among whites, it is considered inappropriate to see each other without clothes on."

"I'm not White."

His gaze kept straying to where her breasts floated in the chest-deep water. In the end, he looked away, whispering, "This isn't proper."

"I could go away." Willow began scrubbing her long legs, then rinsed the sand from her muscular thighs and calves. The current carried her closer to where he squatted, his feet solidly planted under his tightly tucked body.

He rubbed his face with a wet hand and gave her a worried smile. "No, it's all right. It's me. Not you."

"Ritshard, easy, coon." She gave him an annoyed look. "Why do Whites not bath together? They have separate rivers?"

"No, it's done inside. In a building. It's just not proper, that's all."

"Why?"

"You're not supposed to see another person's brea...body!"

"I did not know this. Among my people, we bath together all the time. Why do Whites think this is bad? Are they all ashamed of being so...white?"

He gave her a miserable look and shook his head, still crouched, arms crossed tightly in his lap. "It's just not proper, Willow. Because...because that's the way it, is."

"You saw Trawis's body when you sewed it up."

"That's different, I didn't see his...uh...man part."

"Are man parts not all the same? You know..." She made a fist with her left hand, dangling the index finger of her right over the top in a semblance of a penis over a scrotum.

"I suppose."

"Then why are you so afraid I might see you?"

"Because it makes a man think of things he shouldn't." He squeezed his eyes shut. "And I'm *not* thinking the things I'm thinking right now. I'm not. I'm really not thinking them—not even a little bit."

A slow smile curled her lips. "Ah." This time she wrapped the fingers of her left hand around the index finger of the right and made suggestive sliding motions. "How silly." Willow splashed him with water and shook her head. "I will never understand Whites."

"Well, don't try this with the engagés. At least, I'm a gentleman. And right now, I'm concentrating on Saint Jerome, on Anselm, Aquinas, and thinking about what happened to Peter Abelard when he let his carnal desires lead him astray."

"Ritshard," she said wearily, "I am Willow, clothes on or off. Do Whites think a person changes with the clothes they wear? Where does this come from?"

"From two thousand years of Christian thought, from the Bible, from our scholars and teachers."

"I don't know these words."

"I'm starting to wish I didn't either." This time when she looked his way, he was watching her with unabashed interest. His expression of wonder grew as his gaze traveled her body. He wet his lips, taking a deep breath. Her heart skipped, her own interest suddenly perked by his fascination. Not even her husband had ever looked at her with such adoration and longing.

"I understand," she whispered, staring down at her firm breasts. Crystal beads of water caught the sun, contrasting with her smooth brown skin. "What the White man thinks is forbidden, he desires most."

"We have stories about that. Adam and Eve." He raised his hands. "And here I am in the Garden. I guess it's pretty hard for you to understand." He slapped at the water with a cupped palm. "Thinking about it now, I guess I don't understand, either." He paused. "Don't *Dukurika* men want women more when they see them naked?"

She settled back in the water, excited by his desire. "I don't think so, Ritshard. When a man desires a woman, he makes signs that he's interested. She either agrees or not, as is her wish."

"Do your people—when they bathe—do they stare at each other?"

"We grow up seeing each other at the river. It isn't anything strange to us. Not like it is to you. I wouldn't have come here if I'd known."

"But you've been on the boat. You don't..."

"The *engagés* are not my friends. I don't trust them. When they look at me, I see lust in their eyes. That is the word—lust?"

"But you trust me?"

She reached out, touching his arm, smiling. "The eye of my soul has seen into yours, Ritshard."

"And what do you see now?"

"That you want me. In the way that a man wants a woman." She felt him tense, the corners of his eyes tightening.

His voice turned husky. "How does that make you feel?"

Willow, if you tell him, you'll be committing yourself. Are you sure?

Instead, she said, "You're so—white."

"It would be like lying with a corpse? Like mating with your dog?" He repeated her words from the night they'd removed Travis's stitches.

She traced patterns in the water with a slim brown finger. "My husband died six moons ago. He filled my heart so full that I wondered if another could ever find a place in it again. I think about you—as a woman does when she is interested in a man—but I don't know if I want to join with you."

The tension had eased from his shoulders. "That makes me feel better." But she could see that it didn't.

"What would become of us, Ritshard? What I think is all right, you think is wrong. You are not *Dukurika*. You don't know our ways. How could you come and live among my people? What would you do? The men would laugh at you, make you miserable."

He pursed his lips, then said, "I can't be an Indian, Willow."

"Besides, Ritshard, you are going back to Boston. I have listened when you and Trawis have talked about Boston. I don't think I want to go there."

He gave her a weary smile. "I'll admit, I dream about you, Willow. About the way you walk, how I'd love to touch your hair. How I'd love to hold you. And then I think about Boston, about you in Boston. I might be starting to love you, but you're right. I'm not Shoshoni, and you're not white. People would never let us forget that."

She watched a flight of ducks flash past in a pounding of wings. A honeyed sadness filled her. *Why, Willow? This is just the way it is, isn't it?*

"God, how I've changed," he mumbled. "Look at me! Laying naked in a river, talking to a naked woman."

She lifted an eyebrow.

His soft brown eyes had begun to twinkle with amusement. "When I look back at the sort of man I was, and compare that to who I am now, I can't help but wonder." He paused, frowning. "How long were you married?"

"Four years."

"Children?"

"A son. He died when my husband did."

Ritshard frowned, resettling himself. "I never think of you like that. Married, I mean."

"He was a good man. My soul still aches. It always will."

"Obviously you're not a virgin," he whispered.

"I don't know that word."

He gave her an irritated glance. "A woman who's never laid with a man."

"Wirgin." Why did she have such trouble with the V sound? "V-v-v-virgin."

Ritshard tilted his head back. "Well, another dream slips away like mist in the morning."

"I don't understand."

"Oh, nothing," he growled.

She studied him from the corner of her eye, aware that he'd settled back in the water, braced on his elbows, white knees poking up. She could see him now, white like a fish belly except for the black mat of his pubic hair. With skin that pale, she'd halfway thought his pubic hair would be white, too.

"Among my people, we have stories of *Pachee Goyo,* the Bald One. He's an irritating young man who wants everything—and rarely listens to his elders. He sets out on a journey, and never seems to realize how he changes as he travels. It isn't until his escape from the great Cannibal Owl that he realizes he's become a man."

Ritshard watched the water flowing over his hand. "A cannibal owl?"

"Cannibal Owl catches *Pachee Goyo* beside the lake where the Underwater Buffalo live, and carries him far to the north, to an island in the middle of a big lake. There, among the bones of the dead, *Pachee Goyo* makes an arrow of obsidian, and kills Cannibal Owl before it can eat him. To escape the island, he makes a boat from the owl's huge wing and sails for days until he makes shore and can find his way home."

She kicked her legs out to float and studied her toes where they stuck out of the water. "Until I saw *Maria,* I never would have believed anything could float so far."

"Your husband," he asked halfheartedly. "What was his name?"

She fixed her eyes on the sky. "Among my people, we do not say the name of the dead. It can affect the *mugwa.*"

"Mugwa?"

"The life-soul, the spirit. It leaves the body when death comes."

"Ghosts," he muttered, still irritated with himself. Or her. She wasn't sure which. "Do you believe in ghosts?"

She flicked water with her toes. "I don't know, Ritshard. The souls must go someplace when we die. I buried my husband and my son according to *Ku'chendikani* ritual. It was what he wanted. I have to believe it is so for him. By believing, his *mugwa* will find its way to where he wanted to go."

"That isn't a very sound philosophical framework."

"Framework?"

"Uh, basis, foundation, support."

She nodded. "I believe for him, so that it can be true for his souls. I can do that because I still love him."

"But what about for you?"

She laughed, kicking hard enough to splash water in a silver sheet. "For me, Ritshard, I question. I don't know what my *mugwa* will do when I die. If it comes free of my body, fine. If it travels to the Land of the Dead, fine. If it stays in my body and rots with the rest of me, fine." She lifted her hand. "But I hope it goes free of my body, and I can find my way to *Tam Apo.*"

"God? Why?"

"I want to know why He made the world the way He did. Don't you wonder why winter has to come? Why does the world have to freeze? Why do we have to die? Why can't we live forever?"

He leaned forward, brown eyes gleaming, a hunter closing on prey. "What's the Shoshoni reason?"

"In the beginning, *Tam Apo* created the world and all things in it, including Coyote. Some say *Tam Apo* took the form of Wolf to do this. At that time, animals looked the same. How they came to be different is another story. Then Coyote tricked a maiden to get her pregnant, and people were born. Somehow they got out of the basket where the maiden hid them so her mother wouldn't find out."

"Wolf and Coyote," he whispered, gaze unfocused. "Go on, Willow. Tell me about Wolf and Coyote."

"Coyote and Wolf constantly argued about the world *Tam Apo* had created. Coyote looked around and saw people everywhere making more and more children. In those days, when a person died, he could be brought back to life by shooting an arrow into the ground underneath him. Coyote told Wolf, 'We should let some of these people die. The *mugwa* can float away in the breeze, and the rest can turn into bones.'

"Wolf was tired of hearing Coyote complain, so he agreed, but Wolf made sure that Coyote's son was the first to die. Coyote, of course, was very upset, and immediately shot an arrow into the ground underneath his dead son. When the boy didn't come back to life, Coyote ran to Wolf, complaining, 'My son has not come back to life.'

"Wolf told him: 'It was you, Coyote, who complained that too many people were in the world, who asked that when people died, their *mugwa* would drift away on the wind, and they would rot into piles of bones. This I have granted you.'

"And so, death is forever."

Ritshard gave her a skeptical glance. "You don't believe that, do you?"

"Perhaps. I would ask *Tam Apo* about it." She fished a rock from under her bottom and threw it out past the sand spit to splash in the muddy water of the main current. "Why do we have to suffer grief and sorrow because Wolf and Coyote had an argument just after the world was created?"

"The sins of the father..." Ritshard made a face and rolled over to stare at her. His white buttocks bobbed like pale stones. "It sounds like you worry about the problem of God's justice with the same passion that whites do."

She narrowed her eyes. "It makes my people very uneasy when I ask questions like that. That's why I left the *Ku'chendikani*. I was afraid my husband's brother's wife would accuse me of being a...what was the word? Witch?"

"Witch," he agreed.

"That's it. I was on my way back to the *Dukurika* mountains when Packrat caught me."

Ritshard stared into her eyes with that look that betrayed the Power in his soul.

You will dream of him tonight, Heals Like A Willow. You will stare into those eyes, and wish to feel the warmth of his body, the strength of his soul twining with yours.

Her blood quickened. Unbidden, her hand reached out to his, their fingers lacing together.

"So," he mused, "you're an outcast, too. I know how that feels, Willow. To ask questions that make others nervous. I, too, would question God, for if He is all-powerful, all good, and all-knowing the way my people believe, why does He allow suffering to exist? He *must* hear the sobs of a mother weeping over the body of her child...like you over your husband and son."

At his words, the grief tightened in her chest. "I would have given anything to save them. I begged and cried to the Spirit World. I offered anything to save them."

If only I had had the courage to send my soul into the Land of the Dead to bring their souls back.

"But they died. I know." Ritshard tightened his grip on her hand. "God is either a bastard, or He isn't what we believe Him to be. There's always a flaw in the stories we're taught. At least, there is in the Christian dogma. From what you say about the Shoshoni, it's probably the same, right? Always a problem when you really think about what the story means?"

"Yes!" she cried happily. "I was always told to fear the dead. That their ghosts would be angry if they weren't cared for properly and sent across the sky to the Land of the Dead. Why, Ritshard? My husband, he was a good man. His *mugwa* was good, because I saw it reflected in his eyes. Why would it change because of death?" She flicked a fly away.

"Do all Indians have these beliefs? Or are some different?"

"The Pawnee think the world was created by *Tirawa-hat,* 'The-Expanse-of-Heaven,' and Morning Star had to fight a war to mate with Evening Star. And from that mating, the first woman was born. The *Pa'kiani* believe the world was created by *Napi*. In the beginning it was all water, and an animal had to dive to the bottom to bring up mud for the Flat Pipe to rest on. Everyone has a different story. Can they all be true?"

A twinkle glowed in Ritshard's eye. "I don't think any of them are true."

"Why?"

He took her other hand and floated closer to her in the warm water. "Because none of the stories I've heard tell of a purpose."

"A purpose?"

"Why did *Tam Apo,* or *Napi,* or *Wakantanka* create the world? Think about all the stories you know. Wolf and Coyote and death. What is the meaning of all this?" He gestured to the world around them. "Why did God do it? Why does it work the way it does? But the most important question is: What is the *reason* for the world? Does it have a purpose? That's what I want to know."

She matched his smile with her own. "That is why I would seek *Tam Apo!* I'm tired of believing things because the people tell you that's the way it is."

Her spirit felt ready to burst. She had never dared speak these questions aloud. Now, here, so far from her mountains, she'd found a man who understood. They floated closer together, the hot sun beating down to sparkle off the water.

Perhaps he read the glow in her eyes, for his muscles tightened as he held her hands. Honeyed sensations began to stir deep within her, born through her blood by each beat of her heart. The parting of his lips, the pulsing veins in his neck, betrayed his growing want.

His hand rose to stroke the side of her face, his touch

gentle. She closed her eyes, images shifting and whirling within her.

Her arms went around him as they drifted together.

"Willow?" he whispered as their bodies touched.

She savored the sensations as her breasts pressed against his chest. She traced the muscles of his back and felt him shudder. His hardened penis slipped along the curve of her hip as his hand slid over her buttock.

"We've got to stop," he whispered, as if in pain.

"Yes." But she held him for a moment, savoring his male hardness before she turned him loose. She climbed to her feet and splashed the sand from her skin. She raised her face to the sun, letting the sexual tension drain away like the water running down her skin.

When he stood, he staggered like a wounded man, taut penis bobbing.

"It would be very easy, Ritshard." She tilted her head, twisting her hair into a rope to wring the water out.

Large-eyed, he nodded. "I guess now you know why men and women shouldn't take baths together."

Her laughter bubbled up. "It might have happened anyway, Ritshard. I spend too much time dreaming of you as it is." And the dreams would haunt her with greater intensity now, fulfilling in fantasy what they had so narrowly avoided in fact.

"And I you," he replied sadly, reluctant gaze tracing the curve of her breasts, the flat lines of her belly, and the length of her legs. "God in Heaven, Willow, you're beautiful."

"You have your ways, Ritshard…and I have mine." She glanced at him from the corner of her eye. "And I am going away soon. It is better that we do not join in that way."

He nodded distantly, staring at something invisible in the water.

She turned then, wading through the shallows to her clothing. On the sand, she used her hands to wipe the last droplets from her skin, and reached for her dress. As she washed it, she glanced at him.

He stood motionless, calf-deep in the clear eddies of the stream. His hands were clenched at his sides, and the long muscles in his arms flexed. Water had slicked the brown hair on his white legs and chest and beaded like dewdrops in the kinky hair around his softening penis.

Don't even think it, Willow. Coupling with Ritshard would only bring you heartbreak.

Resolute, she pulled on her damp dress and moccasins before picking up her war club and beginning the climb back to camp.

———

"Reckon I seen whipped puppies what looked a heap more pert than ye do, Dick." Travis gave Richard a sidelong glance as they rode their splashing horses across the gravel-bottomed Cheyenne River.

Everything had come undone.

Laura, oh Laura, what have I done?

All those vows of chastity, the promises he'd made himself and her had come so close to disaster that day at the Grand Detour. He'd been torturing himself ever since, trying to find his way—but nothing rational remained to him.

Blessed God, I'm totally lost. Nothing makes sense anymore.

That magnificent clarity with which he'd once viewed the world was gone, and a maelstrom of confusion was unleashed in its place.

Richard concentrated on not losing his seat as his white mare climbed the steep bank in buck jumps. Shouldering through the brush, the mare trotted out onto the cottonwood flats beyond. A series of sculptured bluffs— weathered, scalloped, and grass-covered— rose in the distance. Here, the Missouri had cut deeply into the plains, and the valley slopes were speckled with oak, cedar, and patches of buffaloberry.

Richard watched Travis lead the horses alongside, and gave the scar-faced hunter a sour glare.

"Wal?" Travis asked mildly. "Ye gonna tell this coon why Willow and ye are looking so sad? Hell, fer the past three days, the both of ye've been so damned careful to keep from saying anything, or looking at each other, that Baptiste and me, we're getting a might fidgety."

Richard snorted as he tried to slouch in the saddle the way Travis did. "I should have gone ahead and jabbed you in the eyes during our fighting session this morning. Maybe it would have kept you from seeing more than what's there."

He kicked his mare into the lead, trotting the animal across the flats. For a while they rode in silence.

"Thar's another old Ree village over yonder," Travis said, pointing. "Sioux massacred a big bunch of 'em about twenty years back. Chopped the dead into pieces and scattered 'em. Even the wimmen and kids. The stories say the survivors were too horrified to return. They just left the corpses for the coyotes and the Sioux."

"Why women and children?" Richard shook his head.

"Wanted ter teach the Rees a lesson."

"A lesson? They call butchery like that a lesson?"

"Ye ever read yer Bible? They's butchery akin ter that all through the Bible. And God's work, too. I reckon Sioux just ain't civilized like them Hebrew folks." Travis paused. "I'm kinda surprised we ain't run into more of them coons. This hyar's the middle of their country now."

"And the Rees? Will they be around?"

"Reckon they sneak through here when they have the notion. All this country used to belong to them. Funny people, the Rees. Related to Pawnee, but twice as cussed unpredictable."

"Indeed. Well, we've had enough trouble with Pawnee," Richard muttered. Before the whiskey trip with Half Man, life had been so simple. He could just hate, fume, and plot his escape.

Travis continued to watch him with eyes that sliced past all Richard's defenses.

Just like Willow, he can read my soul.

"I reckon if'n I's ye, I'd tie up with that gal, Dick."

Richard tightened his grip on the wrist of the Hawken. "I don't know what you're talking about."

"'Course ye do. We're talking about Willow and ye."

"There's nothing to talk about."

"Uh-huh."

"There isn't!" Richard glared at his tormentor.

Travis Hartman had an unnatural eloquence of facial expression. Just a slight lift of a ruined eyebrow, the quirk of the lips, and a tightening of the eyes that shifted the scar tissue and declared: "Yer a miserable damned liar."

Richard surrendered. "It won't work, Travis. I know it, and she knows it."

"Knows what, fer God's sake? Hell, coon, if'n she's a-looking at me with them fawn-warm eyes, I'd slip her straight off inta the bushes. Then I'd be right tempted to hightail my cussed butt off ter the Snake lands and never look back."

"You would." Richard shook his head. "And then into

another Sioux woman's bed, and then a Ree's, and Crow's, and whoever's next would be next."

"Something wrong with that?" Travis's voice lowered menacingly.

"No. It's your way is all, Travis. It's not mine. I want more."

"Like a nice wife? One of them white 'ladies'? The ones that talk about tea, and Mrs. Snootbutt's cookies, and lace? Hell, I been a fool fer years dreaming about finding me a white wife, of being all them things a man's supposed ter be. It's shit, Dick. Can ye see this coon living on a farm someplace back in the settlements? Gee-hawing a damn mule on a plow line? Smoking up a cabin and shucking corn? Naw, coon, that don't shine, not to this hyar child. But nigh onto twenty years now, I been a-believing it."

At that moment a small band of whitetailed deer broke from a thatch of brush. They dashed away in zigzags, white tails flagged high. "I'm trying to decide if I believe you."

"I don't give a damn if'n ye do or not."

"I guess I do. You told me all this when you were delirious."

"Ye mean raving? When I's fevered?"

"Yes."

Travis worked his jaws, squinting into the distance of his mind. "Reckon I remember." A pause, then he gave Richard a slit-eyed look. "So, why not Willow and ye?"

"Dear God, Travis! I couldn't take her to Boston. She's a savage. She eats with her fingers! She's...she's an *Indian!*"

"That's it, ain't it?"

"No, that's *not* it. I made a promise, that's why. A promise to myself and Laura."

"Who the hell's Laura?"

"A woman...the one I want to marry."

"A rich Boston lady?"

"What if she is?"

"Wal, she ain't hyar, for one thing. But Willow is. And don't give me no shit about yer not in love with her, neither."

Richard's desperation goaded him. "She's been *married,* Travis. Another man's wife. How could I marry a widow? It's not proper. Don't you understand?"

Travis nodded, face suddenly expressionless. "She ain't a virgin."

"That's right!"

"Packrat took her, too."

Richard lost his train of thought. "What?"

Travis continued to give him that cold stare. "Why'n hell did she hate him so much? Come on, coon. She's a slave to that Pawnee kid fer nigh on three months. What in hell do ye think? He lay in his robes each night choking his chicken? She's been used. And that just makes it worse, don't it? A pure man like ye, a plumb dainty Yankee Doodle, wouldn't dare stick hisself where some other coon pumped his come, would he?"

"It's not that! I tell you I—"

"Ain't it?" Travis barked harshly. "Yer a stinking hypocrite, Dick. A damn liar! Fer all yer fancy talk about life and justice and morality, yer nothing more than a Doodle Dandy, as stuffed full of shit as the rest of 'em. Ye makes me sick. And sure as hell, ye ain't worth Willow's spit."

The tone in Travis's voice was too much. "Get off that damn horse!"

Travis kicked a leg over and dropped lightly to his feet.

Richard leapt from the mare, facing the hunter. "You don't *ever* use that tone of voice with me again, you hear?"

"Yer a two-faced, double-tongued hypocrite, Dick. And Willow— and maybe this Laura, fer all I know— deserves more than a crawling worm like ye."

The rage broke. Richard struck, whipping a balled fist at Travis's head. The hunter blocked it, and jabbed at Richard. Knuckles glanced off Richard's cheek, but he was already kicking out, letting loose of the Hawken to gouge those angry blue eyes.

He never got his grip; a knee jacked into his crotch. The force of it lifted him into the air. He was doubled up with agony by the time he slammed the ground. For long moments he could only writhe in the grass, tears leaking from his eyes and breath stuck halfway down his throat.

Travis stood over him, fists knotted, a soul-deep sadness in his eyes.

Richard managed to gasp a breath. The cool air only relieved the paralysis of his sick stomach. He vomited weakly, then lay in limp misery.

"Sorry, Dick." Travis bent down. "Tarnal Hell, coon, I figgered ye's ready ter kill me."

"I was," Richard squeaked. "Damn, Travis, what did you do that for?"

"Stopped ye cold, didn't I?"

Richard rolled onto his back, hands probing his genitals, feeling for blood or...well, who knew what.

"Reckon yer gonna be a mite tender fer a couple of days. Is yer sack swelling full of blood?"

"No."

"Wal, that's a relief. I'd hate ter doctor ye. I seen fellers hit hard down there, and the sack fills up with blood. Sometimes the only thing ye can do is take a knifepoint, or a steel awl, and drain it out. Sort of like popping a big tick."

"Please, God, *no!*" Richard probed again, then dragged a sleeve across his tear-blurred eyes.

Travis walked over to catch up the horses and tied them off while Richard stifled grunts of pain, wiped his mouth, and rocked tenderly.

When Travis returned, he offered a thin tin flask from his possibles. "Hyar, coon. Reckon a sip'll cure ye."

Richard took the tin in trembling fingers, lifted it, and almost threw up again at the sticky pungent odor. Seeing Travis's scowl, he took a taste, gulped it down, and tried to keep his eyes from crossing.

"What in the name of God is this?"

"Castoreum, coon. It'll fix yer *cojones* and pizzle if'n they's mashed."

"Where on earth do you get something that tastes that vile?"

"Off'n a beaver's balls, pilgrim."

Richard suffered a heaving of his gut, but kept it down through sheer force of will. God alone knew, the stuff was bad enough the first time; the second might kill him.

Travis offered a hand and pulled Richard to his feet. Step by wobbly step they made their way across the knee-deep grass to a gnarly old Cottonwood. There, beneath the spreading branches, Travis helped Richard to settle, then dropped down so they both sat with backs to the thick bark.

Butterflies fluttered across the grass, the sound of grasshoppers, and bees filling the air with life. In the branches above, robins and a grosbeak fluttered to nests hidden in the deltoid leaves. A fox squirrel leapt nimbly from branch to branch, pausing crosswise to stare down at them with uneasy black eyes.

"Set ye off, didn't I?"

"You did," Richard said wearily.

"Good, 'cause yer being plumb stupid. Now, what's this shit about marrying a virgin?"

To kill the cloying aftertaste of castoreum, Richard pulled a grass stem from its sheath and chewed the sweet pith before saying, "Laura Templeton is my best friend's sister. She's just seventeen and the most beautiful woman in the world."

"Yer promised? Arrangements made?"

"Well, no, not exactly. She said she'd wait for me. That I could pay court to her when I got back from Saint Louis."

"An what if ye go home ter Boston and find she didn't wait? Hell, ye'll be nigh to two years gone, Dick. Reckon she'll wait that long?"

"I don't know."

"Wal, I don't figger this'll come as a surprise, but yer not the same Doodle lad that left Boston. Ye've become a man, and a heap different one than she knew. Even if'n ye went back, do ye reckon ye'll see her the same way? Folks change, grow, turn into something different.

"Meantime, what about Willow? I seen that look in yer eyes. Ye got a hard case, coon. Why in hell cain't ye love her when she's loving ye back?"

"I made a promise to myself, to Laura, that I would keep myself for her." At the skeptical look in Travis's eye, he added, "It's just the way I am. In this sullied world, is it so terrible to keep yourself for your true love?"

"And this Laura, she's yer true love? Yer sure of that?"

"I am. And it's about my children, Travis. About who their mother is. What sort of person. It's...Oh, God, I'm not sure I really understand, but, I tell you, it's important."

"Why?"

"Because it is, that's why. I don't want *my* child growing up the way I..."

"Go on."

Richard's heart had begun to hammer, and he closed his eyes, shaking his head.

"Is it about yer mother?" Travis asked gently.

Richard wiped his face and sighed. "She was a wonderful lady, Travis. From the finest Boston family. She died giving birth—to me. I never knew her. And all those years, my father would leave, late at night. It was only when I was older that I found out he had a mistress."

"Ain't nothing wrong with that."

"I guess not," Richard lied.

"Ye *guess* not? Shit! Tell me straight, boy, why did it bother ye that yer father let hisself be a man every now and then?"

Richard's jaw tensed. *Dear God, why?*

"Because..."

"Ah, he wasn't being loyal to the dead, huh?" An eyebrow raised, rearranging the scars on Travis's face. "And ye don't think Willow had a covenant with her husband? Or is it that he's an Injun?"

Richard twirled the grass stem between his fingers. "I don't know."

"Reckon ye do."

"Do you know what she did? Back at the Grand Detour, she came down to the beach. She took off all her clothes, Travis, and waded into the water. She said that Shoshoni do it that way all the time." He pitched the grass away. "And I wanted her. I wanted her so badly that I almost gave in to what I knew was wrong."

"Ye were gonna take her against her will?"

"No. She was willing, Travis. I'd never force myself on a woman. But it's just impossible. She knows it, I know it, and I think you know it."

"Because a fancy Boston nob like yerself can't lower hisself to marrying an Injun?"

Richard nodded slowly. "My father—imagine the expression on his face. It would only be worse if I married a Negro."

"It ain't yer father, Dick. It's you."

"It's me," Richard whispered. "It's about the kind of life I want. Laura is that kind of wife, one suitable to a professor of philosophy. When I get back, I *will* marry her. Travis, you know me. How can I hold her, love her, knowing that when I was with her I'd be thinking about an Indian woman? And if Laura ever found out..."

Travis tapped at his knee with thoughtful fingers. "Ye don't have to go back, hoss."

"I have to, Travis. My life is back there. That's who I am." Richard dropped his hand down to massage his tender testicles. "If *anyone* ever found out. Travis, you've got to understand. I'm a *gentleman*."

"Is that another word fer silly idiot?"

"You know what I mean."

"Yer being a fool." Travis stared down at his sun-browned hands. "Ye come from the top, and I come from the bottom of what's back there. Lookit, hyar we are, jawing up a storm, and back thar in Boston, ye wouldn't give me a nod in the street. And Baptiste, ye'd figger him worse than shit on yer heel. Nothing but a nigger, free or not. Tell me, coon, with all yer savvy about mankind and culture and morality, which way's best? The top on the top like back there, or all mixed up like out hyar? Who's free, coon?"

"Is it freedom, Travis? Or a lack of responsibility?" Richard winced as he straightened his legs.

"Huh! I figger it's freedom. Life don't let nobody skip outa responsibility. Take me and Green. It don't matter that I owed him, I'd a took this trip on account of he's my friend. If'n the play was turned around, if'n it was my boat, Davey Green would be thar. Baptiste is stringing along looking fer fun, and ten percent, sure. But if'n I wasn't with this company, nine outa ten says he wouldn't be hyar. Don't matter where ye are, ye gotta be responsible ter yerself and yer companions. That, or ye ain't a man."

"All right, accepting that argument, I must be responsible enough to say no to the temptation Willow offers. In the end it would only hurt us both."

Travis sighed in defeat. "All right, I can accept that if'n that's how ye reads sign. That's a man making a choice to keep a friend from trouble. Willow would savvy that"—Travis's eyes hardened—"so long's it ain't that she's spoilt goods, and a damn Injun in yer eyes."

Is that it? Was that why I wanted to kill Travis? Because he spoke the truth, and I really am a hypocrite?

Travis grabbed futilely at a big black fly that buzzed around his head. "White men have got some tarnal strange ideas about what's what, and right, and proper ways fer folks ter act. Same fer Injuns; just ask that Packrat. Hell, maybe ye can't make it work without breaking each other's hearts. On the other hand, coon, maybe yer gonna throw away the best woman ye'll ever meet."

"What will people say, Travis? A white man...married to an Indian."

"Thar ye go again." Travis waved toward the west. "Ain't nobody out there gonna care. Baptiste figgered that out long ago. Yer only in trouble if'n ye goes back ter America."

"But I *must,* Travis."

"Wal, ain't no man can walk yer road fer ye. How're ye feeling? Reckon we otta drop back toward the river, see if'n the sneaking Sioux's wiped out the *engagés.* Can ye walk?"

Richard stood slowly and made a face, legs bowed. "I'll say this, Travis, I sure won't have to worry if Willow catches me in the river again. You took care of any concerns in that regard."

"Sorry, coon. I figgered I'd take ye out afore ye fooled around and hurt me."

"It's going to be a long afternoon on the back of that bony mare."

Travis's face had resumed that flinty look. "Yep. Ain't nothing come free, hoss. Trail's never easy ter follow, and being a might uncomfortable of an occasion makes a coon think a little clearer."

"I'll remember that," Richard growled, as he eased himself onto the mare's back. But all he could remember was the look in Willow's soft eyes as she walked away that day.

CHAPTER SIXTEEN

Man being born, as has been proved, with a title to perfect freedom and uncontrolled enjoyment of all the rights and privileges of the law of nature, equally with any other man or number of men in the world, hath by nature a power, not only to preserve his property, that is, his life, liberty, and estate, against injuries and attempts of other men, but to judge of and punish the breaches of that law in others, as he is persuaded the offence deserves, even with death itself.

—John Locke, *Liberalism in Politics*

Baptiste led the way, trotting his horse ahead, rifle butt propped on his saddle. On the right, Travis rode with his Hawken across the saddle bows. With each movement of the horses, their long fringe swayed, beadwork glinted, and long hair danced in the wind. To Richard's eyes, they looked like barbarians crossing the flat floodplain.

This was Ree country. From the time they'd crossed

the Grand River, about five miles back, Travis and Baptiste had been increasingly worried. They'd ridden warily through the scrubby bur oak, green ash, and elms that fringed the base of the cedar-studded bluff that rose like a wall to the west.

What a hot, sweltering day. The sun stood straight overhead, and through a faint tracery of high clouds, burned the sky white. Silvery mirages shimmered as heat waves played across the hot ground. Insects buzzed and the horses' feet swished through the brittle grass.

"Ain't no telling about these hyar Rees," Travis warned. "Best check yer load."

Richard did so, making sure the priming powder still filled the pan on his Hawken. Then asked, "Maybe you'd better tell me about the Arikara? Related to the Pawnee, correct?"

"Uh-huh." Travis barely nodded. "Baptiste, hyar, he lived with 'em fer longer than this child. Hell, he talks their talk, knows most of 'em fer the thieving souls they is."

Baptiste shrugged, squinting around from under the brim of his black hat. "I don't cotton to them being called thieves. Hell, they just been pushed too far, coon."

"Pushed?" Richard asked.

"They been on the river foah years." Baptiste waved back toward the south. "Remember all them old villages we seen? The houses has caved in and weeds has growed up, but you'll see them big round holes in the ground. Time was, they had more'n thirty villages stretching up from the Platte clear to the Mandans. Then the Missouri and Osage come. The Omaha and Sioux and Iowa. Sickness come, too. One by one, the Rees quit their villages, moved in with kin foah protection."

"Why were the other Indians so mad at them?" Richard glanced around at the foreboding flats.

"Injuns don't need ary a reason," Travis muttered, "They enjoy killing each other just fer the fun of it."

"Sort o' like a white man, if'n you ask me." Baptiste snorted irritably. "Man can't live without the itch to whack another man and take what's his'n. Don't make no matter. That's just the way men are. So the Rees come heah, to this part of the river...mostly 'cause the Omaha and Blackbird didn't want it. Look around. Not much wood grows here. Not like back south on the Platte, or up north in the Mandan lands. But the Rees hung on, fighting fer their lives against the Sioux and the others. Then the smallpox come. Blackbird died, and the Omaha didn't control the trade no more. The Sioux beat Hob outa the downriver tribes and the Rees figgered their day'd come."

"Tell him about the chiefs." Travis tightened his grip on his sweat-stained Hawken.

"Rees is different," Baptiste said as he scanned the brush. "They set right store by chiefs. Descended from *Nesanu*..."

"Who?"

"*Nesanu*. That's the Ree name fer God. Some Injuns out heah, Sioux, Cheyenne, Omaha, they picks a chief by what he says and does. Not the Rees or the Pawnee. If'n yer daddy be a chief, you'll be a chief, and yer son after that. Nobles, that's the word Lisa called 'em. It's passed through the family, and each village had a chief. Like a son from God. So they call their chiefs *Nesanu,* after God."

"That doesn't sound so odd. People have been doing that in Europe for centuries." Richard wiped at the sweat that trickled over old mosquito bites. His horse shied and side-stepped nervously as a coiled rattlesnake buzzed at them.

"Wal, coon, imagine thirty villages mixed inter just two. And each chief plumb equal with every other one. It's like having fifteen different captains in one boat. All they do is fight with each other. Hell, give a Ree chief a chance ter lift hair on a Sioux or another Ree chief, and sure as sun in the morning, he'll take that Ree's hair."

"That's lunacy!" Richard swatted at a fly that persisted in buzzing around.

"Ter yer way of thinking," Travis agreed, "but it's plumb normal fer Rees."

"Why did they attack Ashley?" Richard watched three buzzards spiraling on the hot air. A sign? Since his encounter with the *wechashawakan,* he'd begun to wonder about such things—much to the disgust of his rational side.

"Trade. What else?" Baptiste cocked his head to glance at Richard. "In the beginning, Lewis and Clark come through and told 'em that the Americans was a-coming to trade. The Rees figgered it was their chance. Then the Americans started passing right on by, headed foah the Mandans and Hidatsas. Rees watched all them goods going upriver, and no letup in the Sioux attacks, and all that was left was being poor and dirty. Hell, the Sioux call the Rees their 'women,' 'cause the Rees plant the corn, tan the hides, and the Sioux come take 'em whenever they wants."

"Don't matter," Travis replied. "Rees is cutthroats and thieves. A Ree brave will sell ye his woman, and cut yer throat as soon as yer pizzle's pumped dry."

"So do Sioux," Baptiste shot back. "And Mandan, and Hidatsa, and Crow, and all the rest. So don't ye go on about—"

"They don't cut yer throat the next instant!" Travis retorted hotly. His horse tossed its head and pranced wide around a patch of brush.

"Wal, coon," Baptiste growled, "we'd best not be fighting over it. You've yor way of thinking, I's got mine. I reckon we just ain't never gonna see eye to eye on Rees."

"Reckon not," Travis groused, then gave Baptiste a sly grin. The two rode close enough to playfully box each other's shoulders.

"Travis, why don't you like the Rees?" Richard asked.

"Rees have wiped out too many good friends over the years. I reckon it fogs a feller's thinking."

"Thar she be." Baptiste pointed across the flats.

Through the glassy heat waves, Richard could see the village: several rounded houses on the dusty bluff that overlooked the river. The palisade still stood in places, charred black, and gaping like broken teeth.

"Someone's thar!" Baptiste cried, pulling up his horse.

Travis slowed his animal and slumped in the saddle, inspecting the flats with uneasy eyes before squinting at the distant remains of the Ree village.

"Tarnation and brimstone," Travis growled. "I never did figger all them coons had hightailed after Leavenworth shot 'em up."

Richard swallowed hard, realizing that these weed-filled flats had once been cornfields. The ruined village, the desolate fields, the heat, all seemed nothing more than a pale reflection of Hell.

"What now?" Richard asked. "Will they attack us?"

Travis licked his lips, his gnarled thumb curling around the cock on his rifle. "Wal, coons, we got ter foller the river. The *Maria's* gonna make camp right about hyar, tonight. If'n there's ter be Ree trouble, we'd best find out."

"You mean ride in there?" Richard glanced back and forth between the men.

Baptiste flashed white teeth in a wide smile. "You figger since I lived with 'em, they might not shoot us right off?"

"Crossed my mind, coon. What's in yer noodle?"

"Oh, I reckon they won't shoot *me* right off—leastways, not till they shoots you and Dick fust."

"Yer sure sassy fer a black beaver." Travis slapped his leg. "All right, let's ride easy. First sign of trouble, we break and run like Hell's jackrabbits fer the boat. Dave'll need all the warning he can get." '

Travis dropped back beside Richard, pointing at the ruined village. "During the Leavenworth fight, the chief hyar was called Little Soldier. About the time it looked like they was nigh ter getting wiped out, he come out under a flag of truce to talk. Told old Leavenworth that if the army'd hide him from the Sioux, he'd help destroy the village. Ye can't trust a Ree, Dick. Never fergit that."

"He was trying to save his kin," Baptiste called back. "White folks don't never seem to understand what kin can mean to a man."

Travis said nothing in reply, but narrowed an eye.

"The place looks deserted," Richard noted as they rode closer to the remains of the charred palisade.

"Yep," Baptiste said, clipped. "But I make it out to be right around ten lodges rebuilt."

Richard studied the brown mounds Baptiste indicated. Looking closely, he could see a thin strand of blue smoke rising from within the village. Here and there, small plots of corn, beans, and squash were growing—but not very well. Dogs began to bark.

"It ain't the whole tribe." Travis scowled. "I'd guess about fifty people."

A bead of sweat crept down the side of Richard's head. A sinking feeling hollowed his gut, and his muscles tightened. His rifle's wrist was damp where he clutched it.

One shot. Make it count. Remember, Travis says you can always bluff with a loaded rifle.

He nodded to himself, mouth gone dry as dust.

"Hold up!" Baptiste raised a hand. "Somebody's a-coming."

Through a gap in the palisade, a lone Indian man appeared. He wore nothing but a loincloth and short moccasins. In one hand he carried a pipe, in the other a rifle. Behind him, Richard could see heads bobbing as other Arikara took positions in the ditch behind the shattered palisade. Was that sunlight glinting off a rifle?

The warrior walked bravely forward, head high, the sun shining on his blunt brown features. Wide-set eyes seemed to pop out from his face, giving him a frog look. His hair had been pulled into two long braids intertwined with buffalo hair, and his forelocks curled back over his forehead. Stopping short, he called in passable English, "Who comes to the villages of the Arikara?"

Baptiste smiled, urging his horse forward. "Big Yellow, by God! It's Baptiste, coon. With me's Travis Hartman and Dick Hamilton. Dave Green's coming up behind us with a boat."

Big Yellow cocked his head, but no smile of greeting turned those hard lips. "Baptiste. Good to see you." And a string of Arikara talk followed, helped along by flourishes of the pipe in his right hand.

"What did he say?" Richard demanded. Damn it all,

he felt like a target sitting out here in the open. His skin crawled, as if waiting for the impact of a bullet.

"Says he figured someone would come after the army come through hyar a couple of weeks back," Travis said from the side of his mouth. "Say's whites and Ankara are at peace, and he's got a paper from General Atkinson ter prove it."

Baptiste had slipped off the side of his horse, walking forward to hug Big Yellow like a long-lost brother.

Richard ran a nervous tongue along the edge of his front teeth. "You believe that?"

Travis pulled at his beard, eyes squinted. "Yep. So long's Atkinson's upriver...and we're armed. Won't be no trouble, Dick. Not with Dave coming up ahind us. Reckon we're gonna be treated like kings whilst we're hyar."

"Food's cooking," Baptiste called as he turned away from Big Yellow. "What do you think, Travis?"

Hartman glanced warily at the heads watching from the broken and scorched palisade. "Reckon we'll palaver out hyar."

Big Yellow shrugged, a weary expression on his broad face. "If you wish, Bear Man. Rees are at peace. I am *Nesanu.* I have given my word."

"And if they's another chief in thar?" Travis jerked his head toward the village. "He give his word, too?"

"I am the only *Nesanu* at this place." Big Yellow offered up the pipe. "Ten lodges. All my people, Bear Man. No one will harm you." His smile seemed forced and weary. "Some of us have learned that no good will come of harming a white man. Some of us know that Leavenworth was foolish—but soldier-chief Atkinson is not."

Travis pulled at his beard, and jerked a nod. "All right, hoss, but if'n something goes wrong, I'll kill ye."

Baptiste climbed into the saddle and rode toward the gap in the palisade. Travis lingered long enough to ask, "Want ter philos'phy him fer a while?"

Richard shook his head.

"Best slip that fetish inside yer britches, coon," Travis warned. "And if'n anybody asks about it, ye bought it down ter Saint Loowee, understand?"

Richard turned the fetish on his belt and tucked it into his britches. "But, Travis, what do these people care about skunk hide?"

———

Fat's in the fire now, Travis thought as he passed through the palisade gap.

The Ree village lay in shambles. Here and there, Travis could see the scars left by Leavenworth's cannon. As the army retreated, two of Pilcher's men—or maybe it was the Sioux—had sneaked back and set fire to the village. Big Yellow and his people had salvaged some timbers, and snagged others from the river to rebuild a few of the large round houses. Each measured about forty feet across and perhaps ten feet high at the top of the earthen dome. Around them lay the collapsed wreckage of much larger houses, some sixty feet across.

In silence, men, women, and children watched them pass—and their simmering anger carried to him like a carrion breeze. He could see it in their hard brown eyes, the hands clenching bows, old trade rifles, and war clubs. In their wake, people closed in behind them. Unlike the old days, the Rees wore tattered clothing: frayed, sun-bleached fabric; leather worn full of holes and missing fringe; and scanty hanks of beads. The pitiful garments seemed to hang on their bony flesh. But the hollow-eyed look of the children bored into his very soul.

No way out but to shoot our way.

Travis's gut churned as he glanced back at the Arikara, who followed like a silent army.

This was a damn fool idea.

But up ahead, Baptiste rode unconcerned, talking easily with Big Yellow.

The place smelled. Old curled hides—once the coverings for bull boats—had hardened in the sun. Broken pots lay scattered about, including cracked iron and flattened copper kettles. Scaffolding for meat racks had been rebuilt, but from driftwood that looked rickety. Piles of horse manure were drying in the sun, no doubt to be scooped up and thrown into the ever-hungry cookfires as soon as they cured. Old storage pits lay open, sides crumbled, ready to trap the unwary passerby in their yawning depths.

"This place is huge," Richard cried, staring at a big house that had somehow remained standing. The long doorway gaped like a black socket.

"This is the little village. Big one is a rifle shot up ahead." Travis tried to calm his horse as a pack of village dogs charged out to nip at the hocks.

"It looks pretty dismal," Richard said sadly. "My God, how dirty they are."

"Comes of making war on whites, coon."

"Travis, what Baptiste said? Is that true? That they were just trying to save themselves?"

"Depends on how ye read sign. They's other ways of saving yerself than killing traders."

They'd pulled up before one of the lodges and Travis reluctantly dismounted. A sunshade of poles and woven cattail matting cast a little square of shade. Big Yellow gestured, shouting orders, and a gaunt woman hustled from the throng, ducked into the long entry, and emerged a moment later carrying a buffalo hide. This she spread on the ground under the sunshade.

Travis slapped at a fly that buzzed around his nose. The whole place was curiously silent. How different from the days when Lisa's boats had arrived here. Then the crowds had thronged about the boats; feasting, dancing, and laying in the robes had followed. In those days, like kings of old, the traders had been carried up from the river in buffalo robes born by muscular warriors.

Travis kept his reins in his hand, noting that Richard had learned his lesson—he kept his animal between him and the gathered Rees.

At a gesture from Big Yellow, three boys came to claim the horses. "Don't take them out of sight," Travis told them in Arikara.

The skin on his back was crawling as he motioned to Richard, and took a place on the buffalo robe in the shade. Tarnal Hell, a coon could be shot in the back so easily. All a warrior had to do was sneak around the side of the lodge, level his rifle, and she'd be Katy bar the door.

Cattail leaves rattled in the hot breeze, the sound like dry bones clacking. At the same time the rest of the Rees closed in, seating themselves in the hot sun. For all the expression they showed, those brown faces could have been modeled of clay.

Big Yellow filled his pipe, lit it with an ember brought by a young man, and chanted the blessing to *Nesanu*; to *Atna,* the Corn Mother; and finally to Grandfather Stone. The pipe was offered to the northeast, southeast, south-west, and northwest, the four sacred directions of the Arikara.

Baptiste puffed, and offered the pipe to the directions. His brown eyes had softened as he stared out at the crowd. Then Travis took the pipe, drawing the bittersweet tobacco into his lungs. To his satisfaction, Richard copied every move correctly.

"It is good," Big Yellow began, "to have traders in my village again. Our two peoples have had bad times. Let us have no more." He made a wiping-out gesture with the flat of his hand. "The time for war between us is past."

"There has been trouble," Baptiste agreed. "Big Yellow speaks the truth. We have come upriver with peace in our hearts. We wish nothing more than to pass in peace."

Big Yellow sat thoughtfully, pulling on one of his braids. He looked around at the people squatting in the sun, their empty brown eyes fixed on him. "My people need many of the things the White traders carry. We have no powder for our guns. No bullets to shoot. We are few now. The village Medicine Bundles have been carried away to the four winds. The Doctors' societies are all scattered everywhere. The White man has come like a great wind, one that has broken Mother Corn, who we also know as the sacred cedar—snapped her off clean. On every side, my people are surrounded by enemies. The Sioux come and take what they wish. If we raise a hand in protest, they kill us. We cannot stop them."

Big Yellow indicated his silent people. "My friends can see my children. Their arms and legs are thin, their bellies hang out. Look at the hunger in their eyes. Look at my women. They wear only what the Sioux have left us. Their dresses are worn thin. The milk in their breasts will not feed their children."

Big Yellow fixed Travis with level eyes. "Is this what the White men wished? To see us so?"

"Reckon not," Travis said carefully. "They's hard times ter go around fer everybody."

Big Yellow betrayed no expression. "We have not seen hunger or want in the eyes of the Sioux."

"Them coons take what they want. It ain't just the Rees that they've been raiding and stealing from."

"I do not worry about others," Big Yellow stated. "I worry about *my* people, Bear Man."

"You know the trade," Travis countered. "We got ter go where the beaver is. How many beaver can ye trade?"

The weary smile creased Big Yellow's lips. "The time for easy talk is past, Bear Man. I will tell you how the Rees think about trade. We trade among ourselves, but it is to make things balance. Some do not have what they need, so we trade that all may share. In the beginning, we thought the White men were like *Nesanu*, powerful, surrounded by wonderful things inside and outside their bodies. We did not understand how you could live in our houses, eat our food, and not share everything you had with us, as we share with each other. *Nesanu* taught us to give something to everyone. But you White men keep as much as you can for yourselves. We have never understood how you could be so selfish. Until I met a White man, I did not know the word 'profit.'"

"That's the way of trade." Travis pulled at his beard. "A trader has to take all he can get. If'n he don't, he can't trade fer more knives, guns, and powder. Ree ways and white ways is different. Killing traders ain't gonna fix it. Why'd ye pick a fight?"

Big Yellow rubbed a callused hand on his bare arm. "It was because we thought you were our friends. It was because we offered you everything, and then you left us to be killed by the Sioux. In the beginning, when *Nesanu* made the world, he made it so that people would share with their friends. How does the White man act when a friend stabs him in the back? Does he not pick up his rifle and make war? Is that not what you did when the British came to trade on the river?"

Travis rolled his jaw from side to side. Hell, that's what they'd told the damn Injuns. Lisa had set in this very village and explained the war that way.

"You do not need to answer, Bear Man." Big Yellow straightened his back. "This chief understands now that your ways are different, that you do not have *Nesanu*'s words in your heart. Some of my people have told me I am a fool for coming back here to the river. They have said that I will die here, killed by the Sioux, or by the Whites." He pointed across the heads of the watchers to a low dirt mound. "My ancestors lie there, in that earth. I can feel their *sishu,* their souls. That is why I am here. If we are to die, it will be on our land, among our ancestors. So many of them are dead because of the wickedness in your souls, my life would only be one more."

"Cain't nobody keep disease away." Travis took a deep breath, his nerves tight as fiddle strings.

"Perhaps, Bear Man." Big Yellow's bug-eyed stare drilled into Travis. "We are poor now. You see what we have. When Green's boat comes, will you trade? Big Yellow understands that you are taking most of your wonderful things to our enemies, but we will offer what we can."

Travis chewed his lip, considering. A dirty, moon-faced child watched him with round eyes. The kid's hair was matted, and he sucked on muddy fingers.

"Reckon we'll trade some," Travis admitted. "Ain't much, but it will help."

Big Yellow nodded slowly. "It will help. Your men will have been long time without women. Once, we thought it curious that you had no women of your own. It was believed that a man could give his woman to you, and afterward, he could gain some of your Power by lying with her. I think now that it was a lie. No man ever gained White Power through his woman that way. If we had, we would not be like we are today."

"Boat will be up by dark," Travis said. "Reckon we'll trade what we can. But, Big Yellow, yer a wise old coon. It wouldn't do fer some warrior ter get outa sorts. Let's keep folks separate fer the most part. Less likely ter be an accident that way."

"Reckon so, coon," Big Yellow agreed.

"So, what's happening?" Richard wondered as they walked toward their horses.

"We're gonna trade," Travis answered. "Hell, they ain't got squat but women to offer. Only thing we're getting is free passage and a lighter load."

"But it beats a fight," Baptiste replied, eyes half-lidded.

"Women?" Richard sighed.

"It's about all they got," Travis reminded.

"I'd call that whoring."

"Not according ter their lights, and it'll fill a couple of these kids' bellies."

———

Maria lay tied off on the bank below the Arikara village. Laughter carried on the warm night breeze. A half moon hung low over the dissected buttes east of the river, and stars dusted the sky. Far to the south, flickers of lightning danced, but no sound of thunder reached them.

This is an awful place.

Willow sat on the cargo box beside Travis. She rubbed her smooth shins and watched the firelit bank. Unease, like a subtle undercurrent, twined with her *puha*. She could sense the spirits here, troubled and crying.

It would be better to leave this place of sorrows.

Green stood just below them, a rifle in his hands. Richard sat at the bow, his Hawken across his lap while Henri stood guard at the stern. Baptiste was ashore with Big Yellow, keeping a wary eye on the *engagés* who dallied with the Arikara women.

Bonfires illuminated the ruined village in a ghostly glow; human shadows wavered against the palisade and earth lodges.

"Looks a mite more peaceful than the last time I was hyar," Travis said. "Reckon we'll get nigh away without trouble. Green and me, we done decided, about an hour afore dawn, we're heading out. Reckon them coons best wet their pizzles, 'cause we'll be humping backs upriver hard. Leastways, until we make a distance atwixt us and the Rees."

Willow filled her lungs with the musky scent of the river and slapped a mosquito that landed on her arm. "Can you feel them, Trawis?"

"Huh? Feel what?"

"The spirits. Some angry, others so sad."

He cocked his head, concentrating. "Don't know, gal. I been on edge ever since we got hyar. Reckon this place has done gone sour. It's them kids. The way they was looking at me. I never give much thought to kids afore. That's the saddest part."

"Green did not like giving them flour and so much food."

"Nope. Might make things a tad tight come winter on

the Big Horn. We'd best hope we make a good fall hunt and the buffs is down in the valleys this winter. Bellies might be a shade gaunted up otherwise."

She reached out, laying a hand on his arm. "If you are worthy, *Tam Apo* will provide."

Travis sucked his lip for a moment, then shrugged. "I had me a dream back when ye made that travois. Saw old Manuel Lisa and his coons. They told me the river was dying."

"Baptiste says it is because of the white men. I think he is right. The water may continue to run, but the river's soul will wither."

"Yer a different sort, Willow. Ye see more than most folks."

"I have always been different." She rubbed her hands together. "At times it has made my life hard. I have been told I ask too many questions."

Richard shifted, and Willow couldn't help but watch him. If only...

Travis, ever keen, noticed and studied her from the corner of his eye. "He's a good man. Reckon the two of ye'd do right nice together."

She shifted on the hard deck. "We follow two different trails. He to the east and his people, and I to the west." But her soul was haunted by the warmth in his brown eyes, and the tender way he touched things. If she closed her eyes, she could imagine the sensation of his fingers on her skin, the warmth of his body against hers.

"Different worlds can join, gal. It ain't always a gonna fall apart."

"The White world touched the Arikara. What do they have left? Begging for food? Selling their women? I have heard the talk. The cut-throat Sioux say Arikara are like women to them. They make things just so the Sioux can come and take them away."

"Sioux is tough coons. Trouble is, they's so many of them."

"They have strong medicine."

"Reckon." Travis rubbed his ruined nose and mashed a mosquito that had settled from the humming hoard. "To my way of thinking, it makes Baptiste's notions wrong. Ifn whites destroy everything in their path, the Sioux otta be about wrecked, too. But they ain't. Seems to this child that they just get stronger and stronger."

"Perhaps."

They shared a long silence.

Travis asked, "Something happened back at the Grand Detour. Dick and ye, ye ain't been the same since. Each of ye is sad way down deep in the heart."

"We saw truth in each other's eyes, Trawis." She batted at the cloud of mosquitoes. "I cannot go to Boston. I am told it isn't my place. He would not like life among the *Dukurika*. What more needs to be said?"

"He don't know that." Travis resettled his rifle. "He figgered he'd hate the river. Hell, he still thinks he hates it, but ye've seen the shine come ter his eyes. He's becoming a man, Willow. He just ain't got his sights set straight yet. A feller don't know what he's got until he can see forward and backward. I reckon Dick's still looking back so hard, he can't cotton ter what's right afore his nose."

"I do not understand."

"He's fixed on Boston, and some gal named Laura."

"Who is this Laura?" What was her Power, that she could hold Ritshard from so far away?

Travis shifted nervously. "Wal, she's little sister to a friend of his. Said she'd let him come court if'n he come back. It ain't final, ye understand, just an agreement to pay court. Them Boston folks do things that way."

"What is court?"

"Um, like offerin' hosses to a gal's father so's a feller can try ter make her like him."

"And she is a lady?" Willow's stomach soured at the thought. "Is that what he wants? A lady in a box? To be taken care of?"

Travis plucked absently at the fringe hanging from his sleeve. "He ain't figgered out that his soul's been changed. It'll happen, but he's a bullheaded son of a bitch. Might take a spell yet...and maybe a good whack on the side of the head, but he'll see. He's a right savvy Doodle."

She stilled the whirlwind that churned inside.

What a fool I have been. "

I cannot wait that long, Trawis. I have decisions of my own that must be made. His heart cannot rest until he has gone back to his Boston."

And he can have his White lady, in her house, with her children.

"Mine cannot find peace unless I can smell the trees, hear the birds, and enjoy a warm fire on a cold night."

"Ye sure?"

"Could you live in his Boston?"

"Nope."

She returned her attention to the Ree village, fists clenched at her side. "I think of good things, and they are all in my land. I want to see my father again, laugh with my mother. I want to hunt the *duku,* what you call bighorn. We trap them in pens on the side of the mountain. My best memories are of cold mornings after a good kill. When you cut the animal open, the bodies smoke in the cold."

"Steam. That's the word, gal."

"Yes, steam. You know the smell, don't you? Of blood, and the insides of the animal. Sweet—and all the while, your soul knows that meat will be roasting, and your belly will be full. People will laugh and tell stories around the fires that night. They do not do these things in Boston?"

"Nope. Folks buy meat all cut up."

"That sweet smell, Trawis, that is the smell of life, of the animal's soul that will join with yours. At that moment, I know I'm part of *Tam Apo's* world. I think these people in Boston do not know these things."

Travis exhaled wearily.

"What will happen when the white men come to my country? Will they take that sharing of life away?"

"I don't know."

"I think they will. They put their women in houses. They put their God in a house. I have heard Green tell me that other Injuns, Shawnee, Cherokee, Iroquois, have all been put in places. Is that what White men do? Will they try to put the *Dukurika* in a place, like flour in a barrel?"

"Yer Snakes are a long way away from whites."

After an uncomfortable pause, she asked, "What about you, Trawis? Why don't you go back? You are a great warrior, a hunter, a powerful man. The Whites should make you a gentleman."

He laughed at that, but she could hear the bitterness.

Again the silence stretched.

Finally he said, "Willow, I ain't sure the whites are gonna go clear ter the Snake lands. Traders, sure. But not the farmers. It'd take some doing ter make a living in the mountains. Hell, there ain't nothing there. I seen the Snake country. It's too damn dry fer growing corn. Only thing a body can do is hunt. And I ain't seen a damn thing can be done with sagebrush but burn it in a fire—and hardwood's the beat of sagebrush any old day."

"I think they will come, Trawis." She rubbed her legs harder, as if to scrub the thought away. "I think the White man wants everything he can get—even if it is only sagebrush to burn in the fires."

"Ye make it sound like poor bull, gal."

She pointed at the village. "Is that fat cow?"

Travis pulled at his beard. "The Rees went to war with the whites. That's what comes of killing white men." He paused. "There's other ways, gal. Snakes could join the whites, help fight the Blackfeet. It wouldn't have ter be grief. Yer warriors know the country. And ain't the Blackfeet more trouble fer ye than the whites would be?"

"My people would kill a man like Trudeau. This would not make other White men mad?"

"Hell, I'd like ter kill him, too." But again she heard hesitation in his voice.

"You have answered my question, Trawis. Now do you see why Ritshard and I must go our different ways?"

And I must go mine, at the first chance.

If she didn't, the sadness within would slowly consume her soul.

Laura? What kind of a name was that?

Beside her, Travis stared glumly into the night.

CHAPTER SEVENTEEN

But the most frequent reason why men desire to hurt each other ariseth
hence, that many men at the same time have an appetite to the same thing;
which yet often they can neither enjoy in common, nor yet divide it;
whence it follows that the strongest must have it, and who is strongest must
be decided by the sword.

—Thomas Hobbes, *Leviathan*

 The four days they'd spent
alternately towing and poling
the *Maria* away from the Ree
village had drained everyone's
gumption. Green had finally
called a halt, here, on a grassy
bluff that looked out over an oxbow of the sun-silvered
river.

Richard lay propped on his elbows, chewing the
sweet stalk of a bluestem. The western breeze had
carried the earliest of mosquitoes away. Every muscle

ached from the time he'd spent on the cordelle, adding his strength to the work.

A wasp landed on his thigh. With a thumb and forefinger, he flicked the beast away and squinted up at the triangular cotton-wood leaves. His soul squirmed between his growing desire for Willow and his commitment to Laura.

Across from him, Baptiste skinned a monstrous rattlesnake, peeling the scaly green hide from pink meat.

Travis lay flat on his back in the shade, his worn felt hat pulled low to shield his eyes. The hunter had fallen into a deep sleep, chest rising and falling slowly. The up-tipped face visible beneath the sagging hat brim exposed the crisscross tracery of white scars and bush of beard.

For the moment, Richard envied Travis his lack of responsibility. How pleasant it would be to flit about, never making a commitment to any woman. But how hollow would he feel in the end, when he finally realized that he'd never fully shared his life with a woman?

I hereby resolve I will not make that mistake, Richard decided.

Green and Henri, as usual, sat before the booshway's tent, their talk perpetually on the river and whether the water was rising or falling.

The other *engagés* lay like logs, with only the unlucky mess captains seeing to fires and cookpots. Grasshoppers chirred in the lazy air, while magpies and robins flitted through the bur oak ringing the meadow.

Richard stretched and winced at his cramped limbs. He turned his head, wondering what had happened to Willow—and from the corner of his eye, caught sight of Trudeau.

Something about the man focused Richard's attention. Usually, the boatman swaggered, but now he walked furtively, a slight crouch suggested by his steps as he eased into the fringe of bur oaks.

I'm too damned tired to worry about him.

Richard took a deep breath and lay back on his saddle, happy to let the afternoon sun warm his face. The world was filled with too many troubles as it was: Laura, Willow, his father; he'd begun to fret about all of them.

Furtive?... Trudeau?

He sat up with a grunt, and threw the grass stem away. Trudeau had vanished into the trees.

Richard growled at himself and stood. He massaged the stiffness in his legs with equally stiff hands, and picked up his rifle. He turned his steps in the direction Trudeau had taken, unconsciously adopting the wary hunter's stalk that had become so familiar.

The most likely path was a deer trail that wound westward, away from the river and toward the bluffs. Several of the pale leaves on a buffaloberry had been bruised where Trudeau had passed.

On moccasined feet, Richard followed silently, employing all the skills Travis and Baptiste had tried so hard to beat into him.

The trail wound uphill into the bluffs, past chokecherry and wild grape. It opened into a grassy cove lined with brush. Richard slowed as he spotted his prey. Trudeau crouched several steps ahead, screened from the clearing by a mass of oblate chokecherry leaves.

On the far side of the clearing, Willow plucked the first ripened chokecherries off their stems. She dropped them one by one into a leather sack. Each night, she'd been collecting such foodstuffs, carefully drying them, and refusing to allow anyone to partake of her growing cache.

Travel food for her journey home. Richard's heart

ached all the harder. The thought of her leaving drove him half mad, but what other alternative was there?

Travis had watched her with a curious frown, but she'd only smiled and artfully deflected his attempts to persuade her to stay.

And now, here was Trudeau, sneaking after her. Richard swallowed hard as he studied the boatman's thick shoulders, the muscles bunched under a sun-bleached and frayed shirt. Black hair, like matted wire, covered the *engagé's* powerful forearms. Trudeau moved with a cat's quick agility, and, like the cat, had little mercy in his callous soul for victims.

What do I do? Run back for Travis?

At that moment, Trudeau edged forward, crossing the clearing in carefully placed steps.

Willow remained oblivious, back turned to the *engagé*.

Richard straightened, heart pounding as he gripped his Hawken.

"Trudeau!" He stepped out into the clearing, scared half to death, and part of him suddenly sick from the realization that he'd just committed himself to a beating.

The *engagé* stopped as Willow turned like a startled fawn, chokecherries falling from her container.

"Who?" Trudeau's eyes slitted, shoulders bunched. "It is you, Yankee. Go away. Now! Or I will hit you hard in the stomach again, eh?"

"Leave her alone." Richard pointed at Willow, hoping his arm didn't tremble.

"Willow and I, we have a talk, eh? It is not for you, weak little American. Leave now, and Trudeau will say nothing."

Willow had plucked the war club from her belt, dark eyes narrowing as she gripped it for a blow.

"She'll break your head," Richard warned.

"She will?" Trudeau threw his head back and laughed. "Why do you worry? This woman, she is squaw, *non?*"

"She's a guest. Travis told you. And Green, too."

"Bah! She's running away. What do you think, eh? She makes dried food for the journey. Very well, but before she go, Trudeau will say good-bye! And so will you, Yankee."

"I'll tell Travis."

Trudeau started toward him, hands outstretched. "You'll tell no one anything, Yankee. I think you will not leave here, eh?"

Richard looked past him, shouting, "Run, Willow!" and lifted the Hawken. The cock clicked loudly as Richard thumbed it back. "Not another step."

Trudeau's dark eyes smoldered. "You do not have the courage to shoot me...no matter what hangs from your belt, *crasseux chien.*"

The set trigger clicked under Richard's finger. "Believe what you want."

Willow had cut around to one side, her war club ready. Trudeau sneaked a glance at her, aware of the dark glint in her eyes.

"Lâchement, bâtard!" Trudeau raised his hands, backing slowly away. "Perhaps you should shoot now, *oui?* If you do not, Trudeau will make you pay."

"You talk a lot."

"You will not always have the rifle!" Trudeau pointed an angry finger. And with that, he spun on his heel and crashed off into the chokecherries.

Richard took a deep breath and lowered the hammer to half-cock. A fine film of sweat had dampened his face and neck; now the cooling breeze wicked it away.

Willow lowered her Pawnee war club and chuckled, a twinkle in her eyes.

How can she do that? I'm almost trembling!

He hung his head for a moment, and looked up from lowered eyes.

"Thank you, Ritshard." She stepped close and laid a hand on his shoulder.

"I thought I was going to have to shoot him."

She shrugged. "Sometimes a man does not know when to quit. *Tam Apo* has little patience for fools."

"He doesn't?"

"How many old fools do you know?"

"Quite a few—but they're all back in the United States." He studied her thoughtfully. "You're leaving very soon, aren't you?"

She kicked at the grass with a dainty foot. "My people are far to the west. I must go." Her dark brown eyes bored into his. "My husband and child are dead. I want to mourn them. You have made a place in my heart, but I cannot have you. You will go back to Boston...and Laura."

"Willow, I—"

"And there is more. I have listened to Green and Trawis talk about the Whites, and what will come. I need to think about this. Until I do, my soul will be like a twig on the river, bobbing, spinning, and never resting, never knowing where it is headed. Do you understand?"

"I...I do."

But, oh, God, I don't want you to go.

He reached up, touching the corner of her cheek with the tip of his finger. She closed her eyes as he traced gentle fingers along her skin.

She took his hand, pressing it to her cheek. "Ritshard, you must promise me, after I am gone, tell Green I will send someone to him at the mouth of the river they call Big Horn. Will you do this for me?"

Her touch stoked a hollow tickle under his heart, and

he drew her to him. Her arms went around him, and she buried her face against his neck. How perfectly she fit against his body, as if molded for him alone. Inhaling, he savored her aroma, sweet scent spiced by leather and woodsmoke. He ran his hands down her slim back and let them settle in the curve of her thin waist. He could feel her breasts pressing against his chest, and closed his eyes to savor the sensations conjured within.

Memories haunted him of that day at the river: her lithe body in the sun, and water like diamonds beading on her firm thighs. Dark nipples on rounded breasts, her flat belly accenting the curve of hip and the mystery hidden beneath glistening pubic hair. How proud she'd looked, broad-shouldered, midnight hair shining blue in the sunlight.

She tightened her grip, surprising him with her strength. Her body's heat burned into him, into his soul, and triggered a hammering of his heart. He wanted her, the need building with each pulsing rush of blood in his veins.

She felt him hardening and pushed away, slim hands on his heaving chest. She searched his eyes with hers, seeking desperately...

"Dear Lord God, I...I can't. Willow." He shook his head, panting, dropping his eyes so she wouldn't see the shame, lust, and need all mixed together.

From the corner of his eye, he could see her nod and turn away, walking toward her basket of chokecherries. He knotted his muscles against the ache in his chest and let the fever ebb from his blood.

I must think of Laura, of the promise I made to her. If I can't keep that simple promise, how will I ever look myself in the eye again and still call myself a man?

They walked back toward camp in silence, casting

furtive glances at each other. Everything seemed dreary and confused. So much piled on him: Trudeau at the precipice of a killing; Willow leaving; the horrible emptiness lurked inside—like rot hollowing out an old log.

———

Travis sat in the shadows with his back against a rolled blanket and watched Richard and Willow. Both were seated cross-legged, the fire separating them as surely as the invisible barrier they had erected. Travis braced his left arm on his knee, hand hanging limp but for snatching at an occasional mosquito. In his right, he cradled his pipe, puffing absently now and then to keep the tobacco smoldering.

Dick and Willow had placed themselves to be as far from each other as possible, but so they could watch each other in the least obtrusive manner.

Never known two people as happy ter torment each other as them two.

Once again, something had happened to upset the delicate balance they'd achieved. From across the camp, Trudeau cursed and jumped to his feet, fists balled, head bulled forward.

Just as quickly, Toussaint was up, his deep voice calming.

"Gonna be trouble with that French coon," Baptiste noted amiably as he appeared out of the darkness with a tin cup in his hand. He squatted at Travis's side, eyes gleaming from under the wide brim of his hat.

"Reckon." Travis caught the tightening of Richard's expression as he watched Trudeau. A curl of disgust bent Richard's lips.

Wal, now there's part of it. Them coons has got each other so stiff-legged they's about ter fall over.

And sure as God made sunsets, Willow was in the middle of it.

"You want I should go knock some sense inta his lights?" Baptiste indicated Trudeau with his cup. "A feller can catch a whole heap of sense with a good hard whack to the side of the head."

Travis studied Richard from the corner of his eye. "Let him be fer now."

Baptiste stuck his jaw out sideways, caught the drift of Travis's thoughts, and grunted. "He'll get kilt."

"Yep. Reckon the fat's a-boiling fit ter spatter."

Richard had clenched his fists, a hard-eyed squint fastened on Trudeau. Willow had turned to watch, then regarded Richard with sober eyes.

Whatever was said by Toussaint, Trudeau hadn't wanted any part of it, for he stalked away from the *engagés'* fire. He'd headed for the edge of camp, then, as if on a notion, he changed directions to pass the fringe of Richard's fire.

"Coming ter a head now," Travis murmured to Baptiste. "Let her play out as she will."

Richard had hunched up, jaw set in his thin face. Travis had seen that crazy shine in men's eyes before; the twitchy set of the lips that betrayed a man pushed too far. Willow appeared unconcerned, but her fingers had tightened around the handle of the war club.

Trudeau hesitated as he approached, started to veer off, but couldn't resist, "You 'ave your rifle, *mon ami?* Is that what you stick in your hot Snake bitch? The only thing you own hard enough to make her moan?"

Richard's reaction even caught Travis by surprise. He leapt like a coiled spring, taking Trudeau around the waist.

Richard bulled him back, pummeling with his fists. Instinctively, Trudeau clenched, lifting Richard off the ground as he tightened his grip in an attempt to snap the spine.

Richard kicked frantically and slammed an elbow into Trudeau's head before poking a thumb into his eye.

Trudeau howled, planted his hands in Richard's chest, and shoved him off. Richard tumbled backward as Trudeau rubbed at his eye, roared, and leapt in an attempt to stomp Richard's chest. From flat on his back, Richard kicked Trudeau's legs out from under him.

With a newfound agility, Richard twisted away from Trudeau's falling body. Both scrambled to their feet in a flurry of dust to circle like bulls.

Engagés had come at a run, and now their shouts and whistles added to the din as they cheered Trudeau on.

Richard feinted and grabbed for one of Trudeau's arms. The frantic fingers slipped as Trudeau planted a foot and lashed out with a fist to graze the side of Richard's head. Before the kid could recover, Trudeau was on him.

Travis put a hand on Baptiste's arm as the black hunter started forward.

When Trudeau hammered Richard into the ground, it drove the air from his lungs. Instinctively, Richard tucked his legs up—just in time to block the knee that jabbed for his crotch. Trudeau arched, pulling back a cocked fist. Richard took the opportunity and used the muscles of his gut and neck to butt his head into Trudeau's face. The smacking impact brought a howl from Trudeau.

The *engagés* were dancing gleefully, swinging their fists in mock combat, clapping and shouting. Willow had backed away, lips parted, a gleam in her wide eyes as she clawed for the war club on her belt.

Trudeau was squealing his rage now, slamming his fist into the side of Richard's head. The Yankee gave a gasp, and the pain spurred something down inside him. His expression twisted, demonic, half mad with panic and desperation.

Travis finally moved, stepping up behind Willow as she tore her war club from her belt and started forward. "Leave 'em be," he warned, placing a hand on her shoulder. "Dick's got ter fight her out, gal."

Willow tensed, trembling, but lowered the Pawnee club.

Travis looked down at the thrashing bodies to see that Trudeau was clawing at Richard's face with hooked fingers.

Come on, coon. If a he blinds ye, she's all over.

Dick was flopping like a fish in the boatman's grip, avoiding the gouging fingers. Sweat trickled, mixed with blood on Richard's face. As the inexorable fingers closed, Richard snapped like a turtle for a worm.

Trudeau shrieked, two of his fingers clamped between Richard's teeth. The Yankee bit down savagely, shaking his head like a terrier on a rat. At the same time, he got a hand back of Trudeau's head, and did a little clawing of his own.

Insane with pain, Trudeau bucked like a fresh colt, broke Richard's grip, and pounded a hard-boned left to the side of Richard's head to loosen those terrible jaws.

Trudeau rolled free, scrambling away.

"Dick! Get up!" Travis bellowed as Trudeau stumbled to his feet, careened off the surrounding boatmen, and leapt. Richard saw, rolled to the side, and Trudeau's hard heels slipped off his ribs instead of crushing them. As he sprawled, Richard curled and grabbed up one of the rocks from the fire ring. He grunted with effort as he bounced it off the side of Trudeau's head.

"Goddamn it!" Dave Green bellowed, elbowing through the circle. "Stop this at once!"

"Let 'em go, Dave!" Travis shouted, waving to get the booshway's attention. "They gotta finish it!"

Richard had used the moment to hammer the half-stunned Trudeau in the head again, but the heat from the rock was too much. He dropped it, balled a fist, and round-housed Trudeau in the face. Travis heard the bones in the Frenchman's nose snap. Richard sprawled on Trudeau's chest, hands clamping abound the boatman's throat in a stranglehold.

Travis gauged the glaze in Trudeau's blinking eyes, and stepped forward as Trudeau managed to get a grip on Richard's wrists. To keep from being pulled free, Richard sank his teeth into Trudeau's ear. His neck and back strained as he tried to rip it off Trudeau's head.

"Whoa, now, hoss," Travis soothed, bending down. "Ye've got him, hear? Let him up, coon. Ye ain't ready ter kill him. It ain't what I'd figger a feller from Boston wants told in all them fancy houses on Beacon Hill."

Richard froze, muscles still straining, Trudeau's ear stretched tight in blood-stained teeth.

"Dick, damn it! Turn him loose!" Travis snapped. "That, or I'll whack ye a good one!"

Richard turned loose, rolled back on his haunches, then flopped onto his back to spit blood and saliva. He wiped his mouth and lay there, panting. Trudeau shuddered for breath, his mangled right hand going to his bruised throat, the left to his bloody ear.

"*Sacré enfant du grâce!*" whispered one of the *engagés*. "If I did not see, I would not believe!"

"Break it up!" Green ordered, waving his hands like

shooing geese. "Go on! Morning comes early. Fun's over for tonight."

Willow had dropped down to one knee and dabbed at the blood running from Richard's nose. He winced at her touch, his half-burned hand cradled on his lap. His eyes had an oddly drained look as he stared at something far, far away, and mumbled, "I'm not a dog...not anymore."

Toussaint remained, head cocked, hands on his hips as he studied Trudeau, who lay curled on his side, gasping.

Baptiste gestured. "Come on, Toussaint. Let's get Trudeau down to the river. Reckon a dunking ain't a gonna hurt him none."

They bent down, pulling the blood-spattered boatman to his feet. As they walked off with Trudeau staggering between them, Travis heard Toussaint say, "When did zee little chick learn to fight like zee rooster?"

"Travis?" Green asked, finger flicking back and forth like a blind man's cane. "I take it this is all over?"

"Reckon so, Dave." And Travis couldn't help but smile as if it would break his face in two.

As Green walked off for his tent, he could be heard to mutter, "Massachusetts gentleman? My ass!"

————

Willow lay in her blankets and stared up into the cloud-black night sky. They'd crossed the Cannonball River the morning before. The French called it *Le Bulet,* for the round stones that littered the bottom of the channel. From what Green told her, the Whites had giant guns that could shoot such huge bullets for as far as a man could see. By now, she knew better than to be skeptical of such fantastic stories.

The first of the birds were chirping in the trees, a sure sign that the morning call of "*Levez! Levez!*" was near. She could hear someone stirring a fire and the sound of metal scraped on metal as the pots were laid out.

Willow turned her head to see Richard. His ghostly face was calm now, but in the night his muted cries had awakened her. Only after she'd reached out and taken his unburned hand had his sleep deepened. She rubbed her thumb over the back of his hand, comforted by the touch.

What dreams had haunted him? Boston, with its lighted windows and all the people dressed in fine cloth? She'd listened to his descriptions, trying to place building after building, some with floors on top of other floors like a human beehive. Did the image conjured in her mind even come close to the way Boston really looked?

All of those women, drowning in layers of fabric until they can barely move. What do they think of, so weighted with cloth, living their whole lives in wooden and rock boxes?

Easier to imagine Cannibal Owl swooping over the peaks, looking for anyone who slept in the open, than to imagine living all of one's life inside a box.

She tightened her grip on Richard's hand as she remembered the aftermath of the fight with Trudeau. Like crossing a mountain, it marked a divide that she recognized but could not fully understand. He had fought for more than himself. He had fought for her, and that changed everything.

"I can't believe that was me," Richard had kept repeating over and over as she wiped the blood from his face and daubed poultice on his burned hand.

It was you, warrior. Your courage is rising to match the puha *hidden in your souls.*

Someone coughed, one of the *engages;* the faint burr of

snoring carried on the cool morning. At the river, ducks quacked back in the reeds.

I only wish I could stay to see you find all of yourself.

She shifted onto her hip to see him better. Only here, in the secret gloom of predawn, could she allow the longing in her souls to show. Only now, when no one might witness, could she allow herself to want him until the ache within her finally brought tears.

And that is a lesson for you, Heals Like A Willow. Coyote's lesson. The time to leave has come. For, if you don't, you will slip into his robes some night.

She'd imagined that enough times to know how it would unfold. His eyes would go wide as her fingers stilled the question on his lips. In the beginning he'd fight weakly, trying to protest as she loosened his clothing with her other hand.

She understood him thoroughly, knew that his protests would drop to a murmured "No" that he'd repeat over and over as she pressed herself against him.

He'd gasp when her fingertips traced around his testicles, and found that sensitive place on the underside of the penis.

Lying here now, separated in the predawn darkness, she could see the expression in his eyes as they joined, the question within his soul struggling against the need of his manhood. Such a vision, as clear as if it had happened moments ago. A trick of the soul's longing. A perfect memory of what would never be, despite the warm aching in her loins.

If only you had asked me to stay, Ritshard.

At that moment, he smiled in his sleep, and mumbled. Mostly it sounded like gibberish, and then he said, "Laura...Laura..."

The effect was like ice water dashed on a warm body.

But then, the world was not a perfect place. Coyote had ensured that just after the Creation.

She said, "I can't be a fool any longer," and gently untangled her fingers from his. She slipped from her blankets and rolled them. Her packs lay where she'd left them, ready for the long journey ahead. One by one, she shouldered them for the short walk to the horses.

At the edge of the trees, she stopped, closed her eyes against the pain, and whispered, "Some canyons are too deep to cross, Ritshard. If our differences are too great even for us, how will your people and mine ever find peace?

"*Tam Apo* bless and keep you safe. May the spirits guide you on your journey back to your Laura, and this Boston."

Then she slipped into the trees, following the trail that led to the horse picket. Her mountains lay many days' ride to the west. Dangers would lurk on all sides, but she would manage to find her way. With any luck the way of the land would prove more kind than the way of the heart.

Like Ritshard, she was going home, to her native land and people. Once there, she would weave the loose strands of her life back together, the way the old stories taught.

She had reached out, and the misty white spirit dog had bitten her. He'd been Coyote after all. And perhaps, somewhere in her distant mountains, she would discover a way to heal this newest wound. After all, she was *Dukurika,* and, for a woman of the People, anything was possible.

In the distance, she could hear a chorus of coyotes as their wailing song rose and fell in the still morning air.

This time, she promised, they weren't singing for her.

A LOOK AT BOOK THREE:

A Panther's Scream

The epic begun in *The Morning River* and *White Mist Dog* continues in book III, *A Panther's Scream*.

Having made the decision to leave Richard and the whites, Willow packs, only to discover that all of the expedition's horses, including her own, have been stolen—a fact the scarred hunter, Travis Hartman can't abide! For Richard, the pursuit of the thieves and recovery of the animals will leave him forever changed.

Meanwhile, the Arikara make their move on *Maria*, ending in a bloody battle where Willow crosses a line she never anticipated. Reunited with a wounded Richard, she struggles to save his life. But some bridges cannot be crossed. Heartbroken, she leaves in the desperate hopes of returning to her people. Only to face her biggest challenge yet when a Blackfeet raiding party crosses her path, for they have a captive too dear to her heart to let die.

Meanwhile, the *Maria* struggles to ascend the Yellowstone, where Dave Green will meet the end of all his dreams. And Richard will face the wilderness alone, and battle for his very life.

AVAILABLE JUNE 2023

ABOUT THE AUTHOR

W. Michael Gear is the New York Times and international bestselling author of over fifty-eight novels, many of them co-authored with Kathleen O'Neal Gear.

With seventeen million copies of his work in print he is best known for the "People" series of novels written about North American Archaeology. His work has been translated into at least 29 languages. Michael has a master's degree in Anthropology, specialized in physical anthropology and forensics, and has worked as an archaeologist for over forty years.

His published work ranges in genre from prehistory, science fiction, mystery, historical, genetic thriller, and western. For twenty-eight years he and Kathleen have raised North American bison at Red Canyon Ranch and won the coveted National Producer of the Year award from the National Bison Association in 2004 and 2009. They have published over 200 articles on bison genetics, management, and history, as well as articles on writing, anthropology, historic preservation, resource utilization, and a host of other topics.

The Gears live in Cody, Wyoming, where W. Michael Gear enjoys large-caliber rifles, long-distance motorcycle touring, and the richest, darkest stout he can find.

Made in the USA
Coppell, TX
12 February 2025

45531258R00196